Do the
Math

Do the
Math

A Novel of the Inevitable

PHILIP B. PERSINGER

iUniverse, Inc.
New York Bloomington Shanghai

Do the Math
A Novel of the Inevitable

iUniverse books may be ordered through booksellers or by contacting:

iUniverse
1663 Liberty Drive
Bloomington, IN 47403
www.iuniverse.com
1-800-Authors (1-800-288-4677)

Because of the dynamic nature of the Internet, any Web addresses or links contained in this book may have changed since publication and may no longer be valid.

This is a work of fiction. All of the characters, names, incidents, organizations, and dialogue in this novel are either the products of the author's imagination or are used fictitiously.

ISBN: 978-0-595-46988-8 (pbk)
ISBN: 978-0-595-70688-4 (cloth)
ISBN: 978-0-595-91272-8 (ebk)

Printed in the United States of America

To My Not-So-Gentle Reader

Acknowledgments

Thanks to the Mater for her great proofreading and helping make sure that nothing in the content would displease Queen Victoria. Thanks to my editor, Anonymous, who also wrote all those books that I enjoyed so much when I was a young man. Thanks to Suki for the editorial board meetings. Thanks to Joe Gilmore, who told me so eloquently that he loved his life that it made me want to love mine. Thanks to Pam Topham, a great weaver and a better friend. Thanks to Dan Rattiner, who made me write in the beginning even though I was happier doing paste-up. Thanks to Liz, a fellow recovering playwright. Thanks to Squire, who is my token MBA friend yet remains pretty enough to hang out with. Thanks to Scott, who occasionally scares me into doing the right thing. Thanks to dead James, who taught me that everything is ancient and still the same. I would like to thank Hogan, but he would want to parse the context in such depth that it would have no bottom. Thanks to my stepchildren Stephanie and Andy, who showed me that becoming a dad didn't have to be toxic. Finally, thanks to Emily Nomer, whose arbitrary and capricious comments made the entire writing process odious and hateful.

Prologue

I am standing on a headland overlooking the Hudson River, an hour north of New York City. It is not a palisade. Those dramatic cliffs are to the south. Up here, the sides of the river are more like foothills until High Tor, which introduces you to the ever-rising mountains to come. About twenty minutes north is the most perilous precipice in the world. I once watched a man knowingly step off it. I don't think he had a choice. Fate yanked his chain with a second stab at heaven on earth. All he had to do was play the assassin.

That was in 1978, when I was an eager young graduate student ready to conquer the numbers. Today, I am a tenured professor in mathematics at a fine college in Philadelphia. This is the first time I have viewed the river from this part of the hill in the intervening twenty-five years. I remember that it was much colder on that night when I last stood here.

We are driving north along the Hudson River because my friend Harvey is the best high school math teacher in Canada. It's official. He is getting an award.

I have known Harvey forever. He is among my oldest friends. He must like me too, because he has tolerated me just as long. He is so smart that I am usually nervous talking to him, knowing that he probably regards whatever subject I land upon as lightweight. But I did get one tangible sign of acceptance—and maybe the notion that he didn't think I was a total moron—on his last night in graduate school. I had taken him out to dinner.

"You know what you are?" I observed, sipping one more drink than I needed.

"What is that?" he asked casually, like he always did when he had you under his microscope.

I was used to that. "You are an enigma couched in a riddle wrapped in a fine Cuban cigar."

"You're OK too," he responded with a regal nod.

On our way to Canada, the Thruway would have been faster, but I made the detour. I wanted to stand on those heights and remember who I had been and what had happened so many years ago. My wife doesn't mind. She knows the story.

Years before, I had exploited it shamelessly. What else was I supposed to do? She was a great beauty—still is—but I was only a mere young adjunct, lecturing hourly to a mob of napping freshmen. I was desperate to show her that mathematicians have huge hearts and can act heroically on even larger passions. Suzanne claims that she saw right through my contrivance, but I know that the story captured her as it touches everyone else who hears it.

I skipped the town and turned directly onto Mountain Road. I am not surprised that I remembered every twist and turn of the long climb up the steep hill. Although there are many new homes and some missing landmarks, the large iron gates are right where I expected them to be. I drove past them and parked on the gravel. The bronze plaque on the stone gate read "Mid-Hudson Wellness Center."

When we stepped out of the car, Suzanne said, "You take in the view. I'm going down to the big house to peek in the windows."

"Don't get arrested," I replied.

She grinned broadly.

"Say hi to the desk sergeant when you bail me out," she laughed.

She kissed me then skipped down the hill.

From where I stand, I can see her finally able to spy on the mansion that she drooled over in *Architectural Digest*. I think her only jealousy of me is that I had spent so much time inside that house back then.

The sun is getting closer to its good-night kiss upon the distant hilltops. The river has already started to doze. It is hushed and losing color. Only the red and green channel buoys, which still catch the late rays, are standing out.

I turn around to face the town that held such a huge place in my heart. It was the first town I had lived in where I hadn't been born—where I woke up in the morning and dealt with adults who weren't my parents, a place that knew me for what I thought and did and not for where I had come from.

But this tale is not about me. It is the account of a man who was developing a mathematical theory about the inevitable. He was my mentor, fifty years old, a grown-up in my eyes. I am that age now. At the time, I did not realize how young he was. But I did learn that there is no retirement age for love and want.

There are few things worse, or more tantalizing, than being one step away from realizing a dream. I was there at the end, observing him, as he balanced on the brink, aware that the only safe move would be to fall backward. Yet he took the step forward, placing his foot firmly onto the air in front of him.

1

I will start about three months before the story begins, during my senior year at Garrison College. It was a dreary Pennsylvania Tuesday in February. I was sitting in my advisor's office watching heavy gray clouds dump sleet and freezing rain onto an even grayer landscape.

Dr. Hazlett was an example of everything wrong with the tenure system. His lectures were flat and probably unchanged since he first presented them at the beginning of his career. He was a capable mathematician, but he communicated no joy in it. The only way he kept current with academic journals was to throw them out periodically, which he was doing at that moment.

Sitting in front of a large garbage can that he had borrowed from the custodian, he fanned the pages of each abstract or learned publication for a brief moment before relegating it to the deep. When I got bored watching the freezing rain outside, I started to read titles on the bookshelves around me. It was clear that his specialty was probability, specifically game theory and how to win at blackjack, roulette and craps.

He disappeared behind his desk for a moment to pour something else into his coffee mug. Then he looked up and commented, "We both know why we are here."

"It's mandatory," I replied.

"Exactly," he agreed as he opened the file folder that housed my permanent record. "So what do you want to do?"

"I want to go to graduate school," I answered.

He closed the file.

"That was easy," he said and took a pull from his coffee.

"Not that easy," I said.

He seemed slightly irritated that one of his students would require additional attention.

"Why not?" he asked.

"The graduate schools that will give me money aren't that good," I pointed out. "The good ones won't give me money."

"That's unfortunate," he said. "But not unusual."

He reopened my file and actually looked inside it this time.

"What went so wrong in Probability & Statistics?" he inquired.

"I was bad at it."

"Why?"

"It's boring," I explained.

"But, oh, so lucrative," he murmured as he read on. "Check the odds."

I wasn't only bad at prob/stat, I hated it—thereby becoming the only math major at Garrison whom everyone wanted to play cards with. I have the worst poker face in the universe.

"You were the only student who showed up on time for my early class in logic," Dr. Hazlett noted.

"I was your only student still living with his parents," I replied.

"You did well in it."

"I like logic."

"So do I," he confessed. "That's how I got where I am today."

Those words did not encourage me. I did not aspire to be the next Dr. Hazlett.

"Logic is wonderful," he mused. "Leave the flash and sparkle of fractal geometry to the youngsters. They all burn out by twenty-two anyway."

His droopy eye was running, and he mopped it with a handkerchief. But when he finished reading and closed the folder and finally looked up at me, he was focused.

"I'll tell you a secret," he offered in a conspirator's voice, as he took another shot of coffee. "Every job ultimately turns to crap. It's just a matter of time."

He pushed my file to the side and pulled another stack of academic journals to the center of the desk. He spent the next few minutes weeding through them.

"Let's look at it logically." he finally said. "A simple syllogism. All jobs turn to crap. All men must eat. Men who don't have crappy jobs don't eat."

He looked at me over his glasses, "I got that one from my roommate at MIT. He was a brilliant son of a gun, but a sucker for the contrapositive."

The mere sound of those three hallowed initials made me feel jealous and more hopeless.

"Be a math teacher," he directed as he riffled faster and faster through the shrinking stack of publications. "I will let you deduce the reason."

"Job security?" I guessed.

"Exactly. There are never enough math teachers." He dumped the remaining contents of the mug down his throat. "Do you know why teachers all wear the mark of the beast: 666?"

"No."

"It stands for six hours a day, six months a year and six years before your next sabbatical," he chortled with self-congratulation.

"But how can you stand it?" I asked.

"Stand what?"

"Delivering the same lectures, day after day, year in and year out," I blurted. "Doesn't the monotonous drone of your own voice make you want to blow your brains out?"

Dr. Hazlett's face twitched slightly.

"I see that you didn't do so well in Tact & Civility 101," he noted dryly.

He was right. There was no required course in diplomacy at Garrison College, but if there had been one, I would have flunked. I didn't mean to be rude or insensitive. I simply had a young man's impulsiveness, probably exacerbated by my dad's mantra that "there is no such thing as a stupid question." Unfortunately, he forgot to warn me that there were millions of inappropriate ones. Even now, I sometimes feel that I'm missing a tiny circuit in my brain, the synapse between "wonder" and "ask out loud."

Dr. Hazlett picked up the next journal and opened it in the middle.

"Son of a bitch!" he exclaimed.

He broke the spine and folded the magazine inside out, placing it flat on the table.

"That's him. My roommate at Tech—William Teale—the smartest guy I've ever met. Should have gotten the Comstock Prize. I'll be damned."

He didn't bother with the formality of coffee. Pulling the bottle out of the bottom drawer of his desk, he poured whisky straight into the mug.

"That's your future," he said, jabbing his thumb at the photograph. "Him. Write him a letter. Tell him I sent you. Be an intern. It's Hudson Polytechnic, a good school, and they've got piles of money left over from World War II. He's brilliant."

Dr. Hazlett shook his head in amazement.

2

For non-mathematicians or those who have not studied philosophy on an academic level, the Comstock Prize is the preeminent award given for achievement in logic. It is not the Nobel Prize, but it is as good as you're going to get in the field. There is no Nobel Prize for mathematics, which most entry-level math students like to believe is because Alfred Nobel's fiancée ran off with a mathematician.

To be invited to present to the Comstock Review Board is in itself an honor.

I wrote Dr. Teale, requesting an interview to discuss my qualifications for being his intern. He returned my letter straight off with "Don't need one" scrawled across the bottom of the page.

When I showed it to Hazlett, he handed me a yellowed monograph.

"Read this," he said. "That's his first published article."

Hazlett then wrote Dr. Teale personally. He received a more civilized response than I had. It was written on elegant stationery.

"No, thank you. Don't use them anymore. Wm."

Besides being disappointed, I found his response rude and arrogant. I was in the mood to find even more flaws in his character as well as in his reasoning, so over the weekend I read the monograph.

The paper was entitled "Significant Inconsequentiality." It was short, just over five pages and it blew my mind. What he had constructed was like one of those complicated Japanese wooden puzzles that all fit together perfectly, except when they don't.

I was familiar with every single tool he'd used. Even at my young age, I thought he was a little obsessed with the contrapositive, but his use of the Henkel matrix was clever. Furthermore, he applied Leffert to great effect. I had never seen Eckstein's Parallel show up so unexpectedly.

I could ace a test on any one of these elements. I could parse them. I could define them. I could use them in context. But I had never seen them all so effortlessly deployed in concert.

But there was more. I got a sense as I reread the article for the third time that he was creating a new field. It wasn't just logic. Sure, the thing was steeped in conventional inference, but there were other bits—like algebra and maybe even a quantum thing that I didn't understand. He even had the stones to use a quadratic equation in the middle of a truth table. It was like reading an early paper by Isaac Newton, just before he realized that he would have to invent calculus to solve his problems—mathematics on LSD.

I wanted to work with this man more than anything in the world. When I read in his bio that he was my age when he wrote the paper, I thought my head would explode.

The basic premise of the paper was simple: that a negligible event could have huge consequences. Kind of like, "for want of a nail, the kingdom was lost." That gave me an idea.

"Dear Dr. Teale," I wrote. "What if meeting with me for ten minutes ultimately resulted in your life being changed forever? There could hardly be anything more insignificant in your life than ten minutes with me."

I was flabbergasted when I got my letter back. He had written across the top, "Philadelphia Airport. Gate E9. 3:45 PM. March 19. <u>10 MIN ONLY!</u>"

3

William, I would learn much later, was changing planes on his way back from the annual meeting of the Society for Applied Logic and Inference at Carnegie Mellon.

I was nervous, but not because it was a job interview. I was nervous because over the course of my educational career I had known a dozen math teachers, but I had never met a mathematician. Would he see right through me?

I positioned myself at the bottom of the escalators and intently studied the face of each person who glided by. A colorful mosaic. There were smiles and frowns and inscrutable looks. Strangers passing by, our eyes would catch and our worlds joined, but only for a moment. Then the inquiring look would dissolve into a glance, which would become a blink that would pop like a drifting soap bubble.

As I watched for him, the stream of people was hypnotic, and my thoughts drifted to Teale's paper. What was the force of contact? What would happen if two of these terrestrial bodies collided? Would it just be a longer shared look, still ultimately reduced to a blink and blankness, or would our lives become inexorably linked and new futures born?

What of those whom we missed due to a wasted hour, a late taxicab or a detour of twenty feet? These were the faces that would not or could not be tested in passing. These were the fundamental questions posed in the paper William had written decades before.

I grew weary of the continuous stream of passing faces and my eyes began to wander around the terminal. It was then that I noticed a disruption on the moving stairs. A moment of chaos. People pushed and shoved. Elbows swung. I heard a woman scream and more than one man cursed out loud. The tumult seemed to be moving up the down escalator.

It was over as quickly as it began, after the last straggler mumbled the last complaint. A new group of faces was ignorant of the previous eddy in the stream.

I felt his presence even before I saw him, standing in front of me so close that I could read "Wm Teale" on the conference nametag still hanging from his lapel.

He was over six feet tall when he stood up straight, which he wasn't doing at the moment. Although he had the distant look of a deep thinker, he was muscular and he shifted often with a certain restlessness. There was a constant vibration of strength and athleticism that belied his academic credentials.

He looked about with intelligent eyes. They weren't exactly green or even hazel; they were flecked with green and umbers. His hair was mostly brown, but there was a seasoning of gray around his ears. It was slightly long, like the academic longhair that he was—yet he was a good-looking guy for a college professor. Compared to Dr. Hazlett, he was Cary Grant.

"Dr. Teale?" I asked.

He looked straight through me. He hadn't heard me.

I repeated myself, less tentatively. "Dr. Teale."

"If this is a chance meeting," he said flatly, "I would prefer that you keep it to yourself and simply go away. I don't want to use up my lifetime quota on you."

"Professor, I'm Roger Davison," I said. "We have an appointment."

He finally focused on me, then set off at a smart pace. "Right. I remember. Another misguided youth sent to me for correction. Walk with me."

None of the books on job interviews that I had crammed prepared me to show off my strengths while trying not to lose a fast walker in a crowded airport. It was all I could do to keep my breath.

"How's Hazlett?" he asked over his shoulder.

"Fine, sir." I panted. "He sends you his best."

"'From each according to his ability'," he quipped dryly, then stopped, looked around distractedly and started off in a different direction.

As my mind raced along with my feet, I decided to go with my mom's first principle: that people love to talk about themselves.

"I read one of your papers," I said.

"So I deduced from your letter."

He stopped and turned. I felt the weight of his full attention. "What rock did you find that under?"

"Dr. Hazlett gave it to me."

"Did you give it back?"

"No, sir."

"Good. Burn it," he said as he started walking again. "What do you want to do?"

"Mathematics," I answered.

Looking at me sharply, he warned, "Better think again. Abstractions are nothing to base your life on."

We were so close that I could see his eyes wander to the left as he added absent-mindedly, "Wait for a number you can dance to."

"Don't move," he commanded, as his eyes locked onto their target. "I'll be right back."

I stepped up onto a bench, but he quickly disappeared into the crowd. It was a spectacular display of broken field running from an academic who had never seen a football scholarship.

I sat down on the bench to wait. Time passed and I felt more dejected with every minute. Standing on the bench again, I made one last scan of the terminal before I snuffed out the last flicker of hope. This wasn't my first blind date. I knew when I was the loser, so I left. I had waited so long that I was charged for another hour in the parking lot.

That year, March came in like a lion but went out like a quart of curdled milk. I was so mopey and blue that my mom told me to get outside and run around the house, like when I was eleven. I was dreading the day after graduation. I had no plan. No future.

Things changed in the first week of April, when I got a letter.

"Despite your virtuosity at insignificance," it started out, "my life has not been radically altered."

"What a creep," I thought. "What a smug creep."

"Nevertheless," the letter continued, "an inconsequential moment with you resulted in a glimpse of an alternate universe. A deal's a deal. I will see you in the fall."

Alternate universe? My relief was edged with anxiety. The letter ended with a future sword of Damocles hanging over my head.

"The first semester will be probationary, of course."

"Of course," I replied acridly to his scribbled words. It was like every free offer I had ever sent away for. It was free until it wasn't, and then you were screwed.

4

Hudson Polytechnic Institute was located in New Coventry, New York. The train was the best way to get there. North of Spuyten Duyvil, the tracks ran practically on the river's edge. My eyes were glued to the riverscape outside the window. As I watched the Palisades pass by, the other shore turned into the grand headland of the Tappan Zee. There was a regatta across the river. The water was dotted with small white sails tacking and darting across one another's paths.

I climbed the steps from Track Five and pushed open the ancient door, which groaned and scraped. A flock of pigeons started and flew in a broad swooping circle above the great room. The station at New Coventry was a testament to the salad days of the New York Central, a cathedral in iron and riveted gothic revival, when every thinking man knew that transportation by rail was the state of the art and would rule for the next five hundred years. In the large and open nave, oak benches lined up like pews. High above, skylights and clerestory windows created the golden diagonals of light, which the birds now crisscrossed.

As I looked about for the taxi stand, a couple standing beside the information window caught my eye. He was tall and intent. From what I could see, she was lithe, blonde and spectacular. They were unaware of anything but each other. He was talking. She was rapt, touching him on the arm and chest. They stood silent for a moment, then he kissed her on the cheek. She tenderly took his face in her hands and returned the gesture on the mouth.

There was something very familiar about the man. I peered at him as I passed by, wondering what it was. I was looking over my shoulder instead of in front of me and did not see the wire magazine rack that I crashed into, sending it, me and dozens of colorful publications cascading to the floor.

The next thing I knew, William was looking down at me. He seemed as startled to see me on the floor as I was to see him above me.

"Are you all right?" he asked.

"That was you," I replied dazedly when I saw he was alone. "But there were two of you."

"Are you seeing double?"

"No. A woman."

He assisted me to my feet and we both cleaned up my mess. I bought a copy of *Scientific American* in atonement.

"Don't worry," he reassured me. "She was only a phantom."

"She was a very pretty phantom," I said stupidly, before I had enough sense to stop talking.

He fastidiously straightened out the magazine rack so that it stood square to the newsstand.

"This must have been a unique event in science," he mused. "A shared hallucination."

He was different somehow than when I'd seen him at the airport. I tried to put my finger on it. For one thing, he was standing at his full height. His eyes were dancing and his brown hair was unruly as if it had been mussed by a sultry torch singer at a supper club. He looked very confident. I guessed I would be too if I had such a beautiful woman so recently in my arms.

"Did you bring the paper?" he asked me.

"Which one?" I stammered blankly.

"Mine," he said with a look that implied that I was simpleminded.

"Yes. It's in my bag."

"In that case, I'll give you a ride."

I followed him out of the train station to a white Chevy van with tinted windows.

"Toss your things in here," he said as he unlocked the double doors in back. When they swung open, I could only gape.

Rather than the customary cargo space or bench seats, I saw the world's smallest, plushest sitting room. An ottoman sat at the foot of an overstuffed reading chair in floral chintz. There was a brass floor lamp at its side. An exquisite oriental rug covered the floor.

A pastel of ballet students at the barre in the style of Degas graced one of the dark paneled walls, while a reproduction in oil of Botticelli's Venus faced it on the other side. A miniature television set hung on a bracket from the ceiling across from the chair, and next to that—and I had to look twice in disbelief—was a gimbaled aquarium with an assortment of tropical fish.

"All the comforts of home," I remarked as I climbed into the passenger's seat. "And then some."

"It's my wife's," he replied cryptically.

We drove out of the station, across the railroad tracks and through the town. New Coventry had survived the fate of many of its neighbors following the collapse of both river and rail traffic, but barely. Its two main sources of economic activity were the university and the nuclear power plant just north of town.

We turned onto Mountain Road. "This is the back way," William explained as he switched on the radio.

Like an irritating teenager, he couldn't settle on one radio station or another and he flitted back and forth across the dial until a woman's voice caught his ear.

"I never view it as a job," she said in a soft but practiced voice. "It is more a way of life than anything else."

William stopped fussing with the radio and returned his attention to driving up the hill.

"You are listening to *Page Turner*," a woman's voice said, "a weekly review of popular fiction. Our guest today is Virginia Faye Warner, winner of the Meekham Award for Romance Literature. Virginia, I want you to fess up."

"Now you're scaring me," the writer responded with a nervous titter.

"Seriously, Virginia, to be as prolific as you have been and still maintain the quality that you have exhibited consistently over the years, must demand an incredible amount of work and discipline. How do you do it?"

"Well, Margaret, I can only answer by saying that there is so much joy and happiness in what I do. It is an act of creation. I never regard it as work. I discover two wonderful people whom the Fates have parted. It is my blessing to be allowed to reintroduce them to each other. After that there is only magic. Both my readers and I politely step back into the shadows so that we won't be in the way as we watch two destined hearts rediscover each other and fall even more deeply in love. How can you call enchantment 'work'?"

"I'm sure many of your fans are wondering when they can look forward to meeting you at a book signing."

"I do so enjoy meeting my readers, Margaret, but … and since I have met your adorable husband, I am confident that you especially will understand … it is so hard to be away from the men we love, isn't it? You see, I have my other job—being the wife of a university professor. It's not easy, but we do the best we can, don't we? That's what makes a marriage work."

"I understand that you have a special—and romantic—tradition every winter," the interviewer intimated.

"Oh, Margaret! Your spies are very good!"

"Yes, they are. So it's up to you to tell us in your own words, or I will."

"You trapped me, Margaret. That was very naughty!" The author gave a girlish laugh. "I guess I have no choice."

The author cleared her throat and continued.

"Every year, at first snowfall, whenever that happens and wherever my darling husband and I are, we drop whatever we are doing and rush home. We light a huge fire. Pop the cork of a bottle of champagne. Turn off all the lights and share the magic of the moment."

"Yuck," I blurted out spontaneously. "Stop the car. I'm going to barf."

Stone-faced, eyes straight ahead, William said, "That's my wife."

Holy crap, I groaned inwardly, as my face turned crimson. If I didn't watch my mouth, this was going to be the shortest semester ever.

I imagined my stipend streaming from the van and pouring into the gutter below. I was too upset to notice the twinkle in his eye.

"I am so jealous," the interviewer continued, "and looking around at the many loving touches that grace this exquisite house overlooking the Hudson River, I can certainly see that this marriage is not only working, it is thriving. We have been talking with Virginia Faye Warner, who is currently celebrating the success of her newest book, *Daydreams of Yesternight.*

"If you wouldn't mind terribly, Virginia, we do want you to close out this week's program with your famous catchphrase."

"Must I?" William's wife asked coyly.

"We insist. Don't forget about my spies."

She paused, then stated with breathy earnestness, "True love never dies; it only grows stronger as it lies in wait."

"Virginia Faye Warner, author and romantic, recipient of the Meekham Award, thank you so much for inviting us into your gracious home."

"Thank you for coming, Margaret."

"This has been *Page Turner,* and I am Margaret Entwhistle wishing you happy reading."

"That was taped last month," William remarked as he flipped the dial once again, stopping in the middle of Muddy Waters growling, "You Never Loved Me and You Still Don't."

By Muddy's second complaint about his love life, we had pulled in behind Abbott Hall, which housed the math and philosophy departments on the tree-lined campus of Hudson Polytechnic.

"Home sweet cesspool," William said as he slid out of the van.

"Modest, but cozy," he added as we climbed the stairs. "I'm not greedy. Many careers have been destroyed vying for a view of the quad."

His office was on the second floor and looked down on the Dumpsters. It was a decent space. He had been the acting department chairman for twelve years, so he was not without influence.

The first thing you noticed when you walked into the place was paper. Paper in all forms: magazines, books, loose articles, clippings. Paper in stacks. Paper in piles. Paper drifting lazily through the air whenever a door opened or someone sneezed.

An institutional desk stood in the far corner, buried under even more paper. Stalagmites of books and journals grew from the floor along the right side of the room. On the left was a sofa so covered in mounds of typed and printed matter that it was impossible to determine the color of its fabric.

Hanging just over a bust of Aristotle, who was wearing a gag arrow through his head, was a small portrait of dogs playing poker. Each hand had five aces. But what really stood out was an exquisite Edwardian bookcase, made of mahogany with glass doors. In William's office, it stood tall, proud and totally out of place.

"Do you have a place to live?" he asked.

"Mrs. Slocum's," I answered.

"Best deal in town," he nodded. "What is the old gal charging these days?"

"Sixty-five dollars a month, including the use of her VW bus."

"I know it well," he added. "Half the alumni association has used that car. Eighteen miles to the gallon and twenty-five to a quart of oil."

I peered into the bookcase.

"It's not locked," William said. "The only thing they steal around here is staplers."

He pulled open a filing cabinet. The drawer whined in a metallic sound that hurt my teeth.

"What we are looking for is an article entitled, 'Ultimation in Conditional Probability: Is that your gum on the floor?'"

"I don't chew gum," I said defensively as I opened the perfectly balanced door to the bookcase.

"That was the name of the problem described in the article," he explained. "It was an investigation into ultimate causality as triggered by events of major insignificance."

"Like you," he added.

He peered into the large file drawer.

I pulled out the first book I saw. It had a garish dust jacket and was called *Where Have I Been All Your Life?*

I opened the back cover. The author was sitting in a window seat overlooking a river. She wore a peasant blouse with flowers embroidered around the neck. Her eyes were large and gentle. Her smile was warm and sincere. Her auburn hair was worn in the popular shag.

I don't know when the photo was taken. But even if she'd since bleached her hair, there was no way she was the woman I saw kissing William at the train station.

Very interesting, I thought.

The bio read, "Virginia Faye Warner lives and writes in the Hudson River Valley. Her husband Bill teaches logic and mathematics at a local university. Theirs is a solid marriage and a true romance, empowered by the combination of heart and mind."

I was surprised that William had crept up behind me. He took the book and scanned a paragraph at random. "This was her first period romance."

Returning the book to the shelf, he added, "It was not a happy time."

He closed the bookcase and then turned to me, shifting gears so fast I almost got whiplash.

"The challenge is to codify inevitability, isn't it?" he inquired with shining eyes. "Inevitability is so much more than a short jaunt into conditional probability."

He was so intense that I had to step back a few feet.

"I know what you're thinking," he followed up. "Will the codification stand up to a coherent truth table?"

The back of my skull was getting warm from his gaze.

"Well, Roger, will it?"

I stared back stupidly.

"I don't know," I finally answered in a panic that this would be Strike Two. At this rate, I'd be on my way back to Pennsylvania before I had my supper.

"Exactly," he agreed, pulling open another file drawer, which also protested rudely. "That's why it's hard to do. I was young and full of piss and vinegar when I started this train of thought, so I had no idea how hard it would be to switch tracks."

He went quiet for a time and rooted through stacks of material. A paper cloud built up over him like the anvil of a thunderhead. I was beginning to feel dismissed and was contemplating whether I would be able to lug my suitcase all the way to Mrs. Slocum's house when he finally looked up.

"I actually found support in other dark corners," he added.

I jumped up as he loudly banged on the wall of his office.

"Arlen," he shouted.

"What?" a muffled voice answered back.

"What is your example for preemptive morality?"

"Don't you write anything down?" his neighbor asked querulously.

"Yes, but only with chalk, never in stone," William answered.

"Open your window," his neighbor demanded. "I'm too irritated to holler."

William groaned as he forced the window open five or six inches, just high enough for conversation.

"I am so flattered you asked me," a high-pitched sarcastic voice cut into the room. "Yet again."

"Don't be," William warned. "I have an eager student here."

"Poor thing."

"He is interested in your field," he lied. "He was asking about postponed inevitability."

"Not my problem. You own all that inevitability crap."

"But the postponement is yours, is it not?"

"Bastard."

"So glad you noticed."

"What do you want?"

"Your cautionary tale."

"Why don't you audit my class?"

"Because you're a jerk."

"I can't help that; it's glandular."

"Just remind me of the timeline. At what point does one stray?"

"The time to do the right thing," the nasal voice next door explained, resignedly, "is in the lobby when she tells you her name. Not four hours later and six floors higher when she uncrosses her legs to reveal that she dressed in a hurry.'

"Exactly," William concurred as he slammed the window closed. "Preemptive morality."

He turned to me and grinned. "He loves talking about the magical night when his parents met."

"I heard that," the ethicist shouted through the wall.

5

Mrs. Slocum lived in a white gingerbread house two blocks from Hudson Polytechnic's main gate. A front porch, which ran along the left side of the building, was crowned with hanging baskets of multicolored petunias made even more festive by the afternoon sun. Taped to the beveled glass window on the front door was a note.

"Roger, your key is hidden under the yellow cushion on the wicker loveseat. Please join me for tea at five. Greta Slocum."

My apartment, on the third floor, was converted from the tiny and irrelevant spaces that constituted the attic of a nineteenth-century river house. It was the steep and dramatic slope of the roof that made the room perilous. It was easy to gauge where not to stand, though, if you properly read the repairs in the plaster ceiling. There was a particularly treacherous spot over the toilet in the tiny bathroom. A yellowed piece of paper taped to the wall warned that it was a "Hard Hat Area."

I unpacked the footlocker that I had shipped up the week before. It was filled mostly with books. All my clothing fit in one suitcase. Jeans and blue work shirts were all you needed in those days. At five o'clock, I went downstairs for tea.

Mrs. Slocum's sitting room was a delicate time capsule of civility. She had obviously never built a fire because the hearth contained a large crock of dried hydrangea blossoms. Two comfortable-looking wingback chairs flanked it. Above a crowded collection of miniatures and figurines on the mantle was the portrait of a dachshund sitting happily in one of the wingback chairs. Her collar and tags rested respectfully in a silver tray beneath the oil painting. Her name was Schatzi.

The wallpaper was made up of small pink flowers on a pale blue background that ran down to the cream wainscoting. On the floor, the hand-hooked rug displayed a scene from the English countryside of red-jacketed horsemen and women riding to hounds.

The window was filled with African violets. On both sides of it, curio cabinets with glass doors proudly exhibited ceramic cherubs. Dressed in either lederhosen or dirndls, they all wore whimsical, adorable expressions.

"I cannot imagine that you are as in love with my little Black Forest angels as I am, Roger?"

It was a small voice, but it was unexpected, and I jumped.

One didn't immediately notice that she was plump, because Mrs. Slocum was as tidy as her house. Starched, pressed and very clean, she wore a white lace-trimmed blouse under a yellow jumper with fabric leaves applied to it and blinding white Keds tennis shoes on her feet.

She must have used the same do-it-yourself hair dye that my aunt did, because it had the same orange hue.

I felt comfortable the minute she looked at me. Her eyes were blue and caring. Her face was open and friendly and had those lines that women get from smiling.

"These," she said, nodding at three other mini-cuties, "we bought when we were driving to Munich. The others are from a catalog or were gifts."

"They're certainly more interesting than my mom's spoon collection," I said, once again earning no points for tact.

She put down the tray. "Some people collect these little darlings as an investment, but I enjoy them simply for themselves."

The teacups were decorative with pictures of historic English castles.

"It's Lapsang Souchong," she explained as she poured. "Young men seem to like that better than Earl Grey."

She opened a tin of Scottish shortbread cookies and placed two on my plate. She served herself, then sat back and sighed, "Well."

We both stirred our teacups, me with the excessive zeal of someone who wants to stir it into something more interesting than tea. I was at a loss as I looked around the room. Other than the Black Forest munchkins in their glass prisons, there were few conversation starters. I was further disappointed that there were no books or magazines in view, always a good stepping off point. Even today, I get uneasy when I visit a person's house with no visible reading material at hand.

"So what will you be studying?" she asked, still stirring.

"Mathematics," I answered.

"Lovely," she said. "How practical! You can help me. I am perfectly dreadful at balancing my checkbook."

Math majors hear that one all the time. What we were studying was light years beyond bookkeeping, but I took no offense.

"I am interning for Professor Teale," I said.

She dropped her spoon and her mouth opened wide.

"You are?" she asked in surprise. "*The* Professor Teale?"

I was flabbergasted that this bookless, middle-aged woman knew the name of an obscure mathematician, who even Dr. Hazlett thought had gone missing.

"Do you know him?"

"Who doesn't?" she gushed. "He is married to the best writer alive. She's famous."

"I've met her twice," she boasted as she stood up. "Bring your tea and follow me. This is so exciting."

I obeyed. She led me out of the parlor and down the hall to a door on the right.

"This used to be the sewing room," she said, turning on a light.

It was a small space and it was packed. There was conceivably as much paper per square foot as in William's office, but with no clutter, just organization.

Along one wall, shelves ran from floor to ceiling. So here's where she hid her reading. Practically all of the shelves had books and typing paper boxes neatly stacked on them. The boxes had titles written on them in Magic Marker.

I scanned a few book jackets at random and realized that they were the same titles as the books that were housed in the fancy display case back on campus. But these, by contrast, had been read and reread. Many had bookmarks of torn paper strips. Some had as many as a dozen.

The treadle sewing table, having been liberated of its machine, was home to a powder blue Smith Corona electric typewriter. On its left was an open box of Sphinx-brand typing paper and on the other side, a manuscript.

The notions cabinet nearby still had a few bobbins of colored threads standing on dowels along the top, but the rest was given over to pens, paper, white correction paint and other office supplies. The counter was crowded with small-framed photographs of what must have been Mr. and Mrs. Slocum in various moments of a happy history.

Conspicuously and proudly hung on the wall over the typewriter was a framed black-and-white photograph. I could recognize the woman who was standing next to the smiling Mrs. Slocum from all the book jackets around me. It was Virginia Faye Warner.

Mrs. Slocum took what was (and to this day still is) the largest thesaurus that I had ever seen off the stool and balanced it on top of the typewriter.

"Make yourself comfy," she directed.

As if that were possible, I thought to myself.

But I managed to squeeze into the seat. She knelt and pulled out a large loose-bound volume from the lowest shelf. It was a thick scrapbook crammed with newspaper clippings and magazine articles, snapshots, menus, matchbooks and all sorts of other flotsam and jetsam that serve as reminders of life's significant moments. She rolled over next to me in the steno chair with the large archive on her lap and dramatically raised the cover.

The first page revealed the subject of the homage. In a cutting taken from a glossy women's magazine, William's wife greeted us with a shy smile. The photo was faded, but she was young and eager, probably the same age that I was as I looked at her. The accompanying article profiled "a lovely new talent, writing lovingly about love."

Mrs. Slocum turned the pages slowly and with deliberation as she guided me through every item in this treasure trove of minutiae so that I wouldn't miss even the smallest crumb.

"This is the first advertisement that her original publisher took out," she said, pointing to a scant two column inches of newsprint. "I'm sure they're still kicking themselves today.

"This is the announcement of her first book signing. It was in Buffalo. If only we could go back in time," she sighed and turned over the page.

"Hmmm," she started with concern, "I'm sure this should be in a safer place. It must be worth quite a lot of money at this point. This is the very first *New York Times* bestseller list that she appeared on."

She turned and looked at me.

"Guess how many times she's been on it since?"

"I couldn't," I admitted in a moment of total honesty.

"Take a stab," she encouraged.

"Ten?" I guessed.

"Ha," she exploded gleefully, then did a quick calculation on her finger tips. "More like twelve times that."

Adding, "And still counting."

The page turned.

"This is a collage," she explained. "Do you math types know what a collage is?"

"Yes, ma'am," I said.

"This is only the start," she warned. "You will have to help me take the other boxes down. They are very heavy."

"I'm sure I can manage." I suppressed a yawn.

"It was July when sales went through the roof," she continued, pointing at the review in the upper left corner. "*Publisher's Weekly* made total fools of themselves. Of course they never had the courage to admit that they had been wrong in letting a woman-hater review the book in the first place. They only embarrassed themselves in their pettiness."

As she turned the next page, she got solemn. I was getting tunnel vision.

"The dark days," she sighed.

The headlines from the trade publications reflected a dire moment in a career.

"Masquerade Press Missing Author," reported the *Tannenbaum Book Watch Newsletter*.

"Two Years and Counting. Fans Eager for Next Warner Heart-Warmer," asserted *Heartthrob Market Beat*. "The romance of the decade is followed by the sophomore slump of the century."

"Where's Virginia?" wondered *Romantic News & Views*.

Variety's literary supplement was pithy: "VFW MIA."

Mrs. Slocum looked morose for a few moments, sadly touching the memories, but her mood quickly changed.

"Then it all got back to right," she exulted. "More right than anyone could have ever hoped for."

She pressed down the curling corners of the yellowing newsprint on the next page.

"Love by the Numbers," the headline read, "'Warner-Teale Wedding Defies the Odds.'"

> Fantasy and science came together Saturday afternoon in Fair Haven when author Virginia Faye Warner married William Emerson Teale at St. Michael's chapel.
>
> It has been a busy time for Miss Warner of New Coventry, New York. Two years after the enormous success of her first bestseller, the romance novel, *Tomorrow is Only a Day Away*, she is putting her money where her mouth is in the form of "I do."
>
> Her fans who view her as the "Queen of Hearts" were surprised and elated as she was swiftly swept off her feet by this brilliant—and handsome—academic. Currently the Albert Stengel fellow at Hudson Polytechnic, Mr. Teale is an expert at logic and probability, who according to associates "can't tell the difference between a candlelit supper and a power failure."
>
> When asked about her understanding of what her mathematician husband does for a living, the new and radiant Mrs. Teale answered, "We only hope that one and one make three."

Hitting this point of rapture seemed to quiet Mrs. Slocum. She became thoughtful.

"That's your profession," Mrs. Slocum murmured, pausing so that I could absorb the information before she continued.

"Eighteen short months after that, things took off," she finally said with a dramatic page turn.

"She's back!" trumpeted the lead story in *Tannenbaum's*.

"Worth the wait," gushed *Romantic Times*.

"The *New York Times* knew they couldn't ignore her this time," Mrs. Slocum observed, pointing out three column inches in the "Books in Brief" section.

She turned the page quickly, but not before I had read that "the technical improvement in her prose is quickly apparent and while it remains saccharine, there is nothing overtly embarrassing to the writer."

"The rest, as they say, is history," Mrs. Slocum read. "One shining success after another." Her lips framed the satisfied smile of vindication.

Now she went into hyperdrive. The pages flipped by in a nearly animated stream of glowing press notices and fawning adulation from various celebrities and other writers. The dust jackets in the scrapbook grew more dramatic and sophisticated, the reviews longer and more serious. My tour guide slackened the pace only so a cover review in the *Times* book section did not pass unappreciated. Then the pages flew by again.

When she read about Virginia Faye Warner's seventh book in the Windward Island series, I was experiencing shortness of breath. The walls of the sewing room started closing in. When she reached for the next scrapbook, I realized that the situation was becoming life threatening.

"I've got to go," I blurted out.

"But we've only touched the tip of the iceberg," Mrs. Slocum protested.

I have no memory of what I said next in my growing desperation, but I tried to make it sound sincere.

"I don't believe it!" Mrs. Slocum said accusingly. My heart sank in shame.

She walked over to the photograph above the typewriter. "I'd swear that this house was haunted by smudge ghosts!"

I let out a sigh of relief, which she took to be one of sympathy. She retrieved a bottle of blue cleaner from behind the books and sprayed the glass over the photograph.

"I was so excited to meet her that first time."

She pulled a paper towel from under the table and wiped it down.

"That was a very rare appearance, but it was local—at the school—so she allowed herself an hour or two."

"She really doesn't go on the standard book tours," Mrs. Slocum said as she looked around the room for something else to clean. "She and her husband can't bear to be apart, you know. It's so terribly romantic."

As I made my sheepish and guilt-ridden escape, she was buffing a plaque by the sewing room door.

"I'm especially proud of this one," she beamed.

The award read: "The Meekham Tribute Award presented to Greta Slocum, Best-of Category—Writing Like Virginia Faye Warner."

I tossed expressions of amazement and congratulations over my shoulder as I fled the incredible shrinking room.

6

My first official act as William's intern was to help him pick up six large pies and a case of Cokes at Venice Pizza for the annual math department open house for new and returning graduate students. I didn't mind. At the time, I was determined to make myself indispensable—at least until my stipend was finalized.

"On campus, there are many open houses better than ours," William admitted as he poured sugar into his coffee. "Any one of them, actually."

We were sitting near the counter at a small round table while we waited.

"I am told that we are a punch line for jokes at the engineering school," he added. "That's pretty low."

He stirred his coffee.

"Now the biochemistry crowd—they get wild."

He looked up at me and smiled with amusement.

"They've got a hook." He winked. "They call it experimentation. 'Absorption rates in a controlled environment.' Who can complain about that? It's science, isn't it?"

"Sounds like," I agreed.

He chuckled as he took a sip from his cup.

"The math department did a lot better during the war. But it's easier when you're sexy, isn't it? We had code breakers and radar jocks. Back then there were even some very hush-hush types who did who-knows-what."

He reflected for a moment.

"There was one guy, Hyram Czewitzski. The chancellor told me about him. Got called up to work with Oppenheimer and threw himself a party. Got drunk as a skunk and stood up on a chair. 'The only reason why I'm still a virgin,' he announced to a captivated room, 'is that I haven't had sex yet.'

"Universally loaded by that point, they honored him on the spot by inventing a drink they called the "Vir Gin Fizz." Three parts Beefeater, one part cold shower and a splash of palm oil served in a tall glass garnished with two blue marbles.

"He went on to lose his virginity the same year that he won the Comstock Prize," William said. Then he drifted into a quiet place.

His discomfort made me self-conscious. I awkwardly sat and drank my coffee, studying the gondolier in the wall mural who was having perspective problems reconciling his long oar with the Grand Canal.

William was quiet until he recognized someone entering the restaurant.

"Damn," he groaned. "It's Ambrose."

I turned and saw a large person waddling toward us.

"Billy, thank God. I've been looking all over for you. Don't go away," he ordered as he turned to the counter.

"Three slices. Extra cheese. Twice," he requested, holding up two pudgy fingers for emphasis.

"Don't leave me alone with him," William instructed me.

"I'll also have a large orange soda while I wait," Ambrose added.

He resembled his food, pale and fatty like mozzarella. He tossed the paper plate onto the small table. The pizza slices slid off just inches from our elbows. He dropped the cup of soda with the same lack of care and spatters flew into our coffee cups. Then he dragged his chair across the tile floor and sat on it as if impaled.

"You've got to talk to her," Ambrose said without preamble. Saving time, he didn't bother putting the food back on the plate and ate it directly off the table, shoveling it into his mouth and chewing noisily.

"I do talk to her," William answered. "I'm her husband."

"She's driving me insane."

"You *are* insane, Ambrose."

"You don't know what it's like."

"I do know what it's like. I'm her husband."

Ambrose regarded me with distrust.

Then he turned and said to William, "I need to talk to you."

"Would you like me to leave?" I asked.

William kicked me.

"Ouch," I groaned and buckled over to rub my shin.

I was down for only a moment, but when I sat up, Ambrose was sobbing into his hands. He must have inhaled the first two slices. They were gone.

"There, there," William reassured, looking disgusted as he fiddled with a toothpick.

"This is so unlike me," Ambrose sighed, looking up morosely and pushing the last slice away. "I have no appetite. I must be very depressed."

Then he looked directly at me and asked, "Got any chocolate? They say it's good for depression."

"I understand that she is anxious," he continued to William. "Lord knows, she has every reason to be anxious. But driving me crazy won't help, will it?"

William snapped the toothpick in two.

"As you know," he said as Ambrose took another gulp from his soda, "I don't like to get involved in either Faye's career or the creative process."

Ambrose snorted so violently that twin orange rivulets streamed from his nose. He snatched a napkin and dabbed at his face.

"Creative process?" he started. "Which creative process would that be, Billy? The finger snapping, 'A book please now, Ambrose.' The petulance, 'Where's my book, Ambrose?' Or the hissy fits, 'How dare you call this piece of crap a Virginia Faye Warner original, Ambrose?'"

He stopped and looked at me in a panic. "Does he know?"

"It's all right, Ambrose," William said. "He's with me."

"Who is he?"

"I'm Roger," I said, presenting him with an ancient Hershey bar that I had discovered in the lining of my jacket. "I'm nobody."

He looked skeptical but hungrily accepted the candy bar.

"Don't worry about Roger," William reassured him. "He's a graduate student."

Ambrose unwrapped the candy bar. I was embarrassed at how old it was.

"Goody," he delighted. "I love white chocolate."

He tossed the oxidized squares into his mouth.

"Billy, you know I love her. Talk to her."

"I do," William replied. "Often."

Ambrose finished the chocolate, licked the wrapper and got reflective.

"I do understand why you don't want to get involved. I really do. But you have to this time. There is only so much I can take."

"I understand."

"I mean, it would be a catastrophe if there wasn't a new Virginia Faye Warner original this season, wouldn't it?"

Ambrose looked up and stared directly at William. "One has to wonder. Would it be more devastating to her loyal fans," he mused quietly, "or to the author herself?"

His smile turned sinister as he took another drink of soda.

"Is that extortion?" William asked quietly.

"That's an ugly word, Billy. I prefer blackmail."

"Number seventeen," the cashier paged, "your pie is ready."

Ambrose pulled himself to his feet.

"Got to run," he announced. "I phoned it in. You know how slow they are here."

He retrieved the pizza box at the counter and paused at our table on his way out. He looked at me one more time with suspicion.

"I'm a math student," I volunteered.

"Oh, well, then," he said in relief before he turned to William.

"You will want to help me with this. You do remember how bad the bad old days were, don't you, Billy?"

"I'll see what I can do."

"That would be such a good idea—for both our sakes—but especially yours," he threatened, then turned and left as the cashier announced our order.

William waited a few minutes to make sure Ambrose was gone for good. Then he looked at me hard and long.

"How are you at keeping secrets?" he asked me.

"Good," I answered honestly.

He studied me a little longer.

"I think you are," he finally said. "Which is for the best, because we have a doozy."

William leaned conspiratorially across the table and spoke into my ear.

"My darling wife is a famous author. She has published over thirty books."

"Way over thirty," I corrected him.

"Really?" He was slightly taken aback.

"Really. I read about that in a scrapbook."

"Where?" William demanded, with a sharp intensity.

"At Mrs. Slocum's."

"That makes sense," he nodded. "So you know about her sophomore slump."

"You mean that she couldn't write a word for over two years?" I asked.

"A little longer than that, actually."

William looked both ways, before he whispered in my ear.

"She's still in it. For all intents and practical purposes, Ambrose is Virginia Faye Warner."

My eyebrow rose instinctively in surprise.

"That's right. Ambrose is the true 'Queen of Hearts,'" he said. "You certainly wouldn't want to see that face on a dust jacket."

"Not on anything you would want to touch," I said supportively.

"In her defense," William added, "she did write and sell the first one all by herself. It was after that that she got a little …"

"I'm blind, deaf and dumb," I reassured him.

I wanted to add that if it would get me a PhD, I would strangle Ambrose with my bare hands, or sit him down in front of a typewriter at gunpoint—whichever would make William happier.

"Good man," William replied. "By the way, one peep and her lawyer will take you for every dime you have and ever hoped to have."

He zoomed in for the eyeball-to-eyeball shot.

"Understood?"

I reflexively cowered, but relaxed as the tone of his voice shifted.

"She's—fragile," he said distantly.

For once it was easy to hold my tongue, even though I wanted to ask him about the blonde at the train station. This was when I discovered that having a really deep secret makes it easier to keep your mouth shut. It's the light gossipy bits that fly from your mouth like crumbs.

7

As we crossed the quadrangle, carrying the hot leaking pizza boxes, I experienced the same nervous excitement that a Princeton physics major invited to meet Einstein might have felt, walking next to the great Albert in an afternoon stroll on the campus of the Institute for Advanced Study. Here I was, studying under a man whose mathematical brilliance was legendary in our tiny world. My heart swelled, knowing that in the future my name might be inextricably linked with his—like D'Artagnan, Watson, Tonto or Sancho Panza. Perhaps my head swelled a little bit too.

To be aiding Dr. Teale in his work was a one-in-a-million opportunity. I would hear his first thoughts long before they were fine-tuned and honed for the general population. When inspiration did hit, I would be on the spot. On the inside. At least for as long as he was convinced that I was smart enough to keep around.

"You should know," Dr. Teale told me over his shoulder. "The Math Department open house has another reputation."

Naturally, I imagined that at this high level of intellectual discourse, mathematical discussions would quickly turn into arcane argument that might actually lead to a verbal brawl between warring doctrines. How Pythagorean!

My fantasies collapsed with his next sentence. "They're duller than dishwater."

Inside the departmental library, we put the pizzas down on top of the bookcase housing the thirteen-volume set of the Encyclopedia of Mathematics. The bookcase was covered with Formica and would be the easiest to clean up.

William directed me to stack the Cokes next to the books on negative numbers so "they would stay cold". Since it was still early, we wandered back to his office. I was shocked when he opened the door—his office was clean. There was a huge expanse of exposed desk and tabletops.

"Where did they all go?" I asked in disbelief. "All—those—papers."

He led me to the window. "There," he said, pointing to the left Dumpster in the parking lot.

"I didn't find what I was looking for," he added. "But I will. I never threw them out. I rejected them, but I never threw them away."

I interjected. "And we are talking about—?"

"It was a series of five papers. You brought the first with you. The next two were—"

He thought for a moment and added, "They might be excellent or they might be crap. I need to know. I think the fourth one contains some significant ideas. It set up number five, which codified the thesis."

"Inevitability?" I asked.

"Indubitably," he answered.

"How do you go about proving something like that? I mean logically."

"Well, that would make me the clever boy, wouldn't it?"

"The one I read was pretty good," I offered. "Not that I understood much."

"Exactly," he responded. "Pretty good. But not good enough. That was before I got an editor. She was brilliant. Only had one bad habit. She wrote suggestive and indecent notes in the margins." He smiled pensively.

Then his entire being froze.

"So I hid them," he finally said softly and very slowly. "Somewhere where they would never be found. I couldn't stand seeing them again. But I could not bear to destroy them. They were the only connection that I had with her."

"And she would be?" I asked.

But there was no answer forthcoming, because he was up on his feet and out of the office before he had even heard my query. I followed him.

"The best place to hide a book is in a library, isn't it?" he said as he energetically pulled books off the shelves, looking behind them, fanning the pages, shaking them out by the covers.

"The only comfort I have," he observed, "is that I am not as young and stupid as I might have been when I was young and stupid and wrote the damn paper."

His intimacy was making me feel awkward. I looked at the clock.

"It's four thirty," I said. "Where is everybody?"

"They'll be here. Not everybody, but the hungry ones. No staff, of course."

"No faculty?" I asked in surprise.

"They hate it. I could make it mandatory but they're all so equally unpleasant that there's little point. Why make it a wake for the living?"

As he inspected the last book that he could reach, I figured that the search was coming to an end. But I was wrong.

Stepping up off a chair, he hopped onto the lower bookcase that housed the unabridged *Principia Mathematica* and renewed the hunt heading north. His athletic frame was up to the agile demands of wall climbing. When he ran out of Bertram Russell, he stepped directly onto the upper shelves, finding foot and hand holds among light fixtures and ornamental carving.

"Would you like me to get a ladder?" I asked, concerned that if he came down it would be on top of me.

"No, thank you," he answered. "I don't like ladders. I fell off one when I was young."

"You did?"

"My father kept Lady Chatterley on the top shelf," William explained. "You can imagine my disappointment when I actually read it."

I was beginning to wonder what was so important about these long-lost articles. If the work was so brilliant, why hadn't he continued it? I don't think that he was reading my mind as much as having the same thoughts himself.

"A friend of mine teaches lit at Amherst," he recounted as he hung from the door lintel and swung his leg across to get a toehold in differential geometry. "He lost the only copy of his novel when his summer house burned down. He told me that over the next ten years, those ashes grew into the best thing ever written in English."

He pulled himself up through transformational geometry and climbed toward multiple integrals. He paused and looked at me over his shoulder.

A tall skinny student walked into the room.

"Hello, Professor Teale," he said, unfazed that the acting department chairman was high up and to the right.

"Welcome back, Mr. Weintraub," William answered. "You've got to watch the shelves in non-Euclidean geometry, gentlemen. I think they're warped."

The student rolled his eyes at me.

"You know you're back when you hear that one," he groaned. "Hi, I'm Harvey."

"Nice to meet you," I said and shook his hand. "I'm Roger."

He grabbed a soda and a slice from the only pizza that had anchovies and sat down.

William began his descent.

"All ready to start your dissertation?" he asked Harvey.

"I wrote it over the summer." Harvey delicately peeled anchovies off his pizza and ate them one by one. "It's up to you to understand it."

"I look forward to appreciating the extent of my ignorance," William demurred as he reached the floor. He kept going down until he was on his hands and knees in front of the open cabinets.

Two more students entered. Tiny Swenson weighed over two hundred and eighty pounds and had a very round head. His eyes squinted out through thin fat slits, but he looked relatively harmless. Jerry Ng was a Jewish Chinese guy with bright blue eyes.

Then the first of the department's two prima donnas walked in. He was Leopold Ickies, winner of the Hasbrooke Medal.

"Oh, look here," he announced sarcastically. "It's pizza. This must be a party."

He picked up a box and took it to the conference table.

Thereupon the other "star" walked in. His name was Lewis Embry.

"Welcome back, Lewis," William said. "We are so eager to hear in what delicious ways you exercised your brilliance this summer."

"As if I'd share my work with a bunch of troglodytes," Lewis snorted. "I will only say that it involves pi and a prime number of dubious parenthood."

He walked over to the conference table, flipped open Leo's pizza box, took a slice and hopped up onto the side table and sat cross-legged as he gobbled it down.

They were an ill-matched group of socially inept misfits with no graces and no charm. I was totally intimidated. They were so rude and hostile that I figured they had to be smarter than I was. I could only wonder why Dr. Teale had chosen me to intern instead of one of those brainiacs.

As they all sat chewing pizza, slurping soda and occasionally grunting at each other, William disappeared into the filing cabinets in the corner. These housed the archives of every paper that had been delivered into the room. Much later, I had the job of cleaning out those files, so I know that some were of interest, most were tedious and a few were brilliant—if you were in the right mood.

The students studied William surreptitiously. When they decided that he was suitably distracted, Leopold pulled a bottle of Bacardi from his book bag and poured shots into everyone's Coke.

"Still working on Wittgenstein, Mr. Ickies?" William's voice drifted up from below the conference table.

"Of course," Leo answered as he poured rum into my soda can. "I'm convinced that there are two worlds. The world of problems and the world of Wittgenstein."

As William pulled himself up onto his knees to respond to that one, the rum bottle magically disappeared.

"We're not drifting into the murky world of philosophy now, are we, Leopold?"

"No smoke and mirrors for me." Leo stood his ground. "Wittgenstein discovered, he codified … and wait … he gave us the tools, didn't he? And I've seen you use them. Damned, if he didn't create the very system that you use to formulate logic! In fact, if I'm correct, didn't Wittgenstein codify just about everything?"

"Hands, everyone," William demanded. "Who likes Wittgenstein?"

A forest of arms shot up.

"And who has actually read Wittgenstein?"

Leopold Ickies stuck his hand up with the enthusiasm of a third grader who knew the capital of Montana.

"And who simply likes saying the name Wittgenstein?"

William dropped a huge stack of files on the conference table and started sifting through them.

"I assume that coeds still respond to academic name-dropping as enthusiastically as they did in my day, especially the exotic ones like Wittgenstein. I'll bet at least half of them think he was a beat poet from the '50s."

He looked up at the quiet room.

"It works best with anthropologists, if I remember correctly. Once they get past the hunter-gatherer phase, that is. Nothing like a boozy rite-and-ritual study date on a Saturday night." He leered and winked. "If you know what I mean."

Everyone blinked at him in disbelief. Apparently William had no reputation for ribaldry.

The door opened and the department secretary stuck her head in the room.

"Professor, your wife is on hold in your office."

"Excuse me, gentlemen," he said as he walked out.

A moment later he popped his head back in.

"Oh, by the way," he added. "This is Roger. He is my intern for the year."

He turned and walked away. His footsteps echoed clearly down the hall. The sounds were so distinct because there was suddenly absolute stillness in the room and I found myself surrounded by staring eyes.

"Hi," I offered lamely.

After an interminable silence, Lewis Embry finally broke the crystal goblet.

"Billy hasn't had an intern in living memory," he remarked, eyeing me sharply. "What's up?"

Being an intern meant both reduced tuition and a stipend. These guys might have been dysfunctional, but they could certainly do the numbers.

"What's your specialty?" he asked, meaning, who *are* you?

"I don't have one," I answered, in all sincerity.

That did not satisfy them and they started talking all at once. Sentences of disbelief and consternation flew into each other with no ears capturing them.

Finally, Leopold Ickies held up his hand to still the babble.

"Well, then," he began, "let's look at this logically. You are at least a mathematician, aren't you?"

For once in my life, I followed a basic instinct for self-preservation.

"No," I answered.

The room gasped.

"But I aspire to become one."

I had used the appropriate line at the right time. It played equally well to both super-duper-egos while showing respect to the others. The tension in the room was not entirely dissipated and the long knives were still out, but there was a tacit truce—at least for the moment.

Leopold eventually followed up. "So what's he working on?"

Now while I hadn't yet put my right hand on the Bible and taken the oath of internship, I definitely knew where my allegiance lay. This was treacherous ground.

"I don't know yet," I lied.

"He certainly can't be doing anything new in set theory," Jerry Ng pointed out.

"There is nothing new that can be done in set theory," Lewis scoffed.

"Probability," wondered Tiny.

"What are the chances," Leopold snorted.

At that moment, William strode back into the seminar room. He bundled up the folders he hadn't yet reviewed.

"Sorry, gentlemen. Crisis at home. Got to run," he said. "Welcome back. Have a smashing year."

He had barely turned his back and walked out when the bottle reappeared.

"This is the only dry open house on campus," Tiny explained to me.

"Why is that?"

"Your boss," Lewis explained.

Everyone in the room except Harvey performed the international hand sign for "drinkies."

Then the conversation collapsed into a roundelay of gossip. I tried to stuff myself into the shadows lest a finger point at me.

"Hello," Leo slurred, with a stagger. "My name is Billy and I am a mathematician."

"Went down in flames, didn't he?" another contributed.

"In front of the full membership of the Comstock Review Board, no less," the next chimed in.

"Disappeared for two years. No one seems to know where."

"Returned."

"Married the chancellor's daughter."

"Nobody's better at traditional Aristotelian logic."

"But he will bore the pants off you with the Konigsberg bridge problem."

"Oh my God," agreed Tiny.

"The best topology class in the five schools."

"But he's dry."

"He's tedious."

"He's a pill."

They were full of information. Some of it was perhaps accurate.

I was struck mostly by the fact they all seemed to dislike each other with a certain intimacy, even as they dissected me on the laboratory bench:

"What's going on?"

"What's he up to?"

"What's he working on?"

"What did you score on your GREs?"

They were, excepting Harvey, full of questions, but none had the answer that I too was looking for: namely, why did he hire me of all people?

"It's do-or-die time," Harvey explained to me as we walked out of the building together. "A math whiz loses his luster when he hits his twenties. They're no longer whizzing, going for the gold while still in wunderkindergarten. That's why they're so bitter. Me, I have grander ambitions. I want to be the best high school math teacher in Canada."

8

Once I got past Mrs. Slocum's initial baptism by scrapbook—death by a thousand clippings—I found her quite sweet. Nevertheless, when I saw that her living room was full of people, I tried to sneak past the gathering to get to my room.

It was the local chapter of the Virginia Faye Warner Fan Club. They met here monthly. But she caught me.

"Roger, is that you?" she called out.

"Yes," I answered guiltily.

"Wonderful. Come in and join us. We could use a man's opinion."

"Thank you very much," I heard a male voice grumble.

"Say hello to Roger," my landlady directed the group.

"Hello, Roger," the ladies saluted.

The only man present simply glowered at me.

"Good afternoon," I replied cautiously as I entered into the most obvious no-man's-land since the battle of the Somme.

"I won't bother introducing everyone," Mrs. Slocum said. "That's why we have name tags."

I quickly noticed that the demographic spread through the room was like one of the bell-shaped curves that I had been studying earlier in the science library at Klippman Hall. It was quite a blend: 5 percent Albert (the natty gentleman in the blue blazer and white ducks), 95 percent polyester double-knit. Of the dozen or so ladies in the room, a few were in their twenties and thirties and a few were ladies "of a certain age"; the majority hailed from Mrs. Slocum's generation.

"We have been working on our letter," Mrs. Slocum explained.

"To the board of trustees at SUNY," Joan added.

"The State University of New York," Cindy clarified.

"I still think it should start 'Whereas,'" protested Harriet.

The nametags were indeed helpful.

"We've been through all that," Cindy responded.

"I think it is probably the silliest idea that you ladies have come up with yet," Albert offered and he pulled out an emery board to address a troublesome nail.

"Do you mind, dear?" Mrs. Slocum asked.

"Of course not," I replied gallantly and sat down.

"Dear Sirs," she began. "We demand an explanation of the recent decision taken by the Dissertation Approval Committee at SUNY-Poughkeepsie. We find their actions arbitrary, capricious, unprofessional, without merit and totally unacceptable."

I noticed that the ladies were mouthing the words as she read the document. She turned to me for support.

"How long have you been working on this?" I asked.

"The letter or this version?"

"I still think that sentence should include 'un-American,'" Joan slipped in.

"Aren't you glad you dropped in, Roger?" Mabel flashed me a smile that hung somewhere between sympathy and sadism.

She was the oldest, but she had the keenest eye, like the grandmother who knew exactly what you were up to. The gaze was softened by a conspiratorial twinkle. Sitting to the side, slightly away from the group, she was the only one in the room with gray hair. All the others had blue or orange tints. It was instantly clear to me that she was the spiritual center of the group. Mrs. Slocum might be the chief cook and bottle washer, but Mabel was the power behind the throne.

"Go on with your love note, Greta," she directed.

It was a very long letter. While I wouldn't have been able to pass a test on it, I do think that I understood what it was about. It seemed that Cindy and Maureen were sisters-in-law with a common niece, a graduate student in English going for a PhD at the state university just twenty-five minutes to the north. The brouhaha erupted when her thesis advisor vetoed her proposal to write her dissertation on that great American writer Virginia Faye Warner.

Pouring oil on the flames, the wrong-thinking male admitted that not only had he not read a single one of her books, he had no intention of ever doing so. He further exacerbated the situation when he suggested that she write her thesis on George Eliot.

To which the young woman replied loudly in clear and righteous indignation, "It would be one thing if you redirected me to another great female talent like Georgette Heyer, but I will not write yet one more paper about a dead white male. My paper will celebrate the feminine voice." Then she understandably stomped out of the room.

Upon hearing of this horrible event, the ladies were in quick consensus and found the situation "appalling, galling and totally unacceptable."

Mrs. Slocum soldiered on, interrupted only by the occasional nitpick over the text and two votes. I lost count of what page we were on, but there was a roiling undercurrent in the letter. What started out as a basic complaint had suddenly turned into the dramatic exposure of a huge conspiracy.

"To be frank," Mrs. Slocum read, "we are amazed that you have been successful with your cover-up for as long as you have. But the clock is ticking, gentlemen."

When I realized that I was losing not just the thread of the accusation but an actual grasp of my surroundings, I tried to will myself back into the moment. But apart from the hypnotic drone of the endless letter, all I could hear was the regular throaty ticks of the grandfather clock in the hall, so steady and finite that my pulse rate had regulated itself to sixty. Then my eyes started to fail.

My head sank. Then, on the verge of sleep, I would jerk my head up involuntarily. In the outer fringes, other voices were chiming in. There was an occasional flurry of wings and the pecking sounds of beaks as the letter continued. Finally, the sound of fighting fowl was replaced by angrier voices in argument, and I was brought back to reality. Mabel was patting my knee.

"It looks like a good moment to make your break, hon." She winked.

As Mrs. Slocum tried to restore order, using a teacup as a gavel, I slipped out just as it shattered.

9

The following Friday morning I was late to William's office because I had to drive the bus to take Mrs. Slocum to the podiatrist. When I got to the math department, I leapt up the staircase taking two and three steps at a time. As I entered the office, I found William rummaging in a packing box. He was not alone. Sitting on a stack of three other boxes, swinging his feet, was a small man who turned out to be Arlen Sheffield from next door.

He was properly proportioned. His head was the right one for his body and his arms and legs were the appropriate sizes, but he was small, perhaps under four foot six. He had narrow eyes and a very tight-lipped mouth. His hair was closely cropped but not a crew cut.

"This man has no scruples," William warned me.

"I told you before, Billy Boy, it wasn't my fault," Sheffield said. "They had to remove them when I ruptured my spleen."

"Why are you such an SOB?"

"That question pertains to a condition or a state, not a decision. In my official capacity, I don't have to answer that."

"I take your point," William conceded.

"Thanks for the stapler," the diminutive man said on his way out. "Just try and get it back."

We heard the door to his office close.

"You are blessed," William informed me. "He teaches the ethics course next semester."

"Science and Obligation," he added with a sinister chuckle. "Required for all master's and PhD candidates."

"Lucky me," I agreed.

William's mirth quickly evaporated. "I can't find them," he said.

"What?"

"The next two. I wrote 'Coincidental Logic' when I was in Boston. I did all the math for 'Inferred Fatalism' when I was at the London School of Economics. The concluding paper was magical. That was the proof that closed the door. I wrote that one during the most productive period of my life." He looked smug for a moment, but then folded up. It was a look I was beginning to recognize.

"Before the deep freeze of winter," he added cryptically, moving further into himself.

I was curious to know more, but knew better than to ask. He sat in his desk chair and gnawed at the knuckles of his right hand, brooding.

"What is the difference between coincidence and inevitability?" he asked finally.

I went back to looking stupid until William suddenly slapped the desk. I jumped.

"This won't do," he said. "We've got to find them."

He was up and out of the chair and his face was quite close to mine.

"Don't believe that crap about mathematicians. There is life after twenty-four," he avowed. "It's not that I can't do it again. I know I can do it again. I just did it rather well the first time. I don't like chewing the same meat twice."

He grabbed my shoulders, whether for emphasis or support I still don't know.

"We'll have to go to the house," he said as he released me.

In the moment that it took me to realize that I was meant to follow, he was out the door. I ran down the stairs in pursuit.

Whenever he moved, William was remarkably swift. I was in the parking lot a scant half-minute behind him, but there was no sign of either him or the van. All was quiet.

Then the stillness was ruptured by a wailing fan belt. I followed my ears and walked toward the screech and found William wrestling with a 1965 Plymouth Valiant. His left arm was buried under the dashboard. His other hand was trying to seduce the ignition with the key. All the while, his right foot was pumping the accelerator.

"Don't say a word," he commanded. "These are sacred rites."

Mutely I stepped back. Never have I observed such a fierce and directed concentration. Holding his breath, he slammed his foot hard against the floor, turned the key even harder to the right and held it over.

I watched and waited. I grew concerned as he stopped all movement as well as breathing. Was he having a heart attack? I was about to break my silence and call for an ambulance when the engine coughed twice, turned over and revved madly.

"Haven't lost my touch," he chuckled. He gestured to me. "Get in. Get in. The son of a bitch could stall any second."

We left through the south gate, on the opposite side of campus from the stunning archway that graced the cover of the annual school bulletin. He turned right, driving away from the town and up the hill. The road was steep and winding as it ascended a dramatic headland.

When the Plymouth was finally up to speed, it inspired some confidence but not a lot. I enjoyed the view as we lurched higher into the hills. The campus fell away and the valley opened up. It was a spectacular display of scenery.

Near the top, the trees thinned and we saw the sunlight glinting off the Tappan Zee. The river looked so good at that moment that it should have been photographed by the state board of tourism. To the north you could see the drooping cables of the Bear Mountain Bridge and to the right were the twin-vaulted containment structures of the nuclear power plant. Since it was a warm Friday in late September, a jumble of sailboats darted and tacked against the changeable winds and petulant currents of Haverstraw Bay.

William made a sharp right turn onto an unmarked gravel drive. We pulled up to massive, embellished, wrought iron gates. Cupids hovered around the gateposts and two large conjoined hearts were fabricated into the metal. Above them, in Gothic filigree, was the motto "*AMOR VERUS MORTALIS NUMQUAM.*"

"True love never dies," William explained as he punched a series of numbers into a security pad on an adjacent stanchion.

The gates slowly swung open and the hearts slowly parted. We coasted down the drive. Spinning the wheel to the right, William rolled the car off the noisy gravel and onto a quiet bed of pine needles, pulling up next to the van he'd been driving when he had first brought me to Mrs. Slocum's.

"You live here?" I said stupidly.

"Welcome to VFW Hall," he replied as he climbed out of the station wagon.

I followed him. But it was hard not to notice that the car was still running, coughing and occasionally blasting blue clouds of smoke.

"Don't you want to turn it off?" I asked.

He didn't bother to answer. He just straightened his arm behind him and jingled the key ring at me as he walked away from the rampaging automobile, which finally died.

The main house was chiseled into the rocky terrain just under the brow of the hill. You could make out the terra cotta of the roof through the white pine and hemlocks. William loped down brick steps, hidden among large rhododendrons.

"It takes five minutes longer if we go in through the front door," he explained.

The house was very grand, built in a meandering Mediterranean style with sweeping tile roofs contrasting with pale stucco walls. It was well-sited and folded into the environs so gracefully that it did not appear as vast as it was. Following the ridgeline to deliver a breathtaking panorama of the bay below, the architecture had the dignified demeanor and implied history of an ancestral home.

The landscaping surrounding this classic Italianate villa was exquisite, even though it would be more at home behind an English manor house. There was a grid of low walls made up of ancient brick, marking out a series of gardens in varying degrees of formality. Sprinkled among them there were romantic follies. A crumbling

Gothic ruin graced a small lawn behind the roses. More gardens were terraced into the hillside below.

We turned left at the lily pond and approached the back of the structure. William opened a door near the back of a greenhouse. Working our way through a sequence of utility rooms, we ended up in a pantry.

Over there, he motioned.

He led me up a back stairway, then through a door into a wide hallway. The floor was covered with an array of sumptuous Persian rugs. Rich walnut paneled the dado. Above, the cream-colored wall was home to a magnificent gallery of artwork.

I gawked. I had never seen anything like this. Each painting was displayed in an ornately carved gold-leafed frame. The colors were vibrant. The technique was voluptuous and garish. Despite a wide range of characters and settings, they were all strangely similar. In each, a man and a woman embraced dramatically. Both were superb physical specimens: he, muscular and handsome; she, ravishing and shapely. Only the clothes and the backgrounds differed from picture to picture.

"Book covers," William explained. "From the neo-bordello revival school."

We continued on. It was a long hallway. Although the paintings seemed to merge into a deadening repetition, a few distinctive themes could be identified.

Midway, the men in the paintings became more dashing. There was a sudden glut of pirates, bullfighters and the occasional buckskinned pioneer. Then, in another transition, there was a run of young and manly business executives in gray flannel suits that were almost torn apart by the powerful pectoral muscles constrained within them. Each was sweeping a beautiful career woman off her high heels in a passionate embrace across a wide desk in a corner office.

We arrived at a double door. A dramatic column framed each side. Above the Corinthian capitals, the lintels were populated with more cupids, but this time they were reading books.

Above the doorway in the pediment were carved satyrs. One was standing, playing his pipes. Another was lying on the ground writing in a large volume with a quill pen, his hairy legs and hooves kicking idly behind him.

Over here, William signaled from the other end of the corridor.

He stood on the threshold of a door that would be invisible in the paneling when closed. By the time I caught up with him, he held a finger to his lips. "Shh."

We tiptoed up a long, narrow staircase. William opened the door at the top. I stepped out, suddenly speechless.

When you come into a great space, there is a special feeling. I had felt that way at the Spectrum in Philadelphia, when I passed through the final portal and the full scope of the arena was revealed. I am sure that when a gladiator stepped into the ring, the open expanse of the Coliseum was equally breathtaking. It was like that, albeit on a lesser scale, when you passed through a door opening into Virginia Faye Warner's personal library.

Floor to ceiling, it was three stories high and totally open. There were two mezzanines. Both ran the length of the west wing. The railings were wrought iron with polished mahogany handgrips. Built-in bookcases ran along the wall. Library stacks jutted out from them. Glorious sculptures and paintings, depicting famous lovers of all time, were artfully arranged throughout the room. The most dramatic was a Victorian marble reproduction of a Renaissance Aphrodite and Adonis, positioned and spotlighted in a deep niche over the main entrance. William and I were standing on the top level.

The place was so sumptuous that it could drive the illiterate to love books. Only with time would I appreciate the depth of its catalog: all the classics, as well as contemporary literature, comprehensive science and history collections and a complete reference desk.

Then I looked at the opposite wall. Raising my eyes, I was awestruck.

"Over a thousand window panes," William whispered to me. The view was only river and sky. Man-made splendor shrank to insignificance behind it.

After a breathless moment, I pulled away from the grip of the vista and continued my survey below. To the left of the main reading room was an alcove that jutted out over the great lawn. It contained a huge desk. Behind it were a leather desk chair and a dramatic flower arrangement in an urn, which was so spectacular and large that it looked as if it belonged in the lobby of a grand hotel. I had certainly never seen anything like it in a private home. Of course, I had never seen a private house like this either.

William slipped off his shoes and signaled me to do the same. He also warned me to keep away from the railing. I could hear the low murmur of unintelligible voices two floors below.

Then he disappeared from view. I glimpsed him moving up and down the aisles pushing a shelving cart, which slowly filled as he pulled volumes off the stacks.

I waited, unsure what to do, where to stand. The drone of the voices downstairs lulled me. I settled into a comfortable chair facing west and lost myself in the spectacle that was the Hudson River.

Every one of the panes was sparkling clean and without a streak. I felt myself drawn into the deep blue sky on the other side. Higher up, a swirling mob of Canada geese shuffled and reshuffled until it emerged in an organized v-formation, heading south.

When they had disappeared across the river, the sky was empty, cloudless.

Suddenly there was a brittle explosion of shattering glass. My head snapped upright and I looked frantically for William.

But he was gone. All that remained was a pile of books and papers on the floor next to the book cart. My curiosity overpowered my discretion. I went to the railing and peered down at the scene below.

From the many dust jackets I had seen at Mrs. Slocum's, I knew immediately that I was looking at William's wife. She was perfectly coiffed and made up just like she was in the photos. However, unlike in her publicity stills, she was wearing a baby blue quilted housecoat with pink fluffies on her feet.

Glowering across from her was Ambrose. Even though his face was red with outrage, it retained its pasty complexion. He was wearing a "Kiss me, I'm Irish" baseball cap and a sweatshirt that read "Chaste Makes Waste."

"You are so right," Ambrose snarled at her. "That was completely out of line. This one is so much more apropos."

He grabbed a book from the shelf and referred to the spine. "*Love Has Wings.*"

Then he crouched like a discus thrower, wound up and let go. In a perfect parabola, the book sailed up through the room and found a fresh windowpane, quickly reducing it to flying shards.

"Whee!" he exulted. "Love flies."

"You'll pay for that," Virginia Faye Warner snapped.

"Take it out of my check," he barked.

"First, you need to earn it," she replied icily. "I'm not running a charity here."

"A home for wayward ghouls," he muttered.

"I heard that."

"Now hear this: I'm leaving."

"Good riddance. You're a burnt-out, worthless hack."

"I know you are, but what am I?" Ambrose sneered back at her.

They were toe-to-toe when William suddenly inserted himself between them. Now they had to lean over behind his back to trade barbs.

"You can't quit. Nobody will hire you," she continued. "You're gross and stupid."

"You hired me, Stupid."

William picked up *Bartlett's Familiar Quotations* and slammed it down hard on the tabletop. The loud report made them both jump.

"Enough. Both of you," William ordered. "Faye, sit down. Ambrose, go to your corner."

Ambrose stomped to the other side of the room and stuffed himself into a small antique school desk. He sulked for a while, but then he discovered a bag of unshelled peanuts under the lid. He ripped it open with his teeth and started cracking and chewing. The pile of husks grew as he jawed like a cow and his eyes stared vacantly ahead.

"Disgusting," she mumbled in a bad stage whisper. "Look at him!"

"Behave yourself," William admonished before looking for me on the mezzanine.

"Roger," he directed to me, "pick up the pages I dropped and put them in order."

When William's wife saw me standing at the rail, her eyes seemed guided by laser beams.

"Who is that?" she demanded.

"Say hello to Roger," William said. "He's my new intern."

"Hello, Miss Warner," I called down. "It's a pleasure to meet you."

"Don't pretend that you know who I am," she snapped as she disappeared into her handbag. "You haven't read any of my books, have you?"

"No. I'm afraid I haven't."

There was no reason why I would have ever read a "girl" book like she wrote. Nevertheless, I felt inexplicably sheepish.

"But I want to."

She looked up at me again and a red tide of color spread across my face.

"At least we know he can't lie," she noted, as she lit a cigarette before turning her attention to her husband.

"What are you doing here, anyway?"

I realized then that this unfamiliar level of society would take some getting used to. I had never set foot in a mansion before that morning. I certainly hadn't met anyone famous before. But what struck me the most was the nature of my mentor's relationship with his wife. For being married, they seemed cool and formal, nothing like any of my relatives.

"I'm looking for some papers," William replied.

The chill was drifting toward frosty as they looked at each other until the telephone on her desk rang. He seemed relieved by the distraction. She ignored it.

It rang a second time. She had an idea of who it was because she began to mimic the caller even as it continued to ring.

"Virginia, Aloha," she parodied. "It's me, Frederick. How's my favorite writer?"

"I'm fine, Freddy." She continued her little *theatricale*. "How's my favorite agent?"

"Fabulous, darling," she answered herself, in insincere West Coast banter. "So how's every little thing?"

"Equally fab, sweetmeat," she went on. "Thinking of flying out to the coast and walking into water off the Golden Gate."

"Sounds like a fantastic weekend, sweetie. How's the book coming?"

The phone stopped ringing. The room got still. She lit yet another cigarette. We watched her smoke it down to the nub. It didn't take long. She was a pro.

Glaring at Ambrose, Virginia Faye Warner said, "I hope you're satisfied."

Then she sank down into a chair.

"I must be the only one in the world to have a ghostwriter with writer's block," she announced loudly with an exasperated sigh. "Rich. Really, really rich."

Surprised that William took time out from his domestic crisis to toss me a scowl, I returned to my job of gathering up the books and papers. I temporarily loaded them onto the shelving cart and wheeled it to the end of the stacks near the staircase.

More interesting than the books were the papers and articles still strewn all over the floor. A few had been clipped out of journals, but most of them were original manuscripts. When I read the abstracts, I knew that these were what he was hunting for.

"'A Logical Sequence toward a Proof of Inevitability' by William E. Teale, Professor of Mathematics and Philosophy," read the title page of one article.

I was eager to read that one, but there was no page two. The typescripts were old and seemed to have all given out at the same moment. The floor was covered with crumbly fragments that fell apart when you touched them.

I knew that I could never accurately collate the pile in front of me, but I did my best to preserve it. I isolated the title pages. There were four. That was exciting in itself. Then I carefully tamped the rest into the neatest stack possible and returned to the railing wondering what I should do now.

Down below, the argument had taken a new turn.

"Oaters?" Miss Warner sneered at Ambrose. "You want to write westerns? You?"

"You are in no position to demean," Ambrose answered defensively. "The western genre has a rich history in publishing. That will be my next book. Read my contract."

"I've read your contract, Tex," she answered. "Your spurs are mine."

Then, overcome with curiosity, Faye asked, "What's it called?"

"*Bad Day at Fort Meade*," Ambrose answered proudly.

At that, she laughed so hard that she segued into a coughing jag.

"What's so funny?" the ghostwriter demanded once she was breathing regularly.

"Fort Meade is in Maryland, idiot," she explained. "Everyone knows that."

"Big deal," Ambrose said defensively. "I'll go back to *Boots in Yuma*."

"You can get the boot after you write the next book," Faye explained. "It's in the contract."

"I've been waiting for that contract for seventeen years," Ambrose spat back.

"Don't blame me. Blame the post office."

William pulled his head out of the book he was studying. He was aglow. "This is logical," he announced. "Even I could make it work."

Faye and Ambrose both looked at him with scorn.

William slapped the book closed and read the spine. "*Muriel Meekham's Practical Guide for the Romance Novelist*."

"Don't say anything that you'll regret later," Faye warned.

"Nothing but professional admiration, my dear. She seems to know what she's talking about and she covers it all. Did she ever write anything?"

"Of course."

"*That.*" Ambrose pointed to the book in William's hand.

"Ah." William scanned the manual as he read chapter titles, "Planning the plot … Picking the place … Setting the scene."

He flipped ahead.

"Oh I like this. 'Comic relief is more than just for laughs.'"

Ambrose rose to his mentor's defense. "You can make fun of it all you want," he argued. "But Meekham has been the manual of choice for writers in our trade for over fifty years."

"I'm not making fun of anything," William answered.

"You never do," Faye pointed out. "But that doesn't mean you are innocent."

He didn't seem to hear her. He read aloud, "'When choosing names for central characters, especially the lovers, avoid employing the exotic or unfamiliar.'"

He closed the book.

"Too bad," he sighed. "I guess you can't use Sanjoop Chatterji for the hero."

Ambrose was visibly distressed.

"It's all well and good for you to be sarcastic and cynical and carry on about something you know nothing about."

"That's all right," his boss interrupted him. "I'll take it from here."

Faye looked at her husband. "Mrs. Meckham's manual built this house, Billy. We have followed it chapter and verse on every book we've written, and she has never let us down."

"My point exactly," William said. "It is a formula."

They both started to protest contentiously, until William held up his hand. I was surprised to see them both quiet down.

"Don't let the technical words scare you," he explained. "You both employ formulas every day in your life."

He looked at his wife. "Three parts gin, one part vermouth," he said.

Turning to Ambrose, he added, "Two chocolate wafers and a creamy center."

Then he chuckled.

"If it can be formulated, it can be a mathematical model. All I need is a computer."

10

The next afternoon I stepped into William's office to deliver the finalized course enrollment schedules from the registrar's office. He was on his back on the sofa, writing furiously on a legal pad against his scrunched up knees. Arlen Sheffield was sitting cross-legged on the desktop reading Meekham's Guide.

"It's kind of like *Lawrence of Arabia*," Professor Sheffield explained. "The T. E. Lawrence one—*The Seven Pillars of Wisdom*—except replace 'Wisdom' with 'Romance.'"

"That's so creepy," William commented.

"It's not," Sheffield corrected, looking at the author's portrait on the frontispiece. "She's a dear, actually. A sort of cross between Jazz Age flapper and Queen Victoria."

"That's not what I meant," William explained. "It's the notion of you touching anything that involves love. Like Meals on Wheels being doled out by Typhoid Mary."

"That is totally unfair," the philosopher protested. "I have a heart as big as all outdoors."

"Let it snow, let it snow, let it snow," William sang out as his pencil attacked the yellow tablet in time.

Sheffield ignored that. He was much more interested in the text.

"Sit down," my professor directed when he saw me. "I need you to do something."

"Mrs. Meekham has certainly developed a comprehensive system," Sheffield said in admiration.

He elucidated. "The Pillars of Romance:

> Know your time;
> Know your lovers;
> No marrieds;
> No exotic personalities;
> Keep it simple;
> Keep it clean …

and once joined …

Keep them together forever and ever after. Hallelujah. Amen."

After a quick review, he said, "I count seven."

"That's what I came up with," William concurred, having ticked them off on his fingers.

"Then why did you drag me in here?"

"To torture you until I got my stapler back."

"Over my dead body."

William winked at me. "I think he wants me."

"Can't," Sheffield explained. "Pillar number three: No marrieds."

"But we've got one more," William explained. "Faye's pillar number eight: true love never dies."

"Where does it go when the people do?" Sheffield wondered.

"That is on a need-to-know basis. We are concerned with the before, not the after. Separated for years. Lovers reunited by fluky circumstance. Fate. Kismet. Karma. Take a wrong turn at the bus depot and wham, bam and 'where the hell have you been for half my life, ma'am.'"

"I wouldn't know," the ethicist said, starting to untangle his legs. "You are the probability and statistics guru."

William stopped writing and faced his neighbor.

"Actually, I hate statistics," he said.

I smiled to myself. That confirmed it. William and I were kindred spirits.

"But there is a high probability of profitability," he continued. "A huge market of people wondering 'what if?'"

"What if—what?"

"What if I were a middle-aged hausfrau and I ran into my high school boyfriend, whom I hadn't seen for thirty years? And he still likes me."

"There is no accounting for taste," Sheffield observed.

"Who cares?" William corrected. "The bean counters say we're printing money."

No one said anything after that. The only sound was pencil scratching. Professor Sheffield was reading the book. I was trying to steal glances at what William was working on.

Finally, Sheffield confessed in a sheepish voice, "I had one."

"Had one what?" William asked.

"A love of my life."

"Sheffield in love," William said in amazement. "That must have been a sight to see."

He swung his legs off the couch and tossed the pad on the desk.

"She was perfect. We were together for seventeen months. She was beautiful and funny. She was smarter than I. I called her 'Stretch.' We were fantastic together. People enjoyed being next to us. We were so happy and lively. We had an aura."

As I watched, he seemed to grow more in stature with every new detail of the memory.

"What happened?" William asked in a gentle voice.

"She left."

With those words, he crashed back to earth. I wanted to know why, but I didn't ask.

Eventually, Arlen asked. "What about you?"

"I am lucky," William answered. "Not only did I have a love of my life, but I am married to her."

"No one else before her?"

"Oh, there were some. One or two that flashed and sparkled. A blonde perhaps. Nothing remarkable. The trappings of youth."

"Is that what it's called nowadays?"

"Few are called and less are chosen."

"A blonde, you say?" Sheffield reflected.

"I suppose," William replied. "I'm not completely sure. They tend to blur together. It was a lifetime ago."

The only reason why a Klaxon didn't go off in my head was because my mind didn't process this part of the conversation until later. I was too absorbed in the work on William's yellow tablet. I didn't understand most of it, but some patterns were beginning to emerge.

"No one stands out?" Sheffield pressed.

"Nope."

"From the sea of women that washed over the math department, not a special one?"

William shook his head and shrugged his shoulders. "Sorry."

"I am not surprised that you forget that I was there for your indefensible presentation to the Comstock Committee. I was in the front row." The little man slid off the desk onto his feet.

With the growing cloud of mystery surrounding William's appearance before that august academic review board, my interest was more than piqued. I had already looked for the minutes of that meeting in the basement of Klippman, but the volume that covered that period had suspiciously gone missing.

Here was my opportunity. I turned to see what more I could finesse out of Professor Sheffield. But William was on his feet first. "Enough about us old-timers. We are holding up young Roger."

"Don't worry about me," I said, watching the calculations on the page twist and turn in a hypnotic dance.

"OK, wise man," William asked Sheffield. "What do I do?"

Arlen Sheffield clearly wanted to pursue the previous topic, but he went along with the gear shift. He fanned through the pages of Meekham; then he weighed the volume in his hands, studying it.

"It's hard," Sheffield admitted.

"It certainly is."

"There are so many variables."

"Even though it starts out with only two."

"But it gets compounded with every interchange which would square the set size."

"Cube it, Arlen."

"Cube? Well, that gets big in a hurry."

"So what do I do?"

Sheffield stood next to me, perusing the calculations on the pad.

"Beats the hell out of me. What do you think, Roger?" he asked me. "You're still young and closer to the source. How's your love life?"

"Garrison's a small school," I said. "Our math department wasn't awash with blondes or females."

"But you did the best you could? Regardless of hair color."

"I do have a practical understanding of the mechanics, Professor Sheffield," I replied, intentionally trying to sound inexperienced.

He took the hook.

"You do know where to put it, don't you?"

"Well—" I started slowly. "I think I would start about here."

I pointed at a specific insertion point on the page of William's tablet.

"It's rather straightforward, isn't it?" I said. "You nest the codified rule set inside a random number generator."

I looked up and was taken aback to see astonished looks on both their faces.

"Of course," William slapped his forehead. "He's right."

I was suddenly bursting with the pride of accomplishment.

"Out of the mouth of babes," Sheffield assented, grabbing a staple puller off the shelf on his way out. "I need one of these."

William didn't notice. Before the door was closed, he had retrieved his work and was steadily circling, crossing out and scribbling. He concluded with two bold underscores at the bottom of the page.

"That's good," he said after he reviewed it one more time. "No more probation for you, young man."

My sigh of relief was audible, but I don't think he was listening. He walked to the coat stand and threw me a heavy sweater.

"Wear this," he directed.

"I'm warm enough like this," I said.

"Not where we're going."

11

The computer center at Hudson Polytechnic was tucked between the admissions office and the infirmary. It was originally housed in the basement of the comptroller, but as the field and demand for space grew, the programmers took over the whole building. They were justifiably proud of their new IBM 370/3030. The machine room took up most of the first floor.

"Do you have a reservation?" I asked William.

This was a reasonable question. There was a seven-day wait for processing time on the 370, even well after midnight on Saturday nights.

"Don't need one. We're going to the cellar."

There was no wait for the computer downstairs. Not only did that system predate the new one by more than two generations, it employed so many vacuum tubes that the thermostat had to be permanently set at two clicks below "frigid."

"Here," William said, handing me a pair of gloves without fingertips. "I hope you can type."

The sign-up sheet clipped beside the door informed us that we could have the room until Monday afternoon, when the local high school science club had an ongoing reservation.

William dutifully wrote his name on the schedule and x-ed a large block of time well into the next morning. I groaned internally as he opened the door and I could see his breath. I realized that the tedious work of the night would be made even more miserable by the environment.

The florescent lights did nothing to temper the chill. Their hues were bluish without a single pink tube for balance. Inside the stark room, anyone's skin looked as pasty as Ambrose's.

"You've got to be kidding," I said when I first caught sight of the rusting hulk of IBM iron.

"Don't be seduced by that tart upstairs," William cautioned. "A one is but a one. Zero is nothing the world over."

"Do you really think you can build a mathematical model of something as complicated as love on this heap of junk?" It sounded like a complaint.

"It's all in the code," he said confidently, perhaps hubristically. "I can formulize anything."

He pulled out a steno chair. Its broken wheel scraped across the floor.

"Have a seat."

The keypunch machine had been a loyal ally to the outdated computer next to it. All the letters, digits and symbols were worn off except for "z," "q," and the exclamation point.

Taped on the front of the machine, underneath the pressure plate, was a yellowed sheet of paper. If you looked carefully through the jumble of quickly scrawled phone numbers and under the medley of coffee stains and pizza sauces from over the years, you could barely make out "No food or drinks."

William showed me how to load the blank card hopper and explained the function switches and how to type in the code. He warned me that the punched card stacker would bind up if I let it get too full.

It soon became apparent why we were downstairs. William had never bothered to learn FORTRAN, so he was unable to use the more modern machine even if he wanted to. He wrote in Descartes, which was an arcane—albeit elegant—and now obsolete programming language.

He stood over me while I punched out the first twenty cards. Once he was satisfied that I could fly on my own, he sat at the desk next to the computer and went back to work writing code on his yellow pad.

Initially, I was dreading a long night of meaningless keystrokes, but after the first excruciating hour, I settled into a rhythm. The drone of the fans inside the computer blanketed out any other sound. The wall of white noise was a fertile field for auditory hallucination. As the typing became mechanical, I began to hear snippets of songs that I hadn't listened to for years.

We worked well together. He kept feeding me long pages of code, and I kept banging out punch cards. I got faster on the keyboard, but he had had a head start. I caught up with him just as he was finishing.

When I stood and handed him the last stack of punch cards, my teeth began to chatter uncontrollably.

"Get out of here," William directed. "Go get a bowl of hot soup at the diner. I'll run the program. It will take a while."

As I walked out, the computer center was still a hive of activity. It wasn't until I stepped off campus that I realized it was two o'clock in the morning. I crossed Academy Street, turned left and walked two blocks, shivering the whole way.

The Division Street Diner was a local landmark, which was a polite way of saying that it was old and rundown. It had been most recently renovated sometime in the 1950s. The red vinyl seats in the booths were cracked and patched with tape. Half the stools at the counter had frozen bearings and wouldn't spin. Heavy traffic lanes in the linoleum were worn through to the small black-and-white hexagon tiles of a previous life. The restaurant was also hot and stuffy.

I stepped over to the coat hooks and pulled at my jacket zipper. Halfway down, it jammed. William's thick sweater had gotten stuck in the teeth.

The more I tugged, the more the sweater was enmeshed. I tried to pull the zipper back up to clear it and start all over again, but it wouldn't budge. My hands were cold and clumsy.

I jerked and I yanked. The zipper only grew more embedded. More and more agitated, I squirmed and struggled.

Now I was burning up. I strained. I thought that I felt a slight give, so I prepared myself for the final assault.

I wound up my body like a spring. I took a deep breath. I gritted my teeth. Pulling down at the bottom of my coat with one hand, while pulling at the tiny metal tag with the other, I threw myself into the struggle.

I don't know exactly what happened, but I did achieve sufficient torque to spin me on my feet. I pirouetted, landing with a thud onto a booth seat. It was a moment before I realized that the booth was occupied.

"So glad that you could drop in." A soft English accent welcomed me.

I looked up. I was sprawled across the table from a stunning woman. A bemused smile played on her lips. Her eyes sparkled. I sensed that she was suppressing the urge to laugh at me.

"Might I help?" she asked.

Still struggling to get air back into my lungs, I could only nod stupidly.

"Stand up," she ordered, pointing to a spot on the floor next to the banquette.

Once I had my breath back, I stood at attention beside her seat while she studied the obstruction. At first, she tentatively tested the zipper. Then she pulled at the fabric of the coat. But as her rational approaches failed in rapid succession, she too lost patience and resorted to brute force.

"What a horrid and troublesome sweater," she exclaimed.

"It's not mine," I replied quickly. "Borrowed."

"Well, that's to your credit," she said as she rummaged around in her handbag until she extricated a small manicure set. "As it is as hideous as it is horrid."

She lifted the skirt of my jacket and looked underneath. Slipping her thumb and forefinger into a tiny cuticle scissor, she ordered, "Don't move."

As she leaned close and carefully snipped around my jammed zipper, my heat stroke was replaced with vertigo. The swirling eddies and random sprays of her hair were dizzying. Blonde, full and dangerous. She had it tied in a loose knot, but it was unruly and wayward.

"All done," she announced and gave the zipper a quick liberating jerk to prove that we had succeeded after all.

I pulled my jacket off and carried it over to the coat rack just as a waiter approached the table.

"No point in running off now that I've undressed you," she said. "Would you like a cup of their beastly coffee?"

"Yes, thank you," I stammered.

"Pie?" she asked.

"I can only go four decimals," I apologized. "3.1415."

That brought a grin. I was saved from further embarrassment when she sent the waiter off to fetch my coffee.

"How do you do," she said as she reached across the table with a firm handshake. "I'm Claire."

"Um … Roger."

Her eyes—navy blue and full of magic—were lovely. And they belied her age; she was clearly older than I was, but I couldn't tell by how much.

She moved some papers to one side.

"Let me make some room for you," she said after the waiter had gone. "I'm doing last-minute corrections. I've got a training session in an hour."

She gave another mischievous smirk.

"I can tell you're a student. You understand. This term paper was due yesterday."

I glanced at the avalanche of papers. Some were typed, some hand written. Some were covered with calculations. She started scribbling frantically then pulled up short.

"Damn," she complained as she erased with equal fervor. She began the calculation again.

Looking down at her work, I saw the problem immediately. It was a quadratic equation.

"Plus or minus," I told her, pointing at the error. "That should be '*plus or minus* the square root of b squared minus c.'"

She looked up and smiled. Her face lit up the dingy restaurant. Now that I'd had a chance to watch her and to catch my breath, I realized that Claire was a grown-up. I guessed she was somewhere between forty-five and fifty. But she was so far out of my league on so many levels that her age was immaterial. She was beautiful like the women that I watched on television or saw in magazines.

"So it should be," she said with delight. "Clever you."

She erased the offending operand and made the correction.

"I knew my luck would change if I took a break from the lot that I work with," she commented. "Nothing but physicists and engineers.

"They can only see the physical world," she continued. "If something goes up it must come down. No mystery. No magic. No imagination.

"No 'or.' No plus *or* minus," she noted as she finished off the calculation with a victorious QED at the bottom of the page.

"How can that be possible?" she mused. "It must be Zen."

Her face was exquisite. She was wearing a black turtleneck and a Harris tweed blazer. She was too thin, but her features were rounded off and graceful. Only her lips could distract you from disappearing into her eyes. They were full and soft with the tiniest creases at the sides. Those must have derived from whimsy, because when she caught me gawking at her, they became more pronounced.

Her eyes became even more playful as she put on a sultry look and asked, "Do you come here often?"

"About twice a week," I answered flatfootedly. "You?"

"Oh," she said wistfully, "every twenty-five years or so."

Two sharp honks from the street interrupted our conversation.

"That's my taxi," she explained as she stood up and reached for her wallet.

"Please," I insisted. "Allow me."

She patted me on the shoulder. "You're sweet. Thank you."

I held her coat as she slipped her arms into the sleeves.

"I'm off to train the lobster shift," she said. Then she added, "I do think that is a most unfortunate expression. A lobster shift at a nuclear power plant has a very bad suggestion of superheated steam going awry."

"I don't think you'd prefer the alternative," I suggested.

"What would that be?"

"The graveyard shift."

She laughed and I felt very clever.

After she collected all her things, she turned back to me. "Lose the sweater, darling. It doesn't do you justice."

She shook my hand again. "Thank you, 'um … Roger,'" she said. "Nice to meet you."

Then she was gone.

I'm not sure how long I sat in the booth. My reverie was broken only when William plopped down heavily across from me.

He turned around and suddenly seemed to notice his surroundings.

"Let's get out of here," he said. "This place gives me the creeps."

12

I was still groggy the following afternoon when I was back upstairs in the Virginia Faye Warner library, continuing my archeological reconstruction of William's earlier work. The floor of the balcony was covered with manuscript pages laid out in long rows.

I studied them carefully, moving them around into new combinations. I used whatever criterion came to mind at the moment: their degree of yellowing, the amount of ink left on the typewriter ribbon, a manufacturer's watermark. Ultimately, the best I could do was to match up the staple holes.

Even upstairs, I could feel the weighty air of a bad vibe that morning. William was being pedantic, lecturing his wife. Faye peppered every other line with "Blah blah blah."

Ambrose walked in from the kitchen, stuffing chocolate éclairs into his face, making it two-to-one against William, who was pulling a thick wad of computer paper from a briefcase.

"It's so simple," William protested. "You just need to see it. The genres are arrayed down the y-axis."

Faye and Ambrose looked halfheartedly at the printout.

"We hate Regency," Faye said as she read the first choice.

"Fine," William responded patiently. "No problem. There are six genres here."

"We hate all of them," Ambrose announced.

"I see," William said diplomatically.

Then, looking at them, he added, "I think we are all quite tired of pirates."

They just rolled their eyes.

"We don't have to choose a genre yet," William continued. "I populated the x-axis with thematic content and drove random numbers through a matrix. We have over two thousand story lines here."

He proudly patted the thick stack of green bar on the table.

"At this point it's just a question of picking the one you like best."

Ambrose licked a gob of chocolate out of the empty pastry box.

William flicked through the printout.

"Pick a critical situation to start the ball rolling."

They both looked at him blankly.

"How about writer's block?" William offered.

"Very funny," Ambrose groused.

"Not funny at all," Faye corrected.

William reconsidered for a moment.

"Don't worry," he said. "For the contextual constant within the program I used 'True love never dies.' That is, after all, your trademark. The premise is self-explanatory. Our hero rediscovers the love of his life after n years."

"N what?" Ambrose interrupted. "That doesn't make any sense."

"Just let him talk," Faye advised. "Then he'll go away."

"But the hero doesn't know what to do about it?" William suggested, desperately grasping at straws.

"The hero always knows what to do," Ambrose corrected. "That's why he is the 'hero.'"

From my perch I thought I saw William flare. Thinking back, he might have been angry, but with him it was never easy to tell. His head disappeared into the printout.

"How about this?" He read, "Surgeon loses wife on operating table, but finds his true love is in pre-op waiting for appendectomy."

"Wrote it," Ambrose yawned.

"*Black Scrubs*," Faye offered. "It was terrible. Fifteen thousand units. Total."

"Not to mention total humiliation," Ambrose sighed.

"Remaindered," Faye said sharply.

William flipped through more pages. "How about, nurse discovers long lost love on a gurney double parked in the emergency room."

"Wrote it," Faye informed him.

"Three times."

"*Angel Nurse Wife*."

"That was huge."

"*Bypassed but Not Forgotten*."

"That did OK."

"And *Vital Signs*."

"The girl was deaf in that one. We're staying away from handicaps these days."

"How about, hero discovers his lost love of thirty years in a—"

At this point, his wife interrupted. "It is very sweet of you to try to help us, Billy, but I see you are finally realizing that this isn't as easy as you think. There is something the how-to books don't mention."

"An unwritten rule," Ambrose added.

"Which would be?" William asked.

"These books aren't about the man, Billy," she explained. "Romance is rather one-sided in our business."

"In what way?"

"All men are dogs," Ambrose cut in severely.

"And all cats are girls?"

"Don't be cute, Billy," Faye snarled.

"Fine," William said. "Time to move on. You're through with the medical angle. I can understand that. Three books can exhaust a theme."

Ambrose and Faye erupted in guffaws.

"What's so funny?" William asked.

"Three books?" Ambrose asked incredulously.

"More like seventeen," Faye explained.

"OK. That certainly seems to be a saturation level."

We all waited while William scanned through more plot lines.

"How about the law?"

"Death," Faye declared.

"Death," Ambrose agreed.

William looked up sheepishly. "I guess Holy Orders are out?"

"You guessed right." Faye practically sneered.

"Our publisher wants colorful costumes on the book jacket."

"So I guess no long gray line."

"We tried military," Ambrose said.

"Wasn't terrible."

"Wasn't great."

"But we like ambassadors."

"We love ambassadors."

William was ebullient.

"Ah," he reveled. "Here's one. A woman suffering from amnesia in a foreign land wanders into the U.S. embassy, only to discover—"

"No good," interrupted Faye.

"Why not?" asked William.

"Ran out of countries," explained Ambrose with a smirk.

"Amnesia is for amateurs," Faye added.

The lethal silence returned.

"I guess that leaves the Fourth Estate."

"Oh, we do like the press," Faye enthused.

"Very much. Journalists are so sexy."

"Battlefields."

"Political intrigue."

"Manly tousled hair. Stubble. Turtlenecks!"

"Rockets' red glare."

"Sweaty nights."

"Early mornings, unwashed and under stress."

"Flak jackets."

"The perfect recipe."

William's eyes danced across the printout. He was jubilant.

"Fantastic," he exulted. "I've got nearly thirty reporter stories. Let's write a book."

"Can't," Ambrose corrected.

"Why not?"

"That was the one we just published."

"You told me you had read it," Faye accused with a hurt look.

For a moment, William seemed dispirited. At the same time, the other two looked totally pleased with themselves for having beaten Teacher.

But he was not to be bested. After all, he had taught graduate math students.

"Civil War."

"Nope," they said in unison. "The romantic side lost."

"War of Independence?"

"Margaret Taylor Stanley owns the Revolution."

"That cow," Ambrose added.

"The Crimean War. Nothing like a dose of Florence Nightingale."

"Did it," Ambrose shot back.

"Korea."

"Deadly."

"Boer War?"

"Like it wasn't one?"

"The Great War?"

"Too muddy."

"So all wars are out," William said.

"Vietnam shut the door on war."

"Ruined it for everyone," Faye complained.

William drifted into thought. The two writers were getting tired.

"How about—" William began anew then faded.

After a long pause he suggested, "How about a self-effacing academic type, totally married and honorable, stumbles out of a dark terminal and into the brightness of a clear day in March and almost walks in front of a taxi at the airport, except that he is grabbed by the nape of the neck and is saved by the love of his life, who he lost twenty-seven years earlier."

The quiet continued until Faye said, "Are you trying to help us or what? That's just plain ridiculous. Improbable circumstances are another mark of the amateur."

Ambrose snorted in agreement. "His next plot device will be a homewrecker as a romantic lead."

William seemed to ignore the snippiness. He sincerely asked, "What am I missing?"

"The conflicts," Ambrose replied.

"Conflicts? Plural? There's more than one?"

"There are two," Faye explained. "A big one and a smaller one."

"Mrs. Meekham calls them the 'inconveniences.'"

"One long-term."

"And a recent crisis."

"Can you give me an example?"

"Long term. Girl is trying to save the ancestral home from a developer," Faye elucidated.

"And the short term?" William asked.

"The house is on fire."

"I see," he said and the room went quiet again.

This time even I was beginning to lose interest as William searched through the bottom of his stack of computer paper.

"How about this." He read from the printout. "A crane operator stops the wrecking ball in the very nick when he spies his seventh grade sweetheart looking out of the upstairs window of her father's condemned but landmark hotel in a depressed but soon-to-be-revived seaside resort."

"Do wake me up when this is over." Faye yawned as she crossed to the couch in front of the fireplace. "Really, Billy. We don't do tawdry."

I was ready to go home, so I hurried to finish my work. William had given me a list to pull from the stacks. It was an odd assortment of books.

The heavier ones were Whitehead's *Counting towards Certainty*, which must have weighed twenty pounds, and *The Concise Oxford Book of Chaos*. That came in four volumes. Number three was missing.

I was completing my task pulling Wittgenstein's *De Serendipita* and an old German translation of Aristotle's *Metalogika* when there was a commotion. Shouts. I went to the railing and looked down.

Faye was hugging her knees, rocking back and forth on the sofa. Ambrose was braying. William was saying "calm down" in a very loud voice.

But Ambrose was frantic, almost hysterical.

"It's never been done," he repeated over and over as he paced in great agitation throughout the lower floor. "It can't be done."

He was pulling at his hair.

He stopped and faced William, "No one has ever done that and succeeded. No one."

"It's valid," William explained patiently. "It's the contrapositive: When all premises are false, the result is true.

"It's impossible," Ambrose spat and renewed his desperate pacing.

He was covering the main floor with his anxious walk. Faye had now curled up on the sofa in a fetal position. William studied both of them with a scientific eye.

Ambrose stood at the tall bookcase that housed their collected works. He randomly grabbed at books.

"Lost husband but rediscovered the love of her life in a mortuary."

As he recounted the plots, he tossed each book to the floor in front of him.

"Lost lover is in charge of loser husband's rehab. Hubby conveniently OD's and dies.

"Cop called in for domestic disturbance turns out to be true love from summer camp. Abusive husband conveniently dies.

"Medical examiner of dead husband is girlhood crush and lab partner from ninth grade.

"See any similarities, Professor?" Ambrose glared.

"Dead men?" wondered William. "Should I be worrying?"

The pile of books on the floor was growing.

"Head of abused women's shelter is childhood sweetheart.

"Kidnapped by a pirate only to discover that under the eye patch and parrot is the love she lost in a cotillion fire.

"Loser husband prosecuted for bigamy, but she dated the DA in college.

"Lost in jungle, found by her senior prom date."

Ambrose was growing in volume and desperation. He slammed the next one down especially loudly.

"Stupid woman rescued by total moron!" he screamed.

"Perhaps you should put your feet up for a few minutes," William suggested. "Do you know any relaxation exercises?"

"Don't you understand?" he ranted. "Don't you see the trend, Mr. Science?"

"I do see a trend," William said. "A very clear and obvious trend. In fact, you might even call it a rut. Which is why I'm suggesting that we try something a little different. I don't see what is so terrible about that."

He attempted a pleasingly bland look, which offered no comfort.

Ambrose exploded. "It can't be done. It breaks the rules."

"Right, the seven pillars. Or is that the seven wonders of the world?"

"And one commandment," Ambrose shouted as he slammed his hand loudly against the table to emphasize every word. "The Man Shall Not Leave The Woman."

William listened politely and then said, "Maybe just this once?"

Ambrose leaned in, speaking and spitting into his face with vigor.

"You are a fool," he hissed.

"Oh, well … that. Of course," William conceded .

"You are a toad. You are a clot. You are lint."

William turned and looked out the large window. In a very controlled voice he said, "The last one hurt."

"It might not be the worst idea, Ambrose," Faye suggested. "We could give it a try, couldn't we, sweetie?"

"We?" Ambrose seethed.

"It's only a book." Then she offered meekly, "I can help."

"You're worse than worthless," Ambrose said rudely.

Even though my view was obstructed, I could hear the intake of breath signaling a stifled sob. William reacted immediately.

In what looked like a single stride he was across the room and on top of Ambrose. Clamping the other's elbows in his strong hands, he raised him off his feet and carried him across the room, pinning the terrified ghostwriter against a copy of Rodin's "The Kiss."

William's fury was intense. Ambrose squirmed trying to look anywhere but into his eyes, as the statue's knees pressed painfully into a kidney.

William spoke curtly and pointedly into his ear. Then he lowered him to the floor and released his grip. Without another look, he turned to comfort his wife.

At a safe distance, Ambrose went into a full-blown tantrum. He tore again at his hair and muttered to himself in a whiny voice that went higher and more shrill as he stomped around in circles.

"I don't have to put up with this crap," he chanted in a growing frenzy.

"It's bad enough that I do all the work. It is bad enough that I have to work with her," he shouted across the floor.

"Yes, you!" he said, pointing at Faye, who was now huddled against William. "You are a spoiled little princess and I hate you."

William whispered something to Faye, who laughed, despite herself.

"It's not like I don't know how crappy this crap is," Ambrose continued. "I do know and it's crap. C–R–A–P. Crap."

He backed up the spiral staircase, positioning himself in a higher pulpit so he could more dramatically rain down his vitriolic torrent.

"Crappy crap," he screamed down from the landing.

Faye began to sob. William gave Ambrose a steely look.

"Dog crap. Horse crap. Bull crap."

Anger flashed across William's face. He tenderly deposited his wife back onto the sofa and started across the room with deliberation.

"Bird crap! Frog crap! Turkey crap! Weasel crap!" Ambrose screamed as he backed up the stairs toward where I was standing with an armful of books.

William put his hand on the iron railing and said, "Stop right there, please."

A chill ran through me. Even though those words were not directed at me, the force of their underlying threat turned my blood cold. At that point and just inches from me, Ambrose abandoned his cautious backpedaling and turned to flee.

To this day, I don't know why I did what I did next. It's the sort of thing that is generally unremarkable, certainly nothing that should put anyone in the hospital.

As the menacing sound of William's heel rang on the metal rung below, Ambrose looked up and his face went white. He had been so caught up in his own diatribe that he was completely unaware that there was anyone else on the stairs. When he turned around, he looked crazed—like he had just seen a ghost.

His surprise surprised me.

"Boo!" I said reflexively.

He gasped. His eyes rolled back in his head. Then he collapsed, clutching his left arm as he slid and bumped down the iron staircase, arriving in a pile at William's feet.

I was at the railing above just in time to see Faye pull herself off the sofa and shuffle over in her pink fluffies. As William dialed the telephone for an ambulance, she stood looking down at Ambrose gasping at her feet.

"Serves you right," she said.

13

My classes were difficult, but that only made me work harder. William was not prone to showering anyone with praise, which made me more eager to please him. I didn't mind a few weeks later when he asked me for a favor.

"Can you drive a standard shift?" he asked.

"Of course," I answered. "I drive Mrs. Slocum's bus."

"That doesn't count," he replied. "Shifting that Volkswagen is like stirring rice pudding."

"I can parallel park," I protested.

"Good. Tomorrow in the afternoon—"

"I can't," I said. "I have your seminar."

"I've canceled my seminar."

"Do I still have to read the book?"

"You can read it in the van while you are waiting for Faye at the doctor's office," he said.

"By the way," I added. "I think we're missing something."

"Where?"

"In the algorithm, we're missing something important."

"I think you might be right," he agreed.

I was pleased that he took my point. It relieved some of the anxiety that I was feeling at the prospect of being alone with his wife.

The next day, William picked me up at Mrs. Slocum's and drove me to the house.

"More family secrets," he said in an exaggeratedly ominous tone.

"Is she sick?"

"No," he explained. "Therapy. All creative types have to go for therapy."

"About the writing thing?"

"Everything is about the writing thing."

On the other side of the iron gates, we turned left onto a drive I had not noticed before and coasted down a gravel track that hugged the outline of the rambling building. Pulling up under the overhang on the second floor that was the master bedroom, he pushed a button clipped to the sun visor, and hidden garage doors opened automatically. He put the van into reverse and backed it under the house.

Inside, there was a loading dock at the same height as the floor of the vehicle. It was carpeted with matching Persian rugs. This way Faye could get on board with the impression that she was simply moving from one room to another within the comfort and privacy of her home.

"Good afternoon," she greeted me as she lowered herself into the easy chair in the van.

"It's a beautiful day," I said.

"Whatever you say," she replied.

She nervously fidgeted with a white carnation.

"Scoot over," William directed as he climbed out of the driver's seat. He closed the back doors.

"I had to cancel a seminar," he announced as he pulled himself up into the passenger side.

"I'm sure your students are devastated," Faye replied. "Are you devastated, Robert?"

"Of course." I knew better than to correct her about my name. I was delivering a fragile hothouse flower. I needed all my concentration as I carefully drove out of the garage.

William reached across me and pushed the button to close the door.

"I don't know why I couldn't blow her off on the telephone," he complained.

"That wouldn't be nice," his wife insisted. "People are entirely too cavalier about rejection. You know my views on that subject." She sighed. "Furthermore, it's not her fault that Ambrose got better."

"You acted quite rashly," William said. "I wish you had talked to me first."

"I am quite capable of making decisions for myself, Billy," Faye replied. I saw her look toward the aquarium in the van. The fish were swimming in confused disarray as we bounced over the uneven gravel drive.

The gates closed behind us, and we turned down Mountain Road toward the campus.

"You should have talked to Freddy," William said. "He would have found someone."

"Freddy doesn't know about my ... problem."

"It's not a problem; it's just a question of volume. Freddy knows you need an assistant."

"Freddy has been smelling a rat for years. Don't think I don't know what happens when they reduce your advertising budget."

"Well, you could have at least talked to me."

"I'm so sorry that I am taking an hour out of your busy day."

"That's not what I meant."

I was glad that I was invisible.

"It was very rash," William said.

"It was one classified ad. Do I need your permission to place a classified ad?"

"It was a public thing to do."

"It was only four lines."

"It was the *New York Times*."

"How would anyone know?"

"Fine," William concurred, employing the most toxic word in a marriage.

"I'm not a moron, Billy," Faye stated coldly.

"I didn't say you were a moron."

"I know you were thinking it. You always do when you use that patronizing tone."

"I wasn't patronizing."

"I really don't need this, today, of all days."

"You set up the interview for today."

"You could be a little more helpful."

"You only had to ask. I did find Ambrose."

"That worked out just fine, didn't it?"

William didn't say anything. From the corner of my eye, I saw the face of a soldier looking toward a distant defeat.

"I thought it was very subtle," she continued. "It didn't say 'Virginia Faye Warner needs a ghostwriter,' did it?"

"It might as well have. You included our phone number."

"Which is unlisted."

"But not unknown."

"That's not the point."

"That's exactly the point," William said. "Off the top of my head I can give you the names of three romance writers who would go to your funeral just to make sure you were dead."

"I can give you five."

"So you agree."

"I'll never agree with that tone of voice."

I could hear her unfolding a newsprint tear sheet.

"Technical Writer Wanted," she read. "Must be able to write to spec and take detailed direction. Fast study. Nonsmoker."

I pulled the van up in front of the student union.

"I figured that anyone who knew me would be thrown off by the last bit," she said proudly.

William turned and faced his wife.

"Fine," he said. "I'll deal with it. But do me a favor. Don't help anymore, OK?"

"Don't be mean on therapy day," she said in a quavering little-girl voice. "You know how fragile I am."

"Sorry, sweetie. We'll patch it all up tonight."

William stepped out of the van, his manner businesslike but softened. He slid open the side door of the van and climbed in.

"How will I recognize her?" he asked.

"She'll recognize you," she explained. "Lean over."

While Faye pinned the carnation to the lapel of his tweed jacket, she asked, "Don't you want to know her name?"

"I'm only going to fire her," he responded. "I'd just as soon not know anything about her."

"Be nice about it."

"I will," he reassured her as he stood to leave. "Have a productive session, sweetheart."

"Thank you."

He bent over and kissed her.

She said nothing as he slid the door closed. He started into the student union as we pulled away and headed downtown. It was a short drive to her doctor's office. She sat quietly in the back lost in her own thoughts, which was fine by me.

Finally she broke the silence. "Is this all terribly tedious for you, Roger?"

"Oh, no," I explained, catching myself from correcting her now that she got my name right. "I'm invisible and nameless. I'm the driver."

"It may seem that way. But you're not."

"Then who's driving?" I asked.

I looked in the mirror and saw her shake her head.

"A word of advice," she started. "Don't be flippant with someone who has been in therapy longer than you've been in long pants."

"Yes, ma'am."

"And don't call me ma'am."

"OK."

"Do you know why I like you?"

"No, ma'am. Sorry."

"Because I trust you."

"I'm glad," I said, thoroughly puzzled.

"Do you know why I trust you?"

"No."

"It was the first time I met you. You couldn't lie to me about reading my books. You blush when you try to lie," she said. "That's so sweet."

"Actually, it can be grossly inconvenient at times," I answered.

That in itself was a lie, proving that she was wrong about me. I didn't turn colors when I said it. The only reason why I turned red in the library was because I had told the truth about not reading her books when I should have been diplomatic.

Her erratic behavior, I now realized, was a mark of the fragility William had mentioned. I wanted to help protect her.

"I don't really trust Ambrose," she confessed. "Of course, I love him to death, but he does have a jealous streak. I guess we're just too close."

She shook a fresh cigarette out of the pack.

"He's being written up in some medical journal, by the way."

"Ambrose?" I wondered aloud.

"Yes, our own Ambrose. It turns out that his heart attack was psychosomatic. Yet it still required surgery."

I glanced at her in the rearview mirror. She looked very proud.

"He is supposed to be released tomorrow," she added.

"What good news." I was feeling a little guilty that I was partly—maybe even mostly—the cause of Ambrose's condition, even though no one else had seemed to notice.

Faye was rocking slightly in her chair and thumbing through a copy of *Vogue*.

"I'm so glad that Billy has a little friend," she said. It took me a moment to realize that she was referring to me. "He seems much more happy now that he's doing his projects again."

She closed the magazine.

"I don't know how long it's been." The quality of her voice softened as she reminisced of happier times. "He was a lovely young man when I met him, you know. So ambitious."

I wanted to be polite, but her conversation made me feel so awkward that I couldn't find talk small enough to respond.

"He could have had it all," she noted, letting out another deep sigh.

"What more could he ask for?" I said sweetly. "He's got you and a perfect life."

"Yes," she agreed. "You'd think that would be enough, wouldn't you?"

She went back to her magazine.

"Of course, it all changed after the fiasco in front of the Comstock Committee. You do know about that, don't you? Everyone does. I was still flying high on my first book. He looked like a lost wet puppy when I first met him. I remember I said to Daddy, 'He followed me home. Can I keep him?' Thank God—Daddy was Chancellor by then so he could save the day. A bad business, though. Billy should be happy about what he has. He was so close to losing it all."

She continued to talk. I couldn't tell whether she was talking to herself, to the magazine in her hands, or to an imaginary friend, but it was totally lost on me. I tuned it out as she continued on about bad outfits, bad hair, bad faces, bad handbags and bad feet.

I was relieved when we arrived at her therapist's office. Following William's directions, I drove the van down behind the building and parked by the basement door. By the time I had opened the van's back doors, she had already put on her large sunglasses.

"You don't mind holding an old lady's hand, do you, Roger?" she asked in a little voice as I helped her out of the van.

"What?" I asked. "Is your mother here?"

"Corny and trite," she commented. "Sweet."

I led her across the asphalt and into the building's basement. At the door to her therapist's office, I left her.

"Fifty minutes," she reminded me.

I looked at my watch. There was just enough time to make a quick visit to Ambrose.

14

Ambrose was in a VIP room. As a member of Miss Warner's household, he was a Very Important Patient, convalescing on the top floor of the new wing, riverside, with a view. When I got there, he was sitting in bed, propped up on three pillows, reading Zane Grey. His color wasn't good, but then again it never was.

I was a little nervous when I knocked on his open door.

"Hello," I said, sticking my head into the room. "Are you talking to me yet?"

"Only when I'm lying down," he said into his book. "That way, you can't sneak up from behind and try to kill me."

"I'm really sorry about that."

"You and me both."

He made a determined effort to lose himself in his book.

"What are you reading?" I asked.

"*Riders of the Purple Sage*," he answered. "I've read it seventeen times. It relaxes me. Especially in moments of great stress."

At a loss for words, I held out my offering.

"Here," I said. "I've brought you something."

He didn't even deign to look up.

"What?" he asked, his eyes still glued to the book.

I stumbled forward, offering the bakery box. "A present. Pastries."

At that word, he held out his hand and greedily accepted the gift. He peered inside, and a new day dawned on his face.

"Close the door," he said. His smile was genuine, his voice conspiratorial.

I did as I was told. When I turned back into the room, I was reminded of a contest I'd seen in my youth. Ambrose was gobbling chocolate cannoli with the same gusto with which my cousin consumed pie at our county fair in Pennsylvania. I stepped away just in case there was a similar unfortunate result.

Halfway through, he put the box down.

"Keep those coming," he said, loudly licking his fingers, "and I might forgive you some year. It was all your fault, you know. You're lucky I didn't press charges."

I sat for a few moments watching him catch his breath and wondering why hospital gowns were not made of a thicker material, or at least enough of it.

"Bring éclairs too next time," he mumbled before sinking down into the pillows and drifting into a deep sleep.

It was time to return to the professional building. I knew that Faye had little patience. I quickly left the hospital. Fortunately, I made it in time. She staggered quietly out of the therapist's office, whiter than pale. Her eyes weren't focused on anything, and she barely recognized me.

Moving straight past me, she went through the secret corridors that she knew so well to exit through the back of the building. I followed. She opened the side door to the van, climbed inside and sat down in her chair.

I hopped into the sitting room and crouched beside her chair.

"Are you all right?" I asked. I was genuinely worried.

"Nothing good will come out of today," she augured as she lit a cigarette.

She smoked. I rested on my haunches, oddly chilled by her pronouncement and unsure what to do next.

Finally, she broke the silence. "That sadistic head-shrinking witch doctor has given me an assignment," she burst out. "The rat."

"Can he do that?" I asked.

"He can do anything he wants. He's the doctor."

She had trouble lighting the next cigarette. I moved to the driver's seat and turned the key in the ignition. The van roared to life, accompanied by a rolling string of mumbled curses while she fought with her Dunhill lighter.

"Where are we going?" I asked.

"That's the $64,000 question, isn't it?" she replied.

She continued. "I am assigned to go and buy a cup of coffee."

She inhaled deeply then let the smoke escape her open mouth in a defeated sigh.

"In a public place."

The van idled quietly as I waited for her to continue.

"Do you know what agoraphobia is, Roger?" she asked suddenly.

"Of course I do," I answered. "The fear of farming."

Her laughter sounded like rustling leaves.

"That was a noble effort," she said. "But it's not agricultural. It's fear of open spaces. Fear of the marketplace. Fear of buying a lousy cup of coffee."

Her explanation had drifted into self-criticism.

"Maybe you should go someplace you've been a thousand times before," I suggested. "Then it won't be so scary."

"I like that," she said. "In just one sentence, you've been a lot more helpful than fifty minutes with Dr. How-does-that-make-*you*-feel."

"Do you have to do this now?" I asked, hoping that I could just deliver her back to her husband. Being the driver was suddenly a larger responsibility than I had bargained for.

Her voice was deadly serious now.

"He told me to do it on the way home. Just like that. No big deal."

I knew I was out of my depth. She wasn't smoking now. She sat perfectly still, paralyzed by fear.

"Where have you been a gazillion times?" I asked. "You've lived in this town forever. At some point you must have bought a cup of coffee somewhere, before you developed ... your fear of farm equipment," I hoped for a small smile.

"Well," she thought aloud, "I grew up in the student union. I had lunch there every day when I was in high school. Maybe there."

"Just what the doctor ordered," I said effusively, spinning the van in a tight U-turn.

We drove down Fermi Boulevard, turning right at Steinmetz, which brought us the back way onto Division Street.

"Daddy is at New Paltz today. We can park in his space," she instructed. "I'll show you where."

We turned into the campus through the north gate. As we approached the student union, Faye said, "Keep going. Take the next left and then turn right."

"There," she pointed as we turned behind the building.

We took the down ramp a few turns into a parking garage in the subbasement. Now she was crouched behind me, her chin on the back of the passenger seat as she gave directions.

"Jeez." She exhaled. "I haven't been here in years."

"There," she said, pointing over my shoulder as we came up on a space with a sign that said "Reserved for the Chancellor." It was right beside the elevator.

15

The student union was located in an extension that jutted out from a large amorphous gray granite-clad building. Its two floors were dedicated to social and student government organizations. There were meeting rooms and a small theater, a poet-infested coffeehouse and a busy snack bar called "Pi Are Round." The higher floors above housed the nonacademic business workings of the college. Faye's father had an office on the top floor.

"Here goes nothing," she said tightly as she stepped out of the van.

"Break a leg," I encouraged her.

"Just my luck."

The short walk across the parking garage was empty and echoing, but also without threat or menace. The elevator was waiting and comforted us on our ascent with a bland rendition of the "Girl from Ipanema."

Then the elevator doors opened.

The main floor of the student union was an architectural wonder. In the design search, the trustees of the school had decided that the competition should be restricted to recent graduates. The winning plan was daring. The space was open, the ceilings were too low, and it was very, very loud. As a result, the soothing rhythm of the bossa nova was immediately drowned out by a cacophony.

There was elevator music. There was a juke box blaring Beatles on the left. There was a flaky burnout with a portable amp playing off-key Dylan on a Stratocaster. On top of all this, a PA system periodically fed back important announcements. There was also constant motion as people wandered back and forth with food trays or threw Frisbees across the length of the room. The remaining decibels were given over to clinking silverware and clattering dishes.

"If you are really, really brave," I encouraged her, "you get rewarded with a bad cup of coffee."

She slowly slunk backward into the elevator.

"Come on in," I said, attempting to rally her. "The water's fine."

She was trying very hard. She looked up at me dazedly and offered her hand. I took it.

"Don't let me down now," I said, looking into her eyes. "This is just a job, isn't it?"

She nodded. But there was terror in her face.

"OK, then. On the count of three," I said.

"One ...

"Two ..."

I moved prematurely. My intention was to surprise her into action and get her out of the elevator before she even knew she was moving forward. But I ended up a victim of my own deceit. When I went to reestablish my grip, my hand came up empty. She had given me the slip and was feverishly stabbing at the garage button. I could only watch her in full terror as the doors closed and she was gone. I had lost her.

I jabbed the down button. I knew I couldn't make the elevator move any faster than its machinery allowed. I also realized that it wasn't going anywhere soon. I heard it stop. The doors opened; I could tell she was holding them. Still I kept poking at the button.

All of a sudden I understood what agoraphobia was all about. The room was too loud and shrinking. I panicked and ran about in tight circles looking for a down staircase. I could not breathe. I could only see a dizzying crowd of swirling bodies, until I saw a hole in the madness. My eye was drawn into that oasis of calm within the din.

I found myself staring at William. He was sitting at a small round table in the middle of the maelstrom, oblivious to the traffic and noises all around. It was as if he—and his companion—inhabited their own personal island, ten thousand miles away from the chaos around them. At that moment and only fleetingly, I was glad Faye had not succeeded at her assignment.

I didn't have to look twice to know who the woman was: Claire, from the diner. Even at a distance and in the light of day, she was very beautiful. Thrilled at the opportunity of meeting her again, I walked up to the table.

In the crowded and overheated cafeteria, it struck me as odd that they were both still wearing their coats. I also noticed that their coffees remained untouched. She was wearing a khaki trench coat. Her hair cascaded out down her back. The strong metal clasp kept it within a roiling channel.

As I got close to the table, I could feel the power of their cocoon. The sound and the fury and all the other distractions that were swirling around the room diminished then disappeared entirely as I stood next to them. They were so involved that I went unnoticed.

I have no idea what they were talking about. But it must have been brilliant and fun because they enjoyed it so much. Without even following, I found myself smiling along with them.

Then Claire happened to look up. I blurted, "What are you doing here?"

"Why, if it isn't my fellow nighthawk," she remarked.

William looked at her inquisitively. I barely noticed. As I continued to stare at her, he became part of the background.

"Maybe if you say something to him, he'll start breathing again," William remarked dryly.

"May we help you?" she asked solicitously.

"No, thank you," I replied dreamily. "I'm fine. So is my zipper."

William looked taken aback. Claire laughed with me and then at him. That didn't seem to help matters.

"I'm surprised to see you here," he said, with a little irritation in his voice.

"I'm surprised to see you too," I answered mindlessly.

"Around this time, I thought you would be driving the van up Mountain Road," William pointed out.

"Oh, my God," I gasped as I suddenly came back to my senses. "I've lost her."

"What?" William asked sharply. "You lost Faye? How did you do that?"

"She ran away. We were stepping off the elevator, and she ran away."

"Why the hell did you bring her here?" he thundered in a fearsome manner.

"Her therapist gave her an assignment. She was supposed to come here and drink a cup of coffee."

"What! Of all the preposterous things!" William barked. "Here of all places. Egotistical quack."

He stood and faced Claire. She rose also.

"I've got to go," he said. "Sorry you can't have the job. Far too overqualified."

"The story of my life," she sighed.

"It was a treat to interview you," he said.

"The treat was all mine," she answered.

They shook hands across the table. Their grasp seemed inordinately long.

Finally, she said, "Right."

He said, "Right."

They both turned away and walked briskly in opposite directions. I struggled to catch up with William. The crowd parted before his determined stride and just as quickly filled in behind him.

"I'm so sorry. I really am. I hope she hasn't gone far," I said.

"Good bet," William answered. "Can't run far when you're hyperventilating."

She hadn't. When the elevator doors opened, she was sitting by a pillar on the concrete floor, hugging her knees and rocking back and forth.

"I'll take it from here," William murmured.

I stood watching as he tenderly approached her. He didn't help her to her feet as much as draw her up into a comforting embrace. It was a familiar place for her. I could see the tension immediately begin to drain from her body as the elevator doors closed.

16

Hudson Polytechnic offered two advanced degrees. The master's took only two years and was popular with high school teachers looking for accreditation. The PhD program was more grueling. For that there were three years of classroom work, nightmarish oral exams and a dissertation defense from hell. The majority of the panel was bitter or drunk or both. William was the nice one, but he actually listened to what you were saying, so it was a mixed blessing.

Because my fellow students were pursuing a variety of career paths, they did not take all their classes in the math department. My friend Harvey Weintraub naturally gravitated toward Skinner Hall for child psychology credits. Years later, I would discover that Leo Ickies had surreptitiously pursued a second doctorate in philosophy, while Tiny Swenson turned out to be an ace at probability and statistics. After getting an MBA in market research, he would go on to revolutionize the telemarketing industry.

What brought us all together was the mandatory and challenging graduate seminar called Advanced Concepts that met every Tuesday.

We sat for two hot and airless hours in a creaky lecture hall. Halfway through there was a ten-minute break that allowed for an awkward attempt at conversation by our miserable group of social misfits, mouth-breathers and blind-date disasters. I was thoroughly intimidated by them, convinced that every one was smarter than I was. I had not yet learned how to act blasé about something that I was passionate about.

One day, after we had enjoyed our silent social moment on the sunny portico outside, we trudged back into the dark lecture hall to find William and Arlen Sheffield in the middle of a heated argument.

"This isn't worth a heart attack, Arlen," said William at his most arrogant. "We do share Aristotle as a foundation. It only makes sense that we meld back together on the higher levels."

"A-*ha*," the diminutive ethicist emphasized as he leapt up onto a chair to heighten the drama of the moment. "We most assuredly do not. That is the tired old scam that you mathematicians have been pulling for centuries. You are—and have always been—limited. Admit it. You crippled yourself when you learned how to count."

"How did we do that?" William asked with disbelief.

"On your fingers, I suppose. Mathematicians are such dopes. You can only count to ten. A philosopher would have been twice as good."

"In what way?"

"By properly defining his terms," Sheffield pointed out victoriously. "He would include all twenty digits."

"I did hear how difficult it was for you to stop biting your toenails," William commented.

"Moron," said Sheffield.

He turned to us with a little bow. "Good day, gentlemen, and—" he added, looking at our teacher, "good luck."

As Sheffield left the lecture hall, William closed the door.

"Who has satisfied his requirements for the mandatory ethics course?" he asked us. "Raise your hands."

When he saw no raised hands, William let out a sinister chuckle. He wiped half the morning's work from one of the blackboards, Von Steerling's famous disproof of the proof's own existence. Then he reached for the chalk and started writing. Few in the room bothered even to feign interest. Jerry Ng did pay attention, but Leo and Lewis shot paper clips at each other with rubber bands. Resting his head on the seat in front of him, Tiny went to sleep with no shame, while Harvey Weintraub surreptitiously read an education textbook.

After he had covered a blackboard, William stepped back to study his work. I knew immediately what it was about. I had been looking at similar formulae for the last week as we tried to resurrect his early papers.

"I have a problem," Jerry Ng said.

William turned, cupping the chalk in his hand and shaking it like he was about to roll craps, which was what he always did when he was impatient because someone was keeping him away from his thoughts.

"Yes?"

"I can't find the premise."

"Not to fret," William reassured him. "There isn't one."

"I've never seen that before."

"Of course you haven't," William answered, studying his figures with pride. "It's new. It's mine."

"You have to have a premise," insisted Leo.

"Why?"

"You just have to."

William smirked. "I call it the 'deferred premise principle,'" he said.

"You can't have an inference without premises," Lewis said, in rare support of his most hated enemy.

"Why not?" William asked innocently.

"Because that's how logic works," Lewis insisted.

"It's the framework of the syllogism," Leo supported.

"The core of Aristotle," Lewis emphasized.

Adding a calmer voice to the argument, Jerry Ng asked emotionlessly, "Are you trying to undo 'Barbara'?"

"Perhaps only her brassiere," William answered. Then he turned toward me. "How's the new boy doing?" he asked. "Keen and eager and keeping up with the field?"

"I think so, sir," I said.

"Pop quiz," he announced. "Who is 'Barbara'?"

"Aristotle's first syllogism," I answered.

"Excellent. Gold star," William lauded. "Extra credit if you spell her out."

"All men die. Socrates is a man. Socrates will die," I recited.

"Our point exactly," shot back Leo.

"Exactly," chimed in Lewis.

"Premise—premise—conclusion."

"There is no inference without it."

"No chance for validity."

"So you concede the old broad's validity, do you?" William asked, his eyebrow cocked like the hammer of a Colt 45.

"Of course," Leo said.

"No problem with the very first line then?"

"Of course not."

"'All men die.' Not feeling a little immortal today, then?"

"Intellectually, I accept that I am not," Leo asserted.

"But we can't exactly prove it, can we, Leopold. At least not without making your rival over there very happy."

"I would greatly mourn his passing," Lewis, who by all counts was humorless, offered from across the room.

"I know I'm going to die," Leo insisted.

"But I don't know that you are going to die," William reasoned.

"All I am saying is that you can't have an inference without a premise," Leo complained in frustration.

"Of course you can't," William agreed.

"What?" Lewis asked, his head jerking around so fast that his glasses flew off.

"It's called the *deferred* premise principle," William explained. "The emphasis is on *deferred*, gentlemen. I only put it off. You must have a premise by the end of the whole mess or it makes no sense at all, does it?"

Leo and Lewis appeared to be sorely misused.

"Not once have I said that we must 'vacate the premises,'" William offered, trying to resuscitate them. But they were both so deflated that they were the only ones in the room that didn't groan at the pun.

"Lewis, a question for you."

"Yes," he answered, with some apprehension.

"Irrespective of that immortality thing," William said, "do you think that you now know everything that you will ever know in your lifetime?"

"Of course not."

"Another question," he said. "If your work as a logician is dedicated to validating your premises, would those be only the premises that you understand—even though by your own admission you are still ignorant of many things that will ultimately reveal themselves to you in the future? If so, is this necessarily a good thing? Or should I ask, is this good science?"

"Don't answer that," Leo interrupted. "It's a trick."

Standing at the lectern, William milked the dramatic pause. He was in total control of the room, until his eyes wandered over to Harvey.

"What the hell are you reading during my class?" he erupted.

He stomped across the floor and whipped the early childhood development textbook out of Harvey's hands.

"You know I don't tolerate this crap in my classes," William upbraided him.

"I was listening," Harvey said in his own defense.

"Show me," challenged William, slapping a piece of yellow chalk down on the desk.

Harvey begrudgingly took it, got out of his seat and shuffled to the front of the lecture hall. He walked past the jumble of William's evolving theory to the blackboard that displayed the tangled remnant of Von Steerling.

"Do you mind?" he asked, eraser in his hand.

"Of course not," William answered.

Harvey cleaned the entire board, slowly and with deliberation. Then he turned to the seminar.

"I will now prove that men who smoke cigarettes have more sex than men who don't smoke," he announced in his characteristic bored monotone.

Reaching into his breast pocket, he pulled out a small hard pack of unfiltered Lucky Strikes. He held it at arm's length and displayed it. Then he turned it on its side so that we all could read the slogan.

"LSMFT," he wrote in large letters on the blackboard. "Lucky Strikes Means Fine Tobacco."

"OK," he started. "First, we flip it into the contrapositive, which of course is always true."

"If not fine tobacco, then not Lucky Strikes," he wrote on the board, reducing the words to symbology.

"Then, relying on the verisimilitude that we have discussed in this seminar earlier today—sorry Jerry, I know you hate 'truthlikeness,' but I have to use it here—we can establish through inductive validity that 'not fine tobacco' equals 'bad tobacco.'"

He wrote it out.

"We can build a quick Henkel value matrix with coordinates across the top of 'fine tobacco' and 'bad tobacco.' Down the y-axis we array 'smoking' and 'not smoking.'"

He paused for the briefest moment to check his work. Then he stepped back to x out a square in the grid.

"Retrieving the contraposited square, we will call it 's' for smoking."

The chalk broke in his hand. William, who was following the presentation with interest, quickly offered him a new piece.

"Thank you," Harvey said. "Next, we redefine the outboard part of the equation, embracing Leffert's Separation Theorem, bisecting the modified element 'not Lucky Strikes' in two so that we now have 'not-lucky' and 'not-strikes.'"

"Following an application of Leffert's Contraposited Separation Axiom, we can parse 'not-lucky' to 'intentional' and 'not-strikes' to 'balls.'"

He was quiet for a moment while he caught up with the writing and we digested his logic.

"We can then distill the consequent to a 'forced walk,' or as we would technically say, 'an intentional walk on balls.' Either way, of course, the batter is now standing safely on first base.

"Finally, we engage Keppler's Axiom 17, colloquially known as 'the anvil and the gnat,' which will conclude that you can't get either to second or third and certainly not home unless you have at least achieved first base."

"Therefore, we can safely say, with validity and logical proof, that girls will be more prone to have sex with boys who smoke cigarettes."

He made a big swooping circle around his inference and handed the chalk back to William. Then he retrieved his textbook from William's desk and went back to his seat, where he began to study it again in plain sight.

"Well played, that man," William applauded. "So firm. So round. So fully packed."

Harvey waved halfheartedly as he fell deeper and deeper into Early Childhood Development. Leo and Lewis appeared agitated that they were no longer the center of attention.

William, who had no interest in the mood of his students, walked over to Harvey's blackboard. He paused to review it for a moment before moving to wipe it off. Then his gaze seemed to catch on a bramble. His hand stopped inches from the blackboard, and the eraser slipped to the floor.

"Lovely use of the contrapositive," he said.

"Thanks," his student mumbled into his text.

I was so close to him that I could see his eye darting back and forth between the two blackboards in a tight comparison between Harvey's goofy proof and his own flawed thesis.

"Gentlemen," William said quietly, but with such intensity, that every ear in the room quickly tuned in. "I would ask your indulgence to be very quiet and still for just a moment or two."

The quality of his voice said it all. We froze; even Tiny was alert and sitting up at this point.

I couldn't tell whether the idea came down upon William from above, or if it spread throughout his body from his core, but it took over with rapidity and conviction. His eyes lit up, and the corners of his lips started to lift.

"On your marks!" William declared.

We immediately knew that this was going to be important. He went over to the table behind his desk and reached into a bucket. He removed a sponge, wrung it out and attacked his earlier work, returning the blackboard to its purest state. Then he tossed the sponge back into its pail. All in the room, even Harvey, waited in rapt attention as we watched the streaks dry.

He strode to the blackboard with the confidence of a Caesar and raised the chalk. As his hand hovered just inches away from both the blackboard and a watershed moment, there was a tiny discreet tap at the door to the seminar room.

He pounced and rushed to the interruption, nearly pulling the door out of its frame.

"Yes," he roared at the departmental secretary, who stood cowering on the other side of the threshold.

"Sorry to bother you, sir, but your wife—"

"Not now, Mrs. Lowey," he erupted as he stormed back to the blackboard and glowered at it.

"She says it's very important."

"It's always important," he spat with venom, intently focused on the problem before him, poised to strike like a cobra.

He stepped back and studied the board, preparing to strike again.

But he fell back once more.

"Son of a bitch," he said in a powerful outburst, then paused.

He was motionless until he rubbed his eyes like a child waking up groggy from a nap and looked at Mrs. Lowey.

"What seems to be the trouble?" he asked.

"I really do think it might be important, this time," She said apologetically.

"I'll be right out," he replied.

"Thank you, sir," she responded as she left the room.

"I guess that will be all for today," William said.

He halfheartedly tossed the chalk toward the tray under the blackboard, missing it by a wide margin.

After the door closed silently behind him, we all sat and stared at the blank slate. It was only the jarring sound of the hall bell that snapped us out of our stunned reverie. We collected our notebooks slowly, stood up and started out, walking gingerly around the empty blackboard as we would walk around a homeless person sleeping on a city sidewalk.

Harvey and I left the seminar room together. We stopped outside at the top of the stairs so Harvey could light up a Lucky Strike. It was a spectacular autumn afternoon, clear and bright.

"Well," he said, after a few deep and obviously satisfying drags, "it wasn't boring for a change."

"No, it wasn't boring," I agreed.

"He must be a good teacher. He makes you wonder."

"Yeah, he does that."

"Wonder whether he is a mad genius or just plain crazy."

"My thoughts exactly."

"It's all about the five corners," Harvey pointed out.

"I have no idea what you are talking about," I confessed. "I'm the new boy, remember."

"The five corners of knowledge. It's an ongoing saga," Harvey explained. "According to legend, he wrote these five papers, each one more brilliant than the last. They were going to be the foundation of a stellar career. Even better, it would be the cornerstone of a whole school of thought. But 'Holy Shit, Batman'—he loses the whole bunch of them mid-bar crawl during a night of drunken excess on the eve of his meltdown before the entire board of the Comstock Committee."

"He crashed and burned?" I asked, recognizing a recurring theme. Finally, I was with a person I could ask outright about the mysterious review.

"Exactly. In public. Just like those tiny incinerated orts that you dump from that little pull-out tray from your toaster," he elucidated. "Only more humiliating."

"What could have happened?" I mused aloud. "I thought they were rather good. At least the one that I read."

"Which one?" he asked.

"Which one what?"

"Which one did you read?"

"The first one," I told him. "'Significant Inconsequentiality.'"

"Probably a parlor game or sleight of hand," he replied. "Or he hypnotized you. The papers don't exist. Maybe they never existed. He could be stark-raving mad. Think about that."

I had known Harvey for only a few weeks, but I did like him. I thought that he was very smart. Yet I was confused about his eagerness to dismiss William's academic past.

"It sure seemed real when I held it in my hands and read it," I answered him.

Harvey stopped in the middle of the quad and turned to face me. He looked unusually shocked for how nonchalant he preferred to be.

"I don't believe it," he said with obvious sincerity. "You actually saw it?"

"Yes, I saw it. I read it. It's only a paper."

"Right. A paper. Not a movement."

"Well, not just one paper," I corrected. "At the moment, we are trying to reconstruct four others, up at the big house."

"So that's why he needed an intern," Harvey said, suddenly understanding.

I shrugged. "I guess."

"Let's grab a beer," he suggested.

"Why the hell not?"

17

The Crypt was a generic bar like any other found near every place of higher education throughout the country. Only the names differed: The Cave, The Tunnel, The Cavern, The Tomb. They were all pretty much the same place, a basement beer joint with a stained plywood bar, sticky tables, a pinball or a video game, a bitter owner and bathrooms that should be condemned by the Board of Health. The main room smelled like a morning after.

We stepped up to the bar. Harvey was two years older than I and worlds more sophisticated.

"Two Ballantine Pale India Ales," he told the surly man behind the bar.

"I've never had one of those," I confessed.

"You'll like it," he guaranteed. "They have clever Rebus puzzles inside the bottle caps."

It was the middle of a school day in a college town, so the place was only half full. A couple of goons were playing air hockey, and others draped themselves across various pieces of furniture.

We carried our beers to what seemed to be the most hygienic table in the place. I took a couple of sips from the bottle. I hadn't eaten breakfast or lunch that day. The brew was cool and refreshing and very tasty.

"Why does William get so irritated with you?" I asked.

"Because I'm really smart," he answered frankly, "and I want to teach high school math."

He added with a grin, "That pisses him off."

We sat and drank, and when our bottles were empty, we returned to the bar for another with the understanding that we were reasonable men and that a second would fulfill our set limit for the afternoon.

"So you've met his wife?" Harvey asked after we had finished off the next round.

"I guess," I answered. I was feeling a little light-headed.

"What's she like?"

"I'm not sure," I replied. "She is very successful, isn't she?"

"Is she as nutty as they say?" Harvey probed.

"Not at all. She's just a little—" I grasped for the word. "She's just not exactly what you would call thick-skinned."

Some time and many pale ales later, I found myself sitting next to a sophomore, embroiled in an impassioned discussion on how it was so lousy that girls didn't come to bars in the afternoon.

Harvey came up to me at the bar to tell me he was leaving.

"How can you take a test now?" I asked him as I tried to focus on any one of the four eyes that were spinning around behind his glasses.

"It's only psychology," he explained as he walked away.

18

It was a long enough walk to Mrs. Slocum's front door that I had somewhat collected myself by the time I got there. The cold late afternoon air helped.

My face was no longer beet red, and I was not staggering. I reached for the large brass doorknob, only to watch it slip through my fingers.

As I stared at my hand in disbelief, I saw another hand wrap around my wrist. It was Mrs. Slocum. She had a very strong grip.

"We were so worried about you," she said through clenched smiling teeth as she pulled me inside with quiet maternal force.

"Where were you?" she whispered loudly, more disappointed than angry. "Everyone's here. They are all waiting."

"Trouble up at the Warner estate." I hedged in a panic, still not sure what I was late for. "Sorry I wasn't on time."

I felt guilty about the lie but was amazed at how successful it was. Mere mention of that locale was enough to relax her grasp on my arm as she propelled me forward.

"I knew there was a reason you didn't call," she said as she patted my wrist. "You're a good boy. I hope it isn't anything serious."

Relieved that I was no longer in trouble, I felt better as we walked into the living room. Then I saw how big trouble could be.

There were rows of folding chairs and a makeshift podium. To the side was a small table with a glass water pitcher and a yellow rose in a bud vase. At the back of the room she had covered the dining room sideboard with a festive tablecloth and set out her famous deviled eggs and other assorted treats.

What made it an extra special occasion, however, was the dazzling presence of a decanter in the center of the spread, ringed by her tiny, precious sherry glasses. I focused on the cut glass in order to distract myself from the fact that every seat in the room was occupied.

"Make yourself comfortable," said Mrs. Slocum as she directed me to one of the two chairs next to the podium.

I did as I was told, sitting down across from Albert, who had a strangely blood-thirsty look on his face as he gazed upon me from the front row. Even his outfit was funereal. He was wearing a three-piece charcoal gray suit. I thought it was from

Brooks Brothers, but I might have been wrong. The silk tie (it looked so fancy it might have been a cravat) was yellow with dark green chevrons.

Mrs. Slocum moved to the podium, and the room quieted.

"Ladies. Gentleman," she began. "I welcome you all to this extraordinary meeting of the Mid-Hudson Chapter of the Virginia Faye Warner Fan Club. I would also like to greet our special friends from across the river. A big hello to the Virginia Faye Warner Fan Clubs of Rockland and Bergen Counties. I hope that you didn't have any trouble clearing customs."

There was polite laughter, accompanied by polite applause.

"For almost ten years," she continued, "I have been renting the upstairs room in this house to students who have attended that big school across the street. Generally, I have been lucky. They have been clean and well behaved. But this year, my luck has turned to gold." She paused and looked at me in a way that embarrassed me a little.

"It is my pleasure," she continued, "to introduce this year's tenant, who is not only a handsome and honorable young man, but someone who also spends most of his days within the sphere of the greatest writer writing in the world today: Roger Davison."

She sat down, only to leap up almost immediately.

"Of course, I didn't mean to imply that Roger Davison is the greatest writer writing in the world today," she explained.

She sat again, to jump up again in order to add, "Not that he won't succeed at anything he sets his mind to. He's such a nice, clever young man."

As Mrs. Slocum stammered and staggered toward the end of the introduction, I stared out at the small pool of expectant faces. They were all looking at me. My mind raced as I tried to remember why I was here. Finally, when it was obvious that it was my turn to be awkward, I stood up.

"Roger Davison," Mrs. Slocum said again and sat down in relief.

I studied the podium in great detail for a few moments, but then I made the mistake of looking up at all the seated people.

While it seemed like hours to me, I'm sure it must have been a few moments that I stood and gazed back at them blankly. Mrs. Slocum was twitchy and politely coughing like a tubercular behind me, but those in the chairs in front of me were very quiet.

I nervously played for time with the water glass until I spilled most of it. I stared again at them and they all continued to stare back.

Then my uncle's voice drifted through my beery fog and into my inner ear, and my head rang with his First Rule of Survival.

When in doubt, the voice echoed in my head, *confess to something. Preferably something small. It doesn't have to be true.*

Inspired, I blurted out, "My name is Roger and I am a mathematician."

"Hello, Roger," everyone answered.

That was it. I had absolutely nothing more to say. I stumbled, wasting valuable moments of brain processing, when I should have been collecting my thoughts. It was worse than my worst nightmare, which was standing up for my oral exams, totally unprepared—except this time, I had my pants on.

Finally, I squeezed out, "I have known Virginia Faye Warner for two months. I was amazed by her really amazing house and her writing. Her writing is amazing. It's all over the place."

I grinned sheepishly. My stomach churned and flipped.

Oh God, I silently prayed.

But when I next looked, I saw a roomful of eager eyes and ears.

"I mean," I added feebly, "maybe if I was as good a writer as she was, I could come up with a better way to say how amazing it is to sit in the same room where she writes all those amazing books, but I'm not. So I can't. I'm sorry."

At that moment, I hoped that I would be vaporized by Klingons.

So it came as no small surprise when I saw Albert smile at me warmly and put his hands together, an act that quickly inspired friendly applause throughout the room.

Once again, beer was my friend. The alcohol in my system delivered a timely and spectacular reddening of my face that apparently passed for a profoundly self-conscious blush. I looked over to Mrs. Slocum, who was beaming at me, and the blushing became sincere.

"Please," I begged. "I'm just a very lucky guy to be in that amazing room at the right amazing time."

They settled down. Now they were looking at me with eager expectation. I was in a worse place than when I started out. The last thing you want to hear when you have nothing left is, "Please continue."

Just a few moments into the next extended pause, the ticking of Mrs. Slocum's grandfather clock made the silence intolerable. Every second wielded and lowered a sledgehammer strike into the epicenter of my brain. I realized that I would have to admit to something else.

"As I have said," I confessed, "I have known Miss Warner for only two months. But while I might be young, I am not so young and stupid as to think for a second that I truly know her."

"Furthermore," I pandered, "some of you have been reading and living her books since I was knee-high to a grasshopper. Who am I to pretend for a minute that I have a deeper understanding of the mind and talent of Virginia Faye Warner than you do?"

I could feel my ears pop as the air pressure in the room changed as a result of their collective "Ahhhhhs."

"Therefore," I concluded, aware from their response that a conclusion was actually possible, "instead of embarrassing myself talking about things that you are far more familiar with than I am, I think we should skip my prepared statements entirely and go straight to questions and answers."

I looked out into a sea of approving faces.

"That is, if it is acceptable to you," I added.

It seemed to be OK with them, so I stepped to the side of the podium. I had noticed from talks that I had previously attended that the speakers always stepped to the side to await questions when they were through with their prepared comments. At the time, I could feel the stepping aside giving me added credibility, and I was prepared for a bit of a wait.

The other thing that I had noticed at lectures was that there was always an awkward pause until the first questioner got up the nerve to raise a hand. Luckily, it was only a short wait this time.

"Would you tell us what her next book is about?" a woman whom I did not recognize asked.

I stepped back to the podium.

"I'm sorry. I'm not at liberty to discuss her current projects," I said, wearing my serious face.

"So you have read it?"

"Sorry," I repeated. "I hope you understand."

The mood of the place sank.

"Go on, junior," Mabel directed from her perch in the wingback chair in the corner, knitting as usual. "Throw them a crumb."

"Well," I started. "I can tell you one thing."

Immediately, I could feel the room rally and electrify.

"It's not about pirates." I looked up in time to watch the room slump in disappointment.

"But it is very, very good," I reassured. "Personally, I think it's her best yet."

"So you've read it?"

"Not entirely. It's not done, you know."

"You've read some of it."

"I have sat in on story conferences."

"That must be very exciting."

I nodded, sagely, I hoped.

"But she is writing?" someone desperate for confirmation asked.

"From what I understand," I reassured. "She hasn't been so involved in a title for many years."

"When will it be done?"

"Look at me," I said. "I'm a math geek from Pennsylvania with three mechanical pencils in my top pocket. What do I know about the creation of great literature?"

They all appreciated my realness.

"But here is where I'm lucky," I added. "While I know that your wait for her next book must be excruciating, fortunately for me there are so many others that I haven't read even for the first time that I have plenty of wonderful stories to fill the time."

"I've been rereading the 'Queen Anne's Parish' series," someone volunteered.

"I love those," somebody else answered.

Another added, "*Chance Meeting in …*"

Others quickly ticked off the books in that collection.

"Paris."

"Rome."

"Peking."

"Rio."

"How many titles in that one?" Cindy wondered.

"Seven."

"*Lovers' Arithmetic,*" a new voice chimed in.

Upon which a dozen ladies chanted in unison, "One past and two hearts plus one love equals four-ever."

Spontaneous applause and laughter followed. It was very uplifting. Slowly they settled down again. Maureen raised her hand.

"Yes?" I acknowledged her solicitously.

"What is she really like? I mean, I've read all the magazine stories and all that. But what is she really, *really* like?"

"She's everything you want her to be … and more," I answered.

I glanced around the room and saw that the ruse had worked; their faces were rapt and attentive. This focused attention continued for the next thirty-five minutes while they barraged me with hundreds of personal and professional questions about Faye, and I made up answers that seemed to fit her persona the best I could.

"How long does she write every day?"

I had no idea. "She demands at least three hours from herself," I said. "But when she is inspired, it is up to the rest of us to make sure that she eats and sleeps."

I got that bit from a biography I read about Thomas Alva Edison.

"Where does she write?"

"In her window office, overlooking the Hudson River on a Royal typewriter that she bought from the estate of Zelda Fitzgerald."

I could tell that they liked that. I had no idea how I managed to pull Zelda out of a hat. I hated having to read *Tender is the Night* in the tenth grade, but it seemed to make the ladies happy. When the ladies were happy, I was happy that they were happy.

"Does she have any vices?"

"The only one I know of is bacon, lettuce, and tomato sandwiches."

"What time does she wake up in the morning?"

"That depends on William's class schedule. Despite the fact that she has a domestic staff, she always prepares his breakfast personally."

I was starting to cross my fingers behind my back to keep my soul safe from liar's damnation.

"What time does she go to bed?"

"To bed or to sleep? They always read to each other for twenty minutes before they turn out the light. Sometimes it is what she wrote that day. Other times it could be from newspapers, magazines, or books, whatever they want to share. In mid-December they start working through Shakespeare's sonnets so that they will hit the "Marriage of true minds" on New Year's Eve, which they always spend alone together."

My ears popped again on that one. I could tell things were going well. I looked over to Mrs. Slocum. She was delighted. She rose from her chair to close things down and finally let me off the hook. I took my last question and answered, "Whenever she finishes a book, she traditionally takes a glass of champagne and some caviar on thin melba toast. Thank you so much for inviting me here this afternoon."

"Remember," I added as I made a zippering motion across my mouth. "Everything I told you this afternoon is strictly off the record."

I sat down. I was amazed that I had pulled it off.

The gathering then dispersed for refreshments. Mrs. Slocum brought me a glass of sherry.

"Thank you," I said.

"No," she answered. "Thank *you*," touching my hand tenderly as she passed the glass.

Being dehydrated, I downed the glass and then compounded the mistake with a return visit to the decanter. I soon discovered an inherited biochemical peculiarity in my family's DNA.

At first, my reaction was euphoric. I felt as if I were drifting on a magic carpet, blissfully watching life stories as they floated by. It was all benign, until the jagged edges of acrimony ripped the outer layer and let reality flood back inside.

The loudest voices that disturbed my reverie were from Cindy and Maureen. They were in full diatribe, once more ranting against the SUNY trustees. Still on my dreamy high and the feeling of oneness with the group, I felt that their fight should be my fight. All for one and one for all.

When offending things happen, offense must be taken, and the board did offend. It had responded to the group's letter protesting the niece's rejected thesis proposal on Virginia Faye Warner.

Calling it a response was polite. They didn't even take the time to be condescending. It was an insult. Who did these people think they were?

It was not even an original form letter. It was a Xerox copy of a form letter.

"Arrogant SOBs," I said to myself. "Spineless, gutless bastards."

All around me, the voices stopped and the room went still. They were again all looking at me. My inner dialogue seemed to have leaked out of my ears.

"Well, it doesn't seem right," I added sheepishly.

"It isn't, dear," Mrs. Slocum said. "That's why we are writing another letter. It is much more vocal this time."

Here is when I finally understood why my mother always warned my siblings and me, "Beer and sherry—very scary."

The Spanish wine on top of the earlier beer diet was like spraying gasoline on a brush fire.

"That's not good enough," I stated. "They don't care about letters."

"We're going to be very forceful this time," Maureen insisted.

Cindy was more to the point. "We are going to threaten them with a chain letter."

I was on fire now.

I walked up to Cindy and said, "You've got that only half right."

"What do you mean by that?" she asked, barely covering irritation at the perceived insult.

"Not chain letters," I answered in excitement. "Chains."

Once again, I had the attention of the entire room. Even though I knew that I was out of control, I continued on crazily.

"This is the sort of stuff that TV news lives for. Respectable senior citizens, ladies, chained together at the front gate of SUNY-Poughkeepsie in protest over a great injustice. I'll drive."

I knew that I volunteered to drive only because Mrs. Slocum reminded me about it when she graciously brought tea up to me the next afternoon, while I was still in bed.

"Thank you," I mumbled as she handed me the cup and saucer.

"No," she replied. "Thank *you*. You were brilliant. We will all be ready at ten o'clock next Saturday morning."

I drifted back to sleep and dreamed of taking my oral exams without my pants on.

19

"Let this be a lesson, Roger," Virginia Faye Warner cautioned me, her large eyes emphasizing her concern and warning. "You are still young and trim. You are also innocent. Always be on your guard against Italian pastries."

"They are tempting and exotic," she added, "but oh, so dangerous."

She lit a cigarette and inhaled for emphasis.

We were on the main floor of the library. I now had my very own carrel in the stacks above. At least for the moment, I was on Faye's good side. She had admired how supportive I had been when Ambrose had drifted into diabetic coma.

I didn't try to deceive her. She had simply confused my acts of contrition with kindness. She was unaware that I had slipped him the poisonous cannoli in the first place. I went to the hospital nearly every day to read Louis L'Amour books to the sleeping Ambrose. That in itself put me in the credit column of her mental ledger.

The use of Faye's reference room alone was more than I could dream for. It was, after all, William's library too. It was stocked with any math book I would need in my first—or any other—year of graduate school. I went to the library in Klippman when I was on campus or when William required some exotic tome by an unrecognizable name. The fact that Ezeki, the housekeeper, was always standing by with sandwiches and coffee made the Teale-Warner library far superior.

William and I were both a little frayed. Following the analysis and deconstruction of nearly fifteen of his wife's books, along with five of the competition, he expanded the scope of his mathematical model of Muriel Meekham's *Practical Guide for the Romance Novelist*. It was a lot of work, but I wasn't complaining. I was a willing participant. I was flattered.

In recent days, we had spent over thirty-six hours in the frigid basement at the computer center to run his programs. Each night, around the same time, I made sure to happen by the Division Street Diner. If Claire had answered Faye's ad, I reasoned that she must live fairly close by. But I did not see her there again.

The stack of computer paper representing the calculations of our last run was four inches thick. William seemed pleased with the result. He actually bragged to Arlen Sheffield about the model. At that point, I thought he was premature. It was still missing something. I knew that in my gut, but I couldn't put my finger on it. It was elusive.

The library was quiet. William was sitting at the reading table, a copy of Meekham and the printout side by side, flipping through each in turn while idly fidgeting with his reading glasses. Faye was lying on her chaise with a cool compress on her eyes, fighting off a headache.

Outside the windows, a tug was towing three pairs of barges downriver. They were filled with gravel and slammed hard into an oncoming tide, throwing up curtains of spray for the effort. The late afternoon sun found an open slot in the thickening clouds, and for a few moments the river was plugged in, an electric slate gray, touched by liquid gold from above. But not for long. The lights soon went out, and the valley prepared itself for a night in November.

Faye's voice brought in an even chillier draft of reality.

"Frederick called this morning," she said from under her compress.

"How is Frederick?"

"He wants to know where the book is."

There was a brittle pause.

"What did you tell him?" William asked.

"What could I tell him?"

William closed Meekham and walked over to the chaise and sat down beside his wife.

"You don't have to write this book," he said.

"As if I could," she replied mournfully. "Oh, Ambrose."

"Not to worry," William said encouragingly.

He went behind the palms and rolled out his own personal blackboard. It was of far higher quality than those at the school, with a mahogany frame and sturdy brass hardware.

"They say a picture is worth a thousand words," he proudly explained. "Look, I've diagrammed it. May I present the mathematical model of the romance novel?"

If there was a picture on the blackboard, it was of a catastrophic explosion at a pasta factory.

"My God, Billy," Faye protested. "Can we afford the chalk?"

"I really think I've got it this time," he said.

"I know that tone of voice," she stated. "You're missing something, aren't you?"

"Maybe one thing," he conceded. "One small piece of the puzzle."

"Like a woman's touch?"

She walked across the library gingerly, holding her damp compress away from her housecoat. With three broad swipes, she used it to wipe down the blackboard.

"Chalk," she demanded.

He handed her a piece.

She wrote on the board, "Who? What? Why? Where? When? How?"

She walked away and tossed the chalk back to her husband, who caught it.

William studied the blackboard for a long time. On more than one occasion, he nearly turned to me with a comment but thought better of it. He started to say something to his wife, but stopped. He stepped up to study it even more closely, but then drifted back across the room for a longer perspective.

Finally he simply said, "That's very good."

"Thank you," she replied graciously.

He drifted back again and chewed on his glasses as he studied it at even greater length.

"Where did you get that from?"

"Ninth grade English," she answered.

He turned it over in his mind for a few moments longer.

"Even so," he finally concluded. "It's quite brilliant."

"It does the trick."

He jiggled the chalk for a moment and then strode up forcefully.

Next to "who" he wrote "college sweetheart."

Next to "what" he wrote "the love of his life."

Beside "why" he put down "see above."

For "where" he answered "planes, trains and cafeterias."

He was working earnestly. When he hit "when," he looked up and saw us both watching him with great interest. Then he picked up the eraser and cleaned off the right side of the blackboard with great determination.

"Just an idea," he tossed off. "Silly."

He started all over again and worked his way down through the categories.

Who: a Mafia Don.

What: a kidnapping.

Why: revenge for a misdeed.

Then the clock chimed, and I realized that I was late for differential geometry, so I raced to the carrel to get my books. By the time I left the library, William was already building yet another synopsis: *The Pirate and the Stenographer.*

20

Mrs. Slocum and I spent two hours preparing the Volkswagen bus for the road trip to Poughkeepsie. I vacuumed the interior; she painted the outside with protests.

"TRUE LOVE NEVER DIES," she scrawled in large Day-Glo orange letters. In smaller script just below, she wrote: "Melville, Hawthorne and Poe did."

The ladies gathered early the next morning. They stood and jabbered at each other for a few minutes until I encouraged them to get into the bus. It wasn't that we had a deadline; I just wanted to get it over with. By now, I entirely regretted my impulsive commitment and was charting a future life of temperance and sobriety.

A few of them giggled when they saw me struggling under the surprising weight of their handbags. The metallic sounds were ominous, but I was too young and too polite to say anything beyond, "What do you have in here, a set of metric wrenches?"

My comment only made them laugh harder.

"Put them in the back," Mrs. Slocum directed.

We hit the road a little after eight. There were five of us. One seat was empty. Albert had claimed a conflict and stayed away. He did, however, send us off with some excellent box lunches, which the ladies gobbled up even before we reached Cold Spring.

It was a lovely morning. A cold front barreling down the valley the night before had cleaned out all the misty bits, and the sky was a brilliant blue with only the faintest smudge of stratonimbus clouds.

We went north on Route 9, underneath naked trees and over a golden surf of the leaves they had shed. Sunlight dappled and flickered on the windshield. Even though they were embarking on a great crusade, the ladies were surprisingly quiet.

It was not a long trip. Soon we were turning right onto High Street in Poughkeepsie and heading straight toward the meeting site. In one of her little subterfuges, Mrs. Slocum had called the campus and gotten a map, claiming to be the mother of an applicant. She had also contacted all of the local caterers to discover who would be serving lunch to the SUNY trustees so that we knew exactly which building they would be in.

Our arrival reanimated the ladies. They were back to chattering at each other in preparation. They had rehearsed and choreographed this event so many times that they could do it in their sleep. But now that we were there, it was necessary to go over everything just one more time.

Mrs. Slocum had the high honor of actually delivering the letter. Mabel, the consigliere of the group, would be at her right hand. The others would follow in their established pecking order.

Once everything was sorted out and organized, the ladies picked up their clanking hand bags and trooped off to undo a great injustice. I settled back in the driver's seat to await the trip home. In the van, with the windows rolled up, the sun was the great solar mother who brings love and warmth to all her children sitting in cars.

I turned on the radio. It was just traffic and weather. In seconds, my eyes were drooping; I was out cold in less than a minute.

I drifted off into August and a rowboat on a hot and lazy lake in Pennsylvania, enjoying ambient music. It was too early in the day for either frogs or cicadas, but the wings of the dragonflies were making plenty of noise. All around, though distant and quiet, you could hear the discreet splash of a fishhook entering the water and the hypnotic creaking of oarlocks. The distant growl of an outboard motor provided a counterpoint.

Sun warmed my cheek. I drifted down under the lake, to a point so deep that I didn't have to hold my breath. Doing a frog kick, I found that I could swim underwater for miles and miles and miles. I turned my head to the right and saw a smallmouth bass swimming along beside me.

"We found that eighty gauge was much better," the fish said to me in Mrs. Slocum's voice. "It's very heavy, of course, but our research showed that very few patrol cars carry bolt cutters."

I stirred when I first heard her voice and then stretched and moved. She was still speaking when I woke enough to realize that her voice was coming from the car radio.

I woke up fast now. In this fog, I remembered a previous fog. I realized that I had forgotten about the chains.

Then I heard a reporter say, "That—from one of the protestors locked together on the plaza in front of the administration building on the SUNY campus in Poughkeepsie."

"It is a lovely day for it, don't you think?" Mrs. Slocum added.

"I see the police presence is starting to grow," the reporter concluded. "From SUNY Poughkeepsie, this is Sarah Dawn Russell sending it back to Stan Lesher for tomorrow's weather today."

I stepped out of the bus to reconnoiter. The ladies had locked themselves to the statue of a beautiful young Pequot who had stood up to the Delaware Indians early in the city's history. There were only two police officers present.

There wasn't much of a crowd either. It was nothing like one of the antiwar things on campus just a few years before. Those watching who showed any interest merely slowed down briefly or made some clever aside to their walk-mates. Since it was a bright, mild day, there were a few clerks and secretaries from the building enjoying a cup of coffee or a smoke out in the sun.

The older policeman was chatting with Mabel. Since he was capless, you could see his close-cropped gray hair. He had an easy smile and looked comfortable in an open warm winter parka. When she said something, he slipped out of it and draped it over her shoulders. I didn't see anything to worry about there.

The younger cop, on the other hand, hovered around the scene like a humming-bird. His uniform was immaculate, and his cap crowned his head like a storm trooper's. He tapped his nightstick against an open palm with growing frustration as he viewed a situation that was not being confronted. When he couldn't stand it another minute, he approached his partner.

I was too far to hear anything, but his partner whispered something to Mabel, and they both laughed. The younger officer then goose-stepped angrily over to his patrol car and started making calls.

Wondering how I might help end this ridiculous protest, I noticed the glint of the padlock keys lying on the dashboard. I grabbed them and hurried over to the human chain.

"It's Roger," Mrs. Slocum said upon my arrival. "Hello, Roger. We're so glad that you decided to join us after all."

"Roger, this is Arthur," Mabel introduced.

"Hello, Roger," the older policeman said, standing and shaking my hand. "A lovely bunch of ladies you have here."

"I'm just the driver," I replied.

"You take good care of them," he said. Then he confided quietly into my ear: "Watch out for the rookie. He's young and still pissed off that he missed the opportunity to crack open hippie skulls when it was in season."

"I'm on my best behavior," I assured him.

"Just a word to the wise."

"Thanks," I said appreciatively. "I'm hoping that this will all go away quickly." I jingled the keys.

"Good plan."

Then we heard the sirens.

"Shit," the older cop said, then caught himself.

"Pardon my French," he apologized to Mabel.

"*De rien*," she replied graciously.

The wail of approaching cruisers set everyone on edge. It sounded like there were many of them coming from all directions.

"Oh dear," Mrs. Slocum said. "Is the situation worsening?"

"Don't worry," I said. "I'll have you free in a jiffy."

"That kind of defeats the point in getting arrested," Mabel said. "Don't you think?"

I knelt down and tried to grab an ankle, but in the growing anxiety the locks were dancing as fast as the nervous feet attached to them. When I was able to get hold of one, I could not hold it still long enough to insert the key.

As the eager young policeman strutted, the ladies grew more agitated. The cold made my fingers numb. I fumbled. The locks on the chains started to slip from my fingers. I dropped the keys and had to lunge for them.

Over the clinking of the links, I could hear the scream of police cars turning the corner. In a last-ditch effort, I made a dive for Cindy's foot and pinned it to the sidewalk so that I could slide a key into the lock near her ankle. After a little wiggling, the lock finally popped open, and I freed the foot.

That only made matters worse.

The additional slack in the chain made it a nastier snake than it had been before. With the extra length and movement, it became harder to grab.

I couldn't see anything but feet and knees, but I could sense the nervousness of the herd, so I worked quickly. By the time I had released three of the locks, the chain had wrapped a coil around each of my legs.

Four squad cars of Poughkeepsie's Finest screeched up to the curb, lights flashing. Men jumped out, weapons drawn. The ladies leapt up in panic, lifting the chain and pulling my feet out from under me.

I heard a loud crack and things got peaceful again—and remarkably quiet.

As I opened my eyes, the tranquility was disturbed by another irritating siren. I was staring at the ceiling of an ambulance. The lights were really bright.

"You have the right to remain silent," I heard. "Anything you say may be used against you in a court of law."

I rubbed my eyes and shook my head, and things slowly came into focus.

"You have the right to speak to an attorney, dear," Mabel said beside my stretcher, "and to have an attorney present during questioning."

"Why would I need that?" I asked. "What did I do?"

"Sorry, I had to arrest you, son," the older cop explained. "They wanted to throw the book at you. I kept it down to a 12–19."

"What's that?"

"Obstructing an officer's baton with your head."

"Why would I want to do that?"

"Take a gift when offered. It's a lot better than incitement to riot."

"What about the ladies?"

"Don't worry about us, dear," Mabel explained. "You won't get all the glory. We wouldn't leave the scene until we had assurances that they would arrest us too. We're busted. Thank goodness I brought three skeins of wool."

She was casting stitches onto her knitting needles as the ambulance pulled into Vassar Brothers Hospital to take me up to the prisoners' ward so someone could sew up my forehead.

It took eleven stitches. It was a capable job, but fortunately not perfect. It left enough of a scar that I could impress girls for years afterward. Luckily, they never got around to asking exactly what I had been protesting.

Between the blunt force trauma and the codeine, I was pretty stupid for the next couple of hours. Everything was a blur. I wouldn't remember any of it except for my mug shot, which shows the unfocused lazy eyes of a killer and a blood-smeared left cheek, without a doubt the face of a hard-core criminal. The emergency room technicians had shaved a swathe away from the wound, and the rest of my hair was simply wild. I have never complained about a passport or driver's license photo since then.

At the police station, I had one phone call. Who should it be? There was no point in calling Mrs. Slocum since she was standing next to me. I placed the call to Harvey.

"Don't tell William," I told him.

I realized later that it was good for all of us "on the inside" that he did.

Arthur, the older cop, was very helpful. He offered us advice on the best way to get the fingerprint ink off, suggestions on how to keep your pants up after they took away your belt and the best position to sleep in on the benches. He even gave us each a copy of that day's newspaper, first for entertainment and then for something to sleep under when it got colder.

As he walked us to our accommodations for the night, he let us know that we would be staying in the brand-new lockup until the disposition of our case was resolved.

It was not the worst night of my life. The cell was clean and freshly painted in that special institutional green reserved for prisons, church basements and elementary schools. There were benches along the walls and a stainless steel toilet. Above a soapless sink there was an empty paper-towel dispenser. The lights stayed on all night, of course, which wasn't so bad since I think the dark might have been worse.

I didn't go hungry, either. The city of Poughkeepsie served me up a supper of two peanut butter and jelly sandwiches on spongy white bread along with a half-pint carton of milk and a small bag of potato chips. A toothbrush would have been nice, but I had the holding cell to myself, so I wasn't about to complain.

The ladies were in a cage around the corner, so I didn't see them, but I could hear them. They made a picnic of their sandwiches that went on for twenty minutes. After that, they harassed their jailer to bring them tea with lemon. They were loudly appreciative when it was finally delivered.

After dinner, they set out upon the evening's entertainment. They were remarkably good with their Andrews Sisters medley, and the Glenn Miller songbook was delivered with aplomb. My head did stop throbbing during "Moonlight Serenade" and I went to sleep for a while, but I woke up to some well-sung arrangements from both Dorsey brothers. I stayed awake for the rest of the night. After all, I was in jail.

Eventually, the singing trailed off and went from quartet to trio to duet to none, and the lockup turned into a quiet place. A little before the sun came up, I was surprised to learn that Poughkeepsie had a rooster living within the city limits.

Breakfast was another half-pint of milk accompanying a small cardboard box of corn flakes and a plastic spoon. Using only the spoon, I had a bit of trouble breaking the perforations on the top of the box and cutting the wax paper to make the intended self-contained cereal bowl. But I discovered that if I rubbed the handle of the plastic spoon against the rough underside of the crossbars to my cell door, I could make a shiv sharp enough to do the job.

By the time breakfast was cleared away, the novelty of jail had long worn off. Although I couldn't make out actual words, there was bickering emanating from the ladies' cell down the hall. They did not sound as stalwart as they had sounded the night before. Apparently we all missed the comforts of home.

Many hours later, I was taken from my cell by a new jailer, a woman, who walked me to the visitor's pen. Harvey was sitting there smiling.

"Obviously, you can't be left alone for a minute," he said.

"Hi, Harvey," I replied sheepishly.

"You look like shit."

"You look wonderful to me," I answered honestly. "How did you get here?"

"Train."

"What's in the suitcase?"

"Teale handed it to me at the station," he said. "He said his wife was so frantic at the news that she smashed her piggy bank. It's the biggest pile of cash you've ever seen in your life. If you weren't in the can we could take this to some island and live like kings."

It took about an hour to get us all signed out. The ladies were delighted to meet one of my little friends—oh-so-impressed to learn that I knew someone from Canada. How sophisticated, how international.

As we walked to the VW bus, Harvey looked into my eyes and made me focus on his finger as he moved it back and forth in front of my face.

"Give me the keys," he demanded.

I guess it was a lovely morning. I think I heard the ladies saying as much. But that's the totality of what I do remember about the drive back until we pulled up to Mrs. Slocum's house and she began to fuss about the nice hot bath I was about to enjoy.

"Sorry, Mrs. S," Harvey interrupted. "No can do."

"Why not?" Mrs. Slocum protested. "Poor Roger must be exhausted."

"Orders from on high. 'Poor Roger' is to be delivered up the hill. Not to worry, dear ladies. He will get the royal treatment."

Those last words were unnecessary. It took only "up the hill" to inspire awe in the back seats.

"Your 'Poor Roger' seems to be a hero," Harvey added needlessly.

I didn't need to turn around to know that everyone's fingers were covering their lips in the universal expression of "oh, *my*."

As the group climbed out of the bus, I had to open my door and step out. Not one of them could move on before giving my palm a squeeze, my cheek a kiss and a whisper of "thank you."

"I like your ladies," Harvey said as we started up the hill. "They're a pleasure to be around. Except Mabel. She scares me."

"Join the club."

As we pulled into the drive, the drugs were wearing off, my head had begun to throb, and the sleepless night was catching up with me. I wanted a shower. I was tired, but I figured I should at least thank Miss Warner for bailing me out for the crime of associating with her fans. The ridiculous iron gates were actually welcoming. Before we even rolled to a stop at the front door, Ezeki, the housekeeper, was standing at the passenger-side window.

"Miss Warner says that I should be here to help you upstairs," she informed me. "In my village, I was a fireman volunteer. I carry bigger man than you over shoulder."

"I'm fine," I reassured her.

With a mumbled "Thanks, Harvey," I pulled my sore body out of the bus and followed her.

I went inside and up the grand staircase. As I walked through the picture gallery, the sumptuous colors and rich textures were almost overpowering. I opened the library door.

William was sitting at the table, scribbling on his yellow pad. There was a mug full of sharpened pencils in front of him. The blackboard behind him displayed Meekham's Seven Pillars. His wife was pacing back and forth.

"I feel so close," she said. "All I need is a helpmate."

"That's why I'm here," William replied.

"That's very sweet," his wife explained. "But I mean someone who can actually help."

I coughed discreetly. Faye let out a delighted chirp.

"Hail the conquering hero," she effused.

"You look terrible," William said.

"Billy. Champagne. Now," his wife ordered.

As he walked past me on his way to the wine cellar, he said, "It must hurt?"

"Yes," I answered.

"You'll feel a lot worse tomorrow."

"My brave soldier," she gushed as she took my face in both hands. "My God. Look at you. Those brutes!"

"It was an accident," I explained.

She went to her desk in the alcove and pulled open the top drawer. Sifting through piles of pill bottles, she determined the proper medication and returned with drugs in one hand and a water glass in the other.

"Open wide," she said.

"I'm fine," I insisted.

"Be a good boy and take your medicine."

I was dutiful. I swallowed the pills just as William returned with champagne and three flutes. He worked the cork, and despite his best intentions to remove it gently, it went high into the stacks. But he was quick and poured the frothing wine into glasses before it spilled onto the rug. He handed them around.

"Well," Faye began, holding up her glass. "I think today that I must be the luckiest woman in the world."

"Hear, hear," William answered prematurely to a quick and disapproving glare.

"It is a rare thing," she went on, "when a woman can thank a young man who was chivalrous enough to stand up for her and what she believes in—even though it was something that he knows nothing about."

She raised her glass. "The toast is 'Roger the Valiant—a true knight in shining armor.'"

"Roger the Valiant," William repeated in a voice dripping with more honey than Ezeki's baklava. He raised his glass, but he put it down without taking a sip.

The three of us stood in the center of that spectacular room, above one of the most majestic rivers in the world. I was overwhelmed to be in the company of a brilliant academic and his famous wife, and they were toasting me.

The second glass, combined with the mystery pills that she had fed me, sent me down for the count. Against the north wall of the library there was a lovely sofa in an alcove. It fit me perfectly.

21

The sudden buzz of the front gate intercom jarred the entire room.

William walked over to the box and pushed the button.

"Yes," he said into the intercom.

"Taxi."

"We didn't call a taxi." He glanced at us and raised an eyebrow.

"Dropping off," the box squawked.

"Thank God," Faye said in relief as she rushed over and pushed the button that opened the gate.

"I've got to get dressed," she added as she flew from the room.

William scratched his head for a few moments, standing and staring at the clouds outside. A rising wind and occasional gusts rattled the windows. It made me feel only more comfortable, curled up as I was in a plush and comfy sofa. I watched William watch the sky.

Soon he was back at the writing table. With the steady and sonorous scratching of his pencil point against the legal pad, I was once again mesmerized and floated off into the space between the balconies and the painkillers.

But not for long. "What on earth are you doing here?" I heard William's voice ask sharply in genuine shock.

"I was asked?" replied a woman's voice in a vaguely familiar English accent.

"You could have said 'no.'"

"Lovely to see you again, by the way," she added.

There was a silence. The wind kicked up a bit more, and it sounded like rain or light sleet against the windows. I stretched.

"You shouldn't be here," he said with finality.

I was shocked that he could be so tactless to such a charming woman.

"Of course I shouldn't, but here I am."

"Why?"

"Because I wanted to see you one more time. Sorry."

"No," William corrected her. "I'm sorry."

Marshaling every resource, I stood up slowly, but it could never have been slow enough. All the blood that wasn't yet clotted on my forehead drained from my brain in an instant. The light in the room went flat. I staggered toward the voices, waving my arms in front of me, and my gashed and bruised face like Dr. Frankenstein's monster. Overcome by a wave of dizziness, I grabbed at the nearest chair and fell onto the floor beside it.

As the shimmering mist drifted off from my clearing vision, I saw both of them looking down at me with concern.

"Still beating your students, William?" she asked.

"You should see the other guy," he answered.

I struggled to my feet but went immediately wobbly. Claire lunged forward and caught me.

"Roger," she said. "We can't go on meeting like this."

She was remarkably strong. She raised me back upright and held me still so that I could collect myself. I was in no hurry. It was dreamy in her arms.

I wanted this moment to go on forever. I played possum, but I feigned the faint a moment too long. She caught on, but she didn't expose me. She started to hum in my ear—Strauss.

As "The Blue Danube" began to build in tempo, she slowly waltzed me across the room. I'm a lousy dancer, but she made me feel like I was Fred Astaire. Then she delicately lowered me onto my couch. She lingered, eyeing me, making certain that I didn't need more serious attention.

As she came into focus, I noticed she was dressed with a lot more formality this time. She wore a black suit, and her skirt was medium length with dark stockings and pumps. Her shirt was white broadcloth, set off by a striped club tie. The colors were green, red and gold against a navy blue field.

Her hair was under control, but just barely. It was in a random swirl and clipped in back by a heavy piece of metal. In spite of the outfit, she looked anything but conservative.

"Do you feel as bad as you look?" they both asked simultaneously.

"Water," I croaked.

"Of course!"

"Just the thing."

They practically knocked each other over as they rushed to the pitcher. On their return, which took a few minutes because of the constant editorializing between them in low voices, she handed him the glass and he handed it to me.

"Thank you," I said.

I lay back down, ready to take another spin on my enchanted rug. After she covered me with a blanket, they moved away so as not to disturb me.

"Did he hear anything?" Claire asked with a concerned voice.

"Not to worry, he's a good scout," William reassured her. "Besides, she dosed him up good. He can barely remember his own name."

"What happened to him?"

"It is lovely to see you again too," he confessed. "Even though I dread every minute of it."

"Especially since this is absolutely the absolute last time."

"Exactly."

With difficulty, I lifted my head. They were sitting at opposite ends of the especially wide window seat, so far apart that they could not have touched finger tips if they held their arms straight out.

"I do have a plan, you know."

"I did not know that," he replied. "But I assumed."

"I brought a writing sample. It's horrible."

"I would expect no less," he said.

"After she reads it, there will be an awkward moment. Then she will say, 'Thank you for coming in today, we will be in touch' and imply 'don't let the door hit you on the arse on your way out.'"

"How could I ever doubt you?"

"And then, after that, it's good-bye. The final farewell."

When I didn't hear a peep for a significant interval, I raised my battered head up once more. This time they were standing even farther apart and staring out the windows over the choppy wintry river.

"What's it about?"

"What?"

"Your writing sample."

"It's a little something I whipped up for a power plant in Tennessee."

"What's it called?"

She pulled a file folder out of her satchel and handed it to him. Pulling his reading glasses out of the top pocket of his tweed jacket, he read, "Hot-swapping a tertiary-level subordinated cooling pump from a side-mounted bivalve housing unit."

"When does it come out in paperback?" he asked, then smiled. "This should be a very short interview."

"I hope so."

William started to read, "Due to rivet failure, apparatus name plate might be either missing or unreadable (refer to Technical Note: 49/SCP5F). Warning: following these procedures on a misnamed or unnamed cooling pump may result in personal injury, temporary system failure, or catastrophic damage to reactor core. Read all documentation before continuing."

Looking up, William said, "Oh, that's lovely."

"Keep going, it gets better." She smiled.

"If name plate is unreadable, damaged or missing, pump type can be determined by identifying flange at top of housing. Inductive cooling pump has a rigid pressure release vent hanging down perpendicularly on flange centerline. Whereas action release coil pump is unique because of the two nipples protruding from either side directly above the emergency bleed valve."

As William thumbed through the rest of the manual, he said, "Just as long as there aren't any pirates."

"No pirates," she reassured. "Just safety issues and procedures."

He handed the booklet back to her.

"Well done," he said.

"We added them up. If you followed all the regulations in here," she pointed out, "the average worker would have to take thirty-seven showers a day."

"Sounds like clean energy," he answered.

22

The main and grandest door to the library was rarely used, and it tended to stick. Faye's planned dramatic entrance was accompanied by an ear-jarring screech as she was finally able to get it open. Having thrown her full body weight against it, when it did suddenly give way it cast her unceremoniously into the center of the room.

Looking flustered that her arrival was so far from stately, she stood for a moment, recovering her composure. She smoothed her skirt nervously. Then her hands flew to her head, patting at the perfect shag. Her makeup was immaculate. She was ready for publicity stills.

"You must be Claire." She strode forward with her hand outstretched.

"Miss Warner," Claire acknowledged with a nod of her dangerous hair. "Thank you so much for inviting me here."

She took the proffered hand.

"You are most welcome," Faye answered graciously as she pushed a button on her desk. "Shall we have tea?"

"That would be lovely."

Ezeki entered quietly from a side door carrying a heavy tray, which she put down on the map table. She set out the tea service along with cookies and cakes and then disappeared as unobtrusively as she had entered.

"I understand that you are a very clever writer," Faye said.

"I wouldn't say that," Claire answered modestly. "But I do try to be clear, concise and to the point."

"Do you want me to pour?" William asked.

"Thank you, I can manage," Faye asserted. Her eye briefly caught mine. I could tell she was studying my damaged face and the scabs.

"Stay where you are, dear," she directed. "We will bring your tea over to you."

As they sat down, even I sensed the tension. William sat rigidly, but Claire made a noble effort at small talk.

"I do so love a library that actually has books in it," she said, looking around. "Yours looks especially well stocked."

"Thank you," Faye said.

Sadly, that was the extent of the social part of the proceedings. An awkward pause ensued.

Determined to keep things moving steadily until he had moved Claire safely out the front door, William said, "Have you read her résumé, Faye?"

"No, I haven't," Faye admitted, picking up the curriculum vitae.

As she perused it she complimented, "A master's degree."

"Panic comes naturally at twenty-one," Claire said. "The last thing one wants to do is get a job."

"Is it?" Faye said. It sounded like a little barb. I was never certain of her education, but I don't think there were many letters after her name. "Your degree would be in?"

"Technical financial reporting."

"From?"

"The London School of Economics."

"What a coincidence. Billy taught there once."

Claire murmured something bland and inaudible.

"I can't say that it did him any good," Faye went on. "He came back such a wreck. We had just met, but it took Daddy and me years to put him back together again."

"It was from driving on the wrong side of the road," William offered, surprisingly flat for the circumstances. "Quite disorienting."

"I can imagine," Claire sympathized. "I never conquered it myself."

"How did you get around?" Faye asked.

"I was driven."

"Lucky girl," William observed.

As if on cue, they all sat back and took a sip of Earl Grey.

"Have you brought a sample?"

William passed her the maintenance handbook.

Faye sat back and opened the booklet. William and Claire sat at the table stone-faced.

"Interesting," she said and then read some more.

"Certainly concise and to the point."

She continued reading.

"Well, this could not be more clear."

She read aloud, slowly, tripping over the words.

"A warning. The manifold might be hot. Use caution when sliding the spanner between the opened blades, as there is a danger of electrical arcing."

She flipped a few pages.

"It might be necessary to remove the probe from the main sheath and reinsert with proper lubrication."

She continued further into the text.

"If vibration continues, apply appropriate torque to the uppermost junction point until release is achieved. All measurements are metric."

She closed the booklet with a rude slap.

"There has been a terrible misunderstanding here."

"I'm sorry?" said Claire.

"This seems so—how should I put it? Technical."

"Of course it is," Claire said brightly as she turned the booklet over and pointed to the subtitle. "It's a technical manual."

"Then I'm afraid that we've been wasting your time."

She shot William a hard glance. He responded with a defensive "what did I do?" look.

"In case it was lost on you, dear," Faye explained, "I write romance novels."

"I knew that, Miss Warner," Claire answered. "I particularly loved reading *Day Dreaming in the Middle of the Night.*"

"Oh yes, I liked that one too," Faye gushed, like a schoolgirl, dropping her persona for a moment.

I could tell that William was chomping at the bit, desperate to shut this moment down.

"Well, then ..." he stammered.

"From what I understood," Claire interjected, "what you are looking for is a—"

The room held its breath waiting for the eruption of Mount Faye when that taboo "G-word" was released into the atmosphere.

"—an—assistant," Claire concluded. "Someone to help you with the secretarial aspects of your writing."

"That is correct," Faye acknowledged.

"But writing is writing, isn't it?" Claire said.

"That is a lovely and innocent thought, dear, but I don't think so. What I do is highly specialized."

"You know best," Claire sighed, trying her hardest to seem disappointed. But she continued to look radiant despite herself.

"Thank you for coming." Faye spoke graciously, but her lips were pursed. It was obvious that the Queen of Hearts was not amused.

"Thank you for inviting me."

"Billy, a car, please."

Faye began to leave and then uttered the fateful sentence.

"You seem to be a smart woman," she said to Claire, "but you should realize that there are many forms of writing. Some of them are very difficult. You should restrict yourself to what you do best."

I happened to be looking at William while Faye was talking. I didn't see Claire's reaction. But William looked like a cartoon character watching the fuse burn down on a stick of TNT.

There was a frosty pause until Claire answered graciously.

"I appreciate your advice, Miss Warner, and I take your point. I am constantly made humble with each form I try. As I have only written technical manuals, classical histories, one archeological site plan, two screenplays, four mysteries, some short stories, as well as the annual address for the Lord Mayor of London five years running, I am always eager to learn."

When we turned back to Faye, she was gone.

23

"Oh dear," Claire said sadly. "I have a curious feeling that I blew the interview."

"Well done," William said as he dialed. "You couldn't have blown it better on Guy Fawkes Day."

"Tony," he said into the phone. "How's the family? We need a pickup at the Warner cottage.... No, it's not herself. Send anybody. Thanks."

He hung up and turned to Claire. "Ten minutes."

"Only ten minutes."

"There happens to be a car in the area."

"Just our luck."

"Exactly."

"That's how it is when you're waiting for a taxi. It's either ten minutes or twenty-five years."

They drifted off into different parts of the library but carefully stayed within sight. Despite Claire's brave face, I could tell that she was upset.

I glanced at the wall of windows. The setting sun was making bloody smears across the sky. William and Claire were drawn toward the same window. It was the best sunset window in the house. Before me was a heart-stopping poignant moment: two people silhouetted by the sky outside, the roiling river below, the unmistakable feeling of ambient passion in the room. Perhaps I should blame the drugs, but I was slow on the uptake and I twisted around and turned on the lights when I couldn't see the hand in front of my face.

I realized instantly that that was the wrong thing to do. It took more than a few seconds for my eyes to become accustomed to the light, and when they finally did, the characters of the drama were in totally different places.

William was back on the telephone.

"Where's our taxi, Tony?" he demanded.

Claire sat down at the typewriter.

"I knew a woman who wrote romance fiction once," she said, as she fed a piece of paper into the roller. "Rather pleasant. I don't think she had fifteen cats or anything eccentric like that. She seemed harmless enough. A bit lonely, perhaps. It can't be that difficult."

As she started typing, she mentioned, "I liked her. She was a hard-core Chicago Cubs fan. Got arrested once harassing the third-base coach in the parking lot after a bad steal."

Then there was no more talk, just keystrokes, which were rapid, steady and unrelenting as Claire typed. She did pause for a minute to ask, "Do you have a thesaurus out there? I'm running out of synonyms for 'throbbing.'" But she didn't wait long enough for an answer. The keys were quickly chattering away.

"Oh, I like that," she said as she reread a bit to herself.

"Not sharing?" William inquired.

"I'm only playing," she answered. "I need something to do with my hands when I'm nervous. It keeps them out of harm's way."

She wrote a bit more, then started to read as she typed.

"They could feel that something was wrong with the reactor core. There was a tension in the floor beneath their feet that actually surpassed the moment that had just transpired between them.

"She put on her glasses. Instead of making her look bookish, they only enhanced her natural beauty by bringing out her innate intelligence.

"'Do you mind if I think?' she asked coyly.

"She slipped on her white lab coat with the same grace that he used to cast when fly-fishing in the stream that ran beside his cabin in Montana.

"He looked up, flustered. She looked away so that he wouldn't see her smile.

"But when he pulled on his lab coat inside out, she could restrain herself no longer.

"'If I didn't know that you had won a Nobel Prize,' she giggled, 'I would be embarrassed that Cal Tech ever let you onto the street without adult supervision.'"

"He gave her that adorable cross look that only made him more endearing and she helped him sort out his clothing so that they could start down the ladder into the Dead Zone.

"It was a tight fit in that part of the containment vessel."

"*Why am I perspiring*, she thought to herself. *Is it because I am standing so close to him?*"

Claire stopped typing and pointed to William.

"Or is it because we are standing just feet away from a nuclear core that is about to go critical mass?" he offered.

"Give the man a Kewpie doll. The large stuffed panda if you get the next line right," she goaded.

"Do you think we ought to swap out the cooling pump?" he said, knowing that he was right.

"Well played that man," Claire said. Her fingers seemed to catch on fire. She typed faster than anyone I had ever seen.

"I'm not going to read the steamy bits," she added. "At least not in front of Roger. Don't want to violate his parole."

She banged away at the old Royal for a few minutes longer as William walked back and forth behind her, trying to steal peeks of what was going down onto the page. Without looking back at him, she blocked his view on each pass. Frustrated, he went out onto the porch that hung out over the garden. He left the doors open and stood outside for a few minutes.

Her fingers sped up as she came to the end of a section and then stopped entirely. When the rattle ceased and all was quiet, we could hear William from outside.

"Claire. Out here now."

The voice was so firm and commanding that she made straight for the balcony.

He closed the door with a finality that made it clear that I was not invited, so I quietly stole out to the lower terrace. As I slipped through the French doors, I looked up at something that was so totally out of place—so totally out of season—that a chill shot through my body.

A brilliant white forty-thousand-foot anvil thunderhead was building over the other side of the river. This wasn't summer. This should not be happening. The scientist in me was fascinated; the boy was enchanted.

I glanced up at the upper balcony. Their hands held the railing as they both looked skyward, standing with a close stillness that didn't flinch as explosive thunder crashes followed sky-ripping tears of electricity.

I don't know how many lightning bolts exploded on the ground that night. I didn't count those that I saw. I didn't admit to those that scared me. But I did pray that the moment would go on forever.

I hated it when I heard the buzzer and had to tell them her taxi was at the front gate.

She took a moment to find her purse inside. He stood awkwardly.

"Thank you for coming," he said when it was found.

"I'm glad I came," she said. "Though I'm sorry it was such a terrible mistake."

"In the sciences," William explained, "we allow for 'marvelous mistakes.'"

They stood in the center of the library and shook hands.

"I'll take her down," I volunteered.

"That is a bad idea," William said.

"I'm fine," I insisted. "Really."

They both looked at me skeptically.

"If I fall again, she'll be there to catch me," I pointed out.

Her lilting laughter made me even more light-headed than previously.

She and I were very quiet as we left the library. The taxi was waiting at the front entrance. I opened the door for her, and she turned and faced me.

"Sorry about your hurt," she said as she got into the car. "Take good care of him, Roger."

I nodded, for some reason unable to speak. She rolled down the window, leaned over and blew me a kiss. The taxi churned up gravel as it took off down the hill.

24

The following Friday night, I was squirming uncomfortably on a beanbag chair in the basement of Tiny Swenson's mom's house in Fishkill. The room was dank with mildew.

In those days, there was an event called a smoker or a stag party where young men gathered to drink beer and watch dirty movies on the night before the ball and chain would be locked onto one of them permanently. It was all part of the sacred rite of matrimony. Counting Tiny, there were six of us from the math department—Jerry, Leo, Lewis, Harvey and me—as well as Tiny's brother and a couple of his cousins. None of the math geeks was comfortable at the bachelor party, though Leo and Lewis acted as if this were old hat. I was sitting next to Harvey trying to smoke a White Owl Panatela without throwing up.

"A word to the wise," he whispered in my ear. "Don't inhale."

We drank slightly chilled bottles of watery beer while Tiny's cousins raised a wrinkled bed sheet and his brother stapled it to the wall. Seconds afterward, a flickering 8mm movie projector covered the makeshift screen with a steady stream of carnality.

All the Swensons were enthralled. They whooped. They laughed. They cheered and applauded. The rest of us were embarrassed that we couldn't be at ease watching strangers having sex in the company of people we had never met.

It didn't last long. When we dropped to a single case of Genesee, the brother and cousins panicked and fled to the store, leaving Tiny and us math types to go it alone until the beer ran out.

Even though we weren't good at blue movies, we tried hard. Lewis did his best to sound lecherous.

"This is probably a preview of what Tiny will be up to tomorrow night ... heh heh," he said rudely.

"Eating?" Leo wondered.

"I'm sure that will be the first thing on his mind."

"Don't worry about me," Tiny reassured us. "She's doing the flowers, I'm doing the food."

We turned back to the movie. I have never regretted studying math. It was helpful to my fellow students also. Without our training in analysis, we would have been lost. The film was in bad shape, and the makeshift screen didn't help. We set about trying to determine the gender of each white blob that gyrated through the grainy, flickering images.

It was very difficult at first. Leo wanted to freeze the frame, but we told him that would be cheating. Lewis thought that gender could be determined by position, but Tiny explained that these were trained professionals, and they did things that the rest of us had never heard of.

Leo then implied that none of this was anything that he hadn't experienced personally.

To which Jerry smirked, "Leopold's idea of group sex is doing it with another person."

Then we were riveted to what might have been the orgy scene.

"Is that three or four doing it?" Jerry asked during a particularly active moment.

I was in a position to help. I had no idea what I was looking for. But I knew that it had nothing to do with the formula that I was working on. The only missing link here was the blob on the right with a single eyebrow across his forehead.

"The white mass on the right is a refrigerator," I explained. "The door has been open for some time and swinging back and forth. It's confusing because it is exactly the same height as the white blob on the left that is now doing something to the blob on the dinette."

"Thanks," Jerry concurred. "I believe you're right."

"This is so hot," Tiny drawled. "I think I might be a blobophile."

My eyes were getting tired. Watching the movie took the same concentration as driving in dense fog.

"They seem to be enjoying whatever it is they are doing," someone observed.

"I'm glad someone is," Harvey whispered to me.

The quality of the film deteriorated to the point that none of us could make out anything that was going on, but our hearts were pounding and our breathing was short. We could sense the moment of climax was approaching when Jerry Ng suddenly leapt to his feet.

"The one wearing socks is the man," he shouted.

That would have been a brilliant resolution to the evening, except for the fact that we had six more reels to slog through. Thank God I was sitting next to Harvey.

"Don't be judgmental," he warned me as I groaned at the introduction of yet one more set of twins. "The temples in southeast Asia are covered with naked women. They're sacred."

"I've got more women than I need, thank you very much," I said testily.

"Clearly not the right ones," he said. He turned to look at me. "Are you all right?"

"No," I admitted. "I'm tired—bone tired. They all want a piece of me, and they all want it on Tuesday."

"Who?"

"Who doesn't?" I complained. "I've got that paper on fractional integration due on Tuesday. The test on tangled string theory is on Tuesday. I have to drive Mrs. Slocum to the podiatrist on Tuesday morning. I've got to drive Faye—that's Mrs. Teale, and you didn't hear it from me—to her shrink on Tuesday at noon. William has booked six hours in the computer center for me to input code early Tuesday morning. Before that, he expects me to have the Dead Sea Scrolls glued back together. The Virginia Faye Warner Fan Club is expecting me to be guest of honor at their gala at the Route 9 Holiday Inn on Tuesday night."

I must have looked pretty helpless. All Harvey could come up with in support was to ask, "Can't you call in sick?"

"Maybe deceased would work better," I replied in defeat. "Fortunately, the appointment with the lawyer in Poughkeepsie to keep me out of jail isn't until Wednesday morning."

By the time Tiny's brother and cousins returned with the beer, we were sitting in the kitchen upstairs. They retreated to the basement, no doubt relieved to be rid of us dorks.

We drank coffee.

"I can't believe that Tiny is a married man," Leo mused.

"Not until tomorrow," the big guy pointed out.

"How do you know she's the right one?" Lewis asked.

"I love her," he answered.

"Haven't you been in love before?"

"Have you?"

"Dozens of times," Lewis answered.

"Twelve times a year," Leo pointed out. "Lewis is in love every time there's a new *Playboy* on the newsstand."

Lewis glowered.

"All kidding aside," Jerry asked. "Doesn't it bother you that you are never going to have sex with any other woman, ever?"

"It wasn't that easy to get her to do it, either," Tiny answered.

Changing the subject, I raised my coffee mug and said, "The toast is the bride and groom."

"The bride and groom," everyone answered.

"I think it must be wonderful to know that you have found the right woman," Leo confessed. "But how do you know it's true love?"

"I'm not worried about that," Tiny answered. "I topped three hundred pounds for a few hours last month. I'll take any kind of love I can find."

We nodded at the logic of his argument.

"But it does exist, doesn't it?" Leo wanted to know.

"What?" Tiny said.

"True love."

"Is this girls' night out?" Lewis complained.

"It's just a question," Leo pouted.

"It's a huge question," Jerry agreed.

"I truly love lasagna," Tiny admitted.

"But how do you know when it's truly true love?" Jerry continued.

"He's right," Leo went along.

"That's the real question," Jerry reiterated.

"We should ask Roger," Harvey advised provocatively.

"Of course. Roger's the expert," Lewis said. "He spends all day up at the love factory with Mrs. Heartthrob and The Man."

They all turned toward me.

"So what's the story?" Leo asked.

"The story?" I repeated. "You mean the new book?"

"We mean with Professor Billy," Leo explained, as if to an idiot.

"Like we care about Mrs. Billy," Lewis snorted.

"He's been teaching the same master's seminar for thirteen years," Leo concurred.

"We all bought the notes," Jerry lamented.

"And the test questions," groused Tiny.

"I paid big money for a paper that he has consistently given an A since 1973," Jerry further bemoaned.

"Me too," Tiny commiserated. "Now it's worthless."

"So what's going on?" two or three asked in unison.

"I don't know," I said. "Maybe he got bored."

"That's not his job."

"That's our job."

I suddenly felt a little sorry for William, everyone just wanting him to be predictable. I knew that was not the sort of inevitability that he had in mind.

"I don't know what has happened, but I think he's gone back to being a mathematician, Jerry," I offered.

"Shit," everyone in the room groaned at the same time.

"Sounds like a lot more work for us," Jerry decided.

"He should lose his mind on his own time," someone said.

"I should have gone to MIT," Tiny groaned.

"You got accepted to MIT?"

"I mean, I should have tried harder to get into MIT," he said.

"It's very hard to distract him from his work. He is very excited." I added.

My words were met with only stares and glowers.

"He's got me running up and down stairs like crazy," I explained, trying to stir up some enthusiasm. "He's pulling out every old academic paper he's ever written. We are recreating every detail and event that led up to his submission to the Comstock Committee."

What magic those words were. The room had been getting restive. Now it was all quiet at the mention of that august body.

"Jeepers," Tiny erupted. "Do I have a film to show you guys."

His huge girth charged out of the kitchen on his way up to the attic.

I was relieved to be temporarily off the hook when Lewis unexpectedly volunteered, "I was in love once."

"But then her daddy put up curtains in the bathroom," Leo explained.

"I really was," Lewis said with such hurt sincerity that he got an apology from Leopold. "It was a long time ago, at science camp."

"If this were a Virginia Faye Warner romance," I said, "you would run into her ten or twenty years from now and get back together."

"Why would I want to do that?" Lewis asked. "She threw me over for a jock."

"I had a girlfriend that I would like to see again," Jerry said. "In fact, I think she might be the love of my life."

"Why don't you look for her?" I asked.

"What if it doesn't work out?" he answered. "Then I'd lose even my fantasies."

"I know exactly who I'm going to marry," Harvey suddenly joined in.

Everyone looked at him in surprise. We had never seen him with anyone.

"Do we know her?" I asked.

"No," he answered. "I haven't met her yet either. She'll be about forty or forty-five, divorced with two children."

As our interest increased, Harvey continued peeling the label off the beer that he had been nursing for the last hour. "It only makes sense," he explained. "She's divorced, so she won't have any unrealistic expectations of what marriage is all about.

"She's over thirty, so she won't have any unrealistic expectations of what life is about.

"She's been on her own for at least some time, so she can manage whatever meager resources she has.

"More important, she will appreciate any monetary contributions in the future, no matter how modest.

"The children are preexisting, so it will be fairly easy to determine if they are creeps or not.

"Being stepchildren, they represent no personal, financial or legal liability.

"Ultimately, every family member or woman that knows or ever did know or care for her—and even strangers that you will meet together in the future—will admire you for taking on such an onerous burden."

"You can't beat the logic of that," Leo said.

"No, you can't," he replied. He finally finished off his beer just as Tiny came rushing back into the room waving a reel of 8mm film like it was the grail.

"I found it," he crowed. "Everyone back to the basement."

"No," they all groaned in protest. "We've had enough."

"If I get postcoital depression one more time, I'm going to slash your wrists," Leo said.

"This isn't what you think it is," Tiny beamed. "It's great."

"Not the midgets again," Lewis wailed.

"No, even better."

25

Tiny stood in the middle of the basement room. His brother and cousins had cleared out when they saw the *Return of the Nerds*. "What we have here is a home movie of then-Assistant Professor William Emerson Teale defending his submission before the Comstock Committee."

You could have heard a pin drop. But not for long. We plopped ourselves back into the beanbag and butterfly chairs. Tiny fiddled with the reel of film. He paused for a moment to ask, "I did tell you there was no sound, didn't I?"

"What!" we all exploded in disappointment.

"It's eight millimeter and over twenty years old."

Everyone groaned.

"Hey. It's better than nothing."

He got it threaded into the projector.

"I've heard there's a transcript that goes with it, but I haven't been able to track that down yet," he added as he flipped the switch.

What started out as a flicker soon filled the screen with a title card that announced "Candidate Presentations. The Comstock Committee. May 5, 1953."

That was enough to revive us. We whooped. We howled. This was history come to life, and in Technicolor to boot.

We watched the five members of the panel file in and take their seats on the dais. There were three professorial types, a man in a very sharp business suit—the money guy—and a woman in a tight bun and a long tweed skirt.

"She's got to be prob/stat," someone mentioned.

"Probably."

"She took the pencil out of her hair only because it's a formal event."

"Mommy," Jerry whined playfully. "That statistician is scaring me."

The panel adjusted their chairs, filled their water glasses from their pitchers, settled in and looked up expectantly as their leader, the man in the suit, made a few remarks.

Next, the most rumpled and tattered academic, and obviously the top-ranking one, said a few words. The entire panel laughed politely. After he sat down, the camera panned a small but full lecture hall, coming to rest at the presenter's area in front of the committee. It was a podium with a long table to one side. The camera lingered for a few moments.

After a while, it took another turn around the room. Those on the panel were fidgeting with pens or looking about in irritation. Then the camera moved back to the audience, which was chatting, or snoozing, or reading books or newspapers.

"Is that Sheffield?" someone asked.

"Where?"

"In the first row."

"Can't be. He's too tall."

"No, it is Sheffield. He's got the seat folded up. He's sitting on the edge."

"You're right. That's Sheffield."

"Go figure."

At last, a door in the far corner of the room opened.

"There he is!" Tiny said, leaping to his feet.

There he was, on the bed sheet before us, William marching with determination down the stairs of the lecture hall. When he got to the front, he dropped a large satchel on the table, then stood at the lectern and addressed the panel.

The camera came in for a close-up. It was definitely William, but not the model that we knew today. He was young and skinnier. He had high cheekbones and a flat-top crew cut and large horn-rimmed glasses. He wore a grey flannel suit one or two sizes too big and a bow tie.

"What a dork!" Lewis piped up.

"That was the fashion of the day," Harvey explained.

"He looks a lot better now," Jerry pointed out.

"There's hope for you all then," Leo encouraged.

William opened the satchel and pulled out a huge stack of papers, tossing them onto the table. Then, with deliberation, he separated them into smaller stacks. Finally, when everything was arranged to his satisfaction, he stood at the lectern, grabbed it firmly on either side and delivered what had to be his opening statement.

"What I would give for a lip-reader," Leopold said. I felt the same way.

William talked for several minutes. Then, something, perhaps a noise, made him turn his head to the audience. He was startled by something he saw. He stood and stared, apparently dumbfounded.

The camera panned to the audience. The film was grainy and the seats were packed. It was impossible to tell exactly who he was focused on, but I was convinced that I caught sight of a riot of blond hair just to the left near the back.

Evidently a panel member spoke. William turned. His hands gripped the lectern, and his eyes blazed. He listened. Then he nodded adamantly.

He turned to the table and collected the first stack of pages. He tapped it fastidiously to tidy it up. Returning to the lectern, he placed it before him and read a few paragraphs, then he looked up. Even in old, grainy and red-contaminated 8mm film, you could tell that he was frantic.

He made a few points while waving the document high above his head and gesticulating. Finally he cocked his arm and let fly so that the papers went soaring into the rafters. Pages drifted down like a late spring snow shower.

He didn't spend much time on the remaining stacks. He launched them in quick order so that a steady stream rained down on the audience. As I watched, I realized that these must have been the missing "five corners" that I had been attempting to reconstruct over the last few months.

When William ran out of paper, he stood for a moment and surveyed the chaos.

Someone on the dais said something, but he just stared.

Then he paced, mumbling or ranting by turns. He frequently looked up in agitation and fired back responses to all parties whether they were from the panel or the general audience. It was obviously a vigorous debate. As it progressed, he appeared to calm down. Someone must have said something to soothe him.

We were finally able to read his lips.

"OK," he said.

He picked up the satchel and put it on the table. He took out a tall drinking glass, a large rubber mallet, a wooden elementary school ruler and a liter of Russian vodka. Standing at the table, he began to speak.

He opened the vodka bottle and poured it, filling the large tumbler. Then he took the ruler and measured the level. Holding the mark with his thumbnail against the ruler, he raised the glass and showed it to all corners of the room.

Then he brought it to his mouth. His gulps were large at first, smaller later. Between each swallow, he measured the height of the remaining liquid in the glass. When he reached the halfway point, he stopped and returned to the lectern.

Although it is hard to judge the quality of a man's words when you can neither hear his voice nor see them in writing, I have always been convinced that what I was watching in those silent, grainy, flickering images was not anger or bitterness. It was pure and simple heartbreak.

Holding the glass in his left hand, he indicated the length of the glass in between his right thumb and index finger. Then he closed his digits like a caliper to the empty half. Putting the glass down on the table, he made one more comment before he picked up the mallet beside it and smashed the tumbler repeatedly, rendering the glass into a pile of glittering shards.

William turned and appeared to thank the committee for hearing his presentation. Then he proceeded to clean up, sweeping most of the debris into the satchel and mopping up the spilled liquid with his jacket sleeve.

The camera caught his face in close-up, and his color was rising. The mask of misery grew larger and larger as he charged forward, until the camera shook and seemed to fly up toward the ceiling. Then bright light filled the sheet as if the camera case had cracked open and exposed the remaining film.

We stared at the blank screen long after the scene was over. We hardly noticed when the film started to slap and shred itself against a stationary post in the projector, as the take-up reel spun faster and faster.

Tiny finally reached over and yanked on the cord, pulling the plug out of the wall. It had been unexpectedly depressing. We sat silently for a few moments longer, and then we went our separate ways.

Fortunately it was a cold night, which brought us back enough to remember why we were there.

"Have a nice wedding, Tiny," we said.

He was gracious. "Thanks, guys."

I got a ride home from Jerry Ng.

Usually three beers was a general anesthetic for me, but that night I slept with William's tormented face spinning around in my dreams like a bad drive-in movie horror sequence.

26

Mrs. Slocum knocked on my bedroom door early the next morning.

"I've brought you tomato juice," she said generously. "I do so worry when my guests cry out in their sleep. Are you all right?"

"Yes, Mrs. Slocum," I replied. "It was just another jail flashback."

"You poor young man," she said, patting my cheek. "You must have felt so alone. We had such fun in the little girls' cell. But never mind. Breakfast is ready when you are."

After a fitful night of replaying that movie in my head, I was in no hurry to see William. I knew he had left the "Math for Poets" exams on my desk upstairs in the library. It was the most successful course in the department because it satisfied the school's math requirement. William taught the class because no one else in the department would.

"I don't mind lecturing their blank faces," he told me. "But I certainly won't be the one to cry over their work." That was why I had to grade the tests and homework.

When I got to the library, I snuck up the back steps. I was surprised to hear music. I had never heard the sound system in the library before. I didn't even know it had one. It was playing Tchaikovsky. I couldn't tell whether it was about dead swans or dead Capulets, but it was very romantic. I peeked over the railing.

Faye was lying on the velvet chaise in the corner. William was sitting at her desk flipping *Bartlett's Familiar Quotations*, reading out familiar ditties about love. He'd toss one up and she'd shoot it down with a short sardonic dismissal.

William switched to his most mellifluous baritone to read the famous line by Tennyson. "'Tis better to have loved and lost than never to have loved at all."

"'Tis also tedious," his wife replied. "Why are you doing this?" she finally asked, irritated. "I don't see the point."

"I'm looking for a basic understanding of the subject," he explained.

"Ah," Faye said as she swung her legs over the edge of the chaise and sat up to light a cigarette. "Now I see it."

"See what?" her husband asked, missing her sarcasm.

"The reason for this exercise in futility," she replied. "You're looking for the meaning of love. Good luck, Professor."

"I'm sure it's in here somewhere."

"Don't waste your time."

"I can't help it. From where I come, that's how we work. We are very keen on defining our terms."

"You're on a fool's errand," she snapped. "First of all, we don't give a fig about love. It's romance. You're looking at somewhere between fifty-five and seventy thousand words."

"Exactly," he agreed. "But which words? We are talking about the greatest human emotion—and the most primal animal appetite."

"Wrong again, Billy," she said as she lit up. "We don't come even close to primal. That violates more than two-thirds of our publishing guidelines. We are not concerned with what love is. We only care what love looks like."

He digested that for a few moments and nodded his head.

"I take your point. Might you offer some examples, please?"

"That's no problem at all. It's just a turn of the crank. That's what we do."

She began. "It's all about the woman, isn't it? If she is shy, she can't keep her mouth closed. If she is articulate, she can't talk. Her mouth gets dry, her palms get sweaty. Knees get weak, her breathing constricts. Her circulatory system, however, is always robust. Blood is constantly rushing to every body part imaginable, coloring her in love's colors: pink, crimson, red.

"But most important, she's amazed that this is happening. She doesn't want it to happen. Yet she dreads more than anything that it will stop happening."

"Oh yes," she added. "Somewhere in the middle, she has to hate him a lot. Where did I put my lighter?"

"That was most helpful," her husband complimented.

He returned to his yellow pad to jot down these new revelations.

"I think I've got it now. Thank you."

"No problem," she replied.

I could tell that she was bored. It was in the way she spoke. It was in the way she wandered around the room. She looked out the windows for a while, and then she drifted over to the Royal typewriter and played with the keys. She fidgeted with the roller until she had gone too far and the paper inside the machine flew out and floated to the floor.

It apparently took a moment for her to decide whether to go to the trouble to lean over and pick it up. When she finally did, it took a little longer for her to cast an eye over it. She stood up quickly and demanded, "Who wrote this?"

"Who wrote what?" her husband asked sheepishly, not looking up.

"This," she waved the paper. "In the typewriter?"

Her voice was steely.

"It's that blonde who was here last week, isn't it?" she accused.

"Maybe," he answered weakly.

"Why are you doing this to me?" Faye asked, shaking her head. "If you don't want to help—fine—don't help. But please, don't sabotage me."

William was at a loss for words.

"Have you read this?" she demanded. "It's perfect. Get her back."

Then she turned on her heel and left the library.

William sat as if carved in stone.

The ticking grandfather clock took over the empty space.

I realized that I was in an awkward position. I had not come in through the front door. I had not made my presence known. I was an eavesdropper. Worse, I was a spy. What should I do?

I sneaked another peek over the rail. William was there physically but not there mentally. He was in some other place or time. I figured it was a good opportunity for me to remake my first appearance of the day.

I slipped off my shoes and catfooted it off the balcony, through the door and down the back way, stopping at the floor below. I stepped back into the public part of the house, walked the long plush carpets of the portrait gallery up to the library's main entrance, put my shoes back on and opened the door with much fanfare and complaining screeches.

"Academic slave reporting for duty," I announced as the door slammed behind me.

William started. His head jerked but he did not leap to his feet.

"The blue books are on your desk upstairs," he ultimately said. "But don't go up yet."

He gestured to a chair at the reading table.

"Sit there."

He stood and crossed in front of the windows over to the biography section and perused the titles.

"Ah," he said. "Carrie Nation."

He pulled a large commemorative folio edition off the shelf and placed it on the reading table. Then he reached back into the void once filled by the book. He groped around until he grasped and pulled out a bottle.

"Yes."

He set it down on the table before me.

Unceremoniously, he dumped two glasses of water into the large floral arrangement.

He sat down and slid one glass in front of me and took the other for himself. He opened the bottle.

"What we have here is a whisky from a part of Scotland known for the bitterness of its inhabitants. It is greatly prized."

He poured a shot into both our glasses. We picked them up.

"Cheers," he said.

"Cheers," I answered.

I emptied my glass. He set his onto the table without bringing it to his lips.

"Have you ever been in love, Roger?" he asked.

His straightforwardness threw me off guard. I said nothing.

He refilled my glass. We sniffed and contemplated the amber liquor for a moment, until he asked, "Do you think Tennyson's right?"

"In what way?"

"'Tis better to have loved and lost than never to have loved at all.'"

I thought for a moment and answered like a scientist.

"That would depend, wouldn't it?" I said.

"On what?"

"On Tennyson. Had he done either?"

"Interesting point."

"I mean, if he had never loved at all, what does he know about it?"

He poured another splash of whisky into my glass.

"There's hope for you yet," he said, toasting me.

I drank.

"It's an axiom, isn't it?" I pointed out. "Like the old bromide about optimism."

"They never got that one right."

He put his glass down untasted and studied it.

"An optimist sees the glass as half full, the pessimist as half empty."

Then he turned and faced me with a familiar ferocity in his eye. He was immediately thirty years younger.

"But a realist," he emphasized, "knows that it can all shatter at any moment."

He sat back in his chair, spent. "At that point it is one-half divided by zero. The result is impossible."

His demeanor was so serious and intense that I found it impossible to do anything but sit.

"Love is a great leveler, isn't it?" he observed, breaking the silence. "Ergo, the next logical question would be, is love a gift for the less fortunate because it is a prize so cherished by even the high and the mighty?"

He swirled the liquor for punctuation.

"Or is it the bane of the rich and powerful that it can reduce them to the level of the meanest?"

With each comment, I watched him drift further and further away.

"It must inspire the most basic human compassion, even more than watching the death of innocence, to watch a truly hateful and arrogant man undone by love."

Even the clock now seemed muted in the pauses.

"It is the pinprick that deflates the most established and entrenched hubris."

The next interval was so long that I began to consider which would be the best way to leave. But then he turned and faced me.

"Do you know what is worse than losing the love of your life?" he finally asked.

"What would that be, sir?"

Then he was gone, lost so far in his thoughts that I wondered if he was breathing. I wanted to shake him.

I wanted to demand, "Who? What? Where? When?"

But I didn't have the heart. He looked like he would fly apart like an old rag doll if mishandled.

I don't remember how long I sat next to him.

Later, I stood up and walked across the floor to the staircase in the corner and to my carrel among the books above.

When I brought the graded exams down to leave in his briefcase, he was gone. The entire time, I hadn't heard a sound other than the muffled jotting of my felt-tip pen.

The whisky in his glass remained untouched. I carefully poured it back into the bottle. After returning it to its hiding place behind Carrie Nation, I turned off the lights and closed the library door.

27

Mrs. Slocum made a late breakfast to thank me for driving them all back from the law offices of Abalone Abalone and Slaughter. The ladies had been pleased to discover that their case had been thrown off the official city docket. The district attorney was smart enough to know that prosecuting a bunch of little old ladies and grandmothers was a disaster waiting to scuttle his political career. He withdrew all charges.

That did not mean they were totally off the hook. The board of trustees still had options in civil court if it decided to pursue a charge of illegal trespass.

"But all in all, things look good," the junior associate told us, adding reassuringly, "The trustees seem to want the whole thing to simply go away."

The young lawyer continued to shuffle through the pages in front of him as if he were reading them for the first time. Mabel knitted faster and faster until she could no longer contain herself.

"What about Roger?" she asked.

"Unfortunately, that does not look so rosy," the young lawyer replied without looking up. "They don't like outside agitators in Poughkeepsie."

My episode with the police had been physical. Blood had been spilt—albeit mine.

"He's no radical," Mabel objected. "He helps little old broads cross the street."

"Maybe we can plead out and settle for probation," my counsel suggested.

God, I hated that word.

"Maybe you should be disbarred for being an incompetent pipsqueak," she countered. "That's ridiculous. Hell, he should sue the city for wrongful imprisonment, excess force and civil rights violation."

Mabel started to pack up her needles and wool.

"Go tell that to your boss."

That admonition was unnecessary. The young man was already out the door and halfway down the hall.

Back in her kitchen pouring coffee, Mrs. Slocum slipped a shot of Inlander Rum into my mug. "That'll definitely take the edge off, dear," she said.

It did. Between the liquor and the sunlight flooding in through the window in the breakfast nook, warming my neck and shoulders, I basked in a sense of well-being. We drank our coffee, and Mrs. Slocum set about opening her mail, slitting the spine of each envelope with a long and pointed brass letter opener.

"Any idea what the maximum sentence might be?" I wondered after she reviewed the utility bill.

"There won't be one, dear. You are already a hero." She turned to the next letter.

"Isn't that sweet. A woman from Le Grange has read every book that Virginia Faye Warner has written and asks politely if we would inform her of any future protests. She would love to join us on the front line. How nice."

She flattened out the letter neatly and opened the next one.

"Oh my," she remarked as a small newspaper clipping fluttered from the envelope.

It was the short mention of our protest that appeared in the *Poughkeepsie Journal.* The story couldn't have been more than four column inches long.

"Ladies Deliver 'Chain' Love Letter to School Heads," it read.

The correspondent had circled the headline in angry red ink and written next to it, "Hear us roar!!!"

"This is certainly unexpected," Mrs. Slocum commented as she opened another.

This time cash fell out. Mrs. Slocum's hand covered her mouth.

"Well, I *never*," she said in surprise. "We must certainly pay attention to this one."

She went to the bookcase in her kitchen and scanned through her cookbooks until she found what she was looking for. She returned to the table with a black-and-white marbled composition book.

Uncapping a marker, she wrote "VFW HONOR ROLL" on the cover. Then she carefully entered the names and addresses of each of the ladies who had written to her.

She pulled out a small metal box from behind the cookbooks, dumped its contents into an empty oatmeal canister from the pantry, slipped in the sent money and locked it up.

Next to the last entry in the composition book, she carefully wrote, "$5."

Finally, she stuck the newspaper clipping on her refrigerator door using her most cherished kitchen magnet, conjoined hearts intertwined with the word "Forever."

"Ah," she sighed happily. "I think we will do better with bicycle locks the next time."

We both stood rereading the article until the phone rang.

"Hello," Mrs. Slocum answered, then held it out for me. "It's for you."

"Hello," I said.

It was William.

"What are you doing?"

"I was reading one of your wife's books."

"You're kidding."

"No, it's true."

It was true. Over the last ten days, I had read six Virginia Faye Warner titles—well, actually, it was only five. I didn't realize until the very end that I had read one twice, but since then I began to put light pencil marks on the flyleaf so that I would know.

I was determined to find the missing link and crack the formula before William did.

"Can you go to the house?"

"I thought you were in your office."

"I am."

"Am I meeting you there?"

"I'll be along later."

"What do you want me to do there?"

"Look busy," he answered.

"How do I do that?"

"You'll think of something. Shuffle paper." Then, he added, "Keep your ears open." He hung up.

"Do you need the bus?" I asked Mrs. Slocum.

"I wouldn't think so, dear. I have to write thank-you notes, don't I?" she answered, gesturing to the opened envelopes.

The moment I opened the library doors, it was clear why William had gone underground. It also was clear why he wanted a pair of ears and eyes present where he couldn't be.

The lights in the room made the silver tea service sparkle as it was intended to. Wearing a fashionable tweed ensemble, Faye was playing grande dame in full battle dress, her makeup once again perfect. Claire sat diagonally across the table. I noticed that her hair was under full lockdown, braided then clipped back onto itself.

Her black slacks were tasteful and tailored but unremarkable. The white turtleneck, however, existed solely to highlight the slightly large club blazer that she wore. The crest on the breast pocket was intricate with a lot of gold embroidery and was totally commanded by two crossed rowing oars. The jacket must have been a man's. The buttons were on the wrong side. Although her outfit attempted to conform, it didn't succeed.

When I stepped into the room, they both turned and faced me.

"There he is," Faye gushed. "Roger the Valiant."

I bit my tongue. That routine was getting old.

"How is your 'eye the blackened'?" Claire asked me dryly.

"Come over here," the lady of the house gestured. "Let me inspect you."

Self-consciously, I shuffled up to the table, where she made a big deal out of studying the wound. She then went on to verbally admire my resilience, my loyalty and loyalty in general, then segued to betrayal and back stabbing, then quickly back to loyalty and finally, to absent friends.

When it was clear that she had run out, I asked, "Is it all right if I work upstairs?"

"Of course you can work upstairs," Faye cooed. "After everything you've been through on my behalf, you have the run of the place."

"Thanks," I said.

Claire turned toward me and fluttered her eyelashes with such saccharine sweetness that I had to make tight fists in my pockets to keep myself from laughing out loud.

As I crossed to the staircase and made my way to the stacks, I couldn't help but be puzzled by this new transformation. Faye was a different person from the day before. The anxious bundle of nerves in a tattered bathrobe had been replaced by a smartly dressed woman who from all appearances was fully capable of walking out the front door on her own steam at any time she so desired—agoraphobia be damned. She exuded confidence and talked in a comfortable, commanding fashion.

"Needless to say," she continued with Claire, "it is two weeks overdue. We have to move very quickly. I hope you are a fast typist."

"I have speeding tickets," Claire replied.

Faye ignored the flippancy. She was in control and enjoying it.

"I would prefer if you worked here," she said. "But if you can work faster at home, I will allow that part of the time."

"Whatever suits you. After all, your name is on the book and the paycheck."

"Yes, it is," Faye agreed firmly. "Having said that, now I'm sure we will work well together."

"That is my first priority," Claire responded.

"Watercress sandwich?"

"Thank you."

They nibbled and sipped for a few moments until Faye said, "There might be just one little itsy-bitsy fly in the ointment."

"That would be?"

"My husband," Faye answered. "Billy's got the crazy notion that he is going to colaborate."

"Has he ever done that before?" Claire asked coolly. "Did he do that with your previous assistant?"

"Ambrose?" Faye laughed. "They hate each other."

She lit the first cigarette that I had seen in her hand since I had walked into the room and then chattered on blithely. "But if he does hover at all, it certainly won't last long."

She shifted to the seat next to Claire.

"He didn't want me to hire you. He was going to write the book himself. What would he come up with? Star-struck chemists separated by an unkind fate, reunited while waiting in line at the slide-rule repair shop."

She allowed herself an unattractive titter as she blew smoke toward the ceiling. She coughed. "Imagine!"

"I don't mind," Claire said. "It might even be helpful, having a man involved."

"Oh, that's the last thing we want," Faye quickly insisted. She crossed to the glass-enclosed display case and pulled out a copy of Meekham.

"There is no place for the male point of view in a Virginia Faye Warner book." She placed the book on the table. "It says it right here. Read that tonight. It will be your bible."

She went back to her seat and lit her next cigarette. I could tell by the slight fumbling with the lighter that her poise was beginning to crack.

"Anyway, by tomorrow, he probably won't even remember that he wanted to help. At this very moment, he's involved with yet another project he will never finish. He's obsessed with it, in fact. He's running poor Roger quite ragged."

I could see shades of the other Faye returning. "It's only a matter of hours before he loses interest in that too. He's never finished anything he's ever started."

She picked up her cigarettes and the lighter and made quickly for the door. "Let me know when you have something to show me," she called over her shoulder.

28

I was down the stairs and sitting at the big table before the door swung shut.

"Hello, Roger." She greeted me with an exquisite smile. "You must think I'm the 'bad penny.'"

"Oh no," I admitted. "You're the best penny I've run into since I came to this place."

"Don't let her know that," Claire cautioned. "She's the queen bee around here."

"She wouldn't care," I said. "I'm a small bug at her picnic."

"There's no such thing as a small bug. Trust me."

She looked up at me with the strained patience of someone who wanted to get to work. I knew I should walk away, but I had so many questions. I wanted to know everything about her.

I was very flatfooted.

"May I ask a question?"

"Yes it is my real hair color," she replied. "I dye it myself."

"Are you English?"

"No. I'm from Massachusetts."

"Then why do you have that accent?"

"I married into it," she explained.

She inclined her head. I could see a lifetime of memories instantly flash through her mind. As the briefest glimpse of sadness crossed her face, she quickly dispelled it with a small smile.

"Say hello to Mrs. Chips," she explained. "I was married for twenty years to Trinity College, Cambridge. My husband was a brilliant man. He knew everything there was to know about nuclear physics and almost nothing about people. It was my job at dinner parties to turn the science into a language the guests could understand."

She added wistfully, "He died in the spring."

"I'm sorry," I said feebly.

She grabbed at the chance for transition.

"Little did I know that translating physics into English for my husband would save my bacon when the money ran out."

She opened her notebook.

"Is there anything you would like to know about generating safe, clean nuclear energy, Roger?"

"Not at the moment," I confessed.

I knew that I had been dismissed, but I couldn't move my feet.

Then, to my surprise, William came in. He looked at both of us and then turned to address Claire.

"I gather we are writing a book together," he said.

"So I understand," she replied, then smiled. "Your wife also informs me that you are a bit of a flibbertigibbet."

"I can only aspire," he confessed dryly.

He turned to me and said, "We will need the entire table."

I was disappointed as I trudged up the stairs to the stacks. I hadn't been sent to the kiddie table since I was ten.

They both watched me until they thought I was out of earshot.

William looked at Claire and demanded, "What are you doing here?"

"I did everything you said."

"Did you ask for an obscene amount of money?" he asked.

"I doubled obscene and added 50 percent."

"What went wrong?"

"She gave it to me."

"Can't you fail at anything?" he asked, exasperated.

They were standing some distance apart. Even from a distance I could see her body shudder under the impact of his words.

"I have failed at many things, but it has been a total joy just to see you yet again," she finally said.

Spontaneously, he seemed to deflate. "Yes, it is. Forgive me."

"Surprisingly complicated, isn't it?"

He started to explain himself, but when their eyes locked there was no need. They stood for a long moment without sound or movement.

She finally broke the look.

"I actually need the money, William."

"Then you shall have it," he said quietly.

They stood in the same frozen moment until William crossed to the table.

He broke off a bit of muffin and placed himself at the other end of the long table.

"It can't be that difficult. I've read one a day for the last two weeks. Assuming my studies and analyses are correct—"

"As if you could get any of that wrong."

"So let's write it."

"And then—"

"Well, it won't be like the last time."

"No, it will be worse."

They drifted back down into their private space as alarm bells went off in my head.

The last time? I analyzed that phrase. It didn't take a Leibniz to realize that they were talking further back than the fiasco at the student union.

I studied them once again. There was nothing in their body language that betrayed anything but innocence. It was William who next interrupted the quiet.

"There is no reason why we can't have a little fun," he said.

Her face lit up like it was springtime.

"Oh, yes, please. You were always brilliant at fun, William."

"Was I?"

"Of course."

"That must have been the other William."

"I only knew one," she said.

"I'm glad."

He crossed over to her.

"I assume you have read Mrs. Meekham," he said as he dropped the book on the table.

"I've also read *King Arthur and the Knights of the Round Table*," she said. "I couldn't believe it when she dragged out this fossil."

"Muriel has been kind to us all. I have been so informed repeatedly and often. But all good things must come to an end."

"What do you have in mind?" she asked.

"Violating Mrs. Meekham."

"Oh, William, no. Have you ever seen a picture of her?"

"I meant metaphorically."

"What a load off my mind. Do we have any idea what we are writing about?" she asked.

"We certainly know what we are not writing about," he answered.

When they started to speak so quietly that I couldn't make out a word, my focus returned to my work. But I was back in my ringside seat when I heard William's chalk against the blackboard.

"Meekham's Seven Pillars. Yakety yak," he said as he wrote. "Now, the trick is to break all the rules. If you only violate some of them it won't work."

"I remember," Claire reassured. "It's all about the contrapositive, isn't it?"

"She remembers," he said glowingly.

He stopped writing on the blackboard and underscored the last line three times.

"This is my favorite pillar. No exotic names."

He strode over to the reference section and grabbed a volume off the shelf.

"Perfect," he said as he read the title, *"Horrid English Common Names."*

"Boy's name first?" He flipped through the pages until he landed on a candidate. "Beverly?"

"Not on this continent."

"Leslie?"

"No."

"Robin?"

"You're not even trying."

"Baldric."

"Jesus Christ."

"Now it's you who is picking names that we can't use," he said, shaking a finger at her.

"Innocent?" he continued on.

Claire raised an eyebrow and broke into peals of laughter.

"Lancelot?"

"That's a verb, not a name," she answered.

I slunk back to the long gallery, where I was trying to reconstitute William's earlier brilliance. I grumbled to myself as I looked down at all one hundred seventeen pages of my mentor's four papers that were laid out on the floor in conceivably the world's most complex game of Concentration.

If you're so goddamn smart, I thought to myself, *why didn't you number your goddamn pages.*

When I heard one more mumbled aside and mutual laughter from the floor below, I could stand no more. Anyway, I had a deal with Mrs. Slocum. In return for the use of the bus for the entire holiday weekend, I had to pick up her turkey by five o'clock at Hudson Meats. I pulled on my coat and leaned over the balcony.

Claire looked up.

"Have a nice Thanksgiving," I said.

William spun around in surprise.

"When?" he asked.

"Tomorrow."

"Oh, what a bother. I'd forgotten. I hope it doesn't take too long." His eyes returned to the blackboard as he wrote out, "Angus MacStrood."

I heard their spirited banter echoing through the large room as I made my way out.

"He was MacStrood of the Yard, wasn't he?"

"Oh, *that* MacStrood."

"The same."

"Not the one who tracked the Butcher Barrister of Bournemouth to Blackpool?"

"The very one."

"A lion of a man."

"A manly man."

"A man as handsome as he was brave and resolute."

"Sister, you've said a mouthful."

It was playful banter. They were easygoing and comfortable together. I felt a chill, worried that Faye might get the wrong impression.

29

Pennsylvania was repainting its landscape, preparing its bleak palette for winter. But despite the poetry in its dreariness and the opportunity to reunite with my family—I especially enjoyed the long walks listening to my cousin discuss his various suicide options—I quickly realized I missed the river and the headlands. By the time Saturday night rolled around and my uncle dragged me out to his regular bar so that he could "buy the jailbird a drink," I was chafing to get back.

I left at four in the morning and crossed the George Washington Bridge by six. As I hit New Coventry a little before seven, I knew that Ezeki would already be in the kitchen working on breakfast. My hunger, even more than my mom's locally famous signature pumpkin chiffon pie sitting on the passenger's seat beside me, made me decide to swing up the hill before I unloaded my stuff at Mrs. Slocum's.

I was halfway down the drive when I realized that something was out of kilter. It was still early, yet the house was all lit up as if no one had gone to bed.

"Everyone in big book room," Ezeki explained to me. "Very crazy since pretty blonde lady show up."

Without even thinking of putting the pie down in the kitchen where it belonged, I hurried toward the library. When I opened the door, I was astounded.

The room was ablaze. The Rolling Stones was blaring from the sound system. William's cherished blackboard, still sitting in the center of the room, was covered with a tangled diagram and overwritten with notes and symbols and huge swooping arrows and lines, some of which actually leapt across open space in the form of strings, which were stuck to secondary pages that were taped to window panes, bookcases, plants and anything else nearby.

On either side, there were two easels. Both displayed large panels of poster board with even more scribbled notes and more arrows and even more strings pointing back to the center blackboard.

The reference section was in complete disarray. There were more books stacked on tables and chairs and even the floor than were left on the shelves. A coffee urn surrounded by used mugs had taken over the large table. The place looked like a vast dorm room during exam week.

As I climbed the stairs to park my coat in the carrel, the sun was just rising on the other side of the house, lending a rosy hue to the clouds and a golden highlight to the hills on the far side of the river. Claire sat at the Royal typewriter. Her hair was tightly braided and double-clipped. Her face was fresh. She was wearing a large gray MIT sweatshirt and blue jeans. I don't think she was wearing an undershirt. When she leaned forward to untangle two jammed keys on her typewriter, I caught a glimpse of collarbone. Spectacular.

Faye sat next to her. She was wrapped in a royal blue kimono with a dragon richly embroidered on the back in gold, red and green. There was a large stack of manuscript pages in front of her that she was devouring as soon as they rolled out of the typewriter.

"Well," she finally said as she came to the end of a section. "That was surprisingly excellent."

Claire looked over.

"Which?" she asked.

"The scene in the train station."

"Oh, yes. We like that one."

"It's wonderful."

"Thanks."

"I must say I am very happy with your work so far," Faye complimented stiffly.

"Oh, I didn't write that," Claire said brightly as she fed the new pages into the typewriter.

"What?"

"William wrote that bit."

"Billy wrote this?" Faye answered, waving the pages with incredulity.

"Right. Same chap, different moniker." Claire lined up her margins, but politely held her fingers off the keys, waiting to see if her employer had anything else to say before she got back to work. "Though I did edit him."

There was a pause. "How much has he written so far?" Faye asked.

"About half," she answered. "We would be farther along, but we have been fighting over the typewriter. It's a beastly tug of war."

She went back to work as Faye hunted for cigarettes just as the main door screeched open and William entered carrying a small round tray over his head.

I was shocked. He looked twenty years younger. He stood straight to his full height and moved with agility and power. His stylishly brushed hair seemed to have lost its gray. The Radcliffe T-shirt he wore made it quite clear that he was still taking full advantage of the school's tennis and squash courts.

He went straight to the reading room table and put the small round platter down on one corner, giving it a spin.

"What's that?" asked Faye, inhaling.

"Stop writing for a moment, please," he directed.

Claire lifted her fingers from the keys. William picked the typewriter up and put it onto the turntable.

"It's the lazy Susan from the breakfast nook," he explained. "I had to give Ezeki my watch as security, but I think it will be worth it."

He positioned two chairs diagonally across the corner of the table and demonstrated how easily the Royal pivoted from one seat to the next.

"This will speed things up, I think," he said, sitting down. He studied the text in the machine, banged out another sentence, then spun it around so it was ready for the person in the next seat to keep on writing.

"Brilliant. That deserves a drink," Claire announced as she moved to an urn and flicked the spigot. When nothing poured into her mug, she hoisted the coffeemaker up onto her shoulder and set off for the kitchen.

William sat down at the table and earnestly edited Claire's writing, working fast and furiously to do as much damage as he could while she was out of the room.

I was just about to start down the stairs to deliver my pie and make my presence known when Faye spoke.

"Billy." Her voice was so ominous that I crept back to my hiding place in the periodicals.

She confronted her husband head-on.

"I know all about you two," she stated coldly.

I held my breath.

"What exactly are you talking about, dear?" he asked with remarkable presence.

"I know exactly what's going on. She even confessed."

"I don't understand. What is upsetting you now?"

"Why are you being so hateful?" she complained. "You know."

"No—I really don't know."

"When did you learn how to write?" she asked accusingly.

"Oh, writing. I actually could write before we met. Before we got married, I wrote five papers that some people thought were rather good. You didn't read them, did you?"

"Don't play all innocent with me, Billy. You're doing half the work—and I'm paying her full fee. This is not helpful."

She stood up and paced the floor in short circles. William walked over to the boxes along the windows that held the typing paper, the carbons and the second sheets. He collected an ample supply of each.

"Actually, I thought that was exactly what I was doing."

He sat down and drummed the paper, fed it into the typewriter and began to type.

At that moment, Claire returned with a full urn of coffee. I took this as my cue to come downstairs and present the pie.

"This is some of my mom's best work," I explained. "She hopes that you enjoy it as much as she enjoys your books."

For once my timing was flawless. Faye looked at the pie and looked at me, and her eyes went damp.

"What a wonderful family you must have," she said. "Everyone stop everything and have some of the delicious—wonderful—pie that Roger has brought us."

Dutifully, they all gathered around the pumpkin chiffon, which, thank God, was as good as advertised.

We stacked our dishes onto a tray, and Faye exhorted, "Back to work, troops."

"Aye aye, skipper," William said, and he saluted, giving Claire the opportunity to make it back to the typewriter first and get a two-hundred-word head start.

Glancing down from the balcony, I could see them both. They were like large cats ready to pounce. The one who had control of the typewriter was working frantically to capture as many words as possible before the machine was whisked away in a brief moment of weakness.

Faye drifted around, studying the display's complicated lines and presentation. She wandered to the periphery to look at the various notes and papers. Claire noticed her interest and offered a tour.

"The red yarn is the primary conflict, and the blue is the secondary. The yellow strains are interesting thematic pieces to pick up some good press," she explained. "We were going to color code the index cards by character, but by that point it was Thanksgiving and the stores were closed."

"I love color coding," Faye said.

"The bits over on the bay window, joined by green, are a subplot that we weren't sure of at the beginning—but now we are convinced is essential."

Faye took it all in.

"The book is 95 percent complete," Claire bragged. "All that's left is the writing."

That stopped Faye in her tracks.

"Are you kidding?"

"I don't kid when I'm on the clock," Claire answered.

With a new respect, the famous writer took another tour of the outline. She touched some of the subplots with her fingertips and studied others with curiosity.

"I like this chance meeting," she remarked.

Moving on, she commented, "That's a lovely twist."

And, "Oh, I love what she's wearing here."

Or, "He really is quite handsome, isn't he?"

She came to a stop in front of a blank wall where all the strips converged.

"What happens here?" she asked.

"The ending."

"I don't understand," said Faye. "How does it end?"

"That's the missing five percent."

"It's a happy ending, of course?"

"Of course," Claire reassured her. "We're just not sure how happy."

"Make sure it is very, very happy."

She took one more walk around the diagram.

"You won't mind if I get back to work," Claire said.

She successfully snagged the typewriter back, and it didn't take very long for her to get up to speed.

Faye devoured page after page, while William and Claire spun the shared Royal in a near trance of competitive touch-typing.

Periodically, one or the other would shout, "Break!"

Then they would both stand up and walk around the room for a moment, sometimes conversing, sometimes not. It was during one of those brief pauses that Faye asked, "When do we get the first love scene? They usually come around page eighty-five."

She was too caught up in the manuscript to notice their response, but I did. They turned to each other briefly and smiled.

"They're in there," one said.

"They start out small," the other said.

"But they grow on you," they said in unison, but it went unnoticed.

Faye picked up another page. "I like this," she said and began to read aloud.

"It was only a small round table on a balcony in the front window of a coffee shop, but for her it might as well have been a secret bungalow on a beach in Bora Bora. This was the first time since their chance reunion that they'd had any privacy at all, if you could call this private. Yet she admired him for his discretion, placing their intimate moment, as he did, in the front window. What could be more innocent than a public place?

"If anyone walking on the Strand that rainy Thursday afternoon cared to, all they would have to do would be to look up into the window above to see a presentable couple chatting pleasantly to each other. But that would certainly be the most pedestrian view of the situation.

"She was amazed that he was even more handsome than he had been twenty-five years before. Certainly, there were a few new creases, but his jaw was firm and his eyes were sharp. Such eyes. Was it the glint or the twinkle that made them dance so magically? The only thing she was sure of was that when they did dance, they were dancing for her."

Faye tapped those pages back into a neat stack.

"Well, it seems that we are finally heading in the right direction," she said. "I can't wait to get the next section."

"Then stick around," William advised.

"But that's days away," Faye said. "I do know a few things about difficulties of writing and how long it takes."

"Fortunately," Claire answered, "we know nothing about that."

"Which is in no way a criticism," her husband qualified quickly.

"Of course not," his coauthor agreed.

"We are only trying to meet your new deadline," they said together.

Faye was so distracted that she didn't notice their faces go red at yet another unwanted coincidental unison. They covered their discomfort with work, taking turns at the typewriter, sometimes reading the words out loud. The typewriter spun back and forth between them with the rapidity of the dialogue.

Claire read, "'Very clever to hide us in plain sight,' she said."

William answered, "'Exactly the same way you would have handled it, I dare say,' he replied."

"'Maybe.'"

"'What is it that we are hiding anyway, if I may ask?'"

"'Absolutely nothing.'"

"'That is just what I thought too.'"

"At that, she stood up and pulled her seat around to his side of the table, dragging it so close to his that the chairs exchanged a wooden kiss.

"'Why should you be the only one with a view?' she asked as she lithely slipped beside him to watch the world pass by on the street below."

"Then it happened," William typed, "without warning but with the same inevitability as a match held to a fuse."

"It was a simple-enough gesture," Claire continued as she spun the typewriter back. "She merely leaned toward him."

"But in so doing, she set off a quiet but catastrophic chain of events."

"It wasn't that there was a sound or a crash or even a blow or concussion."

"In fact, when her shoulder finally touched his, there was no impact at all."

"It was more of a melding."

"The fit itself was as pleasing and basic as finding an errant puzzle piece and finishing up the sky on the Sunday afternoon of a long rainy weekend up at the lake."

"They did not fit so much as join."

"They stayed that way for what seemed an eternity."

Claire wrestled the typewriter away and slammed the carriage return, then turned the roller back one line. She violently x-ed out the offending text.

"That is not only terrible," she said, "it is also hateful and crummy."

"I know. I know. I know," William replied, backpedaling as fast as he could.

He quickly went to the next line.

"Don't even think of saying that 'time stood still,'" Claire warned.

"What is wrong with that?" Faye protested. "We love stopping time. Stopping time and racing hearts. They go together."

"It's a grammar thing," William explained kindly. "We used a metaphor in the previous sentence."

"Simile," Claire corrected him.

"You see how complicated it is," he pointed out.

He read as he began to type. "It was as if a leg that had been lost in an accident had suddenly grown back, and only then did he realize what phantom pain was because it had been assuaged."

"Disgusting," Claire interrupted, forcibly twisting the typewriter away from him again. "Could that be more gruesome?"

"I'll have to take her side on this one," Faye agreed.

William was embarrassed.

"It's a very complicated concept," he explained.

"We don't do complicated," Claire stated simply. "Or prostheses."

"She's right again, Billy," Faye noted.

To save the scene, Claire set off in a flurry of typing that could only be described as virtuosic. The pace of her fingers was so rapid that there seemed to be multiple hits at any given moment.

Slowing as she came to the end of her thought, she capped it with a concluding sentence. She took a moment to reread what she had written and seemed pleased and at ease with the work as the grandfather clock chimed the hour.

"Bloody hell," she groaned.

She saw their concerned eyes, and she explained.

"Not that," she said, pointing at the work in the typewriter.

"That." She gestured toward the clock, grabbed her handbag, left her chair and crossed the library floor.

Standing under the balcony and looking up at me, she asked, "How long are you going to be here?"

"Not long," I answered.

"Can you give me a lift?" she said.

"Sure."

"Now?" she asked.

"Why not?" I answered.

She rewarded me with an incandescent smile. "I'll get my things."

She walked under me and out of the room. William and his wife studied the page in the typewriter.

> "It wasn't so much that they fit perfectly as it was a perfect fit," Faye read.
> "When she draped against him, their contours traced each other's. They were in total harmony. For a brief time, they could dare to dream … What if? … If only …
> "They didn't care. They were together, no matter how alone.
> "They did not speak. They drank their coffee in silence. At last, they walked down the incredibly long staircase from the balcony. At the door, he took her hand in his. They both knew they would never see each other again.
> "After they turned, they moved stiffly, comforted only by the lingering imprint of the other's touch. Resisting a last parting glance, they walked away from a past, a future—and happiness."

Faye clicked the roller wheel on the typewriter carriage to get to the next line, but it was at the bottom of the page, and the sheet flew out and onto the table.

"Well that is certainly—adequate," she commented.

"I think it suffices nicely," her husband agreed.

Faye neatly took the new pages and carefully stacked them with the existing manuscript.

"You know," she said, "I'm beginning to feel that there might actually be a book here."

"You're welcome," he said. His firmness seemed to surprise her.

She turned and faced her husband with curious eyes. I wondered what she would say and was so caught up in the moment that the gentle but unexpected footstep behind me made me startle.

"I'm ready," Claire announced.

"Of course," I answered. Reaching for my coat, I spilled the stack of papers that I had spent the last two hours collating. They went all over the balcony floor.

"Oops," she said in sympathy.

"It's not important," I answered stupidly. "They're very old."

"I know," she replied.

Once again, the pages were thoroughly shuffled. She put down her things to help me pick them up. My eyes wandered through the iron railing to the floor below, where William and his wife were quietly discussing something in the office alcove. Claire handed me the pages she had picked up. I scooped up the rest and dropped them on my desk.

Pulling on my coat, I asked, "Do you want me to drive?"

"That was my hope," she answered.

"You must think that I am a moron."

"No," she said reassuringly. "I think you are dear."

She gathered up her handbag and coat and a large yellow envelope. We left by the small door in the balcony. As I reached for the handle of the big door on the floor below, she touched my hand and delicately pulled it back.

"I don't need to say good-bye," she said.

We went out through the kitchen, where Ezeki forced Claire to accept a stuffed pepper wrapped in foil.

"Too skinny," Ezeki said with great concern. "You fall in storm drain and drown, and we all be very sad."

When we got to the driveway, I opened the door to the VW bus. She dropped her bag onto the floor and carefully placed the large yellow envelope on the back seat. It was a bit of a climb into the passenger seat, but she used my shoulder for support and hoisted herself up.

The bus started up with no complaint. As I put it in gear and started down the hill, all I could see was the faded upholstery, the peeling peace decals and the missing sun visor on the passenger side. She was smiling.

"These things are great," she said. "I missed the whole hippie thing. I was playing the dutiful don's wife in Cambridge."

Then she was silent, until we reached the clearing that revealed most of the bay.

"I love this river," she said, with a touch of sadness, as she looked out her window.

"Me too," I agreed. "I haven't even known it for long."

She sighed, reached behind her head and released the two clips that restrained her hair.

Her profile was striking, yet I could not define her beauty in conventional terms. There was no dramatic line to her jaw, or dangerously sharp cheekbones. If anything, her features were rounded. Yet Ezeki was right. She was way too thin. But there was no angularity, no bewitching shadows. Her face seemed to be remarkably open and accessible. She was beautiful in a way that was unfamiliar, unconventional and uncataloged.

"Where are we going, anyhow?" I asked.

"147 High Street. It's across the street from the hospital."

I had no trouble finding the address since it was the same professional building that I had brought Faye to, but this time we could use the front door. When I pulled up, I turned and faced her directly. She seemed to have forgotten about me all together. Her smile was retreating within her. She was concerned about something, but I could tell I shouldn't ask.

"Thanks for the ride," she said as she opened the door and slid out of the bus.

I reached behind me and handed her bag to her and then picked up the large yellow envelope. I couldn't help but notice the bold black type across the top: "X-RAYS. DO NOT BEND."

As I passed it to her, she might have said "thanks" in a soft voice, but I wasn't sure. She walked into the building without a turn or a wave.

30

When I pulled up to Mrs. Slocum's, the place was full of cars. And not just the driveway. They were parked all along the block. When I walked through the side door into the kitchen, the place was packed.

Cindy and Maureen and Harriet and Joan were crammed into the breakfast nook, working on a large stack of mail piled high in the center of the table. Cindy was eviscerating envelopes while Maureen sorted the contents by category. Harriet was recording names and addresses in the composition book. Joan filled out a card and stuck it onto a Rolodex that resembled a Ferris wheel.

Mabel was sitting on a stool next to the drain board counting large wads of money. Albert was at the stove. There was no sign of Mrs. Slocum.

"Whoopee!" Maureen shouted, as she apparently did every time she pulled a bill out of an envelope.

Considering how crowded it was, the room was quiet, almost tense. Still, no one noticed me as I slipped through the room on my way upstairs. I had just reached the door to the hall when the telephone rang. Everyone in the room froze and stared at the phone.

Mrs. Slocum rocketed in through the swinging door. I saw stars.

"You shouldn't stand there, Roger," she warned me distractedly as she hurried to the telephone. "You could get hurt."

"Hello," she answered into the receiver.

"No, we've heard nothing." She looked at the clock. "But there's still twenty minutes to go."

"Yes," she concluded. "You'll be the first to know."

She hung up the phone.

"That was Rockland County," she announced.

There were nods all around as they went back to their appointed tasks.

Mrs. Slocum handed me an ice pack as she walked past on the way to the bookcase that held her cookbooks.

"Let's hope that Roger is our only casualty," she said. "But we need to stand firm. I've been doing my homework and learning from those who have gone before us."

The volume she pulled off the shelf was called *Uncivil Disobedience*. It was a hand-book for successful protests and rioting. She kept it between the *Joy of Cooking* and *Building with Marzipan*.

"We have modified the approach a little," Mabel said.

"We're taking a pass on the tear gas," Maureen added.

Cindy concurred. "Definitely, no tear gas."

"I'm allergic to tear gas," Joan said.

The phone rang again, jolting everyone.

"This is the one," Mrs. Slocum announced. "I can feel it."

All activity ceased. She turned cold and resolute and intentionally let the phone ring three times before crossing the room to pick it up.

"Slocum here," she said. "Good afternoon, Mr. Lathrop."

At that, the ladies scurried throughout the house to all the extensions.

Mabel and Joan stood beside Mrs. Slocum, who held the handset away from her ear so they could hear. Maureen, Cindy and Albert ran upstairs to the phone in the bedroom.

"You won't mind if this is a conference call," she continued. "Yes, I understand. That is only fair. Good afternoon, gentlemen."

I held the ice pack to my forehead.

"That's a wonderful first step, Mr. Lathrop," Mrs. Slocum said into the phone.

She listened for a few moments more. "I agree completely, but it can't really be a first step if it's the only step, now, can it?"

She squinted her eyes as she focused on what was being said.

"I understand, gentlemen."

As she stood and heard more from the other end, I could see the other ladies making concerned faces.

"That is not what I said. That has never been our position," Mrs. Slocum stated. "What I have said, and I will repeat it now for our new friends around the conference table, is that I realize that you have no idea of what is bothering us. Moreover, you have no understanding of the kind of grief that we can rain down upon you."

She referred to the back of the activist handbook. "We are consulting with the same group that shut down your campus for eight days in 1971."

After listening for another moment, she asked, "You are not clear about what?"

Once she digested the next question, she replied. "Over two thousand educated, concerned and voting women who are eager to enact change."

At that point she signaled me with primitive hand signs, and I brought a stool over to her so that she could sit and the others behind her could hear better.

She listened to what was clearly a complicated obfuscation. Finally she informed them, "Yes, I'll be here. No. Not a half hour. There are only ten minutes left on the clock."

She listened again.

"It was your deadline, gentlemen. Not mine," she said. "Tick tock."

Cindy and Maureen couldn't restrain themselves.

"Tick tock," they chanted into the phone. I think the ladies upstairs also were making clock noises.

The next few minutes after that conversation were excruciating for them. To be honest, I was too tired to care that much. They went through the motions of continuing their tasks, but very little was accomplished. They were too agitated. Albert had a total lapse, and the air got thick with the odor of burned whatever-it-was that he was cooking. I was in the way, so I moved upstairs.

There was a crowd in the kitchen, but I had the whole upstairs to myself. The shower more than satisfied my expectations. I turned the faucet to scalding and removed all residue of Pennsylvania. I don't know how long I stood there feeling the sharp needles of water pummel my body, but when the hot water started to run out, I shut off the shower and toweled dry.

Just as I opened the door and stepped out into the hall, shouts and cheers erupted from the kitchen. I dressed and hurried downstairs. The scene was jubilant. Albert and Cindy were hurriedly filling small cordial glasses with peppermint schnapps. Mabel led a spontaneous rendition of "For She's a Jolly Good Fella," after which there were more cheers and hugs.

"Speech, speech, speech," they chanted as the drinks were passed around.

Albert graciously held up an arm so that Mrs. Slocum could mount one of the benches in the breakfast nook with the dignity of the belle of the ball that she was becoming. She was radiant.

"First, I would like to thank the Academy," she said, to much laughter. "Of course, the little people."

"Down in front," Cindy shouted out, adding to the general hilarity. She was five foot nothing.

"Seriously," Mrs. Slocum continued. "While I think we should be very proud of ourselves today, we should also appreciate the great contribution of all the folks who have written in and offered their support."

Polite applause followed.

"Of course, the money don't hurt."

Applause and whoops. She smiled.

"Since there is a quorum present, I propose that we allocate some of those funds to paying Roger's legal expenses."

"I move the question," Mabel chimed in.

"All in favor?"

The vote was unanimous, and I was very flattered. Their generosity and the 100-proof schnapps that I had just tossed back warmed my heart.

When that enthusiasm died down, Mrs. Slocum offered a confession. You could feel the room rally around her.

"I got a little distracted during the negotiations," she explained. "So nervous."

"That's why the gentlemen could still walk to their cars under their own power," Maureen piped in, inspiring a gleeful response throughout.

"Seriously, I really don't have a clue," Mrs. Slocum explained. "I know that we won, but I have no idea what we got."

Their laughter was a testament to their affection for their leader.

"Cindy took the minutes on the bedroom phone," Joan said.

"Where's Cindy?"

"Cindy, come on down."

Cindy walked to the fore, blushing and brandishing a legal pad. Everyone quieted down. She put on her glasses.

"What did we get?" she said. "Only more than we would have dared hope for."

"The trustees understand how often indigenous art forms go unappreciated for too long," she read from her pad. "Then more blarney than St. Pat and a lame excuse about state bureaucracy—and all sorts of legalese—and then we get to the good part. I would love to read it to you, but all of a sudden I've gotten so parched."

"A drink for the secretary," someone demanded. Albert jumped to the task and presented the small glass on a tiny silver tray.

"Sorry for the delay, Milady."

Cindy toasted Mrs. Slocum.

The very air was lightheaded. She raised her glass. "True love never dies."

"Bravo," they hooted and hollered as she tossed it back.

"But seriously now, folks," she continued. "We've hit the mother lode."

There were more smiles all around.

"Of course, they can't come out and say that they are wrong, but they're doing the next best thing. They're going to study it."

"In less than three weeks from today," she continued, "the State University of New York at Poughkeepsie will sponsor a two-day symposium entitled "Romantic Literature?" The panel will include three full professors of English alongside three representatives from within the publishing industry."

She flipped over the page.

"To quote: 'The debate will be open and wide-ranging.'"

There was more applause.

"Yes, that does sound like they are ready to join the sing-along," she went on. "But our fearless leader has an even better sense of pitch than we do. She held out. She went for the high notes."

The room was on tiptoe as she flipped the next page in her pad.

"'We are so close, gentlemen,' Greta Slocum said. 'If only we had a token gesture of goodwill from your side.'"

Cindy closed the pad and slowly looked around the room dramatically.

"And she got it."

Cindy let the tension build for another three beats before she announced: "The keynote speaker to open the symposium on romance and literature two weeks from next Friday night will be—"

You could hear the drumroll churning through everyone's head during the next pause.

"—none other than our favorite local celebrity," Cindy exalted. "Virginia Faye Warner."

That's an out-of-house, out-of-body phenomenon I'd sure like to see, I thought to myself. Everyone else shrieked with delight. I slipped away from the celebration long before it was over.

"I was very scared when I was negotiating with the board," Mrs. Slocum admitted later that night, as I was helping her sort out the dishes. "But whenever I was on the verge of faltering, I just thought of you all alone in your jail cell. Your bravery at that time was just the inspiration I needed to discover my own strength.

"Don't use the blue towels on the dishes, Roger."

31

As the bedraggled members of the advanced concept seminar filed into the lecture hall on the Tuesday after Thanksgiving break, it was hard to tell whom we more resembled: an overworked firing squad or the condemned. Nobody wanted to be there. Worse yet—none of us could remember what it was that we were unprepared for.

William was late. We dropped into our seats like full laundry bags, hoping against hope that he would be even later. It was the unofficial school policy that we could leave if our professor didn't show up within twenty minutes after the bell rang.

This wasn't the first time that William had been late. Typically, if we happened to be sleeping when he did finally show up, he would grab the largest book he could find and sadistically drop it flat onto the podium. I had previously observed him employ that technique in the library at the big house when he was trying to shut up a cat fight between his wife and Ambrose.

This time, I wasn't just dozing. I was lost deep inside a maze of sleep. The heat in the lecture hall added to the vividness of my dreams. I was floating down the Mississippi on the raft with Huck and Jim, lost in a midday torpor. The river was lapping just inches from my ear, and the distant sounds of industry from the shore melded together in a comforting cradlesong.

My head fell forward and jarred me awake. As I opened my eyes, the room came into focus, and the easy drift was quickly replaced with tension. Chalk scratched against two blackboards. Shrill sounds emanated from William and Harvey, who were arguing, or at least in heated discussion.

I wasn't the last one awake, but I was far from the first. Lewis Embry and Leopold Ickies appeared spellbound by the work being laid down in chalk, not to mention the drama of the moment. Tiny was still snoring up a storm.

"How long was I out?" I whispered to Jerry Ng.

"I don't know," he shrugged. "I was sleeping too."

I wish I could say that it was the waking fog that kept me from understanding what was being debated so passionately, but that would give me more intellectual credit than I deserved. The stuff they were writing was still far beyond my understanding.

William had covered just about every inch of his blackboard with small and densely packed scribbles, equations and formulae. Harvey Weintraub's was empty. He was standing by with chalk in one hand and an eraser in the other. William's frustration was palpable.

"A-*ha*," he shouted at Harvey.

William erased a line or two with the sleeve of his jacket and frantically amended the argument with another arcane line of symbols and operands.

"That doesn't do it either," Harvey noted, calmly writing down the disproof on his blackboard, then erasing it cleanly after William had read it.

They had obviously been doing this for some time. For the moment, Harvey was winning.

Another pass of the sleeve and William started, "How about—"

Even before he finished, Harvey was writing. "We did that one twenty minutes ago. Remember. If the probability of p, given not o, is greater than that of its negation, then—"

"I see it," William grumbled as he cleaned that bit off his slate one more time. The sleeve of his jacket looked like he had fallen into a snowbank.

Harvey fastidiously erased his work while William paced around the room. Even Tiny was awake now. Every eye in the place was glued to the blackboard.

As we sat mesmerized by the notations in front of us, I experienced a mini-epiphany. While I had no idea what the big picture spelled out, as I studied the cold and simple scratches on the blackboard, certain patterns began to emerge. They swirled around and revealed connections, and then relationships, and then the lights went on and I realized what I was looking at.

William paced more and more tensely as we got closer and closer to our break. When Harvey asked, "Exactly what are you trying to prove, Professor?"

I answered spontaneously and perhaps a little too loudly, "It's the proof of inevitability."

Although my outburst had broken his train of thought, for once William rewarded my interruption with a smile just as the bell rang. But no one made a move to leave. William stood and stared at the work before him. We followed him with our eyes as he strode from side to side of the lecture hall and then finally climbed to the last row, where he dropped down in one of the creaky older wooden chairs.

He sat there so long that we started to fidget. Other classrooms emptied. But each time we were on the verge of getting up from our seats, William would shift slightly and focus with a little more intensity.

Then I saw it. It was a stupid mistake. A simple mistake. I was amazed that William, the smartest guy I knew, and Harvey, the second smartest guy I knew, had missed it. But you always do miss the really stupid mistakes, don't you?

It was a quadratic equation. I did not know what it was doing in the middle of the spaghetti on the blackboard, but I did know that it was missing something.

Without thinking—if I had, I wouldn't have had the nerve—I walked up to the front of the class and took the chalk out of Harvey's hand.

I licked my finger and wiped off the offending operand and changed it to "plus or minus."

William passed by me as I walked back to my seat, and I heard Harvey say, "How could I be so stupid."

They both studied the proof and then shook hands with great formality.

After that, we less-significant humans all stood up and approached the blackboard to study it closer up. I was flattered to be shown a muted deference by my fellow students.

William showered me with rare praise. "Go to the head of the class."

Lewis and Leo approached and then gushed.

"We like how you invalidated randomness with an application of chaos theory," Leo said.

"It does end up leading us in a new and ancient direction, doesn't it?" Jerry Ng mused aloud.

"What would that be?" William asked as he sauntered in front of the blackboard in a questioning circle, still a little unsure that he had reconciled all the previous weaknesses in the argument.

"It almost reads like one of Newton's laws," Jerry suggested cautiously.

"He's right," Tiny chimed in. "For every action, there is an ultimately disastrous result."

"Which I seem to have proven rather successfully," William interjected with a little swagger. "If I do say so myself."

"Never say die-chotomy," Jerry cautioned.

"What do you mean?" William inquired.

"It smells like rank philosophy to me," Tiny complained. "Excuse me, I need a smoke."

He opened the door and walked out.

"Son of a bitch," Lewis exploded, slapping his head as he studied the writing on the blackboard.

"He's right," Leopold agreed. "Is it determinism?"

"Or free will," Lewis added.

"Did he say 'son of a bitch' because he wanted to?" Leo wondered.

"Or because it was preordained?" Lewis followed up.

Looking from above the fray, I could tell that whatever his students were saying, William was now very comfortable with his work.

"Hold that thought, gentlemen. You will explore all that and more in Professor Sheffield's class next semester."

There was a roomwide groan that was interrupted only when Arlen Sheffield himself stepped in through the open door and asked, "Who dares take my name in vain?"

Nothing clears a room quicker than the presence of future misery. Before we knew it, we were all standing outside on the portico watching Tiny trying to smoke a cigarette. He wasn't very good at it, but he certainly applied himself. He had explained that it was an effort to lose weight to please his new bride.

"It seems to be working. I've already lost seven pounds," he said. "Smoking cigarettes makes me puke a lot."

He could have been a poster boy for antitobacco advertising. Every muscle in his body was focused on trying not to cough, and his skin acquired a pastiness that reminded me that I really should go to the hospital to visit Ambrose soon.

It was a bright December day. The quad was abuzz with students. We were all enjoying the rare excitement that comes with new ideas.

"So what do we think, Harvey?" Jerry asked.

"Interesting."

That cemented it. None of us had ever heard Harvey be that enthusiastic before.

Tiny started to ask a question but dissolved into a coughing jag. He tossed the cigarette away, and raising a finger to hold his place while turning his lungs inside out, he finally asked, "What was it that kept holding him up?"

"It was hurting me too," Harvey admitted. "Sometimes, it takes a new boy to work the numbers, doesn't it?"

My chest swelled with pride.

"So it's good now?" I couldn't help but ask, even at the risk of embarrassing myself in front of the second-year students.

"Very elegant," Harvey said with an admiring nod. "I hope he lets us out early. I have to write a paper on dyslexia."

"You should write it backwards," Jerry joked.

"That's exactly what I'm doing," Harvey answered with a serious face.

We could sense the tension in the lecture hall the minute we walked through the door. William and Arlen Sheffield were sitting on opposite sides of the room, quiet for the moment, but diligently stockpiling ammunition for the next salvo. We all knew better than to disturb them, so we quietly stood against the wall trying to be invisible.

After a while, William finally broke the silence.

"On the other hand—"

"Which would that be?" Professor Sheffield interrupted quickly with a twitch.

"Which what?"

"At last count we were on the fifth or sixth other hand."

"Don't be obtuse."

"I'm only trying to keep up," he said. "You, if anyone, should care about the numbers."

"We like numbers."

"As well you should," Sheffield said, with heavy sarcasm. "All ten of them."

"They're real."

"Except for the imaginary ones."

"Don't be negative."

"How could I? It's all truth and beauty on my side of the street, isn't it?"

"I am being considerate of your feelings," William explained.

"I'm pleased you thought I had any."

William ignored him. "It must be hard to realize that you dedicated your intellectual life to a career with no application."

"You did?"

"Logic is now considered an applied science," William gloated.

"You're kidding."

"Hasn't the philosophy department caught wind of these things called computers, yet? The guys in physics think they might actually be worth something, and they think like we do."

"We are beyond all that," Sheffield dismissed. "We do important thinking."

William crossed to the low bookcase on the right and grabbed a volume.

"*An Introduction to Ethics* by Arlen Sheffield," he read off the spine.

"I'm flattered."

"Don't be," William shot back as he flipped through the book.

"I hope you paid for that," the other said. "You didn't nick it from my office, did you?"

"That would be unethical," William murmured. "Ah, here we go. The ethics of standing in line at the movies. Important stuff."

"That is a classic exercise. Simple enough to be used in practically all entry-level classes."

"Is it? I only thought it was simpleminded."

"Then even you will be able to grasp it."

"How could I not?" William said. "Little did I know that standing in line was so fraught with ethical peril."

"Now you know."

"Let's skip to the study questions," he said as he flipped through the textbook. "While waiting in line for a popular Hollywood motion picture on a sunny, dry day, the temperature in the midseventies. Springtime … a gentle breeze. Birds are singing."

"You're paraphrasing," Sheffield pointed out. "That's not what I wrote."

William ignored him.

"But the beauty of the day is complicated when a wheezing, crippled old crone limps across the street and looks up at you, crestfallen when she realizes how far back the line goes. I'll skip to the problem. Can you offer her the space in line in front of you? Or should you first ask the permission of each and every individual standing behind you on this lovely afternoon?'"

"That is the question," the ethicist agreed. "That is a profound dilemma."

"Then why don't you sex it up a bit?"

"For example?"

"Substitute standing in that line for another one?"

"Hmm," Sheffield thought. "How about waiting for a chopper on the roof of the American embassy during the fall of Saigon?"

"Oops," William stuttered. "I think I have to take your point."

"Why don't you boys take the load off?" Professor Sheffield suggested to us.

Still eager to stay invisible, we shuffled off to our seats as inconspicuously as possible.

"Question?" William posed.

"Ready."

"Was that bit there an ethical issue?"

"Which?"

"When you directed my students to sit down."

"Question?" Sheffield posited back.

"Yes?"

"Is your problem ethical or moral that you think of them as yours?"

"Question?" William followed up. "Is it anything but manners?"

"Well asked," Sheffield complimented. "I will follow up on all my other rude intrusions by commenting on that unfortunate jumble of scratches on the blackboard."

"I thought you'd never notice," William said.

Sheffield approached the work gingerly like a man who didn't want to catch the flu from a doorknob.

"Would you like a stool to stand on?" William asked solicitously.

"No. I like to keep my feet on the ground."

Finally, after a long study, Sheffield admitted, "It's not terrible."

We were dumbfounded. We would have been no more surprised if they had grabbed each other, French-kissed and danced a tango. Even William seemed thrown off.

"Thank you," he said awkwardly.

"Of course, you do know what you've gotten yourself into, don't you?" the shorter man questioned.

"Perhaps a teaching position at a better school?" William suggested.

"You've only taken on St. Paul and over two thousand years of ethical and theological debate on a question that's thornier than Christ's crown."

William sighed and sat down in his chair.

"Well, that was inevitable, wasn't it?"

Sheffield grabbed a handful of colored chalk and decided to drag over a stool as he approached the blackboard. Hopping up, he encircled a large section in blue.

"You might put in a byline for John Stuart Mill on this," he said.

At the mention of philosophy's most famous determinist, Leo and Lewis commenced pounding each other on the back, in self-congratulation, on their perception and brilliance. William's brow became more furrowed as he studied the board.

"That is a no-no in just about any part of the Judeo-Christian world after about the tenth century," Sheffield continued as he made large circles in yellow around a couple of lines. "They take justification by faith very seriously."

William's focus grew more intense as the other man concluded.

"But here," Sheffield said, standing on tiptoes and underlining a core element of the argument with three broad strokes of the neon-red chalk, "is your 'tour-di-saster.'"

As he studied the sequence in question, William's look of concern evolved to one of perplexity.

"I don't understand," he said finally. "What's wrong with it?"

"It's a loop," Sheffield answered.

"It can't be."

"Not directly."

"Not even indirectly," William insisted.

"There's no starting point. It's a loop by implication alone."

Stunned, William threw himself back into the chair. Sheffield grabbed a piece of white chalk.

"Technically the inference is flawless and perhaps brilliant," he said as he wrote "A+" on the upper corner of the board.

"But it's a public relations debacle," he went on, erasing the first grade, "and the best way to get fired even if your father-in-law is chancellor. Therefore: C-."

As if we could be surprised by anything else, he crossed to William and shook his hand.

"An excellent piece of work," he said with sincerity. "It saddens me that it will die here."

"It's not a loop," William muttered, looking slightly shell shocked.

Sheffield was solicitous.

"They're a tough crowd," he consoled.

"Who?"

"The Free Will bunch. They act like they can do whatever they want," he explained.

William looked defeated.

"The problem with inevitability," Sheffield continued, "is 'where does it start?'"

We had all started listening to Sheffield differently. He wasn't simply hateful anymore. He was hateful and smart.

"If Helen was the face that launched a thousand ships—" he began.

"What inspired the face?" William followed up.

"Exactly." Sheffield smiled. "It gets worse. If any act creates a determined series of events, what determined that first act?"

"I take your point."

"Is inevitability a prenatal condition?"

"Was it an accidental pregnancy?" Harvey asked from behind me.

"I am particularly looking forward to having you in my class next semester, Mr. Weintraub," Professor Sheffield said in acknowledgment.

"It's mandatory. Wouldn't you enjoy it more if you knew that I was there because I wanted to be by my own free will?" His bluntness shocked me.

"I like mandatory. Haven't you heard? Free will comes at a price."

William stood up and strode to the blackboard. He picked up the eraser and tilted it on its edge to erase the red chalk lines.

"It's not a loop," he corrected. "There is no prior state. Therefore there is no open sequence. Therefore the inference is valid."

He stepped back, looking a little better with more confidence and color. Sheffield stood up and started toward the door.

"I'd love to stay and finish, but I've got office hours, so I've got to go," he explained. "But in rebuttal I must say there is always a prior state."

"How so?"

He stopped at the door and turned to face us.

"Look at it this way. You are a married man who has been on a submarine for six months. You are alone in a hotel room with a beautiful woman who is not your wife. She uncrosses her legs. Her skirt rises up to show you that she is wearing no panties. You succumb to the forces of nature and your sex. Is that inevitability? Determinism? Preordination? Or simply the power of Jack Daniels?"

"All of the above," Harvey answered, despite himself.

"Here is where we part," Arlen Sheffield said as he put his hand on the doorknob. "I consider it an ethical failure. You should have never bought her the drink at the bar." As he walked out of the room, he said, "That is an example of preemptive morality."

That was when we knew that the mandatory ethics class next semester might be more interesting than we had anticipated.

32

By the third week of December, Mrs. Slocum's house was electric. The phone rang all day long and into the night. People were coming and going at all hours. It was so disruptive that I almost slept through my final in differential geometry. Fortunately, Albert poured hot bacon grease onto his foot while cooking breakfast and woke everyone in the house, so I was able to slip through the closing doors just as the test began.

The excitement came to a head the day before the symposium opened, which coincidentally fell on the last day of school before winter break. Now that all my work was finished for the semester, I was able to enjoy myself a little, beginning with coffee and freshly baked crescent rolls in the crowded and festive kitchen. I needed a good breakfast. I had a busy day ahead.

With William working two jobs, it was now my responsibility to drive Faye wherever she needed to go. It was mostly the same route between her therapist and the house. But there seemed to be a lot less stress than before. She was reveling in her success. Everyone was pleased at how well she was taking her pending public appearance. Instead of cracking under the pressure, she was blossoming.

Even so, she had scheduled a double session with her psychiatrist on the eve of the conference, to help prepare her. I took advantage of the extra time to visit Ambrose at the hospital across the street. I was going to be away for two weeks, and I wanted to wish him the best of the season.

I went straight into his room, barging in on a rotund bald man who was changing his underwear. I quickly excused myself and went to the nurses' station to ask for Ambrose. It took me a little while to find him. He wasn't in a penthouse suite anymore. He wasn't even in a semiprivate room on the next level down.

I finally discovered that he was on the second floor, sharing a room with three other patients. It was pleasant enough, bright and facing west, with a clear view of the parking lot. There was the barest amount of privacy thanks to the thin curtains on tracks.

As Ambrose gave me the grand tour, he informed me that two of his roommates were in vegetative states and that the lung cancer patient in the bed to his right spent most of his time in the stairwell, sneaking cigarettes.

It was impossible to ignore how unhappy he was. There were physical signs also. The sugar-free taffy and candies on his dresser remained untouched, and the parcel of Zane Grey westerns that I had mailed him two weeks before was unopened on the floor of his closet.

He looked great, however. He had lost at least twenty pounds, and his skin had actual traces of color. I offered him everyone's best wishes. I told him that Ezeki had been trying out lavish recipes on us in preparation for his return, that Faye sent her love and that William was helping write her next book. The last news certainly got his attention. He went quiet.

I had been careful not to mention Claire. It never dawned on me that he would be jealous of William usurping his role. If anything, I would have thought that he would laugh or ridicule the possibility.

Finally, he shrugged and then nodded and simply said, "Somebody's got to do it."

He seemed so subdued, so unlike himself, that I blurted out, "Ambrose, what's wrong?"

He turned away. But after a moment, he either decided that he could trust me or simply couldn't hold it back any longer. He looked at me, and his eyes welled up.

"They say that I'm OK," he whispered shakily.

"You're fine," I reassured him, thinking that this was an attack of insecurity.

"No, I mean I'm healthy," he explained.

"That's great," I replied.

"It's terrible. If I take my medication," he sniffed as tears streamed down his cheeks unchecked, "they say I could even live a full and normal life."

I mistakenly took that as even better news.

"Fantastic," I congratulated him. "I'm so happy for you."

He looked at me reproachfully.

"You don't understand," he sobbed. "I don't want a normal life. They're making me leave the hospital tomorrow."

He slumped on his bed, weeping, then wiping his eyes and blowing his nose. I soothed him as best I could. Then suddenly he sat up and pulled himself together. Startled by the instantaneous change, I followed his eyes as an attractive nurse walked through the door.

She was a cute redhead, about thirty-five, with a comely shape. Sexy in a wholesome way, she had an ample bosom, a tight waist and legs that were equally shapely, even in a uniform skirt and regulation white stockings. Highlighted by a winsome smile, every feature of her face was pleasantly animated when she talked.

"Good afternoon, you handsome man," she said cheerfully, with a sweet Irish lilt. "Fantastic supper tonight. Chipped beef on toast."

"Yummy," Ambrose said reflexively in a flat voice.

"Your last supper here, at that. Behave yourself," she admonished. "I'll be back before you know I'm gone."

She disappeared down the hall.

Ambrose threw himself facedown onto his bed and sobbed wretchedly.

"Would you like me to get you a sandwich instead?" I asked, trying to be helpful.

He rolled over, looking at me as if he wondered how I could be so insensitive or so stupid.

"Is there anything I could have said that was more moronic?" he moaned. "'Yummy!' She must think I'm an idiot."

"Don't upset yourself," I comforted him. "She's a nurse. I'm sure she's used to all sorts of things."

"But not from me," he said, wallowing in his misery. "I'm not her usual patient. She's told me so herself."

"I'm sure you are very special. Certainly unusual."

Ambrose shook his head in irritation.

"I'm in love with her, you fool."

He fell back onto his pillow and let loose another torrent of tears. It took a few minutes of soft, soothing words to coax him to sit up and take a drink from his water glass.

"I'm in hell," he said as he wiped his nose on the sleeve of his hospital gown. "Total, complete hell."

"She seems nice enough," I said, trying not to say the wrong thing again.

"Nice?" His eyes flared with a sincere anger. "Nice?"

He was up on his feet. I had never seen him standing that straight. He glared. Then his face softened.

"You are still young," he said patronizingly. "Young and naïve. At some point in your life, you too may experience love with the same intensity that I do now. If you are lucky."

Walking into the bathroom, he added bitterly, "If you are truly lucky, you will be dead soon thereafter."

I heard water running. A few minutes later he came out, patting his face on a towel. I could smell the light scent of cologne. He went to the closet and pulled a robe off the hanger. Slipping it on, he delicately picked specks of lint off the shoulders. Then he tied a surprisingly grand piece of silk around his neck.

"No one seems capable of doing it well," he commented as he inspected himself.

"What?" I asked.

"Writing about it."

"Writing about what?"

"Love," he said as he fumbled about the clutter on his dresser looking for his hairbrush. "They think it's all about sunsets and moonrises and heaving chests."

He finally found the brush, which was military style without a handle.

"It's not about their olive toned skin or jade green eyes, or the surprising contrast to her natural platinum tresses. Even less important are the moonlit scents of jasmine, the expensive champagne, the perfect crescent of beach," he explained as he groomed himself meticulously before the mirror.

"You can take all the country houses and the horses, the boats and the cars, the planes, the elegant dinners and Mediterranean yachts. Add them up. What do you have?" he asked.

I didn't know.

"Nothing more than a really expensive vacation," he answered. "True love is so much more than that."

He put down the brush and faced me. "And so much less. It's the small things that have real value. Stolen moments alone over coffee or a quiet can of soda on a public bench or a simple sponge bath. Those are the places where hearts come alive."

"Let me show you how to make hospital corners," he said as he stripped the bed.

As I inspected his crisp folds, I could tell that his time here had not been wasted.

"I can bounce a quarter off it, it's so tight," he bragged. But when I pressed him to show me, he refused. He didn't want me to muss it.

As the dinner hour was growing closer, Ambrose grew agitated. He paced and he fretted. He vacillated between nervously checking his watch and constantly looking at himself in the mirror. But then, like a dog hearing the special tread of his master's shoe two blocks away, his ears perked up. I think it was a loose wheel on the fully laden dinner cart, wending its way down the corridor, that got his attention.

He smoothed the bed one last time and positioned himself in the visitor's chair, pulling the rolling table next to him so that he would be able to receive his dinner with some appearance of decorum.

Trying to disappear into the shadows, I leaned against his dresser as the trolley rolled up to the open door and a heavy smell of brown food drifted into the room.

From outside, the nurse asked, "Any victims?"

Protecting the daily joke from overexposure, she quickly stepped inside and said, "Oops! I meant to say, 'Who's hungry?'"

"I'm sure it's delicious," Ambrose said, looking stiff in his ascot and dressing gown.

"Hope springs eternal in the human breast," she acknowledged, pausing for effect before she raised one of the covers and looked inside at the food.

"Jesus, Mary and Joseph," she protested. "Have they no compassion? These people are sick already."

We all laughed dutifully, but there was no way that Ambrose could maintain so much jocularity in his mirthless condition.

"I'm not sick," he said sadly. "I am cured. I'm going home."

As I looked at him in his crestfallen state, I couldn't help but feel sorry for him. But the white angel would have none of that defeatism.

"Tell me you're cured," she said as she placed the dinner tray in front of him, "after you eat this."

She smiled.

He smiled.

"How's my favorite patient?"

"Better when you are here."

"I knew you were going to get well for me."

"I did. It makes me sad."

"I have it on good authority from the man upstairs," she said as she put a tender hand on his forehead. "Not only will you get healthy. You will thrive. I expect you and me to have a picnic this spring, beside the river. I will bring the strawberries. You bring the wine."

"I'll be there."

"Enjoy your supper, handsome. I will be back after I tend to your roommates."

As she returned to the food cart to pick up another supper, I was so happy for him. She was vital and lovely. Not the sort of person I would think Ambrose would end up with, but I was starting to appreciate the unexpected twists and turns that bring people together.

While Ambrose attacked his supper, I admired what a caring woman she was as she brought a fresh intravenous drip for each of the comatose patients.

"How's my favorite patient?" she asked as she pulled the tube out of the spent bag.

"I know you are going to get well for me," she murmured as she refitted the needle and flicked and fussed at it.

"I have it on good authority from the man upstairs," she continued as she took a pulse to make sure that this one wasn't dead. "We'll have such a lovely picnic when you're back on your feet. By the river. I'll bring the strawberries."

She took a moment to write something on his chart. Then she moved on to the next bed.

"How's my favorite patient?" she asked.

I stopped listening to her. I was suddenly far more concerned for Ambrose. He seemed to be much more interested in his chipped beef on toast.

"She's an angel on earth," he said as he looked up from his food. "She makes the really sick patients feel that she cares for them as much as she cares for me."

"That's a special gift," I agreed guardedly.

I stayed through supper before I made my desperate getaway. I was so eager to leave that I didn't bother waiting for the elevator.

As I pulled open the exit door, Ambrose's nurse walked out of the room beside it. Surprised by the encounter, I was awkward.

"He seemed very pleased that you came to visit," she said.

"Too late and not often enough," I confessed. "It has been your special kindness that has brought him back to health."

"I'm just doing my job. But you are a friend, and that is so much more," she replied with a melting smile. "Have a lovely evening, friend of Ambrose."

"Good night to you," I replied, squinting to read her ID. "Thanks for everything, Sister Mary Aquinas."

I rushed down the stairs so I would not be late for my other patient.

33

I climbed up the back stairs to my carrel in the stacks and stuffed my coat behind the bronze cupid in the niche next to the alcove. I could hear them working below, ironing out the details of the next day's major event.

"Can she do ten minutes?" Claire asked.

"It has to be at least ten minutes," William answered.

"Would they notice if it were shorter?"

"She's not talking to a room full of puppies," he said, slightly irritated. "These people do have wristwatches."

"Ten minutes is a long time."

"She won't be speaking for the full ten minutes. There will be applause and adulation. She'll like it. It will buoy her up. By the time it's over, it won't have been long enough."

"Ten minutes is nothing."

"We could do it in our sleep."

"I wish."

"Don't start," William cautioned.

There was a squeaky floorboard at the bottom of the iron steps. It creaked on cue and they both looked up.

"How is she?" they asked me together.

"How did she look?" William asked.

"Is she up for it?" Claire asked.

"Seems to be," I answered.

"We were a little nervous that she would be a little nervous," she explained. "We don't want anything to go wrong tomorrow."

"What could go wrong?" I asked.

"Would you like that in alphabetical order?" William replied.

"She did fine," I said defensively. "She walked two blocks along High Street by herself." I did not mention that it happened only because I had been late from visiting Ambrose.

"You're kidding," he said in astonishment.

"Really."

He slid into the chair next to me.

"On her own?"

"Yes."

"She looked OK?"

"She looked fine."

"Not pale or brittle or anything?" he asked.

"Maybe a little pale. It was hard to see her face."

"Why was it hard to see her face?" he demanded.

I had no immediate answer.

"Was she wearing her scarf like a helmet? Those sunglasses, the huge French ones with the bug eyes. Did she have those on?" he asked.

I nodded.

He looked at Claire. "She's doing her invisible woman routine. That never turns out well."

"Sounds like a smashing day out to me," Claire reassured him, and she took control of the typewriter. "Showed a little backbone on the eve of a fabulous victory. No need to panic."

William looked intensely into my eyes.

"Was there music in the van?"

"Yes, sir," I answered.

"Was it loud music?"

"Yes, sir.

"Was it Johnny Mathis?"

"Yes, sir."

"We're doomed," he pronounced.

At that moment, Faye entered the room, showing us how totally wrong her husband could be.

She strode in confidently. The scarf that previously swathed her head was now casually tied around her neck. She wore her sunglasses in her newly blown hair like a tiara. Without the trench coat, her skirt looked smart and stylish.

"Hello, troops," she smiled as she made her entrance. "All ready for our big day?"

Her husband and Claire nodded. I receded upstairs. I had to finish up a proof—or a disproof. I wasn't yet sure of how it would work out.

"What have we got so far?" Faye asked as she dropped into a chair and lit a cigarette. "I must be brilliant, you know."

"We don't want to look too brilliant," William observed.

"I suppose not," she sighed, looking slightly disappointed. "But brilliant enough."

"That's exactly what we're going for," Claire replied. "Self-deprecating brilliance."

"Great minds think alike," Faye said, beaming.

"We're thinking that the speech should last ten minutes," William said.

"That's what I thought," she said easily, but then stiffened. "There won't be a question and answer period, will there? Or those awful men grilling me?"

"Not to worry," William reassured her. "Your Mrs. Slocum turns out to be a brilliant negotiator. She did a bang-up job on the trustees."

"My Mrs. Slocum?"

"She's the president of your local fan club," he explained. "You've met her two or three times."

"Do we have to pay her anything?" Faye asked. "You know that's not my policy."

"No."

"Good job, Mrs. Slocum," she said and relaxed into the overstuffed chair.

After a moment, she asked, "What will I be talking about?"

"It will probably be about writing," Claire said.

"How unfortunate," Faye responded. "Why does it always have to come back to the writing?"

"That seems to be the subject that your audience is most interested in," William pointed out.

"All we need is a hook," Claire said.

"No," Faye said. "I think what we need is a fire. The night is wintry, and I have cold bones.

"I took a walk today," she added proudly.

Even from the cheap seats above, I could see that she was fading fast. It had been a long day. Tomorrow loomed. They both jumped to smooth her way.

"Just the ticket," her husband agreed.

At her side, Claire asked solicitously, "What can I get you?"

Moments of profoundly small talk followed. Tea was requested and served. A quilt appeared and was tucked in around her as William rubbed her neck and shoulders. We could all feel some of the tension leave the room as she settled into a more tranquil state.

Claire had control of the typewriter and was exploiting the moment, typing steadily on. William was at the fireplace, breaking up kindling and stacking it onto the grate. Everything was serene and quiet until Faye mused aloud.

"So is it?" she asked. "Is it literature?"

"Welcome to square one," Claire said under her breath as she continued typing.

"Thank God, we don't have to worry about that," William said as he placed larger logs onto the stack.

"We don't?" Faye asked with surprise. "Why not?"

"Because," Claire said, "we own square one."

Faye looked perplexed and turned to her husband. "What is she saying?"

"She's right," William said as he crumpled up sheets of newspaper into tight balls and jammed them under the grate. "That's the best part of being first."

"If you open the show," Claire explained, "you don't have to answer the big question."

"You can be the one to ask it," William agreed with a smile. "The title is a corker."

Claire pulled the page out of the typewriter with a flourish and read, "The Romance Novel: Is it Literature or Just a Piece of Heaven Captured on Paper?"

"Oh, I like that title," Faye said.

"Good," Claire responded.

"Do you have more?" William asked with skepticism.

"A whole first sentence."

"Let's hear it."

"Before we discuss the relative merits of romance writing," Claire recited, "I think we need to step back just a little and ask first, 'what is literature?'"

"Oh you brilliant, troublemaking she-wolf," William growled. "That will tie them up in knots for weeks."

"And I have the second line," he crowed. "In fact, I think I might have the whole bloody speech."

"Jolly good," Claire applauded.

"We are modest, aren't we?" he continued. "We are awed. We are impressed by this distinguished body surrounding us in this distinguished hall of this most distinguished institution."

"How could we be not?" Claire wondered.

"We are sitting at the feet of the Buddha. Why?"

"I have no idea. Elucidate, please."

"Because," he said. He had that grin that was becoming more and more pronounced these days. "Because we are not professionals. What we do, we do only out of love."

He paused provocatively and repeated for effect and flirtation, "Because?"

The two speechwriters answered the question together in slow unison.

"Because we are *amateurs*."

"Ah," Claire exhaled in appreciation.

"Thank you," William said, bowing. "Define 'amateur' for those in the back of the room."

"'We do it all for love. Because we love what we do,'" Claire answered, already typing. "I can do that one in my sleep."

At that, Faye's head jerked up from a rolling loll as it snapped back to consciousness. "Sleep?" she wondered. "Yes, that's a good idea. I'm so tired."

William was at her side before she was fully standing. They walked across the library floor to the door below me.

"You don't need to take me up," she said.

"Of course I will," he replied.

"I'll call Ezeki. She can turn down the bed. You have much more important things to do here," she said.

"I don't mind."

"But *I* do."

"If you're certain," he replied.

"I am. Thank you, Billy."

"I'll be up soon."

"Don't hurry, I'll be sound asleep. Take your time. Just make me look good tomorrow."

The door closed behind her as she left, and William went back to work.

"What do we want to get out of this symposium?" he asked.

"Respect?" Claire suggested.

"No," he thundered. "We couldn't care less about that. We stand here modestly as the teller of tales. We are humble and honest. Nothing more. Nothing less. We stand on the ground floor of the artistic pantheon. We are simply storytellers."

Claire couldn't contain her smile. Pulling my coat from behind the bronze cupid, I collected my things and started down the twisting stairs. I had finished my work—and I knew that three was a crowd.

"I was so happy," William continued, "to be invited to take part in this symposium. But the true reason I am here might surprise you. I am more grateful for the opportunity to listen than to speak. That is what I plan to do. Because there are so many wiser minds and better writers surrounding me in this room today, that I won't even try to come up with my own words."

Claire hooted, yet captured it diligently in a flurry of typing. But her rattling fingers stopped on a dime when she saw me step off the stairs in my coat. William looked up also.

"Don't go," Claire commanded.

"She's right," William said. "Don't leave us alone."

"I'm tired," I said.

"You are too young to ever be tired," Claire stated.

"It's been a long day," I replied.

"Exactly," William agreed. "Way too long. Time for a break. Sit down in front of the fire. Have a scotch."

Before I knew what was happening, we all were enjoying the roaring fire.

We held snifters of fifteen-year-old whisky. The fire was warm, and its spits and snaps were better music than Shubert ever wrote. The sofa was soft and inviting.

When I woke up many hours later, I didn't know where I was. I was in no hurry to leap up. I heard the rattle of the typewriter keys behind me and the squeaky bearing in the lazy Susan that protested every time they spun the typewriter back and forth. I wanted to lie on that couch forever.

"What the hell is that, you silly woman?" he grumbled.

"It's called style, you irritating man," she snapped back.

More keystrokes and squeaking followed, and I felt myself embraced by the warm comfort of a room that held only a profound affection and respect.

"What do you mean by that?" he demanded.

"I hit the wrong key."

"Cow."

"Don't make me hit you."

By the way they were talking, I didn't think they remembered that I was there. I slithered deeper into the couch and played dead.

"What I wouldn't give for a drink," William said.

"Have a drink then, stupid."

"I don't do that anymore."

"Was it a spectacular crash?"

"Only took five weeks. My liver didn't even know it was in jeopardy."

"Very efficient. How did you know you were in trouble?"

"I was told."

"By herself?"

"Yes."

"Clever girl."

"Don't be rude," William admonished. "She was very helpful. I owe her a lot."

"I'm sure you do."

"That's what makes current events so tricky. I don't skulk about."

"No one is asking you to skulk."

The typewriter keys rattled away for a few minutes before I heard William's plaintive voice. "Question?

"Yes."

"Do I trust you?"

There was something new in the tone of his voice. A texture I had never heard before. I was suddenly alarmed for all involved.

There can be no winners here, I thought.

I stayed stuffed deep into the cushions of the couch. In my involuntary role as drafted chaperone, I was relieved that the rest of the banter was work related and that there was no funny business. I pretended to be asleep for another twenty minutes, until William discovered me and "woke me up."

34

There were no other cars on the streets as I drove into New Coventry so early in the morning. All I could think of was the pleasure of tiptoeing up the back stairs of the dark, quiet house and slipping into the soft sheets of my bed.

As I pulled up in front of Mrs. Slocum's, I could see that I wasn't getting to bed anytime soon. Once again, all the parking spaces on both sides of her street were taken. I had to park three blocks away on Sycamore Place. The house was lit up like a Las Vegas casino.

The winter night was cold, but inside it was so crowded and hot that most of the windows were open. The sounds of many eager and excited voices escaped onto the street. I was relieved for a moment when I looked up and saw that at least my bedroom was dark, but that changed when I walked into the kitchen. Mrs. Slocum saw me, and her face fell.

"Oh, dear," she said. "You came home. I thought you were sleeping out."

"Is that a problem?" I asked.

"Well," she said awkwardly. "We're rather short of beds tonight."

"Any bed in particular?" I wondered.

She looked embarrassed when she replied. "She is very, very nice. She drove all the way from Columbus, Ohio, just to be with us. I just couldn't ..." Her voice trailed off.

"I was hoping to go to sleep," I said, trying not to sound too unhappy.

"There's plenty of time for sleep tomorrow," Mrs. Slocum said breezily. "But now, it's just like the night before Christmas, and all the elves are busy. Let me pour you a cup of coffee. We have a huge urn that the Rockland Chapter has lent us. Albert makes the best coffee. He says it's from Hawaii, but that sounds preposterous. But it is delicious. I can't get enough of it."

"How many cups have you had?" I asked.

"What? Sorry," she replied. "I'll be right back. I have to go to the little girls' room." She trotted off and I was on my own, dead tired and walking into chaos.

If the New Coventry Volunteer Fire Department had put up signs for the maximum occupancy of Mrs. Slocum's house, there would be a violation in every room that night. There were six ladies sitting around the table in the breakfast nook and a teenaged girl sitting cross-legged on top of it. There was another perched on the counter next to the sink.

Every doorway was a bottleneck of women. The sitting room resembled a flophouse for proper ladies of a certain age.

As I wandered through, I recognized some faces from previous gatherings, but for each one of those there were another six that I had never seen before. I squeezed my way along the upstairs hall to my bedroom door. As I heard the deep timbre of the rolling snores within, I went on past. A claim had been staked, and in my current condition, I was entirely too tired to contest it. I forced my way back downstairs, with difficulty, to look for alternate quarters.

In desperation, I went to check out the sewing room. Perhaps I could sleep in the chair in front of the typewriter? It was already occupied. Mabel looked up from her knitting.

"You're up late," she observed. "Can't see your way past the corn-fed bovine beauty that commandeered your room?"

"She seems well established," I admitted.

"Damn."

"My thoughts exactly."

"I dropped a stitch," she complained.

"Is Mrs. Slocum OK?" I asked. "She seems a bit scattered."

"No," she answered as she fiddled with her work. "She's a ticking time bomb."

"What happened?"

Mabel smiled. "They stuck it to her."

"Who?"

"The board of trustees."

"Why? What did they do?"

Mabel grinned broadly. It was the smile of a person who appreciated success, even the achievement of her enemies.

"They invited her to speak at the symposium, right after the keynote speech. It's a tough act to follow. Poor Greta. She's a wreck."

"At least she can write."

"Sure," Mabel agreed, knitting mechanically now that she had sorted out the tangle. "She can write about pounding pulses. But public speaking is a different kettle of fish."

"She'll be fine," I said optimistically.

Mabel put down her work and looked at me with eyes that didn't seem nearly as old as the rest of her.

"In a room full of frustrated academics, she'll be like a salami in a shark tank."

"Has she written her speech?"

"Can't. Dried up," Mabel replied. "Froze like a Haitian in Helsinki."

"What is she going to do?"

"We're working on it. We have teams. They're all writing alternative versions." She looked at her watch. "We're going to vote on them. Any minute now."

She noticed I was run-down.

"On the shelf of the hall closet, there is a sleeping bag," she said. "And when this irritating old broad finally finishes her tedious knitting, there will be more than enough room here for you to unroll it on the floor and get at least twenty winks."

"I'll appreciate that," I said sincerely. "I'm really tired."

"I'm sure you are. You're not looking like a shiny penny."

"Thanks."

My avenue to the closet was clogged. Wandering through the house, beating wooden spoons against pots, the proctors called time and told us to meet in the kitchen. It wasn't the largest space, but it had the most doors that opened onto other rooms.

"Teams, get ready to present your speeches," announced an aggressive young woman I'd never seen before.

Mrs. Slocum was on a bench in the breakfast nook. Mabel slid in next to her. Nearby, sitting and standing, were other members of her group. In the doorways and beyond were clusters of mostly unfamiliar faces. I was impressed at the growing power and involvement of the movement. Cindy had the floor.

"We are here to help Mrs. Slocum select the final draft of comments that she will deliver before the SUNY board of trustees tomorrow—I mean *this*—afternoon," she began. "As you know, this is right and proper, since it is she who we all must thank for the very existence of this special symposium on the placement of contemporary romance literature within the future university curriculum."

She paused for applause.

"However," she explained, "before we get going in earnest, I would like to take a short moment to introduce one of the bravest guys I know and a gentleman that I'm proud to call 'fellow jailbird.' Let's have an enthusiastic welcome and a warm thank-you for everybody's favorite ex-con. Roger, stand up and show yourself."

Much to Mabel's amusement and my astonishment, when I stood up, everyone went wild. Even the new and unfamiliar were clapping and whooping and stomping up a storm.

"Rog-*er*, Rog-*er*, Rog-*er*," they chanted. I waved lamely back at them.

I sat down, but they chanted some more.

"Speech. Speech. Speech."

I stood back up reluctantly and said, "OK, but only a short one. It's way past my bedtime. Lights go out at nine thirty in 'The Joint.'"

They appreciated that and settled down.

"First, I would like to thank you all for finding me a new lawyer. This one is a great improvement. He can spell both my first and last names."

They were generous with their laughter, and I could feel my color begin to rise. I was eager to close as fast as I could before I totally embarrassed myself.

"I just want to say how fantastic the last few weeks have been. Meeting Miss Warner was truly fantastic, and she has been especially fantastic to me. Seeing you all here tonight has been even more—" I paused and thought. "Wonderful."

They admired my eloquent use of a second adjective.

"So thank you. Good night. Have a fantastic day tomorrow. Sorry I can't drive you all."

I finished in a dead heat with the red wave that was climbing up my face to my forehead.

"How was that?" I whispered to Mabel.

"Fantastic," she answered with a wink.

My speech must have been good enough, because it took a minute or two before everyone settled down to address the main business of the night.

"All right, ladies," Cindy said as she recaptured the floor. "We don't want Greta to miss her beauty sleep. So let's get to it. First of all, we will hear from the Putnam County group. Let's hear it for Putnam County."

Two mousy women stood up. There was sporadic clapping.

"We call our speech, 'A School without Love?'" one said. "You will please note the question mark in the title."

"We can't hear you in back."

"Our speech is called—" she repeated, trying to shout.

"Still can't hear you."

Mabel leaned over and whispered in my ear.

"This might be a good time for you to make your escape." She nodded toward the coffee urn. "Once this crowd breaks up, the line to the bathroom will be outside and around the block."

She was right. I worked my way around the edges of the crowded room. The last thing I heard as I escaped was the other mousy woman say, "Which is why we thought it would be best to start with a poem."

I went upstairs to wash my face and brush my teeth. Scrubbed and polished and ready for bed, I felt better. I worked my way downstairs through the crowd to grab my sleeping bag and stake out the sewing room.

The space was small, but I discovered that if I slid my feet behind the iron treadle, I could loop myself around the perimeter of the room in an open arc. It would be impossible to roll over in the night, but it allowed me to be the most spread out in such a small area. I didn't mind sleeping on the floor. Mrs. Slocum was a top-notch housekeeper. Eye level with the casters of the steno chair, I noticed the wheels had recently been cleaned and the hardware polished.

I couldn't find the switch to turn off the light that illuminated the gilt-framed portrait on the wall above. I didn't mind. It wasn't very bright, and although the ambient presence of Virginia Faye Warner gave the place the aura of a shrine, I was confident that it wouldn't keep me from falling asleep.

It didn't. I drifted off the minute my head hit the wadded-up sweatshirt that I used as a pillow.

35

I don't know how long the deep dreamless sleep lasted, but it ended when the room was flooded in blinding white light.

"Don't mind me, junior," Mabel said as she carefully climbed over my interwoven body and sat down in front of the typewriter. "I've got a speech to write."

"What was wrong with the other speeches?" I asked groggily.

"They were giving 'insipid' a bad name," she replied. "That was the only thing we agreed on."

I could hear her take two sheets of typing paper and a carbon and tap them sharply against the table. Sliding them into the roller, she hit the return arm a dozen times to bring the paper up into the machine.

"Hmmm." She thought for a moment and then began to type, mumbling to herself as she went.

"Unaccustomed as I am to public speaking," she began.

With each letter, the impact of the keystroke, completely echoed by the iron treadle table, traveled straight down into the floor, which acted like a sounding board, ultimately driving it back up into my head like a nail. By the time she finished the first paragraph, the percussive effect had become intolerable. I carefully unthreaded myself from my sleeping arrangement and sat up.

"I won't be long," she said as she hunted and pecked her way through Mrs. Slocum's speech. "Just an hour or two."

"Take your time," I answered.

I looked through the windows at the front of the house and saw the first blush of a December sunrise. I was reminded of something my grandmother quoted about the weather.

"Red sky at night, sailor's delight. Red sky in morning, sailors take warning."

The horizon was red, dramatically so, like artillery firing across a distant front. I uttered a quick and silent prayer, hoping that the awful omen pertained only to the weather and that Mrs. Slocum would have only clear sailing ahead of her.

The living room was wall-to-wall sleeping bodies, as were the halls and even the landings on the stairs. But I was no longer concerned with sleep. Once I knew that the sun was coming up, it was the last thing I wanted to do. I had just finished four years as an undergraduate, and I knew that the worst thing you could do when you were up all night was to try to grab a nap. I would stay up now until I went to bed tonight. That way you end up feeling the least worst. I decided to go find something to eat to quiet my complaining stomach.

In the kitchen, I was greeted by an array of delicious smells. Coffee was pumping through the percolator, and bacon was frying in a skillet. Albert was in sole charge. On one side, he was rolling up dough for crescent rolls, and on the other, spooning batter into a muffin pan. He was in his usual Oxford shirt and suit pants, but he had his sleeves rolled up and wasn't wearing a tie. Now that I actually looked at him, he was younger than I had assumed from his formality. I guessed forties and fit.

"Good morning," he said.

"I'm behind," I said. "I haven't said good night and now it's tomorrow."

"Welcome to my world," Albert replied. "Have a bun?"

"Thanks."

"It looks as if you also need a mimosa," he added, reaching for the champagne bottle. "They are so restorative."

I must have looked pathetic. I was tired to the verge of tears. He set the drink in front of me.

He was quiet for a moment—awkwardly. Finally, he confessed.

"I'm sorry I wasn't there," he said. "I should have been."

"Where?"

"In Poughkeepsie."

"You didn't miss anything. The breakfast was terrible."

"But I should have had to endure it with the rest of you," he lamented.

I was too worn out to make him feel better, but that didn't seem to concern him. He busied himself with everything he had to do in the kitchen, and just when I thought he'd forgotten about me, he said, "You must think I'm nuts."

"Not at all." I didn't care enough either way.

"My wife does. She can't stand romance fiction."

"No accounting for taste," I said reflexively.

"Have you read any?"

"Some."

"Did you like them?"

I shrugged.

"Do you like opera, cigars or smelly cheese?" he asked me as he worked.

"No."

"They are acquired tastes. So is romance fiction."

He moved off to stir something that was about to burn.

"That's the challenge, isn't it?" he said from the stove. "Is it a formula?"

"Oh, it's a formula," I said.

"Exactly. That's why it's a challenge to make the expected alive and new. Is it boring Bach, the notoriously dead German, or is it Goldberg doing his variations?"

He put down his whisk and sat down across from me again.

"It's all about finesse," he explained. "It takes some time to develop an appreciation. There's nuance. Flavor. Subtlety. Especially in romance. We know they're all the same story—and it's a good story—but it's so much more than that. It is about how the same can be different."

He was expertly flipping triangles of dough into crescent rolls.

"Yes," I replied. "The formula is clear and succinct. There's just one element that I can't define."

"I know exactly which one you're talking about."

My heart leapt. Did Albert hold the answer to the missing link? I couldn't wait to tell William.

"You do?"

"Of course," he said. "You're talking about the magic."

Magic was the one thing I knew wouldn't fit on an IBM punch card. My short adrenaline spike dissolved, and I became even more weary than before.

The group started to wander into the kitchen, and Albert went about his job brilliantly. If high-end short-order cooking had been an Olympic event, he would have finished with at least a silver medal.

I was crammed into the corner of a bench, but I didn't mind. I closed my eyes, too tired to care.

Everyone spent so much time enjoying both breakfast and the novelty of someone cooking for them that it actually grew late.

"Look at the time," Cindy shrieked in panic, and all eyes were on the clock.

Then we moved quickly. As the hours evaporated, we had to rush everywhere. I drove to Poughkeepsie three times that day.

The first trip was because they voted down every dress in Mrs. Slocum's closet. The second was because after they finally agreed on one in a shop window and bought it and brought it home, they discovered that she had no suitable shoes. The third, of course, was the trip to the event itself.

As a treat and a morale booster, the Fairfield chapter had sprung for a limo. The star would arrive in red-carpet style. Following alone in the bus, I enjoyed the solitude, thoroughly.

36

We showed up two hours early so we could stack the front of the room. We wanted Mrs. Slocum to be able to deliver her remarks in a comfortable environment, surrounded by familiar faces.

The symposium was to be convened at the Alfred E. Smith Convocation Hall high above Poughkeepsie on the upper campus. It offered stunning views of that part of the river valley, with the Mid-Hudson Bridge, toylike below, as a centerpiece.

The conference center was sited to take advantage of its location. The focus of its design was a wall of floor-to-ceiling windows to exploit the panorama to the west. Unfortunately, the recent energy crisis had inspired equally grand draperies, which were drawn in the winter to conserve heat and in the summer to save on air conditioning.

It took us a few minutes to find the lady with the card table and name tags so that we could register.

"You certainly are the early birds."

"We wanted good seats," Cindy replied.

"First come, first served," the lady with the name tags said as she unlocked the door for us. "The symposium doesn't start until four. I hope you brought something to read."

In response, the ladies reached into their handbags and pulled out Virginia Faye Warner romances. The secretary hit a circuit breaker with her fist, which started up the mercury vapor lights hanging from the ceiling. It took almost five minutes for them to bathe the place in a flickering blue-green aura.

The meeting room was large and boxy. The architects were depending on the view to make it work. The mathematician in me quickly did the arithmetic. There were five hundred and sixteen gray folding chairs set out, trisected by two aisles. There was a podium up front, flanked by tables, each with three seats.

The ladies and Albert positioned themselves at the front and then sat back and opened their books. Mabel pulled out her knitting bag. Mrs. Slocum was looking a little pale, though quite chic, in a cranberry red suit. She busied herself reading and rereading the text of her speech. Despite my best intentions, I fell asleep.

As I was waking up, the main door opened and two men walked in.

"Why four o'clock?" the man in tweed wondered. "If it's an evening session, it should start at a civilized hour."

"Like eight," the pinstripe-suited one suggested.

"Exactly."

"If you started any later, you couldn't call it a two-day session, now, could you?" Mabel interjected in clear, ringing tones.

The men turned and looked at the group of ladies and backed out through the door.

I stood up and stretched, then went to the men's room to wash my face. Entering, I walked into the same two men.

"So, what are you?" the man in the tweed jacket asked. "An anthropology major?"

"Actually," I explained. "I'm a graduate student in mathematics."

"What are you doing here?" the suit inquired.

"I'm the driver," I said.

"Ahh," they both replied, assuming, I suppose, that it was a student job or scholarship obligation.

"Actually, they are very nice people," I pointed out.

"Don't worry," the suit answered.

"We will be gentle," the tweed jacket concurred and gave me a conspiratorial smile.

Glimpsing myself in the mirror, I looked a little green. As I splashed water onto my face, I was hoping only that the rest of the day would pass without incident.

I dried off and went back to the conference room. I was happy to notice that there were a few more seats filled. It was twenty minutes until the start. People associated with the school were starting to mill about.

I watched the suit and the tweed jacket hovering near the dais. They whispered into each other's ears, self-important, self-satisfied—smug. I snooped around and discovered that a few journalism students and two reporters, one from the *Poughkeepsie Journal* and another from the *PennySaver*, were sitting with closed notebooks.

The suit mumbled something under his breath to his colleague as they looked at our small pathetic group, sitting isolated in a big empty room. It actually made me angry when both men laughed out loud at what I was certain was a snide aside.

Then the buses began to pull up. First was the Rockland County group. There were seventy-five of them. Then Ulster County: another fifty. Finally Dutchess. What took them so long? They were in their own county. But they were forgiven on account of sheer numbers: over a hundred bodies. Then a loud group from Queens elbowed its way into the room. Fans also came from Pennsylvania, New Jersey and Vermont. We even got a vanload from the Eastern Shore of Maryland. The custodial staff hurried to set up more folding chairs.

Inside the inner circle, I could feel the mood shift. We still all wanted Mrs. Slocum to succeed at her speech, but she was no longer the central focus. We knew who the true star was. She would be standing before us in this room very shortly. Anticipation was building.

Finally, after another long pause, the man in tweed led two other panelists to the table on the left. One was a woman in a denim dress wearing her hair in a circular braid, and the other was a man, a younger version of the man in tweed, but with a goatee that looked like he had slopped his lunch on to his chin.

"That's the pompous SOB that rejected Helen's thesis topic," one of the ladies grumbled.

"He'll pay for it now," her neighbor hissed.

Representing the commercial side of the argument were Faye's publisher and two junior editors. They sat at the table on the right. Not one of them seemed to want to be there. Faye's agent Freddy was conspicuous in his absence. He had announced the passing of a beloved aunt just two days before the event. Faye was skeptical of the aunt's previous existence.

Both tables took their time getting settled. They positioned their pens and pencils and pads with excruciating care and were equally cautious at pouring water from the carafe into their glasses. Once they were established, the man in the pinstripe suit walked to the podium in the center.

"Good afternoon, my name is Harold Lathrop. Welcome to the State University of New York-Poughkeepsie."

To say that there was a smattering of applause would have been hyperbole. But the tepid response didn't seem to rattle him for a moment. He was as professional as his suit.

"Before we introduce our distinguished panel, we would like to thank you all for coming out this afternoon. Over the next two days, we will be discussing a unique and exciting form of expression: the romance novel." He said it with calculated neutrality.

"Such discussion and analysis is totally warranted. The written word is a dynamic and ever-evolving medium, and the question of literary legitimacy is subject to much interpretation."

"What about *your* legitimacy?" a female voice from the back interrupted.

Unfazed, he continued. "Before I even begin to introduce our experts and describe the events and workshops that will comprise the framework of the symposium, I would like to announce a very special treat. We are most fortunate at the outset to hear remarks from one of the form's leading practitioners—" He paused to search through his notes.

He did not need to continue. The crowd knew whom it was waiting for. The place erupted in spontaneous applause, cheers, whistles and whoops.

The man in pinstripes, who turned out to be undersecretary to the provost marshal of the board of trustees, waited as the demonstration died down, only to be replaced by something unexpected. It was hard to tell exactly where it began, because the chant emanated from every corner.

"Vee Eff Double-U. Vee Eff Double-U."

It started out in pockets, but soon filled the entire space, which vibrated with those initials. "Vee Eff Double-U. Vee Eff Double-U."

The suit and the tweeds looked irritated.

"Vee Eff Double-U." The chants grew louder.

Then the foot stomping began. The effect was threatening.

Mrs. Slocum leaned over to me, "I hope that they will be more polite when I try to speak."

Before I could reassure her, William was suddenly standing in front of me.

"We need you," he said, and I followed without question.

"We're doing fine," he said over his shoulder. "She just needs a little encouragement. Along with a familiar face."

He opened the door to a small office behind the hall. A cloud of tobacco smoke rolled over me. I sensed immediately that things were not going well.

Faye was sitting tensely in a chair. Next to her, Claire was hiding behind a copy of *The New York Review of Books*.

I hadn't seen Claire and William together since the night before in the library. I looked for telltale signs on their faces but saw only focused concentration on the job at hand.

"Just look at me," Faye complained to no one in particular.

"You look fine," I said, which was true in theory.

Her makeup was flawless and every hair was in place, but her eyes were frantic. Her lips were pursed, and she was clutching her midsection as if her appendix had burst.

"I can't do this. I feel sick."

William sat down next to her and gently patted her wrist.

"Of course you can," he said in a steady voice. "Just remember your exercises. Remember what Dr. Goldman said. This is a fantastic opportunity for you."

"Oh, Billy," she said in a small voice. "I'm scared."

"You don't need to be. You're among friends."

"I don't know any of them."

"They all love you. They all want to love you."

"I can't do it. I said I can't do it and I mean it," Faye insisted, her voice rising.

"Yes, of course you can do it. These are your fans. It is so simple. You go in. You read your speech. You leave. There you go," he said proudly. "That's my girl."

She slowly stood up.

"Don't wander too far," she said to me, tightly. "You'll be my good-luck charm."

I caught her eye for a brief moment, but I could tell that she was far out to sea with no safe haven in sight.

"I'm ready," she said and took my arm and started to the door, which William opened with relief.

The chants were louder, and there was an echo in the corridor. The impatience of the throng had increased the tempo, adding to the menace. Faye moved forward, and we started toward the noise, William on her other side.

She was tentative at first, then more determined. Suddenly she stopped dead in her tracks.

"No," she cried out.

"What's wrong?" William asked.

"I don't have my speech."

We were both relieved that it was only a detail. Claire handed it to her. "Here it is, Miss Warner," she said.

"Thank you," she said, looking paler by the minute. "Let me just count the pages."

"They're all there," Claire reassured. "In the right order. I checked."

"I don't know that," Faye snapped.

"It is always best to make sure," William said.

But as she began the recount, the door to the hall opened, and the corridor was flooded with the loud reverberating chant and pounding of feet, along with whistles and shouts. She was startled and dropped the speech. Pages flew all over the floor.

As we all rushed to collect them, a large man I had not seen before approached us from the open door. His face was ugly with rage.

"What is taking so long?" he snarled at Faye. "Are you the speaker? Get in there right now and shut them up."

I saw Faye's face freeze and her eyes go wild with panic. Before William could insert himself to protect her, she ran down the corridor and through the safe room door, which she locked behind her.

"You've got thirty seconds," the rude man informed William and returned to the auditorium.

We hurried back to the office.

"Sweetheart," William pleaded. "Please open the door."

We could hear her sobbing inside.

"Faye," he knocked fruitlessly. "Open up."

"Give me a credit card," Claire said.

Without hesitation, he pulled out his wallet.

Plastic in hand, Claire pressed her hip against the door, sliding the card between the door and the frame while manipulating the knob. In a matter of moments, she sprang the lock.

Faye was huddled in a small pile in the darkest corner of the floor next to the couch.

"Wait outside, please," William ordered.

Claire and I went out into the hall. The noise from the conference hall was now deafening. There was a crackle of feedback from a microphone and a very loud, "Will you all please take your seats. She is on the way." Then rhythmic clapping joined the cadence of chants and stamping.

After a few moments, the door opened and William stuck his head out.

"I have to take her home," he informed us.

I felt a little guilty that my first emotion was relief. I was running low on sleep and quite full up on Faye.

We went inside. She was curled up reflexively on the floor, wearing her overcoat and shivering.

Moments later, the large man was back banging on the door.

"We need your speaker, now," he demanded.

"She's on the way," William explained as he held his wife close. "One minute is all we need."

"Half a minute. That's all you get," he warned through the door. "We're calling the riot squad."

Shifting gears, William became all business. Looking around the small office, he wondered, "How do we get her out? The place is crawling with her fans."

I stuck my head out the window. It was snowing, one of those thick serene Hudson Valley snow squalls. For once my grandmother was wrong. This time a "red sky at morning" offered a safe haven.

"I can see the van from here," I offered. "It can't be more than a seven-foot drop to the ground."

William stuck his head out the adjacent window. He turned to me and smiled. The wet snow quickly stuck to his hair and eyebrows. He shook his head like a wet dog.

"I knew you were smart from the moment I first saw you looking stupid at the Philadelphia airport," he complimented me, before he disappeared back inside.

"We need a distraction. You go start talking," he directed Claire. "We'll do the body-snatching."

"They will eat me alive," she replied.

"As if anyone could," he said.

"I understand."

"By the way. Be brilliant," he added. "If they're transfixed, they won't be wandering around the parking lot."

"I said I understand," Claire repeated, with an edge.

"Give me your coat," he directed.

"I've got a scarf too," she offered.

Faye wasn't unconscious, but neither was she animated. It took a little doing, because she was already in her coat, but we finally stuffed her into the second coat. Claire did a quick hair adjustment and tied the scarf around Faye's head. Then William slid on her bug-eye sunglasses.

He tossed me the keys to the van.

"Once they're enthralled," he explained, "drive under the window."

Claire and William looked at each other for the briefest moment.

"Good luck," he said.

"Good life," she replied.

Claire and I went into the big room. Things had deteriorated, but the hostility slackened when Claire walked up to the podium. I was standing in the wings next to Mr. Lathrop, in the pinstripe suit, who was holding a handful of ice cubes wrapped in a napkin against his forehead.

Claire raised her hand, and the room went quiet for a moment out of curiosity, if nothing else.

"The last thing I want to say is that Virginia Faye Warner will not be speaking to you tonight."

Accented with boos and hisses, there was a huge release of frustrated anger. She held up both hands. After a while the audience quieted down again, but this was the last courtesy. The fans were thirsty for blood.

"But I have to, because she won't."

The volume and intensity of complaint doubled.

It was clear that all control had been lost. No word from the podium could be heard, and no gesture would be regarded. They were a roiling torrent.

Claire pulled the microphone out of its stand and walked it over to the side of the stage. Holding it at arm's length, she held it directly up to the large public address speaker.

The resulting feedback was piercing. Claire didn't flinch. She stood steadfast as the acoustical wave twisted and excruciated, demoralized and ultimately defeated.

Finally, she pulled the microphone away. As she returned to the podium, the new silence was almost as shocking. All that could be heard were a few quiet moans.

"If I could have your attention for just a moment," she coaxed in a soothing voice. "You will understand straight away why we have to share her."

Her exhausted audience rustled, not sure whether or not the revolt was totally quelled, but willing at least to see Exhibit A.

"Would you turn off the lights, please," she directed.

"Is she crazy?" Lathrop said.

"Trust her," I said. "She knows what she's doing."

I don't think he gave two figs about what I thought—he just had no other options. But he nodded to the custodian, and the lights went out.

"Now open the curtains, please," Claire requested.

The draperies were heavy and required an electric motor to move them. They rolled apart in a slow and almost stately manner. As they opened, the dark room became illuminated by the reflected light of millions of white puffy snowflakes dancing in a picture-perfect display of a winter's night.

The room clutched and exhaled a collective "Ahh."

There were whispers and quiet talk throughout.

"It's snowing," a voice in the crowd rang out.

"Of course," another answered.

"That explains it."

"How we could doubt her?"

"There's no way she could be here. Not when it's snowing."

Finally there was a protracted, sincere applause. It grew to a crescendo.

"What the hell was that all about?" the assistant to the provost marshal asked me.

"It's snowing," I answered.

"I can see that," he said gruffly. "What does that have to do with the price of eggs in Morontown?"

"It's a tradition," I explained. "Every year at first snowfall, Virginia Faye Warner and her husband drop whatever they are doing, wherever they are, and rush home. They light a roaring fire, pop a cork and toast each other."

"That's just stupid," he commented. "What a load of crap."

"Would you like to say that into the microphone?" I asked.

"No, I would not. Not to these lunatics. Thank you very much."

"I didn't think so." I scanned the crowd trying to determine whether or not this was the time to back the van around and smuggle her out of the building.

It was. I could tell in the first few moments that Claire had the floor enthralled.

"I have every hope that you understand why I am not with you this afternoon," she read from a piece of paper that I knew was blank.

"As you know, I have two jobs. There is nothing that gives me more pleasure than my day job of sharing stories of love discovered and revisited, revived, reestablished and renewed ..."

The ladies were so thrilled to be back in the fold that they applauded again.

"Except," Claire cautioned. "Except for my night job. Which is why I know that you have already forgiven me for rushing home to a warm hearth and the man I adore."

For a second there was complete silence. Then they were all on their feet, shrieking and clapping enthusiastically as tears poured down their cheeks. No one in the room heard the next sentence. I didn't hear it either, but that was because I was running across the parking lot to start up the van and spirit the woman of the hour off home and to bed.

37

The snow was coming down fast and steady. I took an extra minute after I wiped off the windshield to brush off the top.

As I pulled away from the parking place, William was blinking the lights in the office on and off so that I would go to the correct window.

I backed up to the side of the building. I climbed onto the van's roof carefully so that I would not attract attention. One of the useful things about snow is that it absorbs sound.

"Is it slippery?" he asked as he leaned out the window.

"I'm OK," I answered.

"Ready?"

"Yes."

"Here she comes."

He passed her to me. He stepped onto the roof of the van and climbed down onto the ground.

As I held her carefully in my arms, she asked in a small voice, "Are they terribly disappointed?"

"They love you," I answered. I wasn't lying.

"Lower away," William called from the ground.

We settled her into her easy chair in the back.

"Strap her in," he directed as he rushed around to the driver's side.

While I made her as comfortable as I could and made sure her safety belt was secure, the stillness of the night was interrupted more than once by spontaneous applause emanating from the conference center.

"See," I offered as I jumped out onto the snowy parking lot. "They love you."

"Good night, Roger," she said wearily and looked away.

I closed the back doors and beat twice on the side of the van. William sped off, leaving a trailing mist of snow and ice crystals.

I returned to the auditorium just as Claire finished reading the keynote speech. After the earlier enthusiasm, the audience was sedate but still warm. She saw me as she left the podium and walked over to where I was standing.

"I was brilliant," she said offhandedly.

"I'm sure you were," I agreed.

"Everyone get off OK?"

"OK as it gets."

"We can check up on her when we pick up my coat."

She turned and faced me.

"You will drive me to pick up my clothes?" she asked.

"Of course."

At that point, the assistant to the provost marshal was introducing the next speaker. The audience had been disappointed once already that night, and it was eager for something real and immediate—one of its own to be proud of. Mrs. Slocum was the one. In fact, her modest connection with royalty as the head of Virginia Faye Warner's hometown fan club inspired greater confidence and appreciation. Her quiet sincerity was apparent the minute she opened her mouth.

"Unaccustomed as I am to public speaking," she began.

Claire and I watched from the sidelines as she won the room. Due credit should also be given to Mabel, whose speech was brilliantly manipulative.

When Mrs. Slocum argued, "So if we can't determine whether it is literature within our lifetime, should we teach any writer who is still alive?"

"Sorry, Mr. Salinger," she said, shaking a finger. "Catch you in the rye!"

The room exploded. Even a few of the academics smirked.

Her remarks were just the right length and in just the right tone. She walked away with everyone wanting more.

On her way out, Mrs. Slocum came up to me all aglow and kissed me on the cheek.

"Thank you. Thank you. Thank you," she effused. "I hope you don't mind driving back by yourself. They all want me in the limo."

"No problem," I assured her.

I put my jacket around Claire as we walked to the bus, where I wrapped her up in the blanket that Mrs. Slocum kept in the back.

We drove off through a landscape that would make one fall in love with winter. The flakes hung suspended in the lights of the bus as we drove through a black night that existed only to make the white snow even more dramatic.

Pulling up to the big house, we were a little concerned when we did not see the van.

"It's probably parked in back," I supposed. "At the loading dock."

I let us in through the side door, and we climbed up the stairs to the empty library. There was a fresh fire stacked and ready. Claire was shivering, so I took a long match from the mantel and set the kindling aflame.

She sat at the reading table looking flagged and sad.

"Are you freezing?" I asked.

"Yes."

I went over to the temperance section and reached behind Carrie Nation, returning to the table with the whisky bottle and two glasses. I poured and passed. We sipped. The larger logs caught fire and began spitting and crackling.

We didn't have much to talk about, so we didn't. It had been a long day. The whiskey was warm and soothing.

We were so tired, that after I poured a second round, we didn't bother with it. We just sat and stared at the fire.

After an hour or so, the door creaked and William entered, looking old and spent.

"How is she?" Claire asked.

"In medical circles," he replied as he collapsed onto a chair, "they would report that she is resting comfortably."

"Where?" Claire inquired.

"Her home away from home," he answered. "Room 407. New Coventry Medical Center. Only the best."

"By the way," he added as he picked up Claire's drink and toasted me with it. "You did very well tonight, Roger."

He emptied it down his throat without thinking.

He turned to Claire. "How did the speech go?"

"Well enough," she answered. "No one was injured."

"She was brilliant," I put in. "She told me so herself."

As they sat and chatted, I could feel the steam heat of the room, the additional fire in the hearth, my hunger and exhaustion, as well as the whisky, all kick in at the same time. I thought that my head was so hot that it would either melt or explode, but when I looked out through the huge bank of windows, the snow had stopped. A bright winter's night revealed a pristine landscape now blue hued and magical. I could not stay inside a moment longer. I grabbed my coat and fled the stifling indoors into the clear purity of the white night.

I was amply rewarded. The air was crisp. The full moon lit the scene like a sound stage. The light from the big windows of the library spread arcs of yellow across the fresh snowfall.

The mathematician in me was fascinated by the way the moon-generated shadows of many tree limbs intersected with the spreading grid of the backlit windowpanes to create a non-Euclidean matrix.

As I studied it, I saw William's silhouette, centered in the window, stretch and spread across the snow. Caught up in the optics and perspective, I studied it intently and was startled to see that over time, it morphed and separated into two similar shapes. I looked up just in time to see the end of a kiss.

A slight wind shift from the river brought a fresh gust of cold and chilled my face with a spray of icy crystals, just as the library door crashed open. The field around my feet was flooded with even more light.

I turned. Claire was running toward me, her unrestrained hair flying wildly behind her in the wind.

"Can you take me home?"

"Of course," I answered. "When?"

"Now."

"No problem," I said. "Let's go back into the house."

"Let's not."

"Don't you want your shoes?"

She looked at me and touched my cheek.

"Do me a favor?" she asked.

I hurried into the house and retrieved her shoes and coat. My haste had nothing to do with the fact that her feet were freezing. There was something in her eyes that was heartbreaking.

I drove her home, and then I went back to Mrs. Slocum's. I had to pack. I was going to Pennsylvania in the morning.

38

Two weeks later, I was driving northeast, passing exit 26 on the Pennsylvania Turnpike, when I realized that I hadn't graded the "Math for Poets" final exams. They were still stacked neatly on my desk upstairs in the library. Fortunately, it was early in the day. I figured that I could take them home to Mrs. Slocum's and have them back on William's desk before dinner with no one the wiser. The library would probably be empty on New Year's Day. Yet I couldn't be certain. I had been away. Was Faye still in the hospital? How would William and Claire be able to face her?

Since I had no idea what to expect, it made sense to slip off my shoes and sneak up the back stairs like a cat. This turned out to be the right thing to do. When I peered over the railing, I was shocked to see that Ambrose was not only back, he was stuffed between the arms of the big chair in the window alcove office like the King of Sheba. The desk was already buried under mounds of empty wrappers and half-eaten food.

My professor was sitting at the big table glowering at him. William needed a shave and a haircut. He was wearing a flannel shirt, rolled up at the elbows. There were deep shadows under his eyes.

Closer to me, I could see Faye's head sticking out of a pile of museum-quality quilts on the couch.

Ambrose gathered up the pages of the manuscript that he had been reading, tapped them into order against the desk and tossed the stack down dismissively.

"I hope you have the cash to repay the advance," he said. "Because you certainly don't have a book."

Showing remarkable agility for a woman in the throes of her seventh documented nervous breakdown, Faye was up on her feet in a heartbeat.

"What do you mean we don't have a book?" she screamed.

"Of course we have a book," William corrected.

"Not here, you don't," Ambrose said.

"You're mistaken," Faye said. "I counted the pages."

"It might look like a book. It might smell like a book. In fact it might even quack like a book," he explained. "But it's certainly nothing that you can put your name on."

"Why not?" William asked, his surprise genuine.

"Why not?" Ambrose questioned. "Any idiot could tell you that. Even if it weren't garbage—which it is—it's way out of genre."

"It is garbage because?" William asked coldly.

"Because it's useless. I'm sure if I'd gone to a big fancy college like you did and majored in English, I would have appreciated some of the artsy bits that you guys crammed into it," he answered. "But I didn't. I'm just the dumb undereducated hack writer who paid for this house. I'm sorry, but this is not a Virginia Faye Warner product."

He turned away and helped himself to another pork rind.

William crossed over to him and sat down so deferentially that it made Ambrose nervous.

"What do you want from me?" Ambrose asked suspiciously.

"Your knowledge and expertise," William said. "As you pointed out, I am new at this. So I am vulnerable. Be gentle."

"I don't know," Ambrose said, eyeing him.

"Don't be like that," William cajoled. "I'm reaching out. I need you. Faye needs you."

"Well," Ambrose began hesitantly. "For starters, there's the vocabulary."

"What's wrong with that?"

"The vocabulary," he answered with an aren't-you-listening face. "Some words here are so long that they have to be hyphenated."

"I see."

"Then there's the voice."

"Yes?"

"It's so … intellectual. We don't like that in our books."

"Let me get my pencil."

"The girl is wrong, also," Ambrose added.

"How so?"

"She's too outgoing. We like them feisty but not aggressive."

"F not A," William said as he wrote.

"There was something else that didn't work. It was especially noticeable in the scene at the lake house. She was too … too … what is the word?"

"Happy?"

"Exactly. We stay away from that."

"This is very constructive," William acknowledged as he wrote it down. "What else?"

"The way it ends."

"We hadn't written that yet," William protested.

"Doesn't make any difference. You could finish it ten different ways," Ambrose said as he ripped opened a bag of potato chips and poured the contents out onto the desk. "It would still suck."

"We'll sort that out when we get to it," William said. "I think she left some notes around here somewhere."

"The only thing that she left," Faye sniffed, "was in a hurry."

"She couldn't help it," Teale explained. "There was a domestic crisis at home."

"She might have told me to my face," she snorted.

"Mine too," William agreed in a distant voice.

It felt as if my heart stopped beating for the briefest moment. Fortunately, Faye hadn't heard her husband's utterance. At that point, she had no interest in anyone but herself.

"What's wrong with the ending?" she demanded.

"Well, I wouldn't know anything about that, would I?" Ambrose answered. "As Billy has pointed out so accurately, I haven't actually seen the last chapters, since they don't exist."

"But you can tell me what will be wrong with them, can't you?" William said.

"Maybe."

Faye was suddenly all business. "Talk to me," she demanded.

"You're not going to like this," Ambrose started.

"When has that ever bothered you?" Faye lit a cigarette and waved her hand for him to continue.

"Well," he began as he picked up a greasy potato chip off the desk and popped it into his mouth.

He chewed thoughtfully on the chip and carefully selected another. "There is no way you can end this book, without—him—leaving—his—wife."

"That bitch!" Faye erupted and fell back onto the chaise.

"Your words, not mine," Ambrose said as he wiped his hands on the draperies. "I never met the ... ah ... lady."

He searched through the pile of chips on his desk for the largest morsel. That gesture so irritated William that he walked over to the housekeeping closet in the corner of the library. Returning with dustpan and brush, he swept the desktop clean.

"Hey," Ambrose complained. "You're going to pay for those."

"Don't worry," Faye affirmed. "This is going to cost him a lot more than the snacks."

William emptied the dustpan and tossed it into the closet along with the brush, slamming the door for effect. He crossed back to the desk, where he stood like a statue.

"What exactly is the problem?" he snarled at Ambrose.

"It's the commandment," Ambrose replied. "Moses had ten. In this room there is only one. It is clear. It is simple. Man shall not leave."

"Never?"

"Never," Faye agreed. "I need a Valium."

She stumbled to her desk. She swallowed the pill easily without water and returned to the couch with the look of someone who knew that things would soon improve.

"Yummy," she sighed as she slipped under the quilts. "Things are looking up."

"Yes, they are," Ambrose cooed as he knelt beside her. "I'm halfway through a book I began writing after I left the hospital."

"I knew you couldn't let me down, sweetie."

"I couldn't let 'us' down," he corrected, with a mysterious sigh.

"What is it called?"

"The Truth about Love."

"Mmm," Faye responded dreamily. "That sounds wonderful."

The uneasiness in the room faded as Faye floated off the coach and onto the flying carpet that that had been so kind to me after my incarceration.

"I know Freddy will like it," she said. "*The Truth About Love* by Virginia Faye Warner."

"And Ambrose T. Cavanaugh," he stage-whispered into her ear.

"What?"

The magic carpet crashed to the floor.

Faye collected herself. "I think that might confuse my fans. My name is still very important in romance."

"To hell with romance," Ambrose declared. "I can't write that crap now that I have discovered the truth about love. I don't know what you're whining about. I've given you top billing."

"Your crap," Faye said. "My name. My reputation. I am the Queen of Hearts."

"Some queen. Some heart," Ambrose said. "You know nothing about love. You are a hard, cold ice queen locked in her ice house on an icy mountain trying to freeze all love and happiness out of all your subjects. You have a splinter of flint for a heart. My crap—your house."

"As if you needed one. You seemed comfy enough living at home with Mommy," she sneered dismissively.

Ambrose looked capable of murder. His eyes flashed and his fingers curled into fists.

"You should talk. You were incapable of getting a man until Daddy bought you one, albeit a slightly imperfect retread."

"That's not true," Faye protested. "I could have had any man. I was huge."

"That is so right. You *were* so huge," Ambrose leaned in, face to face. "For six months, and then you were nothing until you met me."

The gasp caught in Faye's throat.

William's voice split the room like Moses at the Red Sea.

"Ambrose," he bellowed.

"Sorry, I don't know what I was thinking," Ambrose said sinisterly to Faye. "Let me make it up to you. I'll buy you a cup of coffee."

Faye was visibly shaken.

"Don't want a cup of coffee?" he corrected. "Then how about we go down to the Union."

Faye paled.

"It's a lovely hangout," he said. "It's big and crowded and pushy and loud. But I should warn you, it's not a place for little girls. Daddy can't protect you there, even though it's his basement rec room."

As William rushed to stop the attack, Faye convulsed in agony.

Ambrose looked at him.

"Sorry," he said. "If she has a problem with that, I can always take her to the Dunkin' Donuts."

"You are hateful," Faye rasped hoarsely. "You know that I have agoraphobia."

"Oh, right," Ambrose sneered, then screamed in panic.

We all took a step back.

"Help me. Someone. Help me!" Ambrose continued. "I am being attacked by the frozen foods aisle!"

Faye's upper lip was visibly quivering.

With malicious satisfaction, Ambrose continued calmly, "I do have a question, Billy."

"What?"

"How can you stand waking up next to—that?"

Faye no longer attempted to stifle her tears. The floodgates parted, and she sobbed uncontrollably.

"Oh, please," Ambrose said, rolling his eyes. "How many times do we have to sit through this melodrama?"

Faye sobbed even louder.

"Enough!" William exploded.

He locked his hands around the pudgy man's elbows and forcefully marched him out of the room.

"Don't bother coming back," William warned from the side of his mouth.

The sticking library door groaned loudly as Ambrose was pushed through it. I could hear them arguing as Ambrose was manhandled down the hall.

The shouts subsided, and the room was quiet except for the ticking of the grandfather clock and the pained broken breathing of Faye, crying in her arms on the library table.

William reentered and went straight to his wife.

She looked up. Mascara made wide deltas down her cheeks. Her eyes were red and her hair was in disarray.

"I can't believe what I just heard," she said.

"We always knew that he was a toad," William said.

"Are you crazy? Go stop him right now," she demanded. "Apologize!"

"What?" he asked in amazement.

"We have no choice. That woman you hired has left us in a terrible position."

Teale stared at her.

"It's a fine book," he reassured her. "We just need an ending."

"Ambrose says it's no good."

"Have you read it?"

"I trust Ambrose," she replied. "Hurry, he's getting away."

"We don't need him," William said as he started to embrace his wife to comfort her.

"Don't touch me," Faye screamed, squirming out of his arms. "He cares about me. He's here helping me every day when you are off at school pretending to have a career."

William backed off, speechless.

"I know you never considered my work important," she continued shrilly. "Even though it pays for the food on your table. But now you've managed to wreck everything."

William's face was frozen in a neutral expression, but the hair on my arms stood up as if I were surrounded by an electrical storm. Faye raged on.

"It's not as if I ask for much. But just once—once—it would be helpful if you were actually part of the solution instead of making things worse."

The resignation in his voice betrayed his total defeat.

"Fine," he said as he started toward the door.

"I don't know what you were thinking when you brought that woman here," she added. "What a mistake. And now you've chased off the only person who can help."

He disappeared under the balcony. An instant later, he hit the stubborn sticking door with such force that it slammed hard against the outer wall with a smash that reverberated throughout the building and nearly knocked me to the floor.

I could hear the deliberate clicking of his steps disappearing down the corridor. Oddly, they grew louder the longer they continued.

I looked up just in time. The statue of Venus and Adonis in deep embrace in the niche above my head had been dislodged by the exploding impact of the door below. It was teetering back and forth in a larger and larger sway.

I threw myself against the wall just as I heard the downstairs door slam closed with a screeching thud. Reacting to this final impetus, the loving couple toppled over the edge. The iron railing caught Adonis' toe and flipped them upside down. Headfirst, they crashed to the floor below.

I raced to the railing and looked down. The statue lay in pieces, broken beyond repair. Faye was unhurt. William rushed into the room.

"Are you all right?" I heard him ask.

She stood up and dusted herself off.

"What do you think?" she said and walked out of the room.

I left the library by the side door, quietly working my way down the service stairs. On the landing on the floor below the library, just as I thought my escape was complete, I heard a whisper. "Roger."

I turned. It was William.

"Take this to her," he said, holding out a book.

The sadness in his eyes was devastating.

We turned and went our separate ways.

39

It was a cold night and icy. The roads were miserable. I had a bad skid at the bottom of Mountain Road, and the book flew off the dashboard.

Once I was safely parked, I leaned over to pick it up. I noticed a piece of paper on the floor next to it. I turned on the dome light in the ceiling and unfolded it.

I didn't realize what I was reading until I was halfway down the page. By that point I was incapable of stopping.

> To the most irritating woman in the entire world—and most dear,
>
> You will of course forgive the logician in me but I am after all Aristotelian. I was very clear about that when we met a thousand years ago.
>
> Therefore, on the one hand, as sad as it is to know that I will never see you again, on the other hand, I am now in the happy position to be able to talk freely to you—safe in the knowledge that I will never see you again.
>
> I will start with the most basic premise.
>
> I have gone through hell trying to figure out a way to keep the conversation going without hurting people who are dear to me.
>
> I knew that the last thing I should have done at first snowfall was to kiss you. But with that kiss, I cracked the door open and wanted to rip it off its hinges. It was the pin of a hand grenade.
>
> And then I told you that I have loved you all my life.
>
> So much for "the truth will set you free."
>
> In the past, I have been very unhappy with you on more than one occasion, but I never ceased to revel in who you are and the fact that you cared for me once.
>
> There were two moments of our meeting this time that I cherish.
>
> The first was magic. I said Claire twice. You stopped on the airport steps and looked up. There was only a half second opportunity for recognition.

I knew that was my best smile. I knew you were looking at my best smile.

The second thing and the one that totally broke my heart in a good way was when we were parting at that second reunion in the train station. I discreetly kissed you on the cheek, and you then kissed me on the mouth.

And just last week, when I tricked you into asking, "What was the happiest instant of your life?"

The answer that I withheld at the time was:

"Every evening twenty-five years ago when you would hold up the sheets to invite me into our bed."

Despite my sadness that I have lost you again, I am buoyed by the fact that this time you did not want to leave.

I love you darling.

Good bye.

40

Claire apparently hesitated a few minutes before she opened the door. I stepped back in shock when I saw her.

Her face was ashen. There were deep circles under her eyes, which seemed swollen and red. Her hair was a tangle, haphazardly tied back.

She raised a hand as I opened my mouth.

"Don't say a word," she pleaded. "If you do, I will start crying again, and then I will look even worse than I do now."

Silently I held out the book.

She looked at it quizzically. She opened it and scanned a few pages, still looking mystified, as if she were trying to make sense out of a language that she could not read. Finally, she flipped to the letter.

"Please wait here," she said and left the room.

I looked around the small but tidy apartment and sat down to wait. There was a neat stack of unread newspapers on the table. I was halfway into a report on the local school board meeting when she returned.

"How is he?" she asked as she handed me another book.

"Shaky."

"I had to leave," she explained. "We were beyond reproach—but it was becoming impossible."

We both looked at the book in my hand.

"Give him that when you see him next," she said.

"I will," I assured her, then paused. "I have a million questions."

She shook her head no.

"Thank you, Roger," she said.

Then she kissed me on the cheek. Her trembling conveyed so much sorrow that as much as I wanted to comfort her, I could only turn and walk away.

41

I felt no urgency to return to the big house on the hill. I spent my first weekend back, instead, at Mrs. Slocum's kitchen table, grading exam papers. Then I helped her clean out the office. It was running out of room. We cleared out books and boxes, dragging stacks of magazines to the garage. The books reminded me of the volume that Claire had given me. It was still in my room. Resisting the urge to see what was inside was a constant struggle. I mustered every ounce of discipline I could to protect their privacy.

"Have you ever thought about finding a publisher?" I asked as we neatly restacked her manuscripts.

"Me?" she asked in puzzlement. "Why would I ever do that? I'm not nearly good enough for that."

The following Monday, I drove her back to the foot doctor, so it wasn't until that afternoon that I was able to get up to the campus. I was a little surprised when I walked past Mrs. Lowey's desk. William's mailbox was stuffed to overflowing with letters and memos and manila envelopes. It was even more unsettling in his office. I had to move a large pile of pink "While you were out" phone messages just to make room to put the exam blue books on his desk.

Turning off the light, I opened the door to find Arlen Sheffield standing on the threshold in great agitation.

"Where is he?"

"I don't know," I answered.

"Is he all right?" He looked around the room to make sure that I was not hiding him behind the draperies.

"Did he miss a class?" I asked.

"Of course not," he replied indignantly. "He's a professional."

He turned and walked away.

"Tell him to call me if you see him," he said over his shoulder.

As I passed the department office, Mrs. Lowey ran out.

"Have you seen him?" she asked.

"Not since before break," I lied.

"When will you see him again?"

"I have no idea," I answered honestly.

I was more eager than usual as I sat down for Tuesday seminar, if only to see if William was still alive.

"We saw him Saturday afternoon," Lewis explained. "He was buying a carton of cigarettes at the union."

"He looked like he'd been on a month long bender," Leo added.

"We sure didn't want to be around if he lit one."

"Fire hazard."

"Maybe he's caught the flu," I suggested. "I've heard it's going around."

"Probably caught it from Jack," Lewis suggested snidely.

"Or Johnnie Walker."

The late bell rang. As I looked out the seminar room window, I could see a few stragglers running across the quad to class.

"Start the clock," Tiny directed.

"One down," Jerry Ng reported. "Nineteen to go."

"God, I wish you could smoke in here," Tiny moaned.

"Looking good, Tiny," Jerry complimented.

He was. He must have lost twenty pounds.

"How is married life treating you?" I asked him.

"There are certain aspects that make up for the other bits," he answered with a sheepish grin.

The steam heat kicked in with a vengeance. I opened the window. The air that rushed in was frigid, but it helped keep my eyes open as I watched for William.

"So is he having another nervous breakdown?" Lewis wondered. "Or is he simply back on the sauce?"

"I just concocted a wonderful moral conundrum," Jerry posited.

"What is it?" Leo asked.

"You're working the suicide help line and a guy calls up. He is such a total failure that killing himself seems like the reasonable recommendation of any sane person. Do you lie to him and tell him that he has something to live for?"

"Of course you do," Lewis responded.

"Why?" Tiny asked.

"Anything to get the loser off the phone," Lewis concluded.

There were chuckles around the room.

"Ten minutes to go," Jerry announced.

"I could use it today," Harvey Weintraub said as he scribbled in his notebook. "I've got a lesson plan due."

He was student teaching at New Coventry High that semester. Realizing that we should all take advantage of this unexpected opportunity to catch up on all the stuff that we had planned to do over the break but didn't, the rest of us followed his lead. For the next five minutes, the room resembled a study hall.

"A probability question," Jerry threw out.

"I thought this was a prob/stat-free zone," someone else groaned.

"If William has a psychic collapse, will he grade easier or harder?"

"Better yet," Leopold Ickies gloated. "Let's revive an American tradition and start bringing Teacher a shiny bottle of applejack every morning."

"Hold the phone," Lewis interrupted. "If he goes all gaga and starts drooling, do we have to repeat?"

"He's right."

"Holy crap."

"I hate this seminar enough with William leading it. Imagine how horrible it will be with someone who isn't as good," Leo confessed.

"Five minutes," Jerry reported.

They seemed to lose any elation over the approaching early release. They drifted into concerns of their own personal futures if their teacher ended up in a straitjacket.

"Certainly, this has happened before," Tiny pointed out. "The school must have a mechanism to deal with it. What are the odds that he is the first faculty member to go bonkers in the middle of a semester?"

"Oh yeah," Jerry agreed. "Given their generosity of spirit, they certainly wouldn't want to make us pay for another twelve credits. Would they?"

There were groans and head slapping all around.

"Oh God," Lewis prayed. "Please heal our brother Billy."

"Thank you, Jesus," Leo added.

"Did Billy say anything?"

"We only saw him," Lewis explained.

"Looking like hell," Leo confirmed.

"Can you qualify what hell looks like?" Harvey asked from left field.

"Did he lose his marbles?" Tiny wanted to know.

"Or just his car keys?" Jerry wondered.

"Do we even know where he has been the last two weeks?"

Unfortunately, as questions mounted, all the eyes in the room seemed to gravitate toward me.

"Do we?" Leo asked.

"What have you done with our professor, Roger?" Harvey asked sardonically into his homework.

"Two minutes," Jerry declared.

Both Leo and Lewis approached me.

"This might be a good time for you to decide whose side you are on," Leo said menacingly.

Tiny wasn't part of the Gestapo, but he was clearly concerned about his academic future and his wallet.

"It would help us to know where things stand, Rog," he agreed.

"I've got a contract with Bell Labs," Jerry said in exasperation, "dependent on a degree. I'm on deadline. I can't have some bozo professor screwing that up for me."

I wasn't sure what to do. I understood their concern. They had their futures to think about. They couldn't afford to have them put on hold because the department chairman had come undone. Only I had read the letter and knew that William was in love with a girl he had known more than twenty-five years ago. That he was honorable and married. That those two conditions made him so unhappy that he probably wanted to jump off the Mid-Hudson Bridge.

Then the doors burst open. William and Arlen Sheffield entered the lecture hall in mid argument.

"Can't," William argued.

"No, it's pronounced *Kant*," Sheffield explained in a condescending voice.

William turned and faced him.

"What board certified you to teach ethics? You are an atheist."

"Do you want questions and answers?" the other replied. "Or bad rules that were written over two thousand years ago? I'm paid to teach ethics, not religion."

"You are being legalistic," William retorted.

Sheffield smiled sweetly.

"Of course it's legalistic. They are commandments."

"But only ten," William said defensively.

"Personally, I don't need them," Sheffield answered. "I am not only smart; I am also perfect in every way."

"Why haven't you been smote yet?" William asked.

"Clean living," the ethicist replied with a smug smile.

"You have completely evaded my question."

"Oops," Sheffield admitted with a giggle and a blush. "But that's a hard one, isn't it?"

"Wrong again," William insisted.

He grabbed a piece of chalk at the blackboard on the right. Both he and Sheffield generally used the Diogenesian Universal Ethical Symbology (DUES) so they could understand each other.

"If in fox hole," William translated as he wrote. "And if buddy mortally wounded. Given one time opportunity for escape—"

He wrote a double sigma. "Conditioned on self-preservation."

Then, with a flourish, he laid down three squiggly lines and boldly scrawled, "Survival equals <dies alone>."

Sheffield stepped back and studied the work.

"Well," he finally said after a long pause. "That construction thoroughly sucks, doesn't it?"

"Wait, I've got another one," William said as he wiped down the slate.

"If doctor marries receptionist," he formulated frantically. "And if new wife contracts brain fever—"

"Brain fever?" Sheffield asked. "What doctor is this? Dr. Dostoyevsky?"

"Shut up and be moralistic," William demanded as he wrote: "And if doctor hires new receptionist who is a perfect soul mate then $\|$->?"

"Don't bother," Sheffield interrupted. "I know where you are going."

For the first time, he picked up his chalk and approached the blackboard on the left.

"Luigi Pirandello, Italian playwright," he said. "Have we heard of him?"

"Yes, I have heard of him," William answered.

Sheffield went into full lecture check-off mode. "Nobel Prize for literature, 1934. Married nut case wife 1894, who had a nervous breakdown in 1904."

"Institutionalized 1919. Diagnosed insane with jealous paranoia." He looked up at us humble students. "For those of you in the back, he got the Nobel Prize after she was gone."

William was agitated. He was pacing and rattling his chalk in his fist.

"What exactly is the question, Arlen?"

"Case of brilliant," Sheffield wrote, "and married to nut job is a function of marriage vows. True or false?

William collapsed into his chair.

"I don't know," he said, rubbing his eyes.

"It is a challenging puzzle," Sheffield nodded.

"I suppose," William replied.

I had begun to sense that Sheffield was threading a needle. I knew this for sure when he asked, "But, of course, marriage is a joint venture, isn't it? One is therefore forced to wonder if there is a joint obligation."

William looked up.

"What do you mean?"

"Consider the numeric value of a couple," Sheffield suggested as he scribbled down a string of symbols that none of the graduate students in the room could recognize. William studied them arduously.

"Are you suggesting that it takes two to tango?" he finally asked.

"Or even converse," Sheffield said.

Although pleased that he had gotten the first riddle correct, William was still stepping gingerly into this new mine field.

"Pirandello died in 1936, honored throughout the world, a Nobel laureate. Would he have been better off if he had stayed home taking care of his wife?" Sheffield asked.

"Of course not."

"Why not?"

"Based on your premise, given the bidirectionality of marital responsibility, he owes just as much to himself as to his spouse," William answered innocently, not realizing that he had just stepped on the trip wire of Sheffield's trap.

"Of course he does," he answered with a wry smile. "Your response is totally understandable. It resides squarely and comfortably within the greater strictures of *Ethica Americana*."

"*Ethica Americana*," William repeated. "What is that? Some cockamamie invention of yours, Arlen?"

"It is a wonderful morality system. I've been studying it," Sheffield explained. "It offers a rationale and justification for practically anything you want to do. The inspired thing about the name is that since it's Latin, it might also be the name for an illness."

Everyone in the room was caught up in this unexpected floor show, but my eyes at that time were focused only on William. I could see that he was beginning to unravel.

"Some of the first manifestations of the disease *Ethica Americana*," Professor Sheffield continued, "are self-serving axioms like 'you can't love anyone until you love yourself.'"

I watched William settle lower into his chair.

"Moreover, the impact of *Ethica Americana* on the concept of responsibility is profound," the other continued. "To wit: 'It will only hurt her more if I am unhappy.'"

We would have to wait until later that semester to hear more about the state of the American ethos. Sheffield's wristwatch started chiming like a tiny Big Ben. After he checked the time, he stood up and practically bowed. "Gentlemen, I must away," he announced. "Tempus fugit, and I will fugit along with it. You will forgive me. I teach, therefore I am."

He turned and exited the room. The door slammed behind him, but nothing distracted us from the drama that was playing out on the blackboard before us. We remained glued to our seats. Everyone was staring at the magical formulation, except me. I was studying William, who seemed to be shrinking.

"In the next session," William said into a small area in front of him, "we will look at random numbers and chaos theory."

"We can start right now," Lewis Embry volunteered.

"No problem," Leo added.

"Not at all."

"They're twenty minutes left in this one."

"And we can play through."

"We won't need a break today."

"But I do," William explained gently. "When I said the next session, I meant next week. You are excused."

We packed up our notebooks and pencils slowly, still looking at the exotic formula. When we dawdled too long, William finally commanded, "Now go away."

I don't know why I had the nerve to stay behind. Perhaps it was because I felt I held a special position. After all, I knew "her," and I had spent time with the private "them." Whatever the reason, it wasn't so much that I felt I had the right to linger, as that I found it impossible to leave. I sat in the second row from the back. His eyes were shut, but I knew he knew I was there.

Finally, after an eternity, he flatly stated, "I am in hell."

"Is there anything I can do to help?" I asked.

"Faye's orders," he said shakily. "I have to make nice to Ambrose."

His upper lip curled, but by a sheer force of will he held himself in check. "I hate the disgusting little snot.

"I have to take him out to lunch and apologize for my egregious rudeness. I know what the pasty-faced son of a bitch is going to order."

I had totally misunderstood what had been bothering him, and I was suddenly stupid. I asked, "What?"

"A pound of flesh, medium rare," he answered.

I had no reply.

"Did you give her the book?" he asked after a pause.

"Yes, I did," I answered. "She had one waiting for you."

I pulled it out of my book bag and handed it to him. He handled it tenderly, like a first edition. He flipped it over to look at the spine.

"The Lives of the Saints," he read, and he chuckled. He stood up and walked out of the lecture hall without looking back.

I was glad he was gone. I didn't want to be anywhere near him when he found the letter. I had memorized it. Obviously, I was not as disciplined as I wanted to be.

Dear William,

What saddens me the most is that without me there to defend its virtue, you will certainly ruin my book.

I shall always cherish this brief respite together, much as I still relive the blissful shared days of our youth.

I regret that I am unable to offer a fare-thee-well in person, but the room was starting to get very crowded. I'm certain you understand.

With past and ongoing love and affection,

Claire

Even I could tell that the letter was one big lie.

42

"Roger," Mrs. Slocum said urgently as she banged on my door. "Wake up."

I was slow to respond. She cracked it open and flicked on the overhead light.

"There's a phone call. It sounds important."

It took a few moments for the black balloons swimming in front of my eyes to pop and deflate. By the time I started down the stairs, she was already in the kitchen, pulling a robe over her flannel nightgown. The phone lay on the counter. I picked it up.

"Hello," I said.

"It's me."

It was very noisy on the other end. There were a variety of voices, metallic clanging and distant shouts.

"Who is this?"

"William."

"Do you know what time it is?" I said reflexively.

"No," he answered. "What time is it?"

"What time is it?" I asked Mrs. Slocum.

"Four twenty."

"Are you all right?"

"I think so, but I'm in jail. Ambrose is too."

"They're in jail," I explained to Mrs. Slocum.

"How much money does he want?"

"How much money do you need?"

"How did you know that I needed money?"

Mrs. Slocum went to the pantry and came back with a large canister of Quaker Oats, which she dumped on the counter next to the phone. The contents seemed to be mostly tens and twenties.

"Where are you?" I asked.

"Poughkeepsie," he answered. "Arthur says hi."

"Ask him how much he needs," Mrs. Slocum repeated.

William heard and told me.

I watched her as she neatly stacked the currency in an old Dutch Masters cigar box.

"He's got until tomorrow afternoon, or he pays interest," she explained. Her recent success at the symposium clearly had an effect on her level of confidence.

"What is he in for?"

"What happened?" I asked.

"A seventy-year-old maple tree fell asleep at the wheel and ran a stop sign. We didn't stand a chance."

"How's the Plymouth?"

"Don't ask."

I could hear a quaver in his voice.

"Who was driving?"

"We're still working on that," he explained. "At the moment, there are only four possibilities."

That, in itself, was a bit of a relief. The fact that he didn't know who was behind the wheel was a concern, but that he was still alert enough to do primary set theory was reassuring, at least mathematically.

Mrs. Slocum was wonderful. By the time she loaded me into the VW bus, not only was I dressed for the weather but I was fully outfitted with a thermos of hot coffee, a bag of ham and cheese sandwiches on dense black bread and the cigar box holding more cash than I would see in my first ten paychecks.

"Don't let them get sick in the bus," she admonished as she waved me off.

As I drove up a very deserted Route 9 toward Poughkeepsie, I was glad that this time it wasn't me in the pokey. When I arrived at the heights overlooking the town, the false dawn illuminated the valley. The river looked like mercury. At that time of the morning, there are more shades of gray than there are colors. At that time of the morning, you wonder why you would ever oversleep. It is quiet magic.

William and Ambrose had not been as fortunate as the ladies and I had been. The two of them were not enjoying the freshly painted modern confinement spaces of the city's newest lockup. They were in the old jail, in "the tank."

When I walked in, it was hard to determine which aspect of it was the most offensive. Even at six in the morning, it was noisy. The stained and slimy green walls amplified every shout, scream and echo. The lights were a sickly raw florescent that made every face a doughy tangle of blood vessels. But the winner of the "Most Disgusting Award" had to be the smell. In its better corners, it was like a bad locker room.

I followed the worn yellow footprints on the floor and arrived at a familiar face behind the desk.

"Hello, Roger," Arthur said.

"Good morning, Sergeant," I answered.

"How's the head?" he asked.

"Don't know," I answered. "My attorney tells me that I have short-term memory loss."

"People with lawyers get that a lot," he said, knowingly. He stepped away from the desk to pull a file.

"Here to pick up the boys?" he asked on his return.

"Yes, sir."

"You only have to pay the bail here," he explained as he showed me the paperwork. "The emergency room charges are separate and between you and the hospital."

"I understand," I said.

"That's for Dr. Teale," he said, sliding a form across the desk. "The judge liked him."

I opened the cigar box, ready to do business.

"That's for the other one," the sergeant continued. "The judge didn't like him. I didn't like him either."

I started counting out the money.

"Does he grow on you?" Arthur asked.

"We use a salve," I replied.

Once the city of Poughkeepsie had its money, the two "perps" were officially handed over to me. Even then, I had to wait more than an hour before they were physically brought out.

"How's Mabel?" Arthur asked as he walked past me in the sticky waiting room.

"Sends her best," I lied.

"She's a real piece of work, that one. Give her my regards."

"I sure will."

My lack of sleep was starting to tell. My mouth had gone pasty, and the second hand on the wall clock was slowing by the minute. Around seven thirty, I heard my name called.

"Roger," Arthur announced over his scratchy public address system. "Party of two."

I went up to the desk where William and Ambrose were reclaiming their personal items. William was checking the official receipt and systematically returning all of his things back to their appropriate pockets. Ambrose was grabbing and stuffing. Even from behind, I could smell that that one was still drunk.

"Thanks, Arthur," I said.

When they heard my voice, they both turned around. Both looked terrible. William had a gash in his forehead that looked like it had been closed up with fifteen or twenty stitches. He also had a busted lip. His face had been cleaned around the wounds, but the rest was caked with blood and dirt along with his shirt.

Ambrose's eye was swollen shut. He had two missing teeth and a broken arm in a fresh white plaster cast, which was the cleanest thing on him. He didn't have any blood on his clothes, but there was evidence of a previous meal.

"Mrs. Slocum says no puking in the bus," I cautioned.

"Not to worry," William assured me. "I'm fine and he's run out."

Ambrose nodded. "Nothing but dry heaves for the last hour."

His words were spontaneously confirmed on the spot as he hunched over by the door and loudly vomited nothing.

"No ham and cheese sandwiches on black bread for you," I cautioned.

"That's probably for the best," William said. "Where's the bus?"

The return trip was as colorful as the other had been gray. It was a spectacularly clear morning that painted the valley with a palette of vibrant colors. The quality of light was so intense, and the colors so rich, that anyone should have reveled in being alive.

Except Ambrose. He sat in the back, sniffling and weeping and muttering, "Love is only pain."

43

The third week of January found New Coventry buried beneath a record snowfall. Even though the town could get rid of the white stuff by dumping it into the river, Hudson Polytechnic still had to cancel four days of classes because nobody was able to get to the town.

When the roads were finally clear enough for me to drive up to the big house, it was in my new capacity as chauffeur—a necessary adjustment. After the accident, William's driver's license had been revoked for six months, and he had to undergo psychiatric evaluation. The first was ordered by the judge, the latter by the wife.

I hadn't seen William for nearly ten days, and I was dreading it. He had been looking worse and worse each time I'd seen him before the accident. It was disturbing to think how much further he could have deteriorated.

As I pulled into the drive at the top of Mountain Road, I noticed a tall man, stylishly dressed in a camel coat, standing beside the iron gate. As I leaned over to punch in my access code at the squawk box, he opened the door to the passenger side and climbed in.

"Brrr." He shivered. "I'm glad your heater works."

My head jerked around in time to watch William carefully slip off elegant kidskin gloves.

"Good morning," he said as he loosened the oxblood cashmere scarf from around his neck. "How are the roads today?"

I was so thrown off by his dapper appearance that I took no notice of the magical winter scene all around us. The only deep blue and blinding white I saw were those under his overcoat. He was wearing a crisp starched dress shirt inside an exquisitely tailored navy blazer. My curiosity was piqued. This was another William Teale, one I had never met.

He was pleasant enough, but not chatty. As I turned the bus around, he clicked on the car radio and spun the dial to the classical music station so that we could enjoy a nerve-rattling Bartok string quartet. I frantically tried to keep Mrs. Slocum's VW bus from skidding off the steep and icy road.

"Stop at the Union," he directed. "I'm drinking green tea again."

When we finally made our grand entrance into the lecture hall for seminar, I could tell that my fellow classmates were as baffled as I was by this new manifestation. His pants were pressed with a sharp crease, and in deference to the weather, he was sporting brown Frye cowboy boots, conservative ones without spurs or straps.

His face, so busted up just over a week ago, was not only on the mend, it was rosy-cheeked. The stitches were out, and although the scar was visible, it was minimized by a close shave and impeccably combed hair.

"Good morning, eager students," he greeted the class.

Caught by surprise, in a weird instinctive spontaneity, they replied in kind, "Good morning, Professor."

"I hope you won't mind if I make myself comfortable?" he said as he slipped off his jacket and hung it on a hidden peg that I had never noticed at the back of the little stage.

He then positioned himself in front of the twin blackboards. They were both covered with formulae and calculations. Lewis Embry and Leopold Ickies were sitting in front-row seats on either side. Both beamed with pride. Sipping his tea, William sorted through the complicated and tightly written argument on the left blackboard.

"That is certainly clever, Lewis," William said.

He turned to the right. "This must be Leopold's work. I can always tell your work. Let me fix that for you, Leo."

He licked his fingertip and rubbed off two sides of a modal operator to make it a negation. Then he reflected for a moment.

"I am very pleased with both these arguments, gentlemen," he said.

The entire room seemed to hold its breath as he reached toward the tray underneath Leo's blackboard. We assumed he would take up a piece of chalk and begin a brilliant and arcane critique, so we waited, on the edge of our seats, for the resolution of the problem that had enthralled us all for the last two months.

To our surprise, he reached for an eraser instead. "However, today we are going to leave fantasyland and enter the world of practical mathematics."

He wiped down each board, picked up a bit of chalk and announced, "Welcome to the exciting world of set theory."

The more knowledgeable students erupted with a collective groan that sucked the remaining oxygen from the room. If there had been a canary present, it would have dropped dead on the spot. I would soon understand the basis of their distress.

Within minutes of entering that exciting new world, my eyes glazed over and were soon glued above the door, watching the second hand work its snail pace around those stubborn twelve numbers on the clock face.

After an endless fifty minutes, when we finally staggered outside for our break, Tiny asked, "So what do you think?"

"He's baaaa-aack," Leo said, waving his hands, trying to make scary horror-picture noises.

"I miss the new William," Lewis mourned.

"Me too," Leo concurred.

"I guess it was only inevitable," I sighed.

"At least he's finally teaching us something that we can use in business," Jerry Ng pointed out.

"If you want to make money," Harvey patiently explained, "you should have majored in computer sciences."

"Like I want to be some little techno-zombie," Jerry answered.

We all watched him as he fiddled with the white tape that was holding his glasses together.

"So what happened?" Tiny wondered.

"Who knows?" Lewis shrugged.

"It's like the Klingons beamed him up and replaced him with the old William. Except for the wardrobe," Leo suggested. "The Death Star William."

"Don't mix your galaxies," Lewis corrected.

"Use the farce, Luke," Jerry warbled.

"Actually, it might prove interesting," Harvey said.

"What do you mean?" I asked him, since no one else seemed to care.

"He's added a new qualitative filter layer, hasn't he?" he explained. "Weren't you intrigued that he has developed a method to weigh the relative value of a null set against one with a value of two?"

I tried to be interested in what my friend was saying. But I failed miserably. Harvey did not bother to continue, probably noticing that my eyes were as vacant as everyone else's.

Then the bell rang. We trudged back into the lecture hall like a gulag work gang.

We found that William had been busy while we were out. Both blackboards were covered with a new meaningless jumble. He was refreshed and raring to go.

A lifetime and fifty-five minutes later, the bell rang again. There was no banter or even good-spirited jousting as we staggered into the quad, only droopy nods and halfhearted waves as we went our separate ways. I did happen to catch Harvey's eye for a moment. He looked back with sorrow. I walked to Mrs. Slocum's VW by myself and waited for William.

I looked out over the frozen town and shared in Harvey's dejection. I had thought that William was different. It wasn't just being a math teacher with him. It was an adventure. But now I felt like I had been wrong, and I was particularly saddened because this was the second person I liked whom I had lost in such a short time.

I stood by the bus, remembering the way she effortlessly swung her body into the seat. I saw her unruly hair, her bemused smile and dancing eyes.

My reverie ended when I looked up to see William.

"I hope I haven't kept you waiting," he said.

"Not at all."

We climbed into the bus and started up the hill so we could pick up Faye and come right back down again. He was quiet and thoughtful.

"I found your lecture on set theory fascinating," I lied.

"I could tell that you did, by the way you focused on the clock over the door so that you would not be distracted by the snoring students around you," he replied.

"I have a question," I said.

"I like questions."

"I'm sure that it's only because I'm a first-year student and dense," I said, "but I have a problem with your qualitative filter—"

"Did Harvey put you up to this?"

"No, sir."

"Go on."

I gulped, because I knew I was out of my depth. Set theory was totally boring, but William had never been boring before today. There must have been something else that he was talking about.

"It's about balancing the quality of the empty set against one with two elements," I started out. "That just doesn't make sense."

"No, it doesn't," he said.

Relieved by that concession, I followed up.

"Then how can a set of two elements be qualitatively equivalent to an empty set?"

He smiled wearily. "Unexplored territory, isn't it?"

He thought a moment longer. "It's the wasteland," he said. "We understand the null set. There's nothing there. But a set of two elements which has no connection, or, if connected, no contiguousness, that is, ultimately a set that is in and of itself empty, isn't it?"

I knew better than to ask anything more because we were now hitting the icy patches on Mountain Road, and I had to pay attention to the driving. As we drove, we appreciated the product of last night's freezing rain. Every branch and every twig on every tree was encased in ice. Backlit by the sun, each and every facet competed to be the prettiest gem in the winter jewelry shop.

"Happiness is an anomaly," William said out of the blue.

"I wouldn't know," I said. "I've only done the junior version."

"What's that?"

"I was happy when I got a Davy Crockett coonskin hat when I was six," I explained.

"That's hard to surpass," he said.

As we waited for the iron gates to open, William was slouched and peering forward into an empty void. By the time we pulled into the drive, he was perfectly himself again. I followed him inside.

On the way to the library, he took two steps at a time on the stairs and blew through the doorway like a master of ceremonies.

"It's show time," he announced enthusiastically.

"Give us a minute," Faye said.

"We're busy," Ambrose said petulantly.

The reading table was strewn with books. Judging by the dustcover art, they represented a broad sampling of Virginia Faye Warner titles.

Faye and Ambrose each wielded a large pair of scissors. They leafed through book after book, snipping out pages and slicing them into individual paragraphs and sentences. Skimming the text of each fragment, they made a quick determination and tossed it into one of three boxes marked: "HE SAID," "SHE SAID," and "DESCRIPTIVE."

We watched them work intensely for a few minutes. Then Faye told us it was her idea.

"Yours and William Burroughs'," Ambrose grumbled under his breath.

She shot an icy glance across the table.

"None of this would be necessary if you had done your job," she said.

"I can't help it if you don't like my writing anymore," Ambrose answered defensively. "It would make a good book."

"It's totally unacceptable."

"There's been no problem plastering your name across the last sixty-two that I wrote," he protested.

"Ambrose has another?" I whispered to William.

"Kind of," he answered.

"Let's see what Roger thinks," Faye suggested.

"I'm sure I'm the last person you want to ask about literature," I said cautiously.

Ambrose snorted at the word "literature."

"Why don't we start with the title?" she continued. "The title is always a good place to start in popular fiction. Tell him what you want to call it, Ambrose."

"Kept Alive by a Memory," he replied.

"Cheery, isn't it?" Faye said. "Not exactly the sort of book jacket that flies out of bookstores."

"I wouldn't have any idea about that," I said. "But I do know that you shouldn't judge a book by its cover," I added, lamely.

"Thank God that's not true. I would have been out of business twenty years ago."

She let me off the hook for a few moments and shifted her unblinking gaze to Ambrose.

"Anyway, we don't have to worry about being convicted solely on the grounds of our appearance, do we?"

"It's not as bad as you're making out," Ambrose grumbled as he ripped out an entire page and mangled it. He struggled to use the scissors with a plaster cast on his arm.

"No, it's worse," she said.

She spun toward me, and I was again hooked in.

"Do you want to hear the synopsis?" she asked. Her eyes bored once again into mine.

"I'm not sure I would understand," I said. "I'm a mathematician; I'm not good at concepts."

"It's not that hard to see how ridiculous it is," she said. "Boy meets girl. They have a fantastic seventy-two hours together. Girl dumps boy for a previous commitment. Boy spends the rest of his celibate life reliving a dirty weekend."

I was surprised to see Ambrose flare at that.

"You're hateful," he lashed out.

That was when William walked across the floor and inserted himself into the festivities. The two writers both glowered at him.

"So what's with the boxes?" he asked. "Packing up our dangling participles?"

I took this opportunity to discreetly slip up the side stairs, where I couldn't be called upon to be a tie-breaking vote.

"Actually, I've been rather clever," she boasted.

"I'm sure you have," William said, kissing her on the forehead. "How does it work?"

"It's very simple," she explained. "I got the idea from the town when they sent us that recycling notice."

"Fascinating," her husband said with a camp counselor's enthusiasm.

"So I put one and one together—"

"And came up with eternal love," Ambrose sneered.

In reward for that snide remark, William glared at him. Faye didn't appear to notice this exchange.

"I mean," she said, "we have so much stuff just lying around and out of print, why should it go to waste?"

"Why, indeed," my professor said.

"Look. It's like a Chinese menu," Faye explained. "You take one from Column A, one from Column B, Column C is optional."

"May we have a demonstration?" he asked.

She shook all three boxes in turn, reached inside each one, pulled out a fragment and laid them on the table. She read the passage:

> "I don't know how I can go on," the redheaded beauty confessed as she slumped against his shoulder. Her tears made tracks through the soot on her cheeks left over from the fire.
> "I always wanted a hellcat who was demure and tidy," he answered as he pulled the axe out of the felled tree and tried to pull together the shirt that had been ripped open by his manly activity.
> The threatening clouds finally burst and drove them running under the arch of the old church where they were forced to hold each other close to keep warm against the raging storm.

William clapped his hands in appreciation. "Brava." He squeezed her shoulder. "A tour de force."

"I realized that I would have to come up with the solution on my own," she said, pushing his hand way. "Why not? I have to do everything else around here."

"Write something else," her husband said.

"That dreadful woman you mistakenly hired just about ruined my reputation," she added as she shook the boxes again. "It was hard to tell which one of you was more incompetent."

He appeared unfazed by her remarks, paying great attention to her new project.

She reached into the boxes and pulled out another three snippets, which she set out in order. This time William read aloud:

> "What a ride," she said as she casually tossed her lithe athletically trained leg over the saddle and hopped off her mount.
> "You must be exhausted after eighteen hours in surgery," he said supportively.
> He lifted his eye patch and leered at her with both eyes, which made her feel totally naked as he folded up the Jolly Roger that he had just lowered from the mizzenmast."

"I still have to work out some of the kinks," she admitted.

"There's not a doubt in my mind that you will succeed." He looked at his watch. "But that will have to wait. It's time to buy your shrink a new sports car."

"Yours too," she said.

"Mine too," he agreed amiably. "Go get dressed."

She collected her cigarettes and lighter and started to leave, but as she walked by Ambrose she turned.

"Don't touch anything," she warned him. "You've made a big enough mess as it is."

44

"She'll be sorry when I'm not around anymore," Ambrose said.

William sat down at the long table.

"Going somewhere, Ambrose?" he asked, idly rummaging through the HE SAID box.

"Maybe," Ambrose answered cryptically.

"That's the ticket," William replied without apparent interest.

"I really don't see any other way out."

"The perfect prescription. Wing your way down to some beach bar in the Caribbean. Spend a week floating on your back in a barrel of rum. By the time you come back, you'll feel like a million bucks. Bang out the next story in record time. I do have a suggested change for your title. It's slight, so don't be offended. I know that I'm not the writer.

"No skin off my nose," Ambrose mumbled. "It's not my book."

"All things being equal," William continued. "How about 'A Memory Alive'?"

"That is the last thing I want to be."

I was not sure whether it was his downcast tone or the enigmatic quality of his answer, but I shared William's sudden interest.

"A memory or alive?" he asked.

"I would certainly prefer to be a memory," Ambrose replied. "That is the best possible way to remind, to haunt and to punish."

"Rather grisly, don't you think?"

"I know it is," he replied, looking solemn. "But I know of no other way."

I could see that William was scanning the upper tiers to locate me. I'm sure that he wanted to dilute the situation with another body, but I was in no mood to help. As far as I was concerned, he was on his own.

"I have no idea where you are going with this," he told Ambrose.

"Don't worry," Ambrose replied, somewhat irritated. "I intend to leave a note."

"Is this a call for help?"

"Calls for help are bogus," Ambrose told him. "I've read the statistics in *Time* magazine. Three times as many women attempt suicide. Three times as many men succeed. That's nine to one. You're the math guy. Do the numbers."

He stood up and collected his stuff.

"Nice knowing you, Professor," he said, spun on his heel and walked out the door.

"Ambrose!" William shouted. He jumped up to follow after him, only to crash into the chair that Faye had pulled away from the table.

By the time he righted himself, tested his injured ankle and made it to the door, Ambrose was gone. Limping back into the library, William looked concerned. He dropped down into the seat in front of the old Royal manual typewriter and stared at it.

At first, he just sat there. But after a while, he picked up some typing paper, rolled it into the machine and began to type.

Things went well for the first few sentences as he got up to speed, but then some keys jammed. He reached into the top of the typewriter and freed them. He continued typing, but they jammed again.

He untangled them once again and continued until they tangled yet again.

He cursed. He flipped up the cover and pulled at them.

They remained enmeshed.

He got angry.

Finally, he lost his temper and hit them with a closed fist.

His flesh split and started to bleed. He cursed.

He picked up the bronze Meekham statuette off its pedestal and struck at the hateful typewriter. He smashed it over and over again until the typewriter was mangled beyond repair.

After his rage subsided, he sank back into the chair with a heaving chest. Calm slowly returned and so did some sense of reality.

He stared at the ruined Royal and inspected the shiny scratches on the dark bronze trophy.

He twisted his wrist to look at his watch, holding his other hand beneath it so he wouldn't drip blood onto anything important. Then he stood and began to clean up.

I was sure he had forgotten about me, but I felt guilty about witnessing this latest outburst. Guilty and a little scared—for whom, I wasn't entirely sure.

William pulled the handkerchief from his breast pocket and wrapped it tightly around his wounded hand. Then, opening the cabinet doors under the encyclopedia, he pulled out a huge stack of books and magazines and papers and dumped them on the antique little school desk in the corner. He slid the broken typewriter into the space he had cleared. Fishing around in a desk drawer, he retrieved a black felt-tip pen, which he carefully used to dab new patina on the old bronze. Finally he mopped up the blood with his shirttail.

The gods were with him, because it wasn't until he had tucked his shirt back into his pants, combed his hair and rearranged everything to an acceptable level that Faye strode back into the library. She was fully decked out in battle regalia and ready to travel.

"You look lovely," William complimented.

"I look terrible," she replied. "I feel even worse."

"Roger has gone to fetch the van."

I soundlessly slipped down to the kitchen, grabbed the keys and ran out to the parking bay.

45

I pulled onto Mountain Road and cautiously started down the hill. Now that the sun was behind us, the delicate ice-encased twigs and branches in the trees had lost their magic. What lay before us was a drab and frozen winterscape.

William chattered. He was like the pleasant real estate agent in a car full of strangers trying to fill an awkward forty-minute drive.

No topic was too small for his enthusiastic interest, no subject too banal. He discussed the relative snowfall amount among the river towns. He explained the "lake effect" and why Buffalo got more than its fair share. Throughout it all, his wife sat sullenly encased in her Hermès headscarf and stylish French sunglasses.

"Of course, that is completely irrelevant in our situation," he finally concluded. "We live on a river. Nevertheless, it is interesting. At least meteorologically. Don't you think?"

By the time I turned left onto High Street, the tension in the van was toxic. Things could not have been any worse until I made the last right turn, driving down behind the clinic. The parking lot, except for twelve spaces occupied by other cars, was piled with mountains of plowed snow.

"I don't think I will be able to get in through the basement," Faye said fretfully.

"I don't think you can," her husband agreed.

"I'll take you to the front," I said. I spun the wheel and backed out onto High Street.

"I haven't gone in through the front for years," Faye noted with growing anxiety. "I have no idea where things are. They have remodeled the entrance, I know that. They moved the main reception. I won't know where to go."

I didn't have to look in the mirror at that point to know that she was squirming in her chair.

"I can't go in through the front," she repeated.

"There's nothing to worry about." Her husband turned around in his seat and soothed her as we waited for a taxi to discharge its passenger in front of us. "We've done this many times before, and we can do it again."

"I don't know," she said querulously.

"You'll be fine, Miss Warner," I added in support.

The taxi pulled away, and I headed for the break in the snow wall when I recognized who had just gotten out of the cab.

It was Claire. She was treading carefully through the very narrow trench in the snow.

The last thing we needed that day was another chance meeting. Out of the corner of my eye, I saw the shiny reflection of a patch of ice just ahead of us. I gunned the engine and braked as I hit it with a heavy hand on the wheel, performing a remarkably controlled 360-degree spinout that slammed us into a snowbank on the opposite side of the street.

Everything in the sitting room jumped. Venus fell off the wall. A gallon of water sloshed out of the fish tank, barely missing Faye.

"Sorry," I apologized. "I'm not used to these conditions. We don't get much snow in Pennsylvania."

William looked like he was about to ask me which part of Pennsylvania I came from that didn't get snow, but he simply cocked an eyebrow.

"Billy, do something," Faye cried out. "He'll kill us."

He turned weary eyes to me and said, "See you after the session."

I joined him behind the van to assist Faye out.

"At least clean up your mess," she told me. Then she turned to her husband. "Take me inside now."

Striding through knee-deep snow, I was able to arrive at the entrance before they did. I was relieved to see that the corridors inside were deserted.

The first thing I did was to break into the wall dispenser in the men's room on the first floor. I rushed back to the van with my arms full of paper towels and managed to soak up the water that had sloshed out of the fish tank. Now, to warn Claire. It had been painful enough for them to say good-bye once. I didn't want them to have to go through that again.

I went back into the clinic and studied the registry. There were over a hundred and fifty doctors in the place, representing something like fifteen specialties. Since I had no idea why Claire was there, I knew that I would have to check out every waiting room. Fortunately, many doctors shared them.

I did the math. There were six floors with five on either side of the corridor. I had thirty-five minutes left. That worked out to thirty-five seconds apiece. I couldn't see any statistical advantage in starting at either the top or the bottom, knowing that whatever I did, I would find her in the last place I looked. So I started where I was, on the ground floor.

Although I had so little time to visit each waiting room, it was not without embarrassment. The building was teeming with gynecologists, plastic surgeons, proctologists and doctors who specialized in catastrophic acne. It seemed that there wasn't a single door that I opened where my inquiring gaze wasn't met with distrust, embarrassment, or censure. More than once, I was aggressively asked what I was doing there. I was polite, but hurried. Those episodes used up valuable seconds.

By the time I reached the sixth floor, I was in a panic. I had never been to a psychiatrist. The only thing I'd heard about them was that they were exceptionally accurate timekeepers, and my fifty-minute hour was up. So I tossed away any pretense at civility. I opened doors, leaned inside for a look around and quickly slammed them shut. I was gone before they could protest.

I was close to the last office. The brass plaque read: "Dr. PJ Nairobi, Oncology." I was reaching for the handle when I heard two doors at the opposite end of the hall open. I turned my head to see William and Faye stepping out of facing suites. At the same instant, the door in front of me opened and the only thing that kept Claire from stepping out into the corridor was me standing on the threshold.

"Roger," she said in surprise.

"They are both here," I told her frantically. "Both of them."

"Bugger all," she cursed.

Grabbing me by my parka, she pulled me into the waiting room.

"You're back," the receptionist said cheerily. "You've saved me a phone call. Sloan-Kettering has confirmed your appointment for next Thursday."

"Too dumb to be a doornail," Claire said under her breath.

The receptionist must have heard Claire, because she looked insulted. Claire quickly picked up on my accusatory look.

"It's not only her lack of bedside manner," she whispered into my ear. "The incompetent boob sent my test results to my last place of employment."

"VFW Hall?"

She nodded.

"I'll get them," I volunteered.

"I know you will," she said as she touched her cool palm tenderly to my cheek. "Thanks."

Even though I didn't want to—even though I wanted to stay and find out what was wrong with her and what I could do to help—I had to go. "They will be waiting for me."

"I understand," she replied.

Then she smiled. "You look great without that sweater."

46

The following Monday, I parked by the front gate to wait for the mailman at the road so that I could "save him the walk." It worked like a charm. He handed me a stack of mail without question and thanked me. I slipped the envelope addressed to Claire into the interior zippered pocket of my parka and drove down the hill.

Entering the library, I immediately noticed a new beige IBM Selectric typewriter centered on the reading room table proudly wearing a huge red bow. Faye had reverted to the security of her old housecoat. She was pacing, smoking and biting her nails as she watched William talk on the telephone. The nail biting was new.

"Thank you for your help," he said before hanging up.

"No sign of him at North Hudson Medical," he told Faye.

She registered the comment but said nothing. Cradling the phone, William drew a line across the legal pad in front of him and then flipped the pencil over to dial the next number with the eraser end.

"Good morning," he replied to the person at the other end. "Admitting, please."

Once transferred, he described Ambrose both by name and body type. "Got anything like that?" he asked.

The answer resulted in yet one more cross-off.

"Why won't he call?" Faye said. Her tone was an ambiguous blend of concern and irritation.

"I hope he's not hurt," William said as he dialed.

Faye ignored him. "How can he do this to me? He knows the pressure I'm under."

"Sweetheart," William said, "we don't even know if he's alive."

"He better be," she replied. "Because I want to kill him."

Many, many calls followed. William contacted the hospitals and police departments in every county in the valley, but to no avail. When he reached the end of his list, he sat down and held his head in his hands.

"Have you called his mom?" I asked.

William looked at me blankly.

"Five four oh four," Faye reminded him.

He dialed.

"Ambrose, please."

He held his hand over the mouthpiece.

"She's crying," he relayed to us.

"Damn."

"Do you know where he is?" William asked.

We both waited as he listened.

"I see ... I understand ... we're hoping for the best, too ... of course we will call you, if—no, *when* we hear from him. Thank you."

He hung up the phone.

"He left a letter," he stated tonelessly, looking glum.

"What did the letter say?" Faye asked. "He didn't leave me one."

"He apologized for being a disappointment. Said he was going to a better place. Good-bye and I love you."

A chill ran through the room. I'm not sure how long we stood there with stupid, stunned expressions on our faces, but we were revived only by the loud ring of the telephone.

William picked it up with anxious anticipation.

"Hello. Yes, we'll accept the charges," he told the operator.

He turned to us. "Collect call."

Prepared for the worst possible news, we both watched him. His brows knitted. Then he put a hand over his other ear and paid even closer attention to the phone. We were straining to hear anything, so it was a shock when he erupted in a peal of laughter.

"It's Ambrose," he explained. "He's at a truck stop in Baton Rouge. He's taking a Greyhound to Texas."

"What on earth for?" Faye demanded, a little brusquely now that she knew Ambrose wasn't dead.

"Why are you doing that?" William said into the phone.

He listened to the answer, whereupon he laughed once more.

"To walk the streets of Laredo," he informed us gleefully.

"Backstabber!" Faye spat.

"Faye sends you her best," William responded.

"I want to talk to him," she demanded. "Give me the phone."

"What was that?" he asked into the phone.

He grabbed for the pencil, which had rolled away.

"I'm ready." He wrote something down on the pad. "Yes, I've got it."

He listened for a few short seconds more as Faye started toward the phone.

"Good-bye to you too, Ambrose. Stay away from the rattlesnakes." He hung up.

A look of surprise clouded Faye's face, tinged with anger. "Why did you hang up? I made it very clear that I wanted to talk to him."

"He couldn't stay on the line. His bus was pulling out," William said, chuckling.

"He wants his check sent to this address," he said, holding up the pad.

The phone rang again. "Maybe he forgot something."

As William reached forward, Faye darted in and grabbed the telephone before he could get to it. Her face grew tight and mean as she held it directly in front of her mouth and sneered, "Eat cactus and die, traitor."

She was about to slam the receiver down forcefully when she caught a hint of an unexpected voice from the other end.

"Freddy, hello," she cooed into the phone as she sat down and straightened her tattered housecoat. "Long time, no hear."

She held the phone away from her ear and complained in righteous, or at last theatrical, indignation, "Billy, why didn't you tell me that Freddy had been trying to reach me?"

She put the phone back to her ear and listened.

"Not to worry. Just doing the boring part, the typing. You know how much I hate typing … What?"

We watched as she struggled with the phone call.

"That's the problem, isn't it? My typist dumped me," she screamed in aggravation. "Gone off to become a cowboy. Can you stand it?"

"You are giving me a deadline?" she asked incredulously. "On your desk? When?"

Even from a distance, I could see the blood drain from her face.

"Give me a minute, Freddy," she replied. "I'll be right back."

She pulled the phone away from her ear and made a face, counted to ten and went back.

"Not for nothing," she said. "I think you should remember who paid for your house on Shelter Island. Honestly, Freddy. Sometimes I forget whose side you're on."

Her agent obviously figured this was a good time to reconsider his strong-arm tactics. As he talked on the phone, we saw her smile.

"Nice to hear you say that. For a change … You know how much I like flattery, but I'm going to have to put you on hold."

She sighed in relief, lit a cigarette and enjoyed a third of it before she went back to the phone.

"Have to call you back, Frederick. It's that pushy woman from *People* magazine. But we both know how important she is, don't we?"

She was so pleased with his response that the smile grew.

"Exactly," she agreed. "You're reading my mind, bambino. Ciao."

She hung up the phone and let her smile fade to black.

"I am going to have a soak now," she announced.

She collected her cigarettes and lighter.

"By the way, Daddy is coming for dinner tonight. Do clean yourself up, Billy. At least for me. Even if you don't care what you look like, I do."

"I'll wear the blazer," he replied.

"That will have to do," she responded. "Try to be pleasant for once. We don't want to stay acting department chairman until we die, do we?"

"I'll be on best behavior," he reassured. "Forks and spoons at every course. Keep my feet off the table."

Moving to the door, she pointed to the pile of papers and magazines that had been unearthed to hide the busted Royal. "Clean up that mess," she added.

Her husband turned to look where she pointed.

"Your wish is my command." He clicked his heels and saluted as she opened the door.

It better be, her hard smile seemed to say as she closed the door behind her.

Reflexively, William walked over and sat down at the school desk. He pulled the top sheet off the heap and began to read it. A few lines down, he distractedly picked up a pair of scissors and began to cut across the paper as he read, reducing the page into long slithers.

"If I didn't know that you had won a Nobel Prize she giggled I would be embarrassed that Cal Tech ever let you out onto the streets unsupervised," he read in a monotone, as he snipped away. "As he gave her that adorable cross look that only made him more endearing, she helped him sort out his clothing, and then they climbed down the ladder into the Dead Zone."

He worked fast. By the time he reached "Do you think we ought to swap out the cooling pump?" there was a growing bird's nest of tangled paper on the desk.

When he finished rendering the complete text into strips, he delicately lined them up before him and shredded them, building a small pile. Given his frame of mind, I was concerned. I moved closer to him.

When he finally raised his head, I knew that I was looking at a man who was miles and years away from me.

"Are you all right?" I asked.

"Today is the first day of the rest of your life," he recited tritely. Grabbing the tiny bits of paper in two clenched fists, he tossed the confetti up into the air. "Whoopee."

His despondency was so profound that I looked around frantically for any distraction. I grabbed the heap of papers and magazines from the desk in front of him and moved it onto the big table. It was clear by the condition of the paper that this stuff was old. It would be relatively easy to sort out.

I threw all abstracts straight into the trash. The reams of interdepartmental memos went into the can just as quickly. Doctoral theses written by unfamiliar authors were relegated to a separate pile.

Further down the stack, the material grew more varied. There were crumpled programs of ten-year-old commencement exercises, a wedding invitation from 1957 and a surprising photograph of a thirty-something William standing proudly on the deck of a small sailboat holding a silver trophy. There were ancient takeout menus. Moo shu Pork for thirty-five cents a quart. A large pizza for a dollar seventy. When I reached the bill of sale for the late great Plymouth Valiant, I saw that he had bought it new and fully loaded for just over six thousand dollars.

Beneath the bill for the car was the brochure that came with it. It portrayed an all-American family, blonde and blue-eyed, driving down long straight roads with a happy and successful future before them. I flipped through each page, marveling that such a perfect world had ever existed, even in mathematics.

Cleaning up this archeological treasure trove was a great way to keep my eye on William without openly watching him. He was sinking lower and lower by the minute.

When I returned to the top of the pile, I saw the familiar cover of his academic paper, "Significant Inconsequentiality." At first, I assumed that this was the copy that Dr. Hazlett had tossed to me, but I soon realized that it wasn't.

It was in too good a shape. The corner wasn't ragged where its staples had been torn out and then refastened. There was no yellowed cellophane tape mending a rip across the bottom of the page, nor the pale tan ring in the middle, which was the only evidence of a cup of coffee that had been brewed over twenty-five years ago. Taking it off the stack to study it in more detail, I could not help but notice what lay beneath.

I set the first set of stapled papers aside and picked up another one. If glanced over quickly, it might be easily confused as just another copy. In every way it resembled the first, except for the title, which read "Coincidental Logic."

I felt a chill run through me. This was too good to be true; it was the second of the five corners of wisdom. I started clawing through the remaining pile of papers as if looking for survivors buried under a mudslide. With a little more digging, I found "Inevitable Coefficients." Just a little further and I came across "Inferred Fatalism."

With shaking hands, I carefully stacked up the four manuscripts. I glanced over at William. His eyes were open, but he was blind to the world around him. I knew that he would be as excited as I was at my find. But I didn't want to disturb him quite yet.

Returning to the shrinking stack, I carefully pulled off each sheet of paper, working my way downward. Dare I even hope?

After tossing out a copy of the 1954 math department curriculum, I had to stifle a yelp as I looked down at the thing that had eluded us for so long. It was the last piece of the puzzle. "Ultimation in Conditional Probability: Is That Your Gum on the Floor?" This was the grail.

What surprised me at first was how relaxed I was. After months of searching, I would have expected a rush of exhilaration. Instead, the discovery left me strangely quiet with almost a sense of finally encountering the inevitable.

My heart didn't stop this time. It raced like a thoroughbred. As I approached him, William was frozen.

"I have found something that you might find interesting," I said, trying to sound casual as the blood pounded in my ears.

His glazed stare remained unbroken, focused straight ahead. He either was ignoring me or simply not listening.

"You really should look at this," I repeated.

"Thank you," he replied, unblinking, making no move to take it.

"You must," I demanded.

My forcefulness actually got him to turn his head.

"Must I?" he questioned.

"Please?" I begged.

"That's better," he said. "It pays to be polite."

"Will you?"

"No."

"You're being pigheaded," I said.

That charge actually earned me a wry, albeit tired, questioning look.

"Am I?" he wondered.

"I have spent the last four months of my life looking for these things," I argued. "You could at least have the common courtesy to look at them yourself. As you say: it pays to be polite."

At that, I slammed the series of scholarly papers down on the table before him with the loudest bang I could generate. But the soggy old paper couldn't manage much more than a muffled slap in the quiet air.

Either out of curiosity or to shut me up, he collected them in his lap, scanning each title before flipping on to the next. When he got to the end, he rolled them up and dropped them unceremoniously into the wastebasket at the side of the table. They landed with a collective sigh.

"You can't do that," I gasped in shock.

He looked down into the trash can.

"It seems that I did."

"That's your life's work," I protested.

"My life's work is my life," he explained. "At least it ought to be."

"You were so good," I pleaded earnestly as I fished the work out of the trash.

"I was just doing my job."

He turned and faced me with a low blue flame burning in his eyes. "My job. My dreary tedious unchallenging and dead-end job."

"Don't you want more?"

"All jobs turn to crap," he recited by rote. "All men must eat. Men who don't have crappy jobs don't eat."

"Fine." I seethed. "I won't waste my energy. Why should I? You don't waste yours. You don't care even about yourself. You don't give a damn about anyone else."

"That's not true."

"Isn't it? What about her?"

"I might have lived a wasted life," he answered in a moment of remarkable candor. "But I can pride myself on being a good husband."

"I'm not talking about your wife."

Realizing that I had said more than I should have, I turned away. I was crossing toward the iron staircase to pick up my parka when I felt his iron grip on my shoulder. He turned me around.

"What are you talking about?" he demanded in a threatening voice.

"I think she's sick."

"Sick? What do you mean? Do you mean sick as in—ill? Is it serious?"

"I don't know. I'm taking her the test results."

I pulled the envelope out of the zippered pocket. He made a grab for it. I held it out of his reach.

"That's not yours."

"Give it to me."

"No."

"I must know," he pleaded.

"It's none of our business," I said, defending her privacy pompously.

With those words, he crossed over to the library ladder against the wall. After rolling it to the center of the grand bookcase, he climbed up to the highest shelf and reached behind a row of books.

He returned to me and held out a little box. It was small and old and faded blue. "Tiffany & Co." was printed on the lid. I opened it.

Turning it upside down, I shook out a velvet jewelry presentation case. As I cracked it open, I could not believe my eyes. Suddenly, it all made sense.

I stared dumbfounded at a modest but beautiful diamond solitaire engagement ring.

"For—her?" I asked.

He did not bother with confirmation.

"Please," he said quietly.

A chill spread across my skin. I looked up at him.

"When was this?" I asked.

"You weren't even born," he said quietly.

Numbly, I handed the envelope to him. Returning to his seat, he tossed it onto the table before him and sank into the chair. He covered his face with his large hands and sat rigidly still.

After a moment, he ripped open the lab report.

I had expected him to be stunned or shocked or heartbroken. Instead, he read the results with the cool detachment of a scientist. Finished, he folded the letter and slid it back into the envelope. Then he stood up.

"Take me to her," he said simply.

When I picked him up in front of the house, he was wearing a pea jacket that he had grabbed on his way out through the mudroom.

It was only when we turned north onto Route 9 that he spoke.

"Where does she live?" he asked.

I was surprised that he did not know.

"Wappingers Falls," I answered.

47

Throughout the drive he sat unmoving. He did not speak. Even when we turned left onto East Main Street, he was silent. By the time I turned right onto Market Street, the tension in the car was making it hard for me to breathe.

"Here we are," I announced as I pulled up to the curb in front of Claire's building.

"Keep driving," he commanded.

"Where?" I asked.

He pointed straight ahead.

As I pulled back into traffic, I soon saw what he had seen. I was amazed that he had spotted her at that distance.

"Stop here," he demanded.

Long before we rolled to a stop, his door was open, and he had leapt out. He ran after her. I parked at a bus stop, far out of earshot but with a good view, and I watched him catch up.

He called out. She turned, saw him and stopped dead. Then she flew to him.

He caught her in his arms. He looked down on her and, from what I could tell from where I sat, began to rant at her.

At first, she seemed contrite, casting her eyes down, but she was not able to hold that pose for very long. Her somber face soon cracked and rippled, and a smile blazed forth.

This seemed to incense him. He railed even more virulently.

The more irate he became, the more amused she got. Soon she could no longer hold it back and laughed out loud.

His fury escalated. He reached inside his jacket and pulled out the envelope and waved it accusingly in front of her.

She grabbed the envelope, pulled out the report and read it slowly. She then spoke to him seriously. Having gotten his attention, she stuffed it back into its envelope and casually dropped it in a trash basket. Then, taking his face in her hands, she kissed him deeply.

Half entwined in each other's arms, they talked. Her lips were just inches away from his ear.

After a few moments, they untangled themselves, everything but their hands, which seemed locked in an eternal knot.

They began to walk back to the bus. When she reached it, she gave me a radiant smile that contained all the joy that could fit into one person as she skipped over to the driver's side.

I rolled down the window.

She leaned in and kissed me tenderly on the cheek.

They walked the two blocks back to her door and disappeared inside. I watched in the rearview mirror until I was jolted back to earth by a bus driver honking at me. I pulled away from the curb and drove off looking for a parking space.

There weren't any. I came around behind the block and drifted down another two to bring me up again in front of Claire's apartment. When I got back onto Market Street, my luck changed. Two spots had opened up right in front of her place. I wouldn't even have to parallel park. I sat there waiting for William.

After about ten minutes, it occurred to me that I didn't know if he would be upstairs for a while or for the rest of his life. I decided to go home. I took a right off Market Street and then a right again. But just as I started south on Route 9, on a whim I went back one more time.

When I pulled up in front of her apartment, William was waiting for me on the sidewalk.

"Perfect timing," he said as he climbed in.

It was past dusk as we finally started south on Route 9. He was just as quiet as he had been on the way up. But the panic was gone, and while his body still radiated tension and stress, there was a new aura of peace.

48

By the time we reached New Coventry, the sun had set. The lights in town were on, but the winter sky was eating up whatever illumination they put out. Mountain Road seemed especially dark.

When we got to the house, I pulled off the road next to the gate and turned off the engine.

"I have some questions," I said.

"I thought you might."

After a long pause, he began, "I met her in Oxford."

He looked straight ahead into the night as he talked.

"I had written a good senior thesis at Tech. They tossed me a bone. A year at the London School of Economics. Visiting fellow, room included. I will always remember that damp and drafty flat with the greatest affection. The fine print read that I had to teach probability and statistics to a bunch of stuffed shirts from The City. On the other hand, I was only seventy-five minutes away from Oxford, so it wasn't all bad. I went there regularly to soak up the atmosphere.

"One weekend at the bottom of a Guinness glass, I met a brilliant fellow. He was a don at some college or other and was hosting a panel. There had been a cancellation. They had an empty seat. He needed a body. An American would be especially sporting. So he bought me another pint, and I signed on.

"The following week, standing before a roomful of bored university students, I regurgitated my senior paper one more time and took questions.

"When she first raised her hand, I wouldn't say that I was bowled over. Her hair was wet and tightly braided. She was wearing a large, faded Radcliffe sweatshirt. Her glasses were big and round, and I thought she looked like an owl.

"She posed a valid question. I realized that later. But at the time, I was arrogant and patronizing. That turned out to be a bad idea on my part. She was not about to be dismissed.

"Follow-up question followed follow-up question as she kept turning the debate like a border collie. Before I knew it, I was in a total muddle and had successfully disproved my own thesis. When I found out that she was presenting at the next session, I stayed around for the show. At the time, I don't think my desire was to eviscerate her in public, but on the other hand, I probably wasn't thinking that it wouldn't be fun.

"In that question and answer session, I commended her on the paper. It is a cogent and well-presented argument, I said. Too bad that the logic is circular.

"She thanked me for the compliment, then determinedly set out to disabuse me of any misconception that I might have had. I responded in kind. It was a spirited and lively exchange that everyone in the room seemed to enjoy. For a while."

He took a moment to chuckle to himself.

"The stewards were very polite about it," he continued. "They started out with awkward glances and discreet coughs, but finally they simply told us to go. But that in no way stifled the ongoing discussion, which we continued over pints while waiting for the train, on the train itself, then ultimately throughout the night and well into the next afternoon. At which point we agreed to disagree and went to Paris for the weekend. She had access to an apartment in Montmartre. Not that we saw much of Montmartre.

"Things got a little awkward when the guy whose apartment it was showed up and turned out to be her boyfriend, but she was quick on her feet and technically dumped him before he threw us out. That was the only member of the walking wounded that I ever met. I never knew her husband, either. I understand he was a decent guy—brilliant at nuclear physics. I read one of his papers, once—in a masochistic mood. I always wondered if he loved her enough to get thrown out on the street."

"Where did you go?" I asked.

"Back to my dank and dreary flat in St. John's Wood, where we set up housekeeping for the next nine months."

He turned and faced me. "It was the happiest time of my life," he said simply.

"Why only nine?"

He sighed, and for the first time since he left her that afternoon, his eyes were tinged with regret. "I did something really dumb. It didn't seem so at the time, but it was very stupid."

"What did you do?"

"I came home, back to the states," he replied with resignation. "Once we were together, there hadn't been a night in the whole nine months when we were apart. I thought it would be OK. She was scheduled to follow later." He paused. "Unfortunately, it was too much later.

"It's hot in here," he remarked.

He opened the door and stepped out into the cold night. I followed.

We leaned against the front of the bus and enjoyed the bracing chill as we looked up at the bright canopy of stars overhead.

Eventually he continued. "There are inherent problems with knowing that you have lost the love of your life."

"I would imagine," I said.

"Where do you go next?" he said. "Do you reapply for a discontinued position and force the other person to go from rejection to repulsion? I chose to disappear."

He pointed up to the west.

"Venus is rather radiant tonight," he said and drifted off.

After a long meditation, he said, "She was decent. She actually took the time to fly over to say good-bye. Her timing was pretty lousy, however."

"The Comstock Committee?"

"The Comstock Committee. She showed up a day before my presentation."

"Christ," I groaned.

"Whatever I do, I do very well," he said with a little swagger. "When I lost it, nobody could find it anytime soon."

He laughed.

"I was pleased that she made the effort. I wrote her a rather sweet thank-you note after I got out of the hospital."

Without any wit or artifice, he added, "I never stopped loving her. I have loved her all my life."

I wasn't quite sure whether the shivers were coming from the cold or his story. Either way I was growing increasingly uncomfortable.

"I still do," he added. "Get in the bus. It's freezing out here."

As I started the bus, he explained how everything that had happened was actually my fault. He told me that he hadn't felt any need for an intern this year or any other. He had only met me at the Philadelphia airport as a courtesy to Dr. Hazlett and because I had referenced an obscure early work—which came as a surprise more than twenty years after the publication date. He was on the way to politely blow me off when he slammed right into Claire, not once, but twice. He decided it was an omen—not very scientific—and hired me. Against all probability, he slammed into her again, at the New Coventry train station. The third meeting was a toss-up. He could credit that to me or the need to find a new ghostwriter after Ambrose's nervous breakdown.

"Either way, Roger," he explained to me. "Your heavy hand has been all over this."

"Maybe it was inevitability theory at work," I suggested.

"Maybe."

He thought for a moment. I think he was marshaling his energy.

"Take me to the house now, please," he finally directed. "There is something I have to do."

The iron gates swung open, and we set off down the drive.

49

I parked by the front door and, out of habit, followed him inside and up the long sweeping grand staircase toward the library. He opened the newly repaired library door. We could see Faye standing at the main table sorting through her boxes of random paragraphs trying to pick a winner.

He turned and faced me.

"I don't think you want to be here," he said softly.

"Oh," I stammered. "Right."

His eyes were set. He shook my hand firmly in both of his.

"Thank you, Roger," he said. "For everything."

He turned and walked into the library, closing the door behind him.

I decided to leave the building as swiftly as possible.

The fastest way out was through the door to the library terrace, but the last thing I wanted to do was to walk past Faye. I made a beeline for the door at the end of the picture gallery. It was basically a fire door, unassuming, with a long wrought iron stair leading down to the left under the library's exterior. I would have to walk around most of the house this way, but that was the closest exit.

When I reached the bottom, I could see how black the night was. Even the blanket of snow did not reflect much light on the dark side of the house. I moved carefully. There was no wind. The air was so perfectly still that I could hear the southbound train pulling into New Coventry station down by the water. Other than that, it was as quiet as an empty church.

After I finally worked my way back around under the library, I stepped into a shadow created by the terrace above. I waited for my eyes to get accustomed to the blackness when a sudden heart-wrenching scream slashed through the stillness of the night like a shard of freshly shattered glass.

The wail expanded and grew, interrupted only by the momentary rack of a sob. It grabbed at my lungs and wrenched them, squeezing the breath from my body.

I wanted to run away, but my feet would not obey. I covered my ears, but the piercing lament passed through my hands as if they were tissue. Even after the silence returned, the shriek hung in the air and echoed in my ears.

I slowly lowered my arms. Cautiously testing the air, I waited an additional moment to collect myself and let my heartbeat get back to normal.

Feeling my way in the dark, I was starting toward the parking area when the terrace door crashed open. I was temporarily blinded by the light from inside, but I could hear the sobs and gasps.

Faye threw herself at me, spinning me around. Grabbing me tightly, she released a torrent of tears in my neck, her body convulsed against me as she sobbed.

She stopped and stepped back. The light was now behind me, and I could see her face clearly. She was pale. She covered her mouth with her hands. Her eyes revealed stark terror. I don't even think she recognized me.

I could hear William's approach on the snow behind me.

"Faye," he said. "Come inside. It's cold."

She did not move. She stood frozen.

"Faye," he repeated.

I could see a flicker of recognition. Then the color returned to her face. She charged her husband, screaming at him. She stood in front of him, beating his chest violently with her fists, punching and pounding, until she exhausted herself and slumped down.

He gently wrapped his arms around her. She started to cry again, but she was easy to guide now as he walked her back into the library.

When the door closed, it was dark again. I was blind, but I did not wait for my eyes to get used to it this time. I stumbled forward, arms in front of me. I began to run, but it was impossible to escape the wail of torment that followed me.

I could not get away fast enough. This was not the grim fascination that lures you into watching a hapless window-washer dangling from his scaffold. This was no accident. This was an execution.

I don't remember driving down the hill. But I still remember the sound a person makes when a living heart is crushed. It was reverberating throughout my head when I let myself into Mrs. Slocum's.

"I'm at the typewriter," I heard her say from inside the house.

I hung up my coat. It fell off the hanger. I left it on the floor and went straight to the sewing room.

"I need a drink," I said.

"If you can wait two or three minutes, I'll join you," she replied.

I stood in the doorway and watched her fingers fly over the keyboard as she banged out two paragraphs.

"Ta-da," she exulted as she hit the last period.

She pulled the page out of the typewriter and laid it onto the stack on her right side.

"Stay right there," she directed as she went off into the living room.

Quickly returning with two glasses between her fingers of her right hand and a bottle of peppermint schnapps in her left, she added, "You need a drink, and I deserve one."

She handed me the glasses, which I held as she poured. Glass in hand, she raised it in a toast.

"True love never dies," she said.

"Apparently, it doesn't," I agreed.

We clinked and drank. Under the influence of nearly raw alcohol, I began to feel a little better.

"What are we celebrating?" I asked.

"I just finished another book," she explained. "My best so far."

"How many does that make?" I asked as I looked at the manuscripts stacked up on the gray shelves.

"I'm not sure." She drummed the pages into order before sealing them up in a typewriter paper box. "I don't keep count."

She picked up a wide marker and labeled it, "WHEN WE WERE PIRATES."

I attempted to count the titles. "You need a publisher," I said.

"Who would want to read anything I wrote? I'm strictly amateur."

"Do you mind if I borrow one?" I asked as I pulled a manuscript out of the stack at random.

"Of course not," she said. "I just can't imagine that you would be interested."

"I think I know some one who might be."

"Just keep my name off the best-seller list," she joked.

"You won't have to worry about that."

I took her book upstairs and sat in bed reading it. I was asleep in minutes, and the painful lament in my head abated, at least for the night.

50

The rest of that semester passed with little drama. On Easter Sunday, there was a heavy wet snowfall in Pennsylvania that uprooted a lot of trees. I enjoyed most of my break with a chain saw in my hands. But once spring actually arrived, it flew by. Fortunately for me, Dr. Sheffield took me on as his intern when I became unemployed. We spent all of April and most of May preparing his manuscript on preemptive morality for publication.

In the department of mathematics at Hudson Polytechnic, the first true test of math candidates came in the form of written comprehensive examinations. A year away from that, there was little pressure on me as I packed up for summer. Even that was not very complicated. Since I was staying on with Mrs. Slocum and because of her new, busier writing schedule, she had decided not to take any summer school students that year. With the steady paychecks she was getting from Virginia Faye Warner, Inc., she certainly didn't need the rent money. My stuff could stay in the closet.

I never returned to the big house on the hill. Everything I know about what happened up there I learned from Mrs. Slocum. Yet even she didn't lay eyes on her idol for the first year of her employment. Faye was incapable of leaving the compound even in her comfy sitting room on wheels, so the medical, mental and therapeutic support teams came to her. By Mrs. Slocum's account, when she went to work, it was more like visiting a clinic than a romantic wonderland.

That was Mrs. Slocum acting in her role of seer, because ultimately the big house would become a clinic. That transition began one afternoon when Mabel couldn't stand hearing one more word as Mrs. Slocum recounted the daily saga of her employer's misfortunes.

"To hell with her bellyaching," Mabel erupted. "She's got the house. She's got the money. She should do something with it."

From what I have read in Mrs. Slocum's letters, Faye responded better to Mabel's strong-arm tactics than to any of her teams of doctors. It began when Mabel sat Faye down and informed her that "the area where a break heals is stronger than the bone around it." She then proceeded to drive home her two core tenets of good mental hygiene: knit and garden.

Both seemed to work—although Mrs. Slocum later went on to write that she wasn't quite sure whether Faye was actually better or was just scared of Mabel.

The math camp where I got a job as a counselor/teacher didn't open until July that summer, so I accepted Harvey's offer to stay at a house that he and Jerry Ng had rented on Rehoboth Beach in Delaware.

It was a lovely day to wait for a train. I stood on the platform watching two sailboats practice racing turns around a green can buoy just a few hundred yards away. The channel ran very close to the eastern side at this part of the river.

They tacked back and forth, working their way upwind of the mark, until they each pulled the helm over across the wind. Mainsails flew over the ducking crews as the boats jibed and those on the deck unfurled spinnakers. A brief moment of intense activity was replaced by a serene quiet as the huge headsails ballooned and both boats headed downriver, running before the wind. I caught up and passed them as I rode south on the train.

Although I never went anywhere without a book, it always remained unopened on the seat beside me whenever I traveled along this part of the river. That day was spectacular, even for June.

A bank of white fair-weather clouds not only brilliantly dressed the deep blue sky above, but also added dramatic patterns to the hills and valleys below. As we rolled on, the fantasy castles made perfect picture postcards along the water's edge.

At Croton-Harmon, I transferred to a local train. I was not going straight into the city. I had a stop to make first.

In his last letter, William had told me that he had found a sunny apartment in the Riverdale section of the Bronx, close to both the train and the gardens. When the weather was pleasing and if she had the strength for it, they enjoyed spending a few hours outside there.

The location was perfect for them. It was convenient to Memorial Sloane-Kettering, yet not so crowded and busy as downtown. In the days immediately following her treatments, which were the blackest, Claire might enjoy some peace and quiet. Furthermore, he added, it wasn't as if either of them could afford Manhattan.

Since I was carrying only a light duffel bag, when I got off the train at Riverdale I skipped a cab and walked up. Wave Hill is a city park centered on an old country house that over its history has been owned by a bunch of very rich people and rented to a lot of famous ones. Its gardens have an international reputation, but once I actually stood there, they felt dwarfed by the sheer cliffs of the Palisades on the other side of the river.

I quickened my pace when I spotted the two of them, sitting side by side on a bench, overlooking the water. He was wearing a straw hat. Her head was wrapped in a bold red scarf. I slowed and then stopped when I realized that she was crying.

William had his arm around her and was murmuring something in her ear, but it was clear from her body's response that she was not going to be comforted.

He stood up and waved a stern finger at her. She looked at him in disbelief and then shook her head dismissively.

He leaned over and whispered something else. She looked crossly at him, but it was clear that her heart was not as hard as her expression.

He mimed a light bulb going off over his head and then bent down into a canvas bag near the bench, emerging with a camera.

Vigorously, she waved her hands no. He said something. She shook her head emphatically.

He stood in front and aimed the camera at her. She covered her face with her hands. He clicked the shutter anyway.

She lunged for the camera. He held it a long arm's distance away from her, snapping photos the entire time.

She sat down in resignation. Dropping down next to her, he said something long and involved. She cocked her head, questioning. He mumbled something.

She punched him in the shoulder, thought better of it and punched him again. He smirked and said something short. She laughed out loud.

He rolled off the bench onto his back in the grass, framing the picture so that she was surrounded by the rich blue sky. She started to pose but got self-conscious. He took a stream of snapshots, and then he had to put in a fresh roll of film, which he did on his back. Talking all the while.

She started to reply. They both laughed.

Instinctively, I knew that this was not a moment to interrupt. I decided I would write to them instead. I walked around behind the greenhouse so they would not happen to see me sneaking off.

When I got to the gate, I turned to look at them one last time. They were both on their feet. He was bobbing and weaving like a boxer as he photographed her. She was spinning and dancing barefoot on the lawn.

I could not hear the words, but there was obvious play and laughter. Hopping up onto the bench, she stood up tall and raised her face to the sky.

That was the "eureka" moment—the moment when I discovered what was missing in our mathematical model of romance—William's and mine. It was the leap of faith.

With one swooping gesture, she tore off her headdress, extending her arms wide open to embrace all and everything around her. The red scarf fluttered in the freshening breeze like a pennant as her bald head shone in the morning sunshine.

Epilogue

My wife doesn't mind that we are returning by the same slow scenic route that we had taken north. She is especially pleased to finally visit Wave Hill. She has never tired of this part of their story.

We have found the bench, but we do not sit down on it. It belongs to them, not us. But we do share a kiss nearby—a tender kiss.

"That's not supposed to happen to us anymore," Suzanne observes. "We have twins."

Then we talk about the night before. Everyone involved agreed that Harvey Weintraub's dinner was a great success. The award came from a national organization. It was a major affair, rented tuxedos all around.

Jerry Ng and his wife flew all the way from California. Also at the table were Leopold Ickies and his wife, with Harvey and Rebecca Weintraub, Suzanne and me.

The cocktail hour had been quite festive. We were delighted at this impromptu reunion. We congratulated Harvey, who I think truly is a great high school math teacher. Then we caught up on the latest news and gossip. Finally, we all complained about our children in a way that we could brag without seeming to dote.

By the time we went into the dining room, we had run out of anything to say. To make matters worse, even though we were at the head table, the service was terrible. It seemed as though we would never get a glass of wine. The men squirmed while the wives exhausted their supplies of small talk.

There were two empty chairs.

"They'll be here," Harvey said. "They said so."

There was a slight reprieve when Leo spelled out a litany of things he hated about middle age. We all agreed, and each of us added to the list, until that made things even more depressing and we just sat and looked at anything that was away from the table.

Then William and Claire showed up. They were ninety minutes late.

"Sorry we're late," he said. "But we can only stand these things for a little while."

"We figured we'd come for the speeches," Claire added as she kissed the man of the hour on the cheek. "Congratulations, Harvey."

Once they sat down—they made Leopold move so that they could sit together—the mood of the table flipped. They had brought the celebration with them.

I was amazed and delighted, as I always am every time I see them, that they look as they do, more full of life than I could ever hope to be. He looks ten or fifteen years younger than he really is, still tall—although not as tall as before—and still fit and bouncing on the balls of his feet.

And she? Well, she will always look to me as she did on that first night in the diner, won't she? She is an eternal beauty. Her hair might be silver now, but who cares? Her eyes are what you are looking into.

They seemed to divide the table into territories and talking at the same time, they soon had both sides buzzing with lively conversation. Although they were facing opposite directions, it was clear that they were tuned to each other's words. Each was prone to stop midsentence to turn around and politely correct or rudely contradict what the other had just said.

After Claire began to flirt with the wait staff in Portuguese, the table became crowded with wine bottles and entrées. The next sixty minutes flew by. The lights were brighter, the music got more upbeat and all the high school teachers and administrators that filled the banquet hall were cosmopolitan and scintillating.

Claire's laughter was in every corner around us. She could juggle three or four conversations at the same time. At one point, as she turned her head away from me to answer a question, I was delighted to see the bright twinkle of a shiny silver hair clip in that ever-dangerous silver hair. It was the one I had given her so many years ago, celebrating the day when she had finally grown back enough hair to hold it.

As Harvey's name was announced, we clapped and whooped and whistled. His speech was short, smart and self-effacing. The night was a huge success.

The good humor and high spirits almost lasted through the interminable wait for our cars at the valet parking lot. That is the extra last act that evenings like this never need but always get—when a close-knit group reverts to individuals and the realities of the present muscle out the nostalgia for the past.

As we milled and paced and looked at our watches, William and Claire stood blissfully apart from us. They had now been married for over twenty years, yet they held hands hungrily, clutching each other as if in a panic that at any moment they would wake up and the dream of a lifetime would have flown away.

978-0-595-70688-4
0-595-70688-6

Printed in the United States
135588LV00002B/39/P

9 780595 706884